Rock Chick Rescue

Discover other titles by Kristen Ashley at:

www.kristenashley.net

ISBN: 0-6157-6403-7
ISBN-13: 9780615764030

Rock Chick Rescue

Kristen Ashley

Dedication

This book is dedicated to the memory of
Patricia Ann Mahan Lovell
My Mom

She had a majorette's smile
that could brighten a room and, if she flashed it at you,
I swear, for a moment, you'd be dazzled.

Acknowledgements

First, I want to thank Kelly "Kelita" Brown for being my best friend for over twenty years, demonstrating how the words "as such" can be so danged funny, teaching me how to play the drinking game "Ooblie Dooblie", naming her daughter after me; and editing this book during school holidays.

Second, to my biggest fans and cheerleaders, The Premier Rock Chicks, Cat "Lily-Landa" Kruzek and Dena "Lotus Blossom" Cocetti and my Rock Guru, Will Womack, thank you for reading, liking every word... and telling me you did. Love you guys.

Third, thank you to my readers, my family and my friends for being so supportive of my writing and the first book in the series, *Rock Chick*. By the way, this book you can flip straight forward to Chapter... erm...

No, you don't want to miss all the fun (wink, wink).

Last, to my stepdad, Reggie "Reggae" Lovell, thank you for showing me what unconditional love means after Momma had her stroke. And thank you for taking care of Momma all the years after her stroke (and the ones before). And thank you for loving *me* so... freaking... much.

Rock on...

Chapter 1

My Name Is Jet

Don't get excited, I'm not cool and hip. My real name is Henrietta Louise McAlister, and that suits me a lot better than Jet. Dad was a fan of Paul McCartney and Wings, so he nicknamed me after the song.

I'm not a Jet in any way, shape or form. When someone notices me, which is rarely, and I tell them my name, they look at me funny.

I'm five foot seven, and I have ash blonde hair and hazel eyes. Therefore, I'm an in-between girl; not tall, not short… not blonde, not brunette… not green-eyed, not brown-eyed.

Just kinda *not*.

⌦⌫

This is my story, such as it is.

⌦⌫

I was born in Denver, Colorado (therefore, a rare "native") twenty-eight years ago to Ray McAlister and Nancy Swanowanski. I have a little sister who's two years younger than me. Her name is Charlotte, but we call her Lottie.

Dad started calling me Jet straight away, and Mom went along with it because she'd do just about anything to make Dad happy enough not to leave. He was kind of a lying, cheating sonovabitch (well, not kind of, he *was* one). That's how I got the name, and that's how it stuck.

Anyway, none of Mom's ploys worked. Dad left when I was fourteen. He came back to visit (which drove Mom nuts), sent a few Christmas and birthday cards (none of which had money in them, which drove Mom nuts) and phoned on occasion (usually collect, ditto with Mom going nuts), but mostly he was gone. Since, when he was around, he was pretty hilarious and definitely over the top, Lottie and I missed him.

I did well in school and had friends. I graduated and got a job as a teller at the Arapahoe Credit Union. It was steady, quiet, you knew what to expect and I liked working there.

Lottie, who got all the personality in the family (she was just like Dad), left town the minute she graduated. She went to LA to be an actress. She didn't become an actress, as such. Instead, she got a boob job, got her ash blonde hair highlighted true blonde, and became somewhat famous for being really good at lounging on muscle cars with half her ass hanging out. I see her picture every now and again in a magazine some guy is flipping through, or on a calendar at the garage where I get my oil changed. Maybe I shouldn't be proud, but I am. She's happy, so I'm happy for her.

***

Things were going pretty steady until eight months ago.

I have to admit, my life was kinda boring, and things have certainly become a heck of a lot more interesting.

I'd never want my Mom to go through what she went through for me to have an interesting life, though.

See, Mom had a stroke eight months ago. It was bad. She lost her whole left side. Then she lost her job, her insurance and her apartment. Since she was in a wheelchair, I had to move to a different apartment with Mom—the kind of apartment with rails in the bathroom, and bigger halls and doorways that wheelchairs can get through. A lot of old and disabled people live in our building, either because they have to, or because they're preparing for when they have to.

Anyway, the place was a lot more expensive than what I had. Furthermore, Mom was getting on her feet a bit. She'd never get the use of her arm back, but her leg was moving and she was beginning to get around on her own. So, to keep that good work going, I had to pay for physical therapy and occupational therapy, twice a week each. That's a lot of cabbage to be coming out of the bank account on a weekly basis when there's no insurance to help. So I had to get a second job working nights at Smithie's; good money, lots of headaches from customers and exhausting because I was on my feet the whole night.

Then, I had to quit the Credit Union three months ago because I was falling asleep at the drawer. I needed a stress-free, flexible job. Yeah, right, you say.

But I had my first stroke of luck, and found the coolest job in the world. It was working during the day at Fortnum's.

Fortnum's is a huge, old, musty, used bookstore (in the back) and groovy coffee shop (in the front). The owner, India Savage, known to everyone as Indy, *is* cool and hip. She's a Rock Chick; gorgeous, with a lot of red hair and a killer body. She's absolutely hilarious, and one of the sweetest ladies I've ever met. She inherited the store from her grandmother several years ago, and she put in the espresso counter. She has a bunch of characters working there, and she had some big drama happen to her and her boyfriend Lee Nightingale a couple of weeks before she hired me. Though, if you paid attention, you'd realize that Indy's past was littered with big dramas. This latest one was just the biggest.

Smithie's is a strip joint, better known as a titty bar. I don't dance. I'm a cocktail waitress. The tips aren't bad—they're better for dancers (for obvious reasons)—though they're good enough to keep Mom in OT and PT appointments. Smithie is a good guy and takes care of all of his girls, including me (though I kinda drive him nuts). Surprisingly, he wants me at a pole, dancing. He keeps trying to talk me into it, but I just tell him he's crazy, and he laughs at me. Working there is relatively safe (considering) because Smithie invests in excellent bouncers. Smithie says, "Doesn't do me no fuckin' good to have my girls quittin' every few weeks. It's like anything in life; you take care of it, it takes care of you."

At Fortnum's I work with Duke, a Harley guy; Tex, a crazy guy; Jane, a quiet lady, and sometimes Ally, Indy's best friend. Ally is also a Rock Chick and is a sister to Indy's boyfriend, Lee. They have a long history, Indy, Lee and Ally. I envy them that. They're all real close, including Duke, Tex and Jane. Indy also has other family and friends who come by all the time. Lee's a private investigator, and all the boys who work for him and his friends come into the store, too, including Lee's best friend, Eddie.

⌦⌫

Eddie is where my life gets interesting, even if it's only in my dreams.

⌦⌫

3

See, the minute I clapped eyes on Eddie Chavez, I fell in love with him. Not that he'd ever notice me if I wasn't under his nose. In fact, watching him (which I do, a lot), I think he has a thing for Indy.

At least I thought that in the beginning. He doesn't look at her like that so much anymore.

Anyway, sometimes, I'd catch him looking at her in a way that made my insides feel funny. Sometimes, in the middle of the day (between shifts at Fortnum's and Smithie's, one of the only times I can get any decent sleep), while I was trying to catch some z's while Mom watched soaps, I thought of Eddie looking at me the way he looked at Indy. Sometimes, trying to sleep, I thought of Eddie doing a lot of different things with me and *to* me, but that didn't exactly help me sleep.

⁂

I kinda screwed things up with Eddie.

No, that isn't true. I *really* screwed things up with Eddie.

Though not intentionally.

⁂

See, he's hot. Not hot. *Hot*. He's so flipping handsome it burns your eyes to look at him.

He has to be six foot, maybe six foot one; tall for a Mexican-American. Olive-skinned, with dark hair and even darker eyes. He has a lean body made up of compact, defined muscles, and he's one of those guys who makes whatever he wears look the bomb, instead of one of those guys who looks like he was trying to be the bomb in what he wears.

Eddie's a cop, and from what everyone says, he's a good one, though not a conventional one. He kinda goes his own way, which isn't exactly encouraged by the Denver Police Department.

Anyway, when Eddie's black eyes turn to you, I swear to God, your breath starts burning your lungs, his eyes are so hot.

He's lush.

Since I'm not lush, there's no hope and I'm in love with him—I get a little weird around him.

4

Weird as in, stupid.

⌁

The first time he spoke directly to me was about a week after I started at Fortnum's.

Eddie was waiting at the end of the counter for his cappuccino. I was re-filling the stacks of cups, so I had two big columns of cups in my hands. Eddie was talking to Lee (who, by the way, is also *hot*).

Eddie's eyes cut to me and he smiled, all super-white teeth in tanned face. The effect of this, when trained on me, totally flipped me out.

Then he said, "So, Jet, what's your story?"

Since he used my name, I couldn't exactly ignore him, so I looked at him blank-faced and said, "Story?"

I hadn't told Indy or anyone about anything; not about my Mom nor Smithie's. People had been really nice about Mom, but it was weird, talking about her and us and how we were having to make a go of things. They got this look on their face that said "poor you" and it kind of pissed me off because, you know, shit happens. We all deal.

Anyway, Eddie turned more toward me. Lee's eyes had moved to me and I was beginning to feel the heat come into my face.

"Yeah," Eddie said, "your story."

I started to panic, so I had to find a way to say as little as possible and get the hell out of there. "No story. I'm just Jet."

"Just Jet." His smile didn't dim and I was beginning to feel my insides curl.

"Yeah." I set the cups down and started refilling.

Eddie turned to Lee, and he said, "Don't know about you but I think there are hidden depths to Just Jet."

"There are hidden depths to everyone," Lee replied, still looking at me, and I could swear he could read my mind, and was trying to get Eddie to leave me alone.

"Not me." Tex, Indy's barista, a Vietnam Vet and ex-con who was crazy as a jaybird but you couldn't help liking him, reached across me to give Eddie his cappuccino, "With me, you get what you see."

Eddie didn't take his eyes off me, even as he reached for the sugar (Eddie took lots of sugar in his coffee. I'd memorized this fact right away, as I memorized practically everything about Eddie).

"What about you, Just Jet? Do we get what we see with you?"

Just for your information, I wasn't a virgin and totally unlucky in love. I had a boyfriend all through high school, and three since then, all long-term.

All boring.

All predictable.

All wanting more but not knowing how to get it.

All just like me.

That said, obviously, I'd had guys flirt with me. It was rare, but it happened. I just couldn't believe Eddie was doing it, or at least it seemed like it.

"Chavez, for fuck's sake, quit flirtin'. Christ, you flirt with anything in a skirt." Tex said (explaining the flirting). "She's tryin' to work and you're embarrassin' her. Can't you see her blush?"

At that, my hands slipped on the cups, they went flying in the air, bonking on my head, arms, hands, all over Tex and they fell everywhere. I bent down immediately to hide and to pick up the cups.

Eddie came around the counter to help. He crouched down and said, "Didn't mean to embarrass you."

I looked up. His smile had dimmed to a grin and his eyes looked different. I couldn't put my finger on it but it, too, made my insides feel funny. I couldn't help but think he felt sorry for me, but his eyes weren't exactly saying that, though I didn't know what they *were* saying.

I was mortified, and maybe a little pissed off at Tex, and one look at my face wiped away his grin.

"*You* didn't embarrass me." It came out kind of snappish, which wasn't intentional, more self-defense. Maybe I was trying to convince myself, I don't know.

He handed me the cups and looked at me closely, no smile or even a hint of grin in evidence. I avoided his eyes, avoided him (as best I could with him helping me pick up the cups). When we were done, I got up fast. so fast I made myself dizzy and had to step back or fall over. Eddie's hand came out to steady me and I jerked my arm away, as if his touch would burn.

6

That's when I saw his brows draw together and I stepped around him, giving him as much room as possible. I walked as fast as I could into the acres of bookshelves in the back and hid there until I was certain he was gone.

⌁⌁

That was the first time I was an idiot around Eddie, but not the last.

⌁⌁

Weeks passed, and I got to know the people at Fortnum's.

It was a laugh riot working there. Everyone was hilarious and nice, and you could tell they cared a lot about each other.

It was comfortable and stress free (except for Eddie, of course). You made your own hours, and I started to relax, except when Eddie came around. Anytime Eddie was there (and he was beginning to stop around more often), I stiffened up, shut my mouth and, most of the time, hid in the back.

Lee and Indy had a party about a month after I started, and they invited me.

Of course, I thought I couldn't go. My shift at Smithie's started at seven, and the party started at seven thirty.

Mom was beside herself. She made me go, said I could "just pop by" and tell Smithie I'd be a little late (something he was used to, part of why I drove him nuts).

See, even before Mom had her stroke, she and her best friend Trixie wanted me to find a life and find a man (these were synonymous to Mom and Trixie, by the way). Both of them kept going on about how pretty I was, I just didn't know it. How I didn't have any confidence. How I just needed to brighten myself up a bit. They'd been saying that for years, but then again, everyone said it, even Lottie.

"Sistah," Lottie would say, "you are shit-hot. Even without any makeup on and your hair pulled back in that stupid ponytail. Look in the fuckin' mirror every once in a while, would you?"

Then again, Lottie loved me. So did Trixie and Mom.

Trixie, who's got a license for doing hair, nails, facials, everything, kept trying to give me highlights like Lottie's. "Don't hide your light under a bushel, or in your case, hide that thick, shiny hair in a ponytail. I'm sick of those ponytails! Every day, it's a ponytail! Enough with the ponytails!" Trixie would say (Trixie was a bit dramatic).

She and Mom kept trying to take me shopping for clothes that "fit a bit better" (they meant tighter, which also meant I mainly wore tight jeans and fitted t-shirts and sweaters), tried to get me to go with the girls to parties and out to the bars. They even suggested speed dating once.

"All the men will be backed up at your table, I swear to God," Mom said.

I know Mom felt guilty for everything that happened. It had been a bad few months, and she wanted me to have a break. She was working hard at getting better so she could get on with her life, but more, so I could get on with mine.

Mom had bigger dreams for me than I did.

Not that I didn't have dreams. I used to dream all the time, always had my head in the clouds. When Dad left though, Mom fell apart for a while (okay, so it was a long while).

I had to keep it together, for Mom, for Lottie, and didn't have time for dreams when I was taking care of all of us. When Mom got back to it, she still needed help. By the time Lottie took off to LA, I was used to the way it was and it was comfortable, so why screw with that?

"A party," Mom said, "is just the thing."

I couldn't let Mom down. I could never let Mom down. It was just the way it was.

She made me make her famous chocolate caramel layer squares to take with me. I didn't have time for that either, but at that point I was so exhausted and run down I didn't know which way was up. Finding a spare fifteen minutes to make chocolate caramel layer squares for Indy and her friends seemed the least of my worries.

"Men love those!" Mom added as I walked into the kitchen to make the squares.

As if that was incentive. I barely had time to shave my legs. Where she thought I'd find time to date, I'd never know.

Anyway, everyone loved chocolate caramel layer squares, mainly because there were five ingredients: chocolate cake mix, butter, chocolate chips, condensed milk and caramel. With those ingredients, it could only be good. It wasn't like I was a master chef or anything.

I went to the party and got there late. I had my face all done up, 'cause Smithie liked his girls heavy on the makeup, which meant I had smoky eyes, lashes out *to there*, dewy cheeks and serious red lipstick.

Once inside Indy and Lee's duplex, I stared at the crowd, and the only thing I could think of was where I was going to change into my Smithie's uniform. I didn't like to go back with the dancers. I had enough confidence problems as it was without being confronted with a dozen perfectly toned, tanning-bed tanned, surgically enhanced bodies.

And I couldn't wear the uniform to the party, no way, no how.

Smithie made all his cocktail waitresses wear red micro-miniskirts, black, skintight, shelf-bra camisoles with "Smithie's" written in fancy schmancy script across the boobs, and the shoes could be red or black, he didn't care, just as long as the heel was thin and high.

I only had time to put the chocolate caramel layer squares on the table when I had to find Indy and Lee and say hi and good-bye.

It was a crush, people everywhere. It looked like a good party; folks were laughing and talking, the music was loud, and I could see cashews in bowls here and there.

Cashews were definitely the hallmark of a good party.

I found I was stuck against the dining room table, people having closed in all around me.

Then, Eddie pushed in right next to me, his back to me and he was hand in hand with a fantastic-looking blonde.

He didn't notice me and I thought I'd get away when, on the other side of the table, Indy and Hank, Lee's older brother (who was also *hot*, by the way, and he's a cop and super-nice) came up. Indy saw me, clapped her hands and laughed, getting everyone's attention.

"Jet! I didn't think you'd come!"

Tex lumbered up to the table just as Eddie turned from having his back to me to looking at me. Eddie's expression was kind of benign when he turned (though he also looked kind of curious, or at least it seemed that way to me) but the minute he clapped eyes on me, he froze and stared.

"Jee-zus, woman, look at you!" Tex boomed, "Fuckin' A if you don't clean up good. You look like that behind the counter at Fortnum's, we'd have a line out the fuckin' door!"

I wanted to run. I didn't want everyone looking at me.

I looked at Indy to give her my apologies when Indy said, "Did you make those chocolate caramel things you said you were gonna make?"

"Yeah, right here." I pointed to them and then said, "Listen, I'm so sorry. I gotta go. I've got something else on that I can't miss."

"Hot date?" Tex asked, reaching for a chocolate caramel layer square.

I chanced a look at Eddie out of the corner of my eye and he was still staring at me, no longer a frozen stare. There was activity behind his eyes, lots of it. Just nothing I could understand. I stopped trying to look at Eddie without looking like I was looking at Eddie and answered Tex, "Not exactly."

"Shame." Tex bit into the square, chewed twice and his eyes got huge, "*Fuck!*" he exploded, chocolate and caramel flying out of his mouth. My heart seized. He looked like he was going to have a chocolate-caramel-layer-square-induced heart attack.

"Tex!" Indy yelled, "You're spewing all over the food!"

Tex ignored Indy and was staring at me.

"These are unbe-fucking-lievable. I think I've finally fallen in love, with a fuckin' brownie!" It was a nice thing to say, especially from Tex. I smiled at him, full-on, forgetting for a second that Eddie was there.

Only a second, because Eddie muttered something under his breath and I looked at him, still smiling a bit. Then, I realized where I was, about four inches away from Eddie Chavez, and the smile died on my face. He was still staring at me, but now he was staring at my mouth.

I felt my knees get a bit weak.

There was one thing on my mind… escape, escape, *escape!*

I turned back to Indy, "Thanks for asking me. Please ask me again."

Indy was looking at Eddie when I talked to her and I noticed that so was Hank. Then both Indy and Hank's eyes moved back to me, and they both were sort of grinning.

"You're always invited, girl," Indy said.

It felt tremendously cool that she said that to me, and I smiled at her. Then, there was a break in the crush behind me. I started to go but Eddie grabbed my wrist.

"Hang on, Jet," he said.

I looked down at my wrist, then up at him. I felt his touch *everywhere*. It was like his fingers hit a switch, and I was a light bulb and he turned me on; a total-body, electric shock.

Panic went through me, and I pulled my wrist away. If I hadn't, I'd have thrown myself at him, right in front of his date. That would have been far more humiliating than the cup incident, I'm pretty sure.

His hands came up, palms out, and his face closed down.

"What?" I asked, because I couldn't string two words together. Even if someone told me they could cure my Mom, make her walk steady and give her back her arm, I still couldn't have said more than "what".

"Forget it," he said and turned away.

That's when I fled.

***

That was strike two. Strike three was even worse.

***

For the next couple of months, I totally avoided Eddie.

This was kind of hard to do, considering he was most definitely not avoiding me.

Before Indy's party, Eddie came in every once in a while, got a cup of coffee, had a chat and left. After Indy's party, Eddie came in all the time, got a cup of coffee, had a chat and hung around to torture me.

Let me explain about Eddie Torture.

Once, Jane and I were going through a box of used books that Jane bought. We were going to put some on the shelves, but most of them were going in the dollar bin.

I was crouched down and I had on a pair of those low-rider jeans and a fitted, square-necked, long-sleeved, plum-colored t-shirt. In the crouch, the jeans came down and the hem of the tee went up, completely exposing the small of my back. The bell over the front door jangled, and I turned to see Eddie walk in, cool, mirrored sunglasses covering his eyes. He took them off, looked down at me, and his eyes moved to my behind.

Immediately I said to Jane, "Let's take these to the counter." And I stood, picking up the box.

11

Kristen Ashley

Unfortunately, the box weighed a ton, and I staggered back, right into Eddie, who'd somehow managed to make it the six feet from the door to me in that short expanse of time.

Instead of just putting out a hand to steady me, both of his hands came to my hips, *low* on my hips, fingers splayed wide so his fingertips rested on my pelvic bones.

"Steady," he said, his lips *this close* to my ear, and a shiver went through my body and I swear, I nearly dropped the box.

Then his hands were gone and so was he. He came around, reached under the box, his fingers just barely (but still, it happened, I know it did) grazing my midriff. He took it from me and walked it to the book counter.

Ally was behind the counter and she was staring at me, open-mouthed. I ignored her look, ignored Eddie completely (didn't even say thanks) and walked (quickly) to the back of the store and hid amongst the shelves until I was certain he was gone.

Other times, he would be standing in tight spaces, spaces I had to get through to move around, so I'd have to suck in my breath and squeeze by him so as not to touch him with some protruding part of my body. This did not normally work, and some protruding part of my body touched him which resulted in one of those aforementioned electric shocks.

It didn't help matters that Indy and Ally were constantly asking me out for drinks or to go to the movies, then turning to Eddie and saying, "You want to come?"

I couldn't go anyway, and I was glad I always had an excuse. Although, since they didn't know I had a second job and was taking care of Mom, the excuses were beginning to sound lame.

The Eddie Torture seemed to escalate over time.

For example, a few days ago I was sitting behind the book counter, my legs crossed, my head bent, going through receipts and drinking a cappuccino.

Eddie was talking to Duke, Indy's second-in-command; a Harley guy with thick, long, gray hair, a beard, and an ever-present rolled bandana tied around his forehead. Duke had been at Fortnum's since Indy's grandmother ran it. At first, he scared me. He was tough as nails and had a low, gravelly voice. Then I realized he was an old softie, mainly because of the way he treated Indy, Ally, Jane (the other Fortnum's veteran) and sometimes Tex (though, most of the time, Duke and Tex yelled at each other).

12

Eddie and Duke were standing across from me at the book counter, so that meant I was also engaged in ignoring Eddie.

Then, all of a sudden, Eddie's hand came into my line of vision and, just as suddenly, his thumb swiped my upper lip. My head jerked up and I stared at him, my lip tingling.

"Foam," he said, dipping his head to indicate my cappuccino.

My face started burning, I stared down at my cappuccino, and get this... when I looked back up, Eddie was again listening to Duke, for all the world like I wasn't even there, but he put his thumb in his mouth to suck off my foam.

What was *that*?

This kind of stuff went on all the time. Being me, I had to find an explanation for it. So I decided he was just trying to be nice.

He was a nice guy, I could tell, even if it was in a kind of badass way. Tex held a gruff regard for him, and Duke liked him flat out. It was clear he thought of Ally like his younger sister, and was always messing around with her. I know he thought the world of Indy, and he was always flirting with her in a way that was hot, but controlled. I told myself he was just putting me in my niche, because no matter how significant these torture sessions seemed, nothing ever came of them. So, I figured my crush, and my daydreams (which were coming a lot more often once the torture sessions began) made me make them something they weren't.

Then Indy asked me over to Hank's to watch a football game. It was getting to the point in her frequent invitations where I couldn't refuse or I'd seem rude. It was going to be her and Lee, Ally and her boyfriend, Carl (who was also good-looking and a cop), Hank and some girl I didn't know... and Eddie.

I didn't want to go because it was Sunday. I didn't have a shift at Smithie's, and Fortnum's had short hours on Sunday. I wanted to rest, then sleep, in the night hours, like a normal person.

Nevertheless, we weren't supposed to be there until five and I had plenty of time to get ready after Fortnum's closed. I needed to accept an invitation. Not to mention Mom was all over me.

I'd made the mistake of telling Mom about Tex's response to the chocolate caramel layer squares, so Mom started to think Tex was a possibility for future bliss for me. In talking her out of that, by explaining that first, Tex was nuts and second, he was old enough to date her, I let it slip about Eddie.

Once Eddie was mentioned, however minutely, I had to come completely clean because Mom gave me the third degree. So Mom was all excited about the possibility that I'd catch Eddie's eye. I tried to tell her that Eddie was hung up on Indy, but she wouldn't hear of it. I tried to tell her Eddie was seriously good-looking, sex-in-cowboy-boots and cool-as-hell and thus wouldn't be interested in me, and *that* she really wouldn't hear of.

So, she pushed me into not only going, but also making her sausage, olive and mushroom cups and taking them with me. She was obviously thinking that I'd work my way into Eddie's heart by filling his stomach with sausage, olive and mushrooms, doused in cream, garlic and Parmesan sauce in a toasted bread cup.

I walked into Hank's carrying a platter covered with foil.

It was still hot from the oven and burning through my sweater. I was late (again), I forgot a hot pad and the minute I walked in, everyone smelled the sausage and garlic.

"Fucking hell, what is *that?*" Carl asked, staring at the foil wrapped platter. He was a big guy, tall, with a thick, sexy mess of blond hair. He had a way of looking at you that made your face burn, because I was pretty certain he was undressing you with his eyes.

I set the dish down on a coffee table with kind of a clatter (because, as I said, it was burning me). I pulled the foil off. The garlic smell wafted out with such strength it was like a smack in the face. Everyone leaned back at the smell, then leaned forward and fell on the sausage cups like vultures.

I was holding my arm and biting my lip because the burn wouldn't go away.

Eddie was sitting in a big armchair, holding a beer bottle by the neck with two fingers. He was the only one not sampling the sausage cups. He was watching me, his dark eyes taking my mind off the burning in my arm because he was making the breath in my lungs burn (and he was making other places burn beside).

Suddenly, he got up, walked across the room, grabbed my hand and pulled me into the kitchen. He stopped in the middle, gently twisted my wrist and pushed the sleeve of my sweater up, exposing an angry red welt on the inside of my arm.

"*Dios mio, cariño,*" he said, tugging me to the fridge.

"It's nothing," I replied.

He grabbed a can of Coke and held it against the burn. I had to admit that it felt good, and it felt even better because Eddie was doing it.

"I can hold it," I said, trying to take the can.

"I've got it," he returned.

"No really—"

His eyes locked on mine. "I've got it," he said in a way he never spoke to me before. In a way I'd never heard him speak to anyone before. Quiet, controlled but a little impatient.

Eddie was a good ole boy, up for a laugh, always grinning, teasing, flirting, and messing around.

There was no messing around in his tone.

At all.

I stood tense and stiff, back to biting my lip while he held my wrist in one hand, the can against the burn with the other. I stared at my arm so I wouldn't be staring at Eddie.

The burn wasn't that bad, and felt much better after the coolness of the can took out the sting. Without the pain, all I could think about was Eddie, and being alone in the kitchen with Eddie.

Mysteriously alone.

Where was everyone?

"Where is everyone?" I asked.

"Who do you want?" he asked.

I thought it was a weird question. But then again, my mind wasn't working properly, so maybe it was a perfectly okay question. Who was I to judge?

"I don't know."

Anyone! I thought.

His fingers wrapped tighter around my wrist and pulled me forward. He was already close, but he brought me closer. "You got a problem with me?" he asked when he was so close I could smell him.

He smelled nice all the time, but it wasn't overpowering. You had to be close. During the last couple months of Eddie Torture, I'd been close enough to smell him a lot, and he smelled good. *Real* good. I kind of slipped into a daze, what with his proximity and his smell, and my mind shut down, and he wasn't just the only person in the room. He was the only person in the universe.

"Pardon?"

"Do you have a problem with me?" Eddie asked again, his eyes looking into mine, and I was in a stark realization that I'd never been this close to him. He had great eyelashes, and his irises were so dark, they seemed to go on forever.

I realized he'd asked a question, and I'd forgotten it again. "Pardon?" I asked, well, kind of *breathed* because, at the last second, I realized I didn't have a lot of breath in my lungs.

That's when his eyes changed from assessing to something else. I saw the dimple in his cheek before his lips formed a smile. He tugged on my wrist gently and brought me even closer. So close my body was nearly touching his, and he had to bend his head further to look down at me.

"I asked if you had a problem with me," he said.

"Well, yeah," I answered, my mouth disengaged from my mind.

His head bent a little further, and, I kid you not, he was so close I could almost kiss him.

"What kind of problem?" he asked. His voice was low, almost a whisper. Something was happening to his eyes. They'd gone liquid, and I felt a similar sensation in my bones.

"I have a little trouble with..." How could I put it? "Your kind."

I meant his kind, as in guys who were hot. Guys who were hot made me tongue-tied, clumsy and shy.

I don't think Eddie took it that way, because his liquid eyes turned hard and glittery, and his hand at my wrist tightened, and not in a good way. Still, I was in a daze, so I didn't really register this at first.

"My... kind?" he asked.

"Yeah," I answered.

He let me go, as if touching my skin was like getting burned with acid. He handed me the Coke, and without a word walked out of the room.

As I stood there and the daze lifted, it came to me what I said must have sounded like.

"*Fuck!*" I hissed to myself.

Usually I tried not to say the f-word, but some occasions demanded it. This was one of those occasions, because I'd never have the courage to tell Eddie what I really meant, and now he thought I was a racist.

Indy walked in, looking worried.

"Is everything okay?" she asked, looked over her shoulder then back at me. "Eddie just took off out the backdoor looking like he was going to commit murder. What happened? Are you all right?"

Luckily, I still had my purse over my shoulder; the television was in the back room, and so was everyone else, and there was a direct shot out the front door.

"Gotta go," I said, with no explanation.

I went out the door.

The minute it closed behind me, I ran.

Chapter 2
The Truth Comes Out
(Well, part of it anyway)

I was entertaining the notion (or more like hoping) that the whole idiot episode with me sounding like a racist to Eddie would stay under wraps. Eddie didn't seem like the kind of guy who shared, but I was wrong.

The minute I entered Fortnum's on Monday morning, I saw the looks from Indy, Ally and Tex, and I felt the frosty air.

By the time the morning rush was over, I knew my hopes were dead, and I had new hopes that it would all blow over.

I was wrong about that, too.

As soon as there were no customers at the espresso counter, Indy turned to me.

"I can't fire you, you know, for what you are. But I have a real problem with someone like you working for me," she said.

My heart sank.

"Me too, fuckin' can't stand racists, even ones that make good brownies," Tex put in.

Ally just glared at me.

"I'm not a racist," I said, feeling like crying.

"Sure, you just have a problem with that... *kind*," Ally entered the conversation.

My heart sank further. At the same time my gut twisted.

"Lee caught up with Eddie last night," Indy explained. "Eddie told Lee everything."

"It isn't like that," I said.

"You can work here until you find another job." Indy was done with me and turning away.

"Really, it isn't like that," I said, getting desperate, because I needed that job. It was a great job. I didn't have time to look for another one, and I *liked* them. They were fun. If I wasn't so exhausted all the time and working sixteen-hour days, I would have been having the time of my life. I didn't want them to think I was a racist. That would seriously suck.

"I don't wanna know what it's like," Indy said, moving away from the counter

Tex was staring at me. "I wanna know."

"I'm not sure what to say." Indy ignored Tex and turned back to me. "You always took off when he was around but I thought… forget it. Never mind."

"I still wanna know," Tex said.

"It's hard to explain," I put in.

"I'll bet it is," Ally said.

I closed my eyes and I was pretty sure I was going to throw up.

Then Indy said to me, "He's a good guy you know. His family has been in this country for three generations. He's as American as you and me. His grand-mother is even Irish Catholic, for God's sake!" She ended up shouting.

I winced like she'd hit me.

"You don't have to tell me that. I don't care if he's only just come over the border!" I was getting kind of panicky.

Ally made a noise that sounded kind of like a snort, an *angry* snort.

"No, that didn't sound right. You don't understand," I said.

"No. I *don't* understand," Indy replied, leaning into me.

I tried to explain, "I just have a problem with his kind, his type. I always have. It isn't only him, I have a problem with Lee's guy, you know, the Native American one, Vance."

Indy looked like her head would explode.

"No!" I yelled. "That didn't sound right either. I have kind of a problem with Lee, and Hank too!"

"What the fuck's the matter with you!" Ally yelled.

"It isn't their ancestry. It's that they're hot!" I shouted.

Everyone went silent and stared at me.

I felt like an idiot, but I had to keep going.

"They're hot, Eddie especially. I get stupid and shy around good-looking guys. I always did. Nothing I ever do is right, nothing I ever say. I try to avoid them. I found it's the best way. The thing is, Eddie and I got caught alone in the kitchen, and he was being kinda weird with me. I started panicking and I tried to explain that he was hot but it came out all wrong, 'cause how do you tell a guy he's hot? He got the wrong idea, got mad and left, and... um, that's it."

"Are you fuckin' shittin' me?" Tex asked.

I shook my head and bit my lip.

"You like him," Indy said. She wasn't looking at me like she wanted to strangle me anymore, which I took as a good sign.

"Well... " I replied, "yeah."

Liked him, no. Loved him and wanted to have his babies, um, shit yeah.

Indy smiled. "I knew it!" she yelled. "That's great! You have to tell him, I think he—"

"No!" I shouted, "No, I can't tell him. *You* can't tell him either."

Ally came around by Indy. She was smiling too. "You *have* to tell him."

"I'm not going to tell him. No one can tell him."

"No one can tell who what?"

The voice came from behind us. It was Lee. He was looking at me like I'd crawled out from under a rock.

"Jet's not a racist, she's got a big ole crush on Eddie," Indy announced, all smiles.

I closed my eyes and I felt my face heat up.

When I opened my eyes, Lee was looking at me. "Strange way of showin' it," he noted.

"She's fuckin' shy. Gets tongue-tied. Says stupid shit," Tex summed it up quickly.

"Please, can we stop talking about this?" I asked.

"No way!" Ally exclaimed. "I've been watching Eddie with you and I'm pretty certain—"

"Ally," Lee cut her off.

"Please!" I cried. "Can we stop talking about this, and you all have to promise not to say anything to Eddie."

"You want him to think you're a racist?" Indy stared at me like I just beamed down from Mars.

"No! Of course not but... um, yeah. It would make avoiding him easier."

"You're loopy-loo," Tex declared.

"Shut up Tex." Ally came up and put her hand on my arm. "Seriously, Jet..."

"Please," I said (or kind of begged).

Luckily, Lee came to my rescue, and when he talked, people listened. "Let her be."

"Lee!" Ally dropped her hand from my arm.

"You all have to promise not to say anything," I demanded.

"Sure!" Indy replied quickly, so quickly I thought maybe she was lying. I also saw Lee's eyes narrow on her, and then he shook his head, and the crinkles by his eyes deepened. I got the impression that I was in more serious trouble than I'd been in when they thought I was a racist, but that wasn't even the half of it.

⚞⚟

Later in the early afternoon, Eddie came in.

I didn't expect him to. I thought he would avoid me too but there he was.

He walked in; his eyes scanned the room, cutting across me like I wasn't even there, and I immediately changed my mind that I didn't want him to think I was a racist.

He looked good. Worn Levi's that fit real well (tight in all the right places, loose in all the right places), black cowboy boots, a black, long-sleeved t-shirt that was snug on his chest and biceps, and a big silver belt buckle on his black leather belt. His black hair was kind of messy from something; the wind, his hand running through it, whatever.

He made my mouth water.

I was behind the espresso counter with Tex, and Indy was behind the book counter. Eddie saw Indy and walked right to her, ignoring everyone else.

I was terrified Indy would say something; even more so when Tex elbowed me.

"You should go talk to him," Tex stage whispered.

"I'm not going to talk to him!" I hissed back.

"You're loopy-loo," Tex told me.

Then the bell over the door rang again, and as I was concentrating on semi-arguing with Tex, I didn't look up.

At first.

Then I heard someone sing.

"Jet! Jet!"

I looked up.

Tex looked up.

Indy looked up.

Ally walked to the front from the back where all the bookshelves were.

Eddie turned around.

And there was Ray McAlister, my Dad, standing in the middle of Fort-num's, banging his head and playing air guitar while he hummed, loudly.

My mouth dropped open.

Then Dad went on, singing the Paul McCartney and Wings song "Jet".

He was really going at it. Singing all the lyrics, the "oo-oo's", jamming on his air guitar like there was no tomorrow, snapping his head around so hard I thought he'd give himself whiplash.

When the lyrics included the word "father", he got a big, goofy grin on his face, put his hands on his heart, and, I couldn't help it—I started around the counter toward him.

"Dad," I whispered.

Everyone was staring. Tex in avid fascination with a huge grin on his face, and Indy was giggling. Ally was nodding her head. Eddie's arms were crossed on his chest, watching, blank-faced with his hip leaned against the book counter.

Dad wasn't quite done. More air guitar. More "oo-oo's".

Then, when I made it to him, he grabbed me in his arms, pulled me close and started dancing with me, flipping me around, still singing, but louder this time.

In fact, he was at the part where McCartney begs Jet to love him and Dad was kind of yelling as he always did when he sang this song to me, which was a lot. In fact, it was every time he came back to town and first saw me.

He did the catcall and I started laughing. I couldn't help it. My Dad may have been a crap Dad, but he was crazy and he was funny, and even though he'd only been in my life for what amounted to hours in the past fourteen years, he was still my Dad.

"Dad!" I shouted over him humming the musical part.

He was half swinging me around, half dancing with me, totally ignoring me, and he kept going. He ended the song as usual, on a hug, swaying me side to side and humming the sad saxophone finale.

"Dad," I whispered again, my cheek pressed against his stubbly one, and he stopped swaying and held me close.

"Jet," he whispered back, and tears stung my eyes, a couple leaking out the corners.

We stood that way for a few seconds, holding onto each other, and then he pushed me back, still holding my arms.

"How'd you find me?" I asked, wiping my cheeks.

"Went to that place you used to work. Sweet-talked the old biddy behind the counter into telling me where you were. Why'd you give up a cushy job like that?"

He was wearing an old army jacket, a t-shirt with a Mack truck on the front, a pair of worn out jeans and construction boots. His graying, sandy blond hair was too long, and (if I was honest) a bit dirty. His hazel eyes were dancing, as usual.

I ignored his question.

"What are you doing here?"

"Came to see my girl." His eyes scanned my face, and then went to my hair.

His hand came up and he yanked the ponytail holder out with a tug. Without looking where it was going, he tossed it over his shoulder. I watched it fly and, still watching, saw Eddie's hand reach out and nab it in midair.

"Shee-it. Your mother gave you a beautiful head of hair. Don't know why you're always hidin' it." He arranged my hair around my face. "Much better," he said.

"Dad."

He snatched me in his arms again and gave me a tight squeeze.

"Fuck!" he shouted. "You feel good. Been missin' my girl."

When he let me go, Eddie was right there. Indy and Ally were staring at us, not even trying to pretend they weren't, and I didn't have to turn around to know Tex was watching.

Eddie held out my ponytail holder.

"Thanks Eddie," I mumbled, taking the band and I could feel the heat coming into my face.

Dad looked between Eddie and me.

"Who's this? Your boyfriend?"

My lungs froze and my mouth went dry.

Eddie just stood there.

Dad looked between Eddie and me again.

"Well? Are you gonna introduce me?" Dad asked me.

My mind disengaged.

Dad took matters into his own hands.

"I'm Ray McAlister, Jet's Dad."

"Eddie Chavez," Eddie replied and shook Dad's hand.

Dad nodded and smiled. "Figures. Jet's always had a thing for our Southern brothers."

Oh Lord, please save me.

"Dad."

I could have happily died at that moment.

"What?" Dad asked, all innocent.

"Funny, Jet's explained she has a little trouble with my kind," Eddie remarked.

Dad turned to me, his eyes comically wide.

"Since when? Every boyfriend you've ever had was Mexican."

Nope, I was wrong. It was *this* moment when I could have happily died.

"Is that so?" Eddie asked, his eyes moving to me, and I could swear I heard both Indy and Ally gulping back laughter.

"Yeah. Thought I'd have me some sweet, dark-headed grandbabies way before now, but Jet's taking her fuckin' time. You know, I'm not getting any younger," Dad told me. "Least you finally got a job in a cool place," he said, looking around. "The old one might have been cushy but... hello? *Boring!*"

"Maybe we should go somewhere and talk," I suggested.

"What's wrong with right here?" he asked, looking at the espresso counter. "I could do with a coffee."

"What'll it be?" Tex boomed.

I closed my eyes. When I opened them, Dad was already headed toward the coffee, and all I could see was Eddie. He wasn't smiling, as such, but the dimple was in his cheek.

Guess I didn't have to worry about him thinking I was a racist anymore.

Before I could come unstuck from mortification, Eddie's hand came up and he tucked some hair behind my ear. He scanned my face and hair, then his eyes locked on mine and he said, "I like it."

My stomach lurched.

Without a word, I turned my back on him, pulling my hair into another ponytail, and followed Dad, who was ordering from Tex. When I got to him, he hooked an arm around my neck and kissed the top of my head.

"Ain't she gorgeous?" he asked Tex.

"She's a nut," Tex answered.

Dad threw his head back and laughed. "Ain't that right?"

Indy and Ally both materialized behind the counter. I did introductions, and there was general chitchat while Dad sucked back a latte.

They all drifted away, but not far enough away that they couldn't hear everything we said. I guess this was my payback for being so cagey. People were going to get curious.

Eddie planted himself at the end of the espresso counter and didn't even pretend to pretend he wasn't eavesdropping.

I turned to Dad.

"What're you really doing here?" I asked quietly.

"What? Can't I come see my girl?"

I looked at him.

He smiled. "Okay, you got me. I need a place to crash for a couple of nights."

Panic filled me. Mom plus Dad plus the same apartment equaled disaster.

"I'm not living in the same place," I told him.

"That's okay," he replied.

"I don't really have the room."

"You didn't really have the room before, but you let me stay," he said, looking at me closer, and knowing I was holding back.

"There's something..." I couldn't finish. Eddie was right there. I could feel his eyes on me. Dad didn't know about Mom, and I didn't want to tell him. I didn't want all the big ears around me to hear, either. And Mom would have had a conniption if I invited Dad to stay. One-armed or not, she'd throw everything in the apartment at him and chase him around in her wheelchair.

"Princess Jet, your ole Dad has to crash. Been on the road too long."

"We'll get you a hotel."

His eyes flashed and then shut down.

Damn.

He didn't have any money.

I didn't have any money, either. Every dollar was pinched for every penny I could squeeze out of it.

I stared at my Dad. He looked tired, he needed a bath and last, but not least, he was my Dad. This was gonna hurt, in more ways than one.

"We'll go to the bank machine," I said on a sigh.

I could pick up more shifts at Smithie's.

Maybe.

If Smithie was in a good mood.

"I'll pay you back," Dad told me.

I'd heard that before.

I turned to Indy and saw Eddie, still leaning on the counter, and still watching me. His eyes were sharp, and I knew he'd heard every word. I felt humiliated, this time for myself *and* for my Dad.

"Indy, Dad and I are gonna—" I didn't even finish.

"You know we make our own hours, girl. Go be with your Dad," Indy said.

I turned back to Dad, trying to ignore Eddie and everyone. I put my arm through his.

"Had lunch?" I asked, pretending to be bright and cheerful and someone who could afford to go out to lunch.

"Nope," he said on a big grin. "Your ole Dad is starved."

"My treat."

I walked him out. I didn't have money to treat him to lunch, either, but in for a penny, in for a pound.

⇥⇤

I set Dad up in a cheap motel, and he acted like I put him in the Bellagio. I paid two nights in advance, and I gave him five hundred dollars because a man had to have money in his pocket.

This left me fifty dollars in the bank, groceries to buy and my car needed gas.

Dad and I planned to meet up at Fortnum's the next morning with me bringing the donuts. Luckily, I'd have my tips from Smithie's in my pocket by tomorrow morning, so I could probably afford the donuts.

I went to the grocery store, got necessities, hit the gas station and arrived home later than usual. I needed a nap, but probably wouldn't have time. There was laundry to be done. Mom tried to help, but she got tired quickly. She was trying to get back to doing things around the house and cooking for herself, but was finding it frustrating, so I'd have to hang with her in the kitchen and help when she needed it. We'd need to do some exercises, too, because she had PT tomorrow, and they didn't like it when you didn't exercise in between appointments. Then I had to cake on the makeup for Smithie's and roll back out the door.

The minute I walked into the living room, lugging the groceries, Mom took one look at me and asked, "What's wrong?"

She freaked me out sometimes.

"Nothing."

I had no intention of telling her Dad was in town. Un-unh, no way.

I went into the kitchen and started unloading the groceries. She rolled into the doorway and blocked me in.

"Something's wrong," she declared.

"Nothing's wrong."

"Henrietta Louise," she said.

She always used my real name when she was ticked at me. Either that or "Missy". I didn't know where "Missy" came from, but that name came out when she was super angry.

Mom had bright green eyes and great, thick blonde hair. Blonde because Trixie came to the apartment and gave her a cut and color every six weeks—Trixie also gave her a manicure and pedicure every two weeks. Trixie had been my Mom's best friend since high school, she loved her to death and she was an absolute gem. Mom also had a great smile, before the stroke. Now it was still good, but kind of lopsided. She was a baton twirler in high school, and she said they taught you how to smile when you were a baton twirler. They did a good job. She had a world-class smile. Even Dad said that.

She wasn't smiling now. She was frowning. "You look worried."

I always looked worried. How she could decipher that I was *more* worried was beyond my powers. I had no children, and thus had not yet been instilled with the "Mom Ability" to sense danger, worry, sadness, boyfriend troubles and when girls were bitchy to you at school.

I decided to take the path of least resistance, choosing a topic that would throw her off the scent. In other words, I kind of lied.

"Eddie thinks I'm a racist."

She gasped. "*What?*"

I shrugged.

"What would make him think that?" she asked.

I put away the milk. "It's a misunderstanding."

"I'll say. Do you want me to call him?"

I had my head in the fridge but at that, I straightened and whirled around. "No! *Do not* call him!"

My Mom would call him, no doubt about it. She didn't have his number, but she'd find it. Not only would she call him, she'd call his mother, just to cover her bases and get the mom-to-mom business going. And not only that, she'd get Trixie to call him, and I *really* didn't want that. Then, they'd get my ex-boyfriends, Javier, Alex, Luis and Oscar to phone him as well, as anti-racist character references.

"Indy's straightening it out for me," I told her. This was also kind of a lie, but also kind of the truth, because I got the distinct feeling Indy was the kind of person who meddled.

"Well I hope so. That's awful. No wonder you look worried sick."

I took a mental deep breath.

With that hurdle out of the way, we tackled the rest of the hurdles of the night: laundry, exercises, dinner, dishes and my transformation into Smithie Bimbo.

I was tottering out of the house in a pair of black pumps with three and a half inch stiletto heels and thin straps around the ankles, calling good-bye to Mom when I opened the door and let out a little scream.

Ada, our next-door neighbor was standing outside the door. Ada was older than dirt, deafer than a doorknob and had a soul made of pure sunlight. She smiled at me, looked at my slut attire and remarked, "What a lovely outfit."

I looked down at the ultra-mini miniskirt and the black camisole that showed too much cleavage that was peeking through the opening of the big black cardigan that I had to wear to keep out the late September chill. Then I looked back at Ada. Maybe she was going blind too.

"I'm going to watch television with your mother. There's a good episode of *Cops* on tonight. I don't want to miss it."

Ada was addicted to *Cops* and *America's Most Unbelievable Police Chases* and pretty much anything that had to do with policemen, bounty hunters, high speed chases, drug busts, hand-held cameras chasing after people running through backyards, and people whose faces had to be made fuzzy.

She shuffled in and I went out shouting, "Have fun girls!"

When I got to my car, it wouldn't start.

I tried it again.

It still wouldn't start.

I tried it a third time.

Nothing.

"Piece of shit!" I shouted, slamming my hand on the wheel, and then maybe cursing more and even pounding my forehead on the wheel a bit.

Guess that tank of gas was a waste of good money.

I'd been in the market for a new car before Mom had her stroke, but that went out the window. Mom's car was worse than mine, and we sold it when we moved in for part of the deposit money. Now, the old jalopy that was second-hand when I bought it five years ago was coasting on a wing and a prayer.

I yanked out my cell and called JoJo, one of the dancers who was also always late. JoJo came and got me, and we both hurtled through the doors of Smithie's fifteen minutes after we were supposed to.

Smithie was at the bar and he looked up at us as we came through the door.

"You're fuckin' late, a-fuckin'-gain," Smithie greeted.

"My car wouldn't start," I told him, approaching the bar. JoJo shot like a rocket backstage to avoid the Smithie confrontation.

He gave me my apron. I took out my cell and slid it into a pocket and handed him my purse and cardigan that he put behind the bar.

"At least come up with somethin' original," he replied.

"I'm serious."

"You're a walking disaster."

I smiled at him. Smithie was all bark and no bite, at least with his girls. He was a big, black guy; used to be muscle but he'd gone a little soft. He had half a dozen kids with four different women, and he doted on all of them, including the women.

"Listen, Smithie, I need to pick up a couple more shifts."

He looked at the ceiling. "She comes in late and, right away, she asks me for more fuckin' shifts."

"I have to get my car fixed!" I cried, tying my apron around my waist.

"You work more shifts, I have to pay you overtime. I don't pay overtime."

"Smithie." I gave him a wide-eyed, girlie, "please" look that I saw other girls use on him. It worked, so I'd tried it and found it worked for me, too.

Smithie wasn't in a generous mood.

"You want more money, you work a pole."

I looked at the stage. Three dancers were working poles, all oiled up, all wearing nothing but g-strings and pasties.

Not on your life.

"I'm not working a pole," I told Smithie.

"You'd be doin' me a favor. Mandy told me today she's gotta quit. She's pregnant."

I couldn't help myself. I clapped. Mandy and her boyfriend Ronnie had been trying to get pregnant since before I worked there.

"That's great!" I cried.

"That is not fuckin' great. I'm a dancer down. You work a pole, you'd have my ever-fuckin'-lastin' gratitude and so much money, you could buy a Porsche."

"JoJo's your best dancer and she doesn't own a Porsche," I told him. And she didn't. She drove a Corolla.

"JoJo can dance but her tits aren't real and she's short. Guys can tell the real from the fake. Your tits are real and your legs go on for-fuckin'-ever in those fuckin' shoes. Men look up those legs to those tits and they'll give you fifty dollar tips."

"I'm not working a pole," I said in a way he knew I meant it.

He sighed.

"You want me to have a guy look at your car?" he asked.

See, Smithie was a softie.

I nodded and smiled.

"You're a pain in my ass. Get to work," he ordered.

I got to work and made extra nice with the drunks and idiots who paid good money, essentially for nothing, though they obviously didn't see it that way. Tips were good, gropes were few and it was a decent night.

I arranged for Lenny to take me home and, when everyone was gone, I waited at the door for him.

Lenny was a bouncer, midnight skin and two hundred and fifty pounds of pure muscle on a six foot four inch frame. He was getting a Masters in Biochemistry at Denver University.

He walked to where I stood at the front door. "Wait outside, I'll do a sweep, set the alarm and lock up."

"Gotcha," I said and walked out to stand outside the front door.

Smithie's was on Colorado Boulevard, and even though it was three in the morning traffic was passing steady. The days were still warm, but the nights were chilly, and I pulled the cardigan closer around me. I was tired, my mind beginning to shut down, and found myself dazedly looking to the right.

Something came at me from the left. I was thrown against the wall of Smithie's, and saw the flash of a knife from the lights of the club.

A hand was at my chest, pinning me to the wall. I could feel the cold blade against my throat.

"You Ray McAlister's daughter?"

I was looking at a guy who was several inches shorter than me due to my heels. He had black hair that looked dyed, and it was greased back from his forehead. He was super thin, rodent looking, and sometime in his life his nose had been broken, and not set well.

He pushed up against me with his hand, body and the blade. "You hear me, bitch?"

I nodded, to *both* of his questions.

"You know where he is?"

I stared at him; my breath caught in my lungs, and my heart was beating so hard I thought it'd jump out of my chest.

Instead of pushing for an answer, his head shot around and he looked over his shoulder.

Then he came back to me.

"Tell him Slick wants what's owed him. Got it?" Then he pushed against my chest, hard, which hurt because I was already against the wall and had nowhere to go. Then he took off, got in a car and peeled out.

The next thing I knew, Vance was there like he'd formed out of thin air.

Vance worked for Lee. He had black hair (*not* dyed, definitely the real thing), long and straight and he pulled it back in a ponytail. He was tall, lean, soft-spoken, Native American and *hot*.

I didn't know if I was more surprised to be held at knifepoint or to have Vance materialize just afterward.

"You okay?" he asked, his hand on my shoulder, his dark eyes intense.

I was not okay. I was so far from okay that I might never be okay again, but I nodded anyway.

"What'd he say?" Vance asked.

"He wanted to know where my Dad was."

Vance made no comment to this because he was busy shifting as Lenny came out of the club toward us.

"Hands off," Lenny warned, morphing into bouncer mode.

"It's okay, Lenny. I know him," I said.

An SUV came screeching up to us. Another one of Lee's boys, Matt, was behind the wheel. Regardless of this, neither Vance nor Lenny moved. They were in a faceoff.

"Lenny's taking me home," I told Vance.

Vance looked from Lenny to me and nodded. Once.

Then his eyes moved back to Lenny.

"Walk her to her door," Vance ordered. He moved to the SUV, swung his body in, and Matt took off.

Chapter 3
Then Life Got Really Interesting

Tips were so good at Smithie's, I treated myself to a taxi instead of the bus the next morning. Before going to Fortnum's, I went by LaMar's and bought enough donuts to feed an army. I couldn't exactly get them for Dad and me without getting them for everyone else.

I walked into work at seven fifteen, carrying my donut box and hoping Vance and Matt had kept themselves to themselves and hadn't shared last night's incident with anyone—namely Lee, who might tell Indy, who might tell everyone.

On the way home last night, I told Lenny what happened, and he got all tight around the mouth. We got into a discussion about calling the police (no way, no how, not when my Dad was involved), then calling Smithie (worse than calling the police, Smithie would have a shit hemorrhage). Finally, Lenny walked me to my front door and made sure I was safe inside.

I got approximately seven seconds of sleep, because I was either reliving having a knife at my throat (which was not fun), or worried about what in the heck my father was caught up in now.

Dad was a bit of a bum. Never had any money. Never had a job that I could tell. And I pretty much figured (and some of the comments Mom made confirmed it) he had a checkered past, present and future.

This, however, was a bit different from the usual Dad bumdom stuff.

Since I hadn't had a midday nap, my seven seconds of sleep did not exactly put me in good stead for anything, much less work, but I had to keep going. I didn't have the luxury of taking time off.

Tex, Duke and Jane were all there when I got to Fortnum's. Indy and Ally were nowhere to be seen.

This, I took as a good sign.

The minute the doors opened at seven thirty, the coffee crush came through.

Tex was Indy's main barista and somewhat of a coffee virtuoso. People drove out of their way for one of his creations. This was one of the reasons Indy had to hire me. They became mega busy because Tex was so popular. I was also pretty good with a portafilter, which helped me get the job.

I was cruising through eight o'clock, relaxing a bit and thinking that maybe Vance and Matt had decided not to share, when the bell went over the door and Eddie walked in.

I held my breath when I saw the look on his face. To say Eddie was unhappy would be like calling the Grand Canyon a sweet, little canal. In other words, Eddie was supremely pissed off.

I should have known Eddie wouldn't like someone who might bring unsavory characters and possible danger into Indy's bookstore. I was surprised Lee hadn't come in first.

Eddie's eyes caught mine and burned into me from across the room. I stood frozen to the spot. He walked straight up to and around the counter, and, his eyes still on me, grabbed my upper arm and hauled me out from behind the counter.

"Hey! What the hell you doin'? Do you *not* see the twenty people who want coffee out there?" Tex boomed to Eddie.

Eddie ignored him and dragged me into the bookshelves, back a half dozen rows to the Crime section (which was appropriate, I thought). He turned in, then walked me all the way down the shelved row to the book-lined side wall before he stopped.

We were well away from the coffee crush and well hidden. No one came looking for books during coffee time.

Eddie maneuvered me so my back was to the books then he moved in, his body in front of me, his left hand resting on a shelf by my head.

"What's going on?" I asked, deciding to act innocent.

"You tell me," Eddie replied.

He saw through my act. How I knew this, I was not sure. It could have been either the narrowing of his eyes, or the tightening of his jaw when he clenched his teeth after he was done speaking.

"I was helping Tex make coffee," I told him.

He shook his head. "Let's talk about last night."

My hopes were dashed.

Damn.

"Last night?" I asked.

"Last night."

"What about last night?"

I had to admit, I was feeling a bit like I felt last night. At least my heart was beating as hard as it was last night.

"About you having a blade at your throat," Eddie answered.

I gave up on innocent and tried nonchalant. "Oh, that."

Nonchalant wasn't a good call. If Eddie's eyes were burning into me before, they were scorching now.

"Yes, *that*," Eddie growled.

"I'm sure it's nothing," I told him.

He stared at me for a beat as if antlers just sprouted from my forehead. Then he said a bunch of stuff in rapid-fire Spanish.

I knew a little Spanish, what with having four Mexican ex-boyfriends, and I thought I caught some naughty words, but I couldn't be sure.

He reverted to English. "You call having a knife at your throat nothing?"

I didn't answer, thinking maybe silence was the way to go.

Wrong again.

He got closer, and because he was already pretty close, this "closer" was predatory.

"You had a knife to your throat before?"

"Not that I can recall," I told him.

His black eyes got kind of a scary glitter.

"Would you forget something like that?" he asked.

"Probably not," I allowed.

He came nearer and, at this point, his body was brushing mine.

"Why didn't you call the police?" he asked.

"It didn't seem that big a deal," I answered.

"Someone holds a knife to your throat, it's a big deal. You report it to the police."

Normally, I would agree with him.

"Dammit, Jet, for once, talk to me," he said, and it certainly wasn't a request.

I stayed silent. Not being a bitch. Mainly because I didn't know what to say.

"Do you know Slick?" he asked.

I shook my head.

"Vance says he was after your Dad," he continued.

I nodded my head.

"Do you know what this is about?" he went on.

I shook my head again but then I said, "Slick told me Dad owed him something."

I could tell by the look on Eddie's face that this was not good news, and my heart started beating even faster.

"I know Slick," Eddie said. "And Slick is not a nice guy."

"I got that impression when I met him," I agreed.

At that answer, there was more teeth-clenching.

"Where's your Dad?" Eddie asked.

"He's coming in this morning for donuts."

Eddie's free hand came up and he dragged his fingers through his hair. He did this occasionally, pulling his hand through his hair. At close range, it was fascinating. But then again, at deep range it was fascinating too. It was just that I'd never seen him do it close up.

Eddie started talking again, shaking me out of the moment. "I gotta tell ya, I'm not getting a happy feeling about this."

"I'll take care of it," I told him.

That made Eddie's face change. I couldn't read what it meant but I saw the change.

"How're you gonna do that?" he asked.

I shrugged.

"Do you have any idea what's going on?"

I shook my head.

"So how're you gonna take care of it?"

"I don't know," I answered. "I'll figure something out."

His eyes flashed. "Something that requires another trip to the bank machine?"

I winced, because I felt the question in my gut. I felt it for two reasons. One, Eddie asked it, and it hurt that his asking it, and this whole conversation, meant he knew my Dad was a bum. Two, because there was nothing left in the machine. Whatever it was I did to fix this mess would probably require me taking a trip to the Stripper Boutique and buying a g-string and pasties, which truly was *not* a happy thought.

"Jet," Eddie called, and I stopped thinking my unhappy thoughts and looked at him.

His face wasn't pissed off anymore. His eyes were different. That difference communicated itself to me in physical ways, reminding me of his proximity, and also reminding me that he was hot.

"That wasn't fair," I told him.

He didn't answer.

I carried on, "It's none of your business. None of this is any of your business."

"I'm making it my business," he told me. "Fair warning, Jet. I'm making *you* my business."

I felt a flutter in several areas of my body simultaneously. I wasn't sure what he meant by that, but I was sure it scared the heck out of me.

"Don't worry about it, Eddie," I replied, wanting to make a move, get away from Eddie (far away from Eddie) and find my Dad and sort this out. "I'll take care of it."

"What if you can't?" he asked.

"I can."

"What do you do if you can't?" he repeated.

"I *can*."

I mean, I did have years of sorting out all my family members' problems. It wasn't just Mom's breakdown after Dad left. It wasn't just her stroke. It wasn't just giving Dad cash and a place to crash every time he rolled into town. It wasn't just letting Lottie cry on my shoulder, both close up and long distance, when some guy walked all over her heart. It was everything. In my life, "Who you gonna call?" was not answered with, "Ghostbusters". It was answered with, "Jet".

Eddie didn't know that, of course, and I wasn't going to tell him. But still.

"I'm guessing any problem with Slick is a problem you can't take care of," Eddie returned.

"I'll deal with it."

"Jet."

"I'll deal with it! It's what I *do*! Okay? I deal with things. I'll find some way to deal with this too!" I shouted.

Yeesh.

After my outburst, he watched me for a beat, and I saw his eyes change again. This time, they grew warm. I was finding I wasn't really very good with Eddie's warm eyes on me. It did funny things to my thought processes.

39

His hand came up and he ran his knuckles down my jaw.

"Don't do that," I said, pulling my face away.

"*Chiquita*, when you get done this afternoon, I'm picking you up and taking you to my house. I'm making a pitcher of margaritas, getting you shitfaced and you're finally gonna talk to me."

I stared at him in total shock.

"About what?" I asked, trying not to sound terrified.

"About *anything*."

It was panic time. How it didn't kick in earlier, I'd never know. I was beginning to feel weak in the knees and funny in the belly.

Eddie went on, "We can start with why you're workin' at Smithie's and we'll move on to why you wanted me to think you didn't like Mexicans."

Um, no way *in hell*.

"I can't," I said.

"Why not?" he asked.

"I just can't. I have things to do."

"What things?"

I stared at him for a second. "Just… things."

He ignored me.

"I'll be here at three to pick you up."

I shook my head.

It registered at that inopportune moment that I could smell him. He smelled really nice, and I liked it. It also registered that I liked to feel the heat from his body and the way it brushed against mine. Furthermore, I also liked that warm look in his eye.

I liked a lot of things about Eddie.

No, I liked everything about Eddie.

Dear Lord.

I took a shaky breath. I noticed Eddie was watching me. I had to admit, I liked that too.

"Jet, three o'clock," Eddie said.

"I like how you smell," I told him, just blurted it out like a crazy person.

Once my idiotic comment was uttered, panic started to slice through the Eddie Daze, but he saw it and put his right hand up on a shelf on the other side of me, by my hip, trapping me.

I looked up at him, flight on my mind, but saw his eyes had gone fluid, and he looked so flippin' sexy my bones went fluid too. So much so, I had to grab onto the material of his t-shirt at his abdomen to hold myself up.

His head started to come down and, I swear to God, he was going to kiss me.

"Jet?" It was Indy calling.

I jerked back, hitting the back of my skull on the bookshelf.

When I looked at Eddie, his head was no longer descending, his eyes were closed and I could tell his teeth were clenched again, but he didn't move away.

"Jet?" Indy called again. Then I heard her say, "Oops! Gosh. Sorry."

I got up on tiptoe and looked over Eddie's shoulder and saw Indy and Lee standing at the end of the row.

Lee looked amused. I knew this because he was smiling so much he looked like he was about to burst out laughing.

"Sorry, I wouldn't interrupt but your Dad's here," Indy told me.

"Great!" I replied brightly, letting go of Eddie's shirt and ducking under his arm. "Thanks."

I got a step away when I was jerked back at the middle. I looked and saw that Eddie had hooked a finger in the belt loop at the back of my jeans.

"Hang on there, *chiquita*, I'm comin' with you. I have a few things I'd like to ask your Dad."

I looked up to Eddie. I wasn't sure I wanted Eddie talking to Dad. "He's just here for donuts."

Eddie's eyes locked on mine. "I could eat a donut."

I knew he wasn't talking about donuts. He was talking about giving my Dad the same kind of third degree he just gave me.

Eddie jerked again on my belt loop and my shoulder came into contact with his chest. Then he said in my ear, "We aren't done."

Eek.

A shiver of electricity, starting at my ear, went through my whole body. I ignored it, and ignored him.

We were *so* done. We had to be done. I didn't have the energy for this, I didn't have the time for this and anyway, if I went up in flames of passion, who was going to take care of Mom?

Indy and Lee were walking in front of us. Eddie was beside me, his finger still hooked into my belt loop.

"I don't wanna hear it," Eddie said, apparently to Lee because Lee answered.

"Come on, tough it up. I had ten years. You've had, what? Two months?"

Eddie didn't respond.

Indy fell back a bit and into step beside me.

"What are they talking about?" I whispered to her.

"You don't want to know," she answered.

It was still a coffee rush when we got to the front, but I saw Dad sitting on the back of one of the couches, eating a chocolate iced, custard filled donut and drinking a latte as if he didn't have a care in the world.

The minute he saw me, he shouted, "Princess Jet!"

Eddie still had his finger in my belt loop, so I couldn't rush to Dad and warn him to flee.

Instead I just called, "Hey Dad."

Dad looked to Eddie and saw Eddie's hand behind my back.

"Chavez, looks like you don't let grass grow."

"Ray," was Eddie's reply.

Dad's eyes moved to Indy and he smiled, then to Lee who'd come up with us. "Fuckin' A," he breathed, the smile dying out of his face and he looked almost panicked. "You're Lee Nightingale."

"Yep," Lee confirmed.

"Fuck," Dad said.

I found this confusing. I looked from Dad to Lee and opened my mouth to speak when the bell over the front door rang and I heard someone call my name.

I turned and stared.

It was Oscar, my latest ex. We'd broken up about a month before Mom's stroke. Before that, we'd been together for two years. The break up was by mutual consent (mutual in the sense that I talked Oscar into it) and we'd stayed friends. He helped move Mom and me into our new apartment. He was a good guy, and sometimes I missed him.

Oscar was about two inches taller than me, had warm, brown eyes, fantastic, thick, dark hair and some acne scars which, lucky for him, only served to make him look more interesting.

I turned to him as he walked to us. He looked upset.

This was not good. Oscar had a short fuse which, upset, could quickly grow into something much harder to control.

"Oscar! What are you doing here?" I asked.

"Your Mom called, said some asshole called you a racist. *Mamita* what is *that* shit all about? I wanna have a word with him. Who is this fuckwad?"

What did I tell you?

My mother.

I wanted to run screaming out of the store, but my belt loop was pulled again and again my shoulder came into contact with Eddie's chest. This time, it stayed there.

"I think I'm the fuckwad," Eddie said.

Oscar's eyes moved to Eddie and he saw the way we were standing. I think he misinterpreted it because his temper flared directly to the red zone.

"Get your fuckin' hands off her!" Oscar shouted and everyone (and there were a lot of people) turned to look.

"Calm down, *amigo*, we've straightened things out," Eddie replied.

"Oscar, it's okay," I put in.

Oscar wasn't listening. "You don't call my woman a racist and then *straighten things out*. And I thought I told you to get your hands off her."

I forgot to mention, Oscar also had a possessiveness issue. It was one of the reasons we broke up. Not to mention his confronting Eddie was stupid. Anyone could see by looking at the two of them that Eddie could wipe the floor with him. Eddie was taller, leaner and had about a half an ounce of body fat, which was clear to see from the skintight white t-shirt he was wearing.

"Your woman?" Eddie asked, his body tensing. He looked down at me. "You seein' this guy?"

"We broke up," I shared.

"When?" Eddie asked.

"Nine months ago."

Eddie smiled for the first time that morning and the dimple came out. He turned back to Oscar. "I'd say she wasn't your woman anymore."

Oscar leaned forward and started yelling at Eddie in Spanish and Eddie returned fire.

"Stop!" I shouted.

I'd had enough. I hadn't slept in over twenty-four hours, my car wasn't working, I'd had a knife to my throat and Eddie just announced that he was making me his business. I couldn't stand anymore.

Both men quit yelling.

"It's sorted out, Oscar. It was something stupid I said to make him think it in the first place. But he doesn't think I'm a racist anymore. Just chill," I ordered.

Oscar wasn't done being angry and he turned to me.

"You worry your mother," he declared.

Wonderful.

"Oscar, everything's under control," I told him.

"Bullshit, *Mamita*. Your Mom says—"

"Stop listening to my mother and stop interfering. I can take care of myself," I demanded.

He leaned into me. "Yeah? I don't think so. I got two eyes in my head, don't I? You've lost weight. You look run down and ready to drop. How're you gonna take care of yourself when you're so fuckin' busy takin' care of—"

"Oscar!" I shouted. "*Shut up!* And quit talking to my mother."

He stared at me a beat and then was quiet. The arrow went out of the red zone and dropped down to green. Once it hit green, he looked at me with concern in his eyes.

"Jet, you need someone lookin' out for you."

"That would be me," I told him.

He shook his head and sighed.

"*Mi cielo,* you break my heart."

It was then I knew we were out of danger. Oscar blew quick and blew out just as quickly.

I smiled at him. "Go get a donut."

"Don't have time for donuts. I'm late for work as it is." He leaned in and kissed my cheek, sent Eddie a glare and then took off.

Before I could react, Tex showed up to our little circle.

"Thank Christ for you, Loopy Loo," He boomed, handing me a cappuccino. "Things were beginnin' to get boring around here." Then he went back behind the counter.

Everyone was staring at me, Eddie, Lee and Indy.

"Oscar's a little overprotective," I said to defuse the mood.

"I'll say," Dad chipped in.

Lee and Indy's attention switched to Dad, but Eddie kept looking at me. His eyes were active again and his hand moved from my waistband to hook an arm around my neck, curling me into him. We were nearly chest-to-chest and I had to splay my hand against his abs to push a bit away from him. His arm tightened, holding me where I was.

His head dipped and he said in my ear, "I've just added a couple of things to my list of shit we need to talk about."

That was not a good thing.

He turned me around, still holding me to his side with his arm around my neck, and he looked to Dad.

"Seems we need to have a conversation, Ray."

Dad looked between Eddie and me, a smile playing on his mouth.

"Jet was held at knifepoint last night by a guy named Slick. You know anything about that?" Eddie went on.

The smile left Dad's face. Indy gasped. Dad's eyes moved to Lee, back to Eddie, and then to me.

"You okay?" Dad asked.

"He didn't hurt me," I told him.

"Fuck, Jet," Dad said, then dropped his head into his hand, and wiped his eyes with his thumb and forefinger.

"Says you owe him something," Eddie added.

Dad looked up.

"I'll talk to him," he said to Eddie. Then he turned to me. "I'll talk to him," he repeated.

"You do that," Eddie returned. "Somethin' else, Ray. Jet's involvement in this began and ended last night with her conversation with Slick. Do you get me?"

My whole body tightened and I glared at Eddie.

This was family business. Who did he think he was?

But Dad answered Eddie. "Yeah. Yeah. No problem. It's over. I'll take care of it." Dad looked at me. "I'll take care of it, Jet. I promise."

"Why don't you do it now?" Lee suggested.

Dad looked at Lee and fear came in his eyes. "Now's a good time."

He got up, and I pulled away from Eddie and went to him.

"Are you okay?"

"Fine. Sure." He hugged me. "I'll get this sorted, Princess Jet. Nothin' to worry about." He kissed my cheek, then his hand came up as if to touch where he kissed, but it dropped away.

"Thanks for the donut," he said, then, without another word or even a look, he took off.

The minute the door closed behind him, I whirled on Eddie.

I didn't know what came over me. Lack of sleep, maybe. Seeing my Dad like that. Whatever, I let him have it.

"That was family business!" I snapped.

Eddie stared down at me. "Your family?"

"Mine."

"Since you're my business, then that's my business."

I gaped at him, mouth open and everything.

I shook myself out of my pissed off stupor and yelled, "Stay out of it!"

"I gave you fair warning, Jet. I'm already in it," he replied, cool as can be.

I narrowed my eyes and planted my hands on my hips. "Not anymore. Your role in this scenario has been played."

He rocked back on his heels and smiled, dimple and all. "Never seen you angry."

"This isn't angry. You haven't seen angry yet," I declared.

That was a lie. I tended to be a pretty mellow person, all in all. I didn't get angry often, and that was about as angry as I'd ever been.

"Then, considering you're sexy as hell right now, I'm lookin' forward to angry."

His words threw me and it was a miracle I didn't stagger backward.

Then panic coursed through me and I started to stomp toward the bookshelves, when Eddie said to my back, "This is familiar, guess it's time to hide."

It was likely a mixture of humiliation and heretofore unknown temper that made me swing around and stomp right back to him. That, and the fact I was seeing red. I guess he really hadn't "seen angry yet" but then again, neither had I.

I got toe-to-toe with him and yelled in his face, "Leave me and my Dad alone, Eddie Chavez!"

Eddie leaned into me, so close he was all I could see.

Quietly, he asked, "Is it wrong that I want to kiss you right now?"

I kind of growled, low in my throat, too angry to be freaked out by what he said.

"*Dios mio, cariño,* you're adorable."

"I'm no longer speaking to you," I told him.

"Yes you are. Three o'clock, then it's you, me and a pitcher of margaritas," he responded.

I walked away (well, maybe more like flounced), behind the espresso counter and started banging around, completely ignoring him and everyone.

A couple of minutes later, Tex said, surprisingly quietly, "It's okay, darlin', he's gone."

I looked to Tex and Indy as she came behind the counter.

"What am I gonna do?" I asked.

"Go with it?" Tex suggested.

"Do you want to talk?" Indy asked.

I shook my head.

"Thanks. I need to get my head together. Maybe later," I told her.

"Anytime Jet, do you know that?" Indy asked.

"Know what?"

"That anytime you need to talk, or need anything, you can call me. Do you know that?"

I felt tears sting my eyes. I nodded and turned away, got back to work, and missed the look Indy and Tex exchanged.

I wasn't going to have a nervous breakdown, not now. And if I gave in to everything I was feeling my system would probably shut down for a month.

I needed to concentrate, prioritize.

Stay awake was first. Find out what was wrong with my car was second. Find out if Dad was okay was third. Find a way to make up the money I gave Dad was last, or maybe first.

Or maybe the problem was it was all first.

Chapter 4

Out of the Frying Pan and Into Eddie's Bed

My luck changed when Smithie called me and told me a "friend" was going to be in the parking lot of my apartment building at two o'clock to look at my car.

This meant I had a genuine reason for leaving early, thus avoiding Eddie.

I left Fortnum's at one thirty because I had to take the bus, and I met Smithie's friend at my Honda. He tinkered around under the hood for a couple of seconds, then straightened up and wiped his hands on his greasy, blue coveralls.

"Gonna hafta tow this in," he told me.

Oh no.

"Is it bad?" I asked.

"Can't tell. Need to get in there."

Wonderful.

"I can't tow it today. I'll have the wrecker here tomorrow some time."

"I'd appreciate that."

I called JoJo to arrange a ride while I watched the mechanic drive away. Then I dragged my behind up to the apartment, looking forward to sleeping for a full three hours before having to go into Smithie's.

When I opened the door to the apartment Mom shouted, "Oh good! You're early."

I walked into the living room. Trixie was there and it looked like a beauty salon bomb had exploded.

"Hooray! I'll have more time to work," Trixie cried.

I absolutely loved Trixie. She'd had dyed red hair for as long as I could remember. She wore it teased out big. It looked good on her. She was petite, had happy, brown eyes, and the most beautiful hands I'd ever seen on anyone. She had what I thought of as an artist's hands.

"Trixie, what are you doing here?" I asked as I gave her a hug. Trixie usually came to visit Mom on a Monday.

"Surprise! You're getting a manicure, pedicure, facial and highlights."

I did a mental groan.

"Trixie—"

"Nope. No arguments this time. Your Mom says you're worn out. So today, it's all about you. It's Jet's Day of Beauty."

I needed a manicure and highlights like I needed a hole in the head. Both required maintenance, and maintenance required time and money, and I had neither of those.

Trixie was dashing around the room getting prepared, and Mom was smiling her glamorous lopsided smile. They thought they were doing me a favor. They thought this was a good thing.

Damn. How did you say no to that?

Trixie put one of our dining room chairs in the living room. I sat in it and she swooped a drape around me.

"Oscar came in today," I said to Mom.

"Really? How is Oscar?" Mom replied, feigning innocent surprise.

"I don't know, since most of the time he was there he was yelling at Eddie in Spanish, and the rest of the time he was yelling at him in English, and any leftover time he was yelling at me."

"Oh dear," Trixie murmured.

"That didn't go as planned," Mom said to Trixie.

My mother.

If I didn't love her, I'd kill her.

Trixie started mixing some gunk in a little bowl with a wide flat paintbrush and shrugged at Mom.

"Everything's okay with Eddie so you can stop meddling," I told them.

"I better call Javier," Mom said quietly.

See what I mean?

"How *okay* are things with Eddie?" Trixie asked, giving me a wide-eyed, nosy stare.

I looked to the ceiling and asked for deliverance.

God clearly had better things to do that day.

I guided them off the subject of Eddie. I fell asleep during the pedicure with a head full of foil wrap and had to be woken up to get my hair rinsed in the kitchen sink.

"Voila!" Trixie said, handing me a mirror when she was done.

I stared at myself in disbelief.

Okay, I had to admit, it looked good. No, really, it looked great. She'd cut off a couple of inches so my hair just brushed past my shoulders, and she gave me deep thick bangs that were parted well to the side and looked almost sexy. It did actually brighten me up. In fact, my eyes looked more green than hazel, and my skin looked kind of glowy.

"It's great," I said.

"It is! It's you! It's perfect! You're a whole new Jet," Trixie announced.

I wished I was a whole new Jet with a whole new life, but I'd take the new 'do because I wasn't going to get the other, that was for sure.

Trixie did my makeup for Smithie's, which also looked better than I could ever do, and I was an expert at makeup. I celebrated my new look by wearing my sexiest slut shoes with my Smithie's uniform. They were black patent leather, closed, pointed toe with double-thick straps with a dual buckle at the ankle. Smithie called them my dominatrix shoes, and he wasn't wrong.

JoJo and I were only five minutes late when we swung through the door. Smithie was at his usual place behind the bar. He turned when we entered, opened his mouth to say something smart, and his mouth just stayed open when he saw me.

I put my purse and cardigan on the bar.

"Please tell me you did that to your hair 'cause you're gonna dance a pole."

"I'm not dancing a pole," I told him.

He handed me my apron and, as usual, I slid my cell into the pocket. I always did this. I was never without my cell, just in case Mom needed to call.

Smithie kept talking. "So, then, it was to throw me off the fact that you didn't call me to tell me some dickhead held a knife to you last night."

Damn.

Lenny had given me up.

"It was nothing," I blew it off.

"It didn't sound like nothin', it sounded like fuckin' somethin'. You're escorted to and from the building from now on," Smithie announced.

I opened my mouth to argue but he lifted his hand. Everyone knew you shut up when Smithie lifted his hand.

"Okay," I gave in.

"I take it since you sashayed in with JoJo that your car still ain't workin'," he said.

"Right," I told him.

He put my purse and cardigan behind the bar. "Then one of the bouncers picks you up and takes you home. You don't arrange it, I will."

I nodded, because he wasn't exactly opening it up for discussion.

"Good," he said. "Get to work."

I got to work and knew right away it wasn't going to be a good night. My station included three tables at the front by the stage. Two hours in, those tables were taken up by a bachelor's party. Who on earth would have a bachelor's party on a Tuesday, I did not know, but there they were. They were getting drunk quickly, and I knew by the way they were behaving (giving me winks, calling me "babe", elbowing each other and giggling every time I was near) that they were going to be trouble. In fact, for a Tuesday, it was a busy night. All the tables were full. There were some men standing around, and the bar was two deep.

It was just after midnight. My section had gone from drunk and stupid to drunk and getting rowdy, and I was at the waitress station at the bar. The waitress station was separated from the rest of the bar by two big, brass rails that went up the front of the bar, ran high and curled around the back. I was waiting for an order to be filled and, deciding that even though they were my sexiest slut shoes, I hated them with all my heart, because my feet were killing me. I was dog tired and looking forward to my three hours of sleep, when Tanya, another waitress, slid in beside me.

Now, Tanya wanted to be at a pole. She looked great; lots of dark hair, a fake DD-cup and long legs. She tried the stage once but she was a terrible dancer. Not only two left feet, but also no rhythm, and when she tried to dance sexy, well, there's no way to describe it, it was just plain wrong. It was hard to watch her up there, it was so bad. Smithie took her off the stage and gave her a uniform. It broke her heart. She was now taking salsa lessons in hopes of another go.

"I'm in love," she told me.

"Really? That's great," I replied.

She laughed. "You idiot. Not really. More like in lust. Got a guy at my station the likes you don't see in here very often."

I looked over my shoulder to her station, but there were people standing around and I couldn't see any of her tables. "Who is he?"

Someone shifted and I froze when I saw Eddie sitting alone at a table, his legs stretched in front of him, crossed at the ankles. His arms were crossed on his chest. He had a beer bottle on the table in front of him, his face was blank and his eyes were on the stage. And he was watching the stage like I would guess he'd watch a sitcom, as if it was all the same to him.

"Holy shit!" I exclaimed, turning away.

"I know!" Tanya cried. "Isn't he hot?"

No.

No, no, no, no.

This was not happening.

"Jet, are you okay?" Tanya asked.

What was I going to do?

I couldn't leave. I needed the tips and the hours, and Smithie would lose his mind.

I couldn't stay because Eddie was there, and he was going to see me in my Smithie's uniform, and that did not bear thinking about.

"I know him," I told Tanya.

"You do? Who is he?"

"Pour a beer on him, turn the table on him. Something, anything to get him to leave," I begged.

"Is he bad news?" she asked, looking toward the table.

"Don't look!" I cried, grabbing her face by the chin and making her look at me.

"He hurt you or something?" she asked between smushed lips and I let her face go.

"No. He's just... I... shit!"

I had to do it. I was in a slut outfit and Eddie was there. As fast as I could, I told her my life story, leaving out bits and skipping over bits, but essentially telling her about my confidence problem, my crush and what had been happening the last few months.

"What's wrong with you?" Tanya asked, staring at me like I lost my mind. "Get in there, girl."

"You don't understand," I said.

"No, I don't and I'm not pouring a beer on him, although I'd like to see that t-shirt on him wet. You look fantastic in that outfit and you shouldn't be ashamed of that. Your new hair is killer and he's obviously here to see you, 'cause it's clear he isn't interested in what's onstage. So, he should see you."

"Tanya."

"Un-unh." She shook her head, gave me a "talk to the hand" gesture, grabbed her tray and strutted away.

Wonderful.

I got my drinks order and spent the next hour hiding from Eddie by walking far out of my way, putting people between us. I didn't even look in his direction, although that took a superhuman effort.

I was at the bachelor party, having unloaded another tray of drinks on them when I turned and chanced a glance at Eddie's table. It was now filled with four guys drinking beer, staring at the stage and adjusting their crotches.

I breathed a sigh of relief. Eddie was gone.

Thank God.

I was about to go toward the bar but stopped.

Eddie was leaning on the bar.

I had no time to react because he began to scan the room, looked past me, then his head snapped back and his eyes locked on me. Even in the dim light, I saw his brows draw together and he straightened away from the bar.

I realized then how I'd avoided him. It was the hair. He'd probably seen me but didn't know who I was.

"Damn," I whispered.

At that moment, my luck, never good, turned nasty.

I felt a hand go from the back of my knee, up my thigh, nearly to my miniskirt.

I whirled around.

"No hands!" I snapped to Bachelor Number One, the one I'd clocked as the one to watch. He had greedy eyes, and at first sight I didn't like him.

"Hey babe, why aren't you up there?" He motioned to the stage. "You'd be shit-hot up there."

I started to walk away but was tagged by a hand at my camisole and pulled back.

I turned around.

"I said no hands." I looked around for Lenny or one of the other bouncers, but I saw none. The place was packed.

"You left without your tip," Bachelor Number One said.

He held up a fifty.

A fifty was a fucking great tip and definitely worth the f-word. Even the dancers didn't often get fifties.

I went to take it and he snatched it away.

He folded it in half, lengthwise. "I want you to take it with your teeth."

Then he held it at his fly.

What a jerk.

My eyes moved to his and I couldn't help it, fifty dollars or not, my lip curled.

"I don't think so."

I turned to walk away. He grabbed me by the waist, yanked me back onto his lap and curled an arm tight around me. With the other hand, he slid the fifty between my breasts.

That was the last thing he did of his own accord.

The next thing I knew, a hand wrapped around my wrist and Eddie jerked me out of his lap. The strength of the pull and momentum of my body threw me away from him several feet and I crashed into some guys who were standing around. Still, I saw Eddie yank Bachelor Number One out of his chair by his collar.

Then he held him by his collar and he put his fist in his face. It was not pretty and I winced. You could hear his nose breaking.

The other bachelor party boys rose from their seats in defense of their brethren, and all hell broke loose.

Several guys tried to jump Eddie but he had his eyes on the prize, yanking Bachelor Number One free of the clutch and, still holding his collar, slammed his fist into his face again.

That was all I saw. I was being jostled and pushed back, teetering on my dominatrix shoes. Lenny got to me and pulled me out of the rapidly growing brawl. It started with Eddie and the bachelor party and grew.

I saw one of the bachelor party boys get thrown on stage. JoJo was dancing and he nearly collided with her. She let out a screech and all the girls began running around and then disappeared into the back.

I wanted to try to get to Eddie but Tanya grabbed my arm, pushed my purse into my hands and tugged me out the front door. The other waitresses and some of the dancers were standing outside, taking the brawl opportunity to get a smoke break in, and some of the customers were reeling out to get away from the pandemonium.

"Holy crap! Did you see that?" Tanya asked. "I watched the whole thing. You were in the way so your hot guy couldn't see what was happening with the money. The minute that asshole pulled you on his lap, though, your man threw three guys out of his way to get to you. It was ace!" she shouted, clearly excited.

I felt a thrill race through me that Eddie would do that for me.

Three squad cars pulled up and the cops went in, the customers went out, and we stood around waiting for the all clear to close down the joint.

Eddie came out with a man in uniform, scanned the crowd and hangers on and locked on me. He said something to the cop, disengaged and walked to me. He had blood on his white t-shirt but it didn't look like it was coming from him, thank God. His eyes glittered, even in the dim light of the club sign and street lamps. When he got closer, I noticed his knuckles were bloody, and I was guessing that some of it was his blood.

I didn't think. I just snatched up one of his hands and stared at it, then looked up at him, still holding his hand.

"We need to get you some ice," I said.

Eddie didn't get a chance to respond because Smithie lumbered up.

"How many times do I have to tell you bitches, no boyfriends?" he shouted at me. "Shit, girl. You are a fuckin' pain in my fuckin' ass. Do you know how much damage this badass motherfucker caused?" He turned to Eddie. "I knew you were trouble the minute you fuckin' walked in."

"He's not my boyfriend," I told Smithie and Smithie turned back to me.

"Bullshit. Jet, you owe me. I gotta replace broken fuckin' furniture. Tomorrow night, you're takin' a pole."

"One of your customers was all over her. Where were your bouncers?" Eddie asked, his voice strangely quiet which made it strangely scary.

"The boys were busy, it was packed," Smithie replied. "And Jet can take care of herself."

Eddie moved his body in a way that was openly threatening, even though I still held his hand. Smithie pulled himself up.

"He had her in his lap with his hand down her shirt," Eddie said.

Smithie's eyes got hard.

No one messed with his girls. It was strictly look-but-don't-touch at Smithie's.

He turned to me. "No shit?"

I nodded.

"Goddammit, Jet," Smithie replied. "If you were at a pole, we could fuckin' control it. You're no good on the floor. You gotta take a pole, for my fuckin' peace of mind if nothin' else."

"The other girls get it too," I reminded him.

"Not nearly as much as you," Smithie returned. "You got that girl next door shit goin' on. Fuck!"

"I'm not taking a pole, Smithie," I told him (again).

"Tomorrow, you're onstage," Smithie declared.

Eddie realized what we were talking about and his body tensed. You could see it. You could almost feel it and the open threat to Smithie turned hostile.

"She's not going onstage."

Smithie looked from Eddie to me, then back to Eddie.

He sighed and shook his head.

"You're a pain in my fuckin' ass," Smithie said to me.

"Am I fired?" I asked, fear that I finally pushed him too far tearing at my gut.

"No you're not fuckin' fired. We have a brawl twice a year. We were due." Smithie said while he moved behind me and yanked the ties of my apron, pulling it away. Then he came back around and pointed at me. "But keep your fuckin' boyfriend outta here."

"He's *not* my boyfriend!" I yelled at Smithie's back.

It was kind of a stupid thing to say because I was still holding Eddie's hand, and it might have been that was what it looked like.

Eddie turned his hand around. His fingers curled around mine and he tugged me forward.

"Where's your car?" he asked.

"I caught a ride with JoJo," I told him.

Immediately, he changed directions.

"Where are we going?" I pulled at his hand, to get mine out of his or to get him to stop; either one would work for me.

Kristen Ashley

I didn't succeed, and Eddie kept walking. "I have to go to the station and then I'm taking you home."

Oh no, I couldn't let him take me home.

"Eddie I can get a ride with—"

He jerked me to a halt and gave me a look that shut my mouth. Then he started walking again, pulling me along behind him.

He walked me to a shiny, red, Dodge Ram. It even had those fancy lights on the top. He opened the passenger side door for me and I tried to get into the high seat gracefully, considering my short skirt and slut shoes. I managed it, but just barely.

"Why don't you take me home first?" I asked him when he got in the car.

"Because I missed my opportunity to talk to you this afternoon. So even though it's nearly two o'clock in the fucking morning, I have you all to myself for the first time, and you're gonna answer a few questions."

I buckled my seat belt (safety first) and then crossed my arms on my chest. I didn't have time to talk to Eddie (not to mention, I didn't want to talk to Eddie). I needed sleep. I didn't have a full day off until Sunday.

That was… I was too tired to count them, but it was too many days away not to sleep.

I tried to talk him out of it. "I don't understand why you're so curious about me. I'm just a quiet, normal person. I know you don't want me bringing a bad influence into Indy's store, but—"

He'd started the truck while I was speaking. At my comment, he turned to me, forearm on the steering wheel.

"This doesn't have anything to do with Indy. And, I hate to break this to you, but you're anything but normal."

My head gave a little jerk and I glared at him. "Yes I am! I'm your normal, average, everyday girl."

He shook his head. "Your normal, average, everyday girl does not work in a strip club. She does not get bizarrely serenaded by her father in a bookstore. She does not transform into a new girl every time she does something to her hair or makeup. And she does not guard every scrap of personal information about her life like it's a State secret."

"I do not guard every scrap of personal information!" I snapped.

"Tell me something personal then," he returned.

58

I tried to find something interesting about myself. I was too tired and freaked out, and anyway, there wasn't much interesting about me. So I threw out the first thing that came to mind.

"My favorite color is green," I told him.

He turned away from me, put the truck into gear and said, "Doesn't count."

"Why not?"

He pulled out onto Colorado Boulevard. "Your favorite color is not a piece of personal information."

"Yes it is."

"Okay, then, your favorite color is a boring piece of personal information that doesn't tell me a thing about you."

I gave up and looked out the window. It seemed a good way to go.

We were silent all the way to the station.

When he parked, I jumped down from the truck, wishing my slut shoes resided in perdition. He came around and grabbed my hand again and we walked into the station.

I'd never been to a police station in my life. It was cleaner than I expected it to be. It didn't look like *NYPD Blue* at all. He walked me through the halls and took me to a room with lockers. He opened one, obviously his, pulled out a flannel shirt and handed it to me. "Put that on."

It was a nice thing to do. It wasn't only chilly, but I didn't wear my Smithie's uniform anywhere but at Smithie's, and his shirt would cover me up.

I put his shirt on and it smelled like him. It was then I thought the shirt wasn't a good idea. Smelling Eddie on Eddie was disturbing enough. Smelling Eddie on me was too much of a good thing.

I didn't have a chance to object. He took my hand again and walked me into another room, this one big, mostly dark and full of desks. There was one guy working, typing on a computer. He looked up when we walked in and his eyes took in Eddie's bloody t-shirt and knuckles.

"Tough night?" he asked.

"Yeah," Eddie replied, not inviting further discourse.

The guy's eyes moved to me. "Looks like you won."

Eddie didn't reply, walked me over to a couch and turned to me.

"Wait here. I'll be five minutes." Then he was gone.

I sat on the couch and the guy was watching me.

"There was a bit of a bar brawl," I explained.

"Yeah, I heard," he replied.

"It started for a good reason." I don't know why, but I decided to defend Eddie.

"Eddie start it?" he asked.

"Yes."

"You the reason?"

I bit my lip then said, "Yes."

"That's a good enough reason."

He turned back to work and I took the opportunity to fish the fifty from my cleavage. It was hard won. I should probably give it to Eddie for the trouble I caused him, but I needed it too much. I put it in my wallet and then waited.

Then I waited some more.

Then I looked at the couch and decided it looked really comfortable. So, for research purposes, I decided to check and see if it was comfortable. So, I stretched out on it and within minutes, I was dead asleep.

꧁꧂

I woke up smelling Eddie.

For a second I thought I was dreaming, but I could feel the sunlight against my closed eyelids so I opened them. I saw unfamiliar surroundings and shot bolt upright in bed.

I was in a queen-size bed that had plaid sheets and a denim-covered comforter. There was a dresser with a mess of stuff on the top, hardwood floors with no rugs, mocha colored walls with no pictures, one nightstand with an alarm clock, phone and some change on it. Then I saw, on the floor, my bright red miniskirt, my purse and my slut shoes lying next to a pair of jeans, cowboy boots and a bloodstained white t-shirt.

"Shit!" I jumped out of bed and stared down at myself. I was wearing my black, cotton, bikini briefs, my Smithie's camisole and Eddie's flannel shirt.

I looked back at the alarm clock. It was eleven forty-five.

"Shit! Shit! Shit!" I shouted and ran to my miniskirt.

Not only was I super late for Fortnum's, I hadn't called Mom. She would be worried sick. I'd left my cell phone in my apron (with my tips) and Smithie had taken them away.

I had to get to a phone immediately to let her know I was okay. Then I had to call Indy. Then I had to call a taxi. Then I had to get the hell out of there.

I pulled on my miniskirt trying not to think of how I got from the police station to Eddie's house, to Eddie's *bed,* and out of some of my clothes. I looked back at the bed and saw that only one pillow had a dent in it. I also saw that the other pillow had a note on it. I ran to it, my skirt still unzipped at the back, and snatched it off the pillow.

Gone to work. When you get up, call me. And he left a phone number.

"Shit!"

I ran out of the room, my hands at my back to zip the skirt. I made it to the hall and crashed headfirst into Eddie.

I flew backward a step, which would have been more if his hands hadn't caught me.

"You're awake," he said.

I looked up at him. "I need to use your phone."

No greeting, no nothing. I was close to hysteria and Eddie must have sensed it because he made no comment, walked out of the hall and into the living room. I followed him, finishing the zip on my skirt. He grabbed a cordless phone and handed it to me.

I took it and bent my head over it immediately, wandering away from him and punching in the number to home.

Mom answered on the first ring.

"Mom?"

"Jet! My God, I've been worried sick."

"Are you okay?" I asked.

"No, I'm not. I'm worried sick. Where are you? Are you safe?"

"Yes, I'm safe. I'm sorry. I left my phone in my apron and things got a little strange at the club and I fell asleep at the police station."

What was I saying? She didn't need to know that. I'd give her another stroke.

"Excuse me? Police station?" Mom asked, her voice rising.

"It was nothing, never mind. I'll be home soon."

But I heard the phone being moved around and then I heard Trixie.

"Jet! Where are you? Your mother's been worried sick. What's this about a police station?"

I closed my eyes, overcome with relief that Mom wasn't alone. I sank down on the sofa. Leaning forward, I put my elbows on my knees and my head in my hand. "Trixie, I'm so glad you're there. Is Mom okay?"

"No, she's not okay. We're both not okay. You didn't come home last night."

"I know. I'm so sorry. Is she all right? Was she able to get to the bathroom, take care of herself?" I asked.

"She's fine. She got herself up, walked to your room and saw you didn't come home so she called me. I came over and took care of her."

"Has she had breakfast?" I went on.

"Yes."

"Were you able to get her she dressed?" I kept at it.

"Yes!" Trixie cried. "Where are you? You didn't answer your cell. We called the bookstore. They didn't know where you were. No one was answering at the club. We were scared to death."

It then occurred to me where I was and my head snapped up and I looked at Eddie. He was standing; shoulders leaned against the wall, arms crossed on his chest, watching me.

Shit.

I looked back at my knees. "I'm at Eddie's."

Silence.

"Trixie?" I called.

I heard her say, not into the mouthpiece, "She's at Eddie's."

The phone was moved around again and Mom asked, "You're at Eddie's?"

Her tone was both hopeful and snoopy. Neither of these were good things.

"It's a long story. I'll tell you later. Listen, Mom, I'll be home as soon as I can."

"No, no, don't rush," Mom replied hurriedly. "We're okay. Ada's coming over and Trixie's managed to rearrange her appointments. Take your time."

I closed my eyes and prayed for divine intervention.

I waited a beat and nothing happened.

Guess God was busy with war and famine and the like.

"Mom, I'll be home as soon as I can get there. Okay?"

"Is Eddie bringing you home?" she asked.

"I don't know," I answered.

"Am I going to meet him?" she pushed.

"I don't know. Listen, Mom, I've got to go."

"Okay, dollface," she said, her voice totally changed from pissed off mother on the edge to sweet as pie. "See you."

I pushed the on/off button and looked up at Eddie. "I've got to call Indy."

"I called her before I came home. She's not worried. Her people come and go as they please," he said.

Not me, I worked mornings. She needed me for the rush hours and that's when I worked for her. I'd never been late for Indy.

I got off the couch, put the phone in its receiver and walked across the room, past Eddie, to the bedroom. I nabbed my slut shoes and sat on the side of the bed.

"Your Mom okay?" Eddie asked.

I looked to the side and Eddie was leaning in the doorway.

I bent double and started to slip on my shoes. "Yeah. Trixie's there and Ada's coming over."

The next thing I knew, Eddie was crouched in front of me and he took my shoes away.

My head jerked up. "Hey!"

"I want you to get back into bed," he said, straightening out of his crouch.

"*What?*" I screeched, half flipped out, half angry, jumping off the bed, which placed me standing less than a foot away from him.

"Get back into bed," he repeated.

"I can't get back into bed. I have to get to work." I began to slide away, but he twisted his torso and tossed the shoes in the direction from whence they came. After he'd done that, he came back around and his arm came out, blocking me.

Then he said, "I carried you from the station to the truck, from the truck to bed, took off your skirt and shoes, and you slept like the dead the whole time. Work can wait. You need some rest."

I couldn't think about Eddie carrying me around, or taking off my clothes, or how any of that made my belly feel. So I didn't think about it and focused on the current drama.

"Work *can't* wait. I need the money," I told him.

"How much did you give him?" Eddie asked.

I stared at him. "Who?"

"Your Dad. How much did you give him?"

My blood pressure skyrocketed.

"That's none of your business," I snapped.

He took the mini-step forward which had me moving back. The backs of my legs hit the bed and I had nowhere to go but down, and he was inches away.

"Move back," I demanded.

"I asked how much you gave him," Eddie repeated.

"Move back!"

"How much?"

"Five hundred dollars, okay?"

I gave in. I had to. Eddie was leaning into me and I had nowhere to go, and I really needed room to move.

"I'll give you five hundred dollars to get back into bed," he declared.

My mouth dropped open and I didn't say a word. There were no words to say.

"I'm absolutely serious," Eddie continued. "You get in bed and I'll give you five hundred dollars. I'll go back to work. You rest, eat whatever's in my fridge, watch TV, I don't give a fuck. But you're not going to work today. You're not doing anything today."

I could not believe my ears, mainly because it was unbelievable.

"I'm not taking your money and I'm not resting, I have things to do," I told him.

"What things?" he asked.

"Things! All right?" I mostly didn't answer. "Now back off."

I put my hands to his chest and gave a shove.

He didn't move.

Wonderful.

I put my hands to my hips and glared at him. "I have to go home."

He didn't move, didn't speak, didn't anything. He just stared down at me with a set look.

I closed my eyes and took a mental breath.

"Do you know what I do for a living?" he asked.

I opened my eyes again so I could blink in confusion.

"Yeah. You're a cop," I answered.

"I'm a detective."

"Okay," I said. I didn't know what else to say.

"Jet, my job is to put two and two together and make four."

"And?" I asked, not knowing what he was talking about and thinking this was a strange turn in the conversation.

His eyes got warm, his hand came up and he tucked some hair behind my ear. When he was done doing that, his hand curled around the side of my neck where his thumb started stroking me.

"I just made four," he said quietly.

I couldn't get caught up in Eddie; his warm, dark eyes, his quiet voice or the fact that he'd just figured me out. I'd think about it later. My life was in turmoil, I needed to focus, and I couldn't focus around Eddie. It was impossible.

"Eddie, I need to get home," I told him in a voice that said I meant it.

He looked at me for a beat. Then his thumb came away from my neck, stroked my cheek, and he said, "I'll take you home."

He walked across the room, grabbed my shoes and brought them to me. I sat back down on the bed and silently put them on. I snagged my purse from the floor.

Eddie walked me out the backdoor, helped me into his truck and took me home.

Chapter 5

I Couldn't Buy a Break (Even if I had the money)

I saw the wrecker hooking up to my car when Eddie drove into the parking lot at my apartment building. Eddie saw it too.

I jumped down from the truck, wincing as my still angry feet protested, and looked at the wrecker. Eddie walked around to my side of the truck, his eyes on the wrecker.

Smithie's friend was doing the tow, looking like he was wearing the same pair of filthy blue coveralls as yesterday. He saw me and gave a small wave. I waved back.

"You know him?" Eddie asked.

"That's my car. I'm having slight car problems."

Eddie's eyes moved to me. "Slight car problems require a jump. Serious car problems require a tow," he said.

I shrugged. I wasn't going to argue about it. I'd probably lose. Mainly because he was right, and I was trying not to think about what serious car problems would mean.

I walked to the building and turned to stop at the front door. "Thanks for bringing me home," I said to Eddie, making it clear that the front door was as far as he was going to go.

He looked at the doors then at me. Then his mouth turned up a little at the corners and he shook his head.

"Just Jet, my ass," he muttered.

"What?" I asked.

"Nothin'."

I heard him. I wasn't going to argue about that either. It wasn't as if I got held at knifepoint and was in bar brawls every day, but I wasn't going to point that out. Not a lot of girls would go out of their way to defend how boring they really were, especially not to guys like Eddie. Anyway, I'd gone that route, and I didn't win that battle either.

He took his wallet out of his back pocket and held a card out to me, putting the wallet back in his pocket.

"You need a lift, you call me," he said.

I didn't take the card. "I'll be okay."

"Jet."

"Seriously. I'll be okay."

All of a sudden, he took three steps forward, backing me into the corner of the overhang that shielded the front doors. My back hit the wall. I stopped and Eddie came in close.

I looked up at him to protest and kept my silence when I saw his eyes all pissed off glittery.

"Someone offers to do something nice for you, you take 'em up on it."

"I'll be okay," I repeated, kind of angry myself then, too.

"I think it's pretty clear you won't be okay. You're workin' two jobs. One of them isn't safe. You don't have time to sleep. You don't have a car. You're taking care of your Mom who isn't well. Your Dad blows into town, cleans out your bank account and makes you the target of a thug. That's not okay."

"It'll get better," I told him.

"When?"

"I don't know, but I have to believe that because if I don't..."

Damn!

Tears started to fill my eyes. I bit my lip and turned my face away. Now was *not* the time to lose my cool. Not in front of Eddie.

"I have to go in," I said and I did. I had to get away from him.

There was no getting away from him, because his arms went around me and he drew me into his body.

I looked up at him, surprised, and saw his eyes had gone liquid.

My body tensed when it came into contact with his from our chests, down our bellies to our hips. Electricity shot through me. I tried to pull away, but one of his arms slid up my back, holding me in position while his head came down and he kissed me.

It was the worst kiss in the history of the world. I could not believe he was kissing me. Hot, handsome Eddie Chavez, kissing me, plain, boring Henrietta Louise McAlister. It freaked me out. I went all stiff, and this was not a good combination.

His head came up and he looked down at me.

I felt the heat in my face.

Such a bad kiss was humiliating and I knew it was all my fault. I would have been happy to be running from a charging elephant. Dancing around in a g-string at Smithie's. Anywhere but there.

He didn't say anything. He was just watching me, and I started to squirm to get away, but he held on tight.

"Let's try that again," he murmured.

"No, I don't——" I started to say, and then his mouth was on mine.

Since I was talking when his lips connected with mine, my mouth was open and, right away, his tongue slid inside.

Dear Lord.

The instant his tongue touched mine, my stomach curled, my bones turned to water and I melted into him. My arms went around his neck, my fingers slid into his hair. I tilted my head to the side and that was it.

His hands went under my camisole. I could feel them sliding across the skin of my back and it made me shiver. I pressed deeper into him. I kept one of my hands in his hair and tucked another one under his arm, pulling his t-shirt free of his jeans and then I slid it across the skin at his back. His warm skin felt yummy. In fact, the kiss was pure *yum*, and I wanted it to go on forever.

"Jeez, Jet, get a room."

I jumped and pulled back and Eddie's arms went slack. Though not *that* slack, he didn't let me go. Both Eddie and I turned to see RJ, one of my neighbors, maneuvering out the front door in his wheelchair.

My face felt like it was on fire.

My body *was* on fire.

"Hey RJ," I greeted, still trying to recover from the kiss. This was hard considering Eddie hadn't let me go.

"Who's the dude?" RJ asked, looking at Eddie.

Eddie was looking over his shoulder, his arms still around me.

"The dude is Eddie. Eddie, RJ, RJ, Eddie," I introduced, feeling like a complete moron. I'd taken my hand out from under Eddie's t-shirt but I was now clutching it at his side for fear my legs would give out if I didn't hold on for dear life.

Eddie nodded to RJ, making it plain RJ was interrupting.

In any other circumstance I might find this funny. Eddie and I were necking at the public entrance to an apartment building in broad daylight, and Eddie glared at RJ as if we had a right to privacy.

However, at that moment, I did not find it funny.

RJ did, and his face cracked into a huge smile. "Boy, Jet, can always count on you to be entertaining."

Wonderful.

I was never going to convince Eddie I was your normal, everyday, average girl.

RJ put his gloved hands to the angled wheels of his chair and pushed forward.

"Later dudes," he said, taking the hint, and then he was off.

I looked back to Eddie and he was shaking his head. "I haven't made out on someone's doorstep in... fuck, I've never made out on someone's doorstep."

I smiled at him because he was funny, and the minute I did it his eyes changed and the change made my insides melt.

"Christ, Jet, you should do that more often," he said.

"What?"

"Smile."

That wiped the smile from my face.

Eddie's slack arms tightened around me. "Un-unh, no retreat. I've gained ground here, I'm not gonna lose it in two minutes."

"I have to go upstairs," I told him.

"I'll let you go upstairs when you agree to have dinner with me tonight," Eddie replied.

Eek!

I hadn't had the chance to process kissing Eddie. I certainly wasn't ready for a date.

Luckily, I had an excuse. "I can't, I have a shift at Smithie's."

Eddie was not deterred. "Tomorrow."

Damn, I had the night off from Smithie's tomorrow.

Before I could think of a plausible excuse, Eddie grinned. He knew he had me. "Six o'clock. I'll pick you up here."

He didn't give me a chance to say anything. His lips came down and touched mine. I could feel most of his body pressed up against me; his arms were around me. I could smell him, and he'd just touched his lips to mine. Therefore, I lost the ability to think.

His lips went away and he asked, "How're you getting to work tonight?"

I blinked to clear my Eddie Daze. "Smithie found out about the knife thing. He says I have to be escorted to and from the building, and while my car's out of commission, he's arranging for one of the bouncers to take me to work."

Eddie ran his fingers through my hair at the temple, and I had to admit, it felt nice.

"Maybe he isn't the asshole I thought he was," Eddie said.

"He takes care of his girls," I told him.

"At least that's one person trying to look out for you. Though, if last night's any indication, he's not doing very well."

"Last night was a fluke," I tried to reassure him.

"Last night is every night at a strip club. You dress like that around drunk guys, shit's gonna happen."

I stared at him.

"Do you *want* me to get mad?" I asked.

His eyes changed. They got warm but serious.

"*Chiquita*, I'll take anything I can get from you."

I didn't know what to say to that, so I didn't say anything at all and just kept staring at him.

Eddie let me go and held the card up between us.

"I gotta get back to work. You need anything or your Mom needs anything, call me."

I took the card. Although I kind of wanted a repeat of what happened when I didn't take it, I *really* needed to check on Mom. Then I needed to check on Dad. Then I needed to do a million other things.

"Thanks Eddie," I said.

He smiled at me, dimple and all, ran his knuckles along my jaw, and then he walked away and, without looking back, I *ran* away.

═══

When I hit the living room, Mom was in her chair at the window and Ada was standing beside her.

"Is that Eddie?" Mom asked, not turning her head away from the window.

I went to the window and saw Eddie standing and talking to Mr. Greasy Coveralls.

71

"Yeah," I answered.

"The Mexican man or the black man?" Ada asked, her eyes not leaving the window either.

"The Mexican man," I told her, watching Eddie. He had put his mirrored sunglasses on and his hands on his hips while he talked. He looked very cool and very hot.

"He's cute," Mom said.

Only Mom would describe Eddie as "cute". He was a lot of things, but he was not cute.

Eddie started to move away and looked up at the apartment building. I jumped out of the window as fast as I could, not wanting him to catch me checking him out. I had enough to worry about with the looming date to have him thinking I was some love struck cocktail waitress staring longingly out the window at him.

Mom and Ada were still playing nosy neighbors.

"Get away from the window," I said to them.

"That sure is a fancy truck he has," Ada remarked.

She wasn't wrong. It sure was.

Neither of them moved from the window, and I could swear I saw Ada wave.

I groaned and went to the bathroom, because I was dying to go. Then I looked in the mirror and let out a little scream. I still had half my makeup on, and it wasn't the good half. One word: scary. And Eddie had kissed me looking like this.

How weird was that?

At least my sexy hair held up.

I washed my face, went to my bedroom and put on some jeans and a t-shirt. I rolled up Eddie's shirt and tucked it under my pillow as a keepsake. I'd give it back if he asked for it, but if he didn't I was stealing it, and I didn't care what that said about me.

Then I walked into the kitchen to get some food and I heard Mom wheel in behind me.

"Why didn't you ask Eddie up to the apartment?" she asked.

"He had to get to work," I told her.

Mom wheeled further into the kitchen. "We saw you drive in. You were down there for a long time. Long enough for him to come up and meet your mother."

Wonderful.

She was using her snooty mother tone, reminding me I'd been rude.

"We were talking about something," I explained.

"You could have talked about it up here. I could have made him some iced tea, maybe a sandwich. I'm getting good at sandwiches. It's lunchtime. Everyone has to eat lunch," Mom pointed out.

"He's a busy guy."

"Not so busy he can't take time to eat."

"What's he do?" Ada asked, coming up behind Mom.

"He's a cop," I told her.

Ada's eyes got huge in her wrinkled face.

"Really?" she breathed, her eyes working, probably wondering how she could finagle a ride-along.

"You're ashamed," Mom said.

My eyes moved to Mom and I stared at her. "What?"

"You're ashamed of me. That's why you didn't bring him up here," she declared.

"I'm not ashamed!" I snapped.

And I wasn't. There were far more complicated reasons why I didn't bring Eddie up, and it had nothing to do with being ashamed of my mother.

"There's no other reason," she accused.

"I told you, he had to get to work."

"You didn't want him to see me like this." Mom indicated her chair.

"That's just not true," I replied.

"I don't believe you. You never bring anyone around. I can't help how I am right now, but I'm getting better all the time," Mom went on.

"It's not that," I said.

"Then what is it?" she asked.

"We were kissing, all right!" I shouted.

Yeesh.

Mom's mouth snapped closed and her eyes got all bright and dreamy. Ada clasped her hands in front of her with obvious joy.

This was not a good sign.

"Ladies, don't get excited" I warned.

"How can I not get excited? He's cute. He has a good job and a fancy truck. What's not to get excited about?" Mom asked.

73

"And he looks good in those mirrored sunglasses. I bet most cops wish they could wear those sunglasses like your Eddie can. He can really pull them off," Ada put in.

I turned to Ada first. "Ada, honey, he's not *my* Eddie." Then I turned to Mom, "The reason you shouldn't get excited is because he's a nice guy. That's it, the end. At first, I think he was curious, but now he's..."

I didn't know what he was. I had to find an explanation for it; for the kiss, his defending my virtue last night, everything. I usually did this in my head, where it was safe, not out loud to my mother.

My mind whirled to find an explanation.

He was a good guy, a cop for goodness sake. He had to wonder about me, especially since I spent time with his friends. Now he'd figured me out and obviously wanted to rescue me. And although I wouldn't mind being rescued by Eddie, what happened after that? What happened when he realized that I wasn't interesting and exciting? What happened when he found out I was really Just Jet?

I didn't want to know.

"He's what?" Mom snapped me out of my thoughts.

"Nothing. We'll see. Just don't get excited, okay?" I told her.

She nodded, but she still looked dreamy.

Wonderful.

I thought about the fifty in my wallet. "You've been cooped up in here for days. I'm wheeling you down to Chipotle for lunch. Ada, you comin'? My treat."

Ada smiled. "I'd love to. I never go anywhere."

"All right ladies, we're movin' out," I announced.

Food, I found, was always a good way of getting people's minds off things, including handsome cops with fancy trucks.

I made it to Smithie's on time because Lenny picked me up and took me in.

The minute Smithie saw me, his eyes rolled to the ceiling and he shouted, "It's a fuckin' miracle!"

I smiled at him as I handed him my jeans jacket and purse and he handed me my apron and an envelope.

"Your cell's still in the pocket. The envelope has your tips from last night. Your fuckin' flea-bitten, ratty-ass sweater is behind the bar."

"Thanks, Smithie," I said.

I opened the top of the envelope, which was tucked in and flipped through the notes. I kept a running tally of my tips, mentally paying bills and buying groceries the minute I made the money. As I flipped through the notes, I decided I'd done a miscalculation because, if my calculation was correct, there were two hundred more dollars than I expected to be there, and that was impossible.

I'd remember an extra two hundred dollars. I'd remember an extra two dollars.

It was packed last night but the tips weren't *that* good.

I flipped through it again and the two hundred dollars were still there.

"Smithie, I think you gave me part of my float." And part of everyone else's float too.

Smithie's head was turned away, looking at the stage and he didn't look at me when he spoke. "Nope. That's what was in your apron after I cashed you out."

I stared at him.

"Smithie, there's an extra two hundred dollars in here. Maybe you accidentally gave me—"

His head turned to me. "It was in your fuckin' apron."

"Smithie—" I started again.

His hand went up and he had a funny look on his face. It was then that I knew he'd slipped in the extra money.

I'd started at Smithie's in the days when Mom was still bad. Back then, I'd drag in after visiting her in the hospital. He knew about Mom and my job at Fortnum's, and now he knew about my car.

My heart clutched, my eyes filled with tears and I opened my mouth to speak, but he leaned in to me.

"Don't fuckin' cry and don't say another fuckin' word. I don't want this gettin' around. As far as you're concerned, that was your take last night. Do you fuckin' understand me?"

I nodded.

"Good," he said, turning away from me again. "Get to work."

I was hoping for a quiet night and it seemed to be going that way. It was a completely different experience, working after having a full night's sleep and then some.

Before I went to work, and after I'd taken Mom and Ada to lunch and cleaned the house, I called Dad's hotel just in case he was still there, but they said he'd checked out. Then I called Indy, and she was cool with me making up the hours or not, she really didn't care. Everyone came and went at Fortnum's, and somehow it worked. I asked her if Dad had dropped by but she said she hadn't seen him.

It was close to closing and I'd had a decent night. I had energy. I had two night's tips. And I had Smithie's generosity. If I wasn't in slow-burn, freak-out zone that would likely escalate to complete hysteria by the time my date with Eddie swung around, I would have actually relaxed.

I was coming back from a bathroom break, leaving the restroom and entering the back hall when I was grabbed by the arm and pulled back.

"Hey!" I shouted, turning around, ready to scream, when I saw Dad.

Not good.

I really didn't want my Dad to know I was working in a titty bar and I really, *really* didn't want him to see me in my Smithie's uniform.

"Dad, what are you doing here?" I asked.

"Jet, I didn't want to drag you into this but I have no choice." He looked down the hall, clearly in a panic.

"Dad, what's going on?"

He started pulling me down the hall, toward the fire exit at the back. "We gotta go."

I jerked my arm out of his hand and said, "I can't go. I'm working. Tell me what's going on."

He didn't have a chance to tell me as we both heard someone at the other end of the hall say Dad's name.

Dad shoved me behind him and we both looked down the hall at Slick.

"You're a hard man to find," Slick said.

At that, I realized that Dad hadn't spent the last two days looking for Slick and sorting this out as he promised. Dad had spent it hiding from Slick.

"We got things to talk about, you and me," Slick said.

"Fine. Sure. We'll talk. We'll go back in the club," Dad replied.

Dad was positioning his body in front of me so Slick couldn't get to me.

"Not in the club, here," Slick returned. "This conversation should last about two seconds after you give me the thirty grand you owe me."

Oh... dear... Lord.

Thirty thousand dollars?

I felt my stomach drop to my toes.

Dad put his hands out, palms up. "I don't have it on me, Slick. Who carries that kind of cake around? I'll go get it and——"

"Yeah," Slick said, looking beyond Dad to me. "You go get it and I'll just take your pretty little girl with me, and we'll have some fun while you're gettin' it."

My heart fell to my toes to keep my stomach company.

"Slick," Dad said.

Slick pulled out a knife. "No more talkin'."

Then everything happened so fast, I didn't have time to think.

Dad pushed me back, yelling, "*Run!*"

I would have run (maybe), but instead I teetered on my slut shoes (this time, a pair of forties-style black sandals with peek-a-boo toes and a thin ankle strap) and fell down hard on my behind.

Dad charged forward and I saw the flash of a knife.

I didn't think. I got to my feet, screaming at the top of my lungs, and ran forward, too. Dad had jerked Slick around, grappling with the knife, and Slick's back was to me. I jumped on it, wrapping my arms around his neck, my legs around his waist, and squeezed as hard as I could.

Slick disengaged from Dad, ran backwards and slammed me into a wall. My head flew back and cracked against the plaster.

"Don't hurt my girl!" Dad shouted and lunged forward again.

"Go, Dad! Get out of here!" I yelled.

All of a sudden, there was a bunch of people. I was holding onto Slick in a death grip and he was jerking this way and that, trying to dislodge me. There were men shouting, women screaming, and hands on me trying to pull me away.

Then Slick whirled and began to slash out randomly with the knife and everyone jumped back, including, I vaguely noticed, Vance, the hot guy who worked for Lee.

Then Tanya rushed forward and started beating Slick with her tray, using it when she needed as a shield. Vance grabbed her by the waist, picking her up bodily, her legs pedaling, still hitting out at thin air with the tray, and pulled her down the hall.

Slick turned, ran to the fire exit, and twisted his body so his weight and momentum had me slamming against the door. The crossbar tagged my hip so hard, I cried out and let go, landing unsteadily on my slut shoes, and Slick ran away.

I had no time to think or do anything. The fire alarm went off and it was blaring loudly.

Then Smithie had a hold of me. He shoved me and I landed in Lenny's arms.

"Take her inside and do not fuckin' leave her side," Smithie ordered, then took off after Slick.

Lenny pulled me inside. Vance (without Tanya) passed us at a run, going out the backdoor.

I didn't hesitate. I dragged Lenny around the whole club looking for Dad. I was limping, kind of, because my hip and butt bone both hurt like hell.

There was no sign of him.

When I yanked Lenny back into the club from the dancer's dressing room, the lights were on full and the fire alarm had been turned off. The stage was empty, people were standing around and the cops were there.

I scanned the people to see if I could find my Dad, but he wasn't there.

"Fuck!" I shouted, because it was definitely the time to say the f-word.

Smithie came in from outside, breathing heavy, and bore down on me. "You wanna tell me what in *the fuck* is goin' on?" he yelled.

"I don't know!" I yelled back. "I have to find my Dad. He was here and Slick was after him."

"Forget your Dad. We're talkin' about *you*," Smithie shot back. "That's twice you had some fuckin' guy with a knife after you."

"He isn't after me," I told him.

"No, from where I stood, it fuckin' looked like you were after him," Smithie returned.

"He pulled a knife on my Dad!" I yelled.

"Someone pulls a knife, you get the fuck outta Dodge. You don't jump on his back. Fuck! You're a crazy woman!" Smithie shouted.

"I'm not crazy!" I shouted back.

A plainclothes police officer walked up and interrupted us with a soft cough. He introduced himself as Detective Jimmy Marker and told me he had to ask a few questions.

Smithie pointed at me. "You're a pain in my fuckin' ass." Then he stomped away.

The detective had the opportunity to ask me two questions before his eyes moved beyond me and his chin lifted in that silent greeting men do so well.

Then I felt fingers curl into the waistband of my miniskirt.

I began to turn around when I heard Eddie say, "Give me a minute, Jimmy."

Uh-oh.

Jimmy looked at Eddie, his eyes knowing and maybe slightly amused, though I didn't know what in *the hell* was amusing right now. He nodded and wandered away.

Eddie pulled me back a few steps and moved in front of me. One look at his face and "uh-oh" didn't do it justice. It was definitely the kind of look that garnered a "holy shit".

Eddie was seriously pissed off.

I tell you, I couldn't buy a break.

Before I could say anything, Eddie turned to Lenny, who had still not left my side. He communicated something nonverbally because Lenny said, "I got orders not to leave her."

Eddie fished in his back jeans pocket and flashed his badge.

Lenny nodded, looked at me and moved away.

"Eddie..." I said before he started but he lifted up his hand, Smithie style, and I shut up.

I was getting "the hand" a lot these days, and it was beginning to tick me off.

He waited a beat, hooking his badge onto the belt on his jeans. Then he shook his head.

"You know, I don't even know what to say," he said.

"Let me explain," I requested.

"You got an explanation for this? This I have to hear."

I actually didn't have an explanation so I fell silent.

"That's what I thought," Eddie said.

All right, enough was enough. I mean, what would *he* do?

"What could I do? He had a knife and was fighting with Dad. I had to jump on his back and try to help!" I yelled.

Okay, so before, it actually *was* an "uh-oh" moment and *this* was a "holy shit" moment.

Eddie's face changed and he looked at me like I just told him I wanted to go to Pluto for Spring Break.

"I hadn't heard that part," Eddie said in his scary quiet voice.

"Eddie—" I started again.

He didn't let me finish.

"Have you lost your mind?"

This wasn't said in a quiet voice. This was shouted, and everyone, cops, bouncers, dancers and waitresses, turned to stare.

I opened my mouth to defend myself, as if I had to. I mean, really, it *was* my Dad. But didn't get a word out.

"That's what I'm talking about." As if things weren't bad enough with pissed off, shouting Eddie, Smithie showed up at our tête-à-tête.

"It wasn't like I *asked* to wrestle in the hallway with a guy with a knife," I said to the both of them, pissed off myself now, hands on hips and everything.

"You see a knife, you run as fast as you fuckin' can," Smithie returned.

Now he was repeating himself.

"You run in these shoes," I told him.

"That's it. You wear tennis shoes on shift from now on," Smithie declared.

My eyes widened and I stared. None of Smithie's girls wore tennis shoes. The cocktail waitresses were required to have no less than a three inch heel (I saw Smithie measure once) and the strippers wore sky-high platforms.

"I can't wear tennis shoes!" I snapped. "Do you know what that'd do to my tips?"

Now both Eddie and Smithie were staring at me like I'd donated my brain to science pre-mortem.

Smithie turned to Eddie. "I'm leavin' her in your hands. You fuckin' deal with her." And he stalked away. Again.

Eddie dragged a hand through his hair.

"Eddie," Jimmy Marker was back, "I really gotta ask her a few questions."

Eddie flipped his hand out in an annoyed "go ahead" gesture, but didn't leave my side as Detective Marker asked me questions. I told him my story, feeling Eddie get more and more tense as I told it. Don't ask me how I felt this. Trust me, I just *knew.* Detective Marker took notes and asked me if I knew how to get a hold of my Dad—which I didn't.

He took my number, turned to Eddie and said, "She's all yours."

Not good.

Before Eddie could do or say anything, I walked quickly to the bar to get my coat, sweater and purse. Maybe if I ignored him, he'd go away.

I took off my apron, pulling out my cell and slapped the apron on the top of the bar to begin cashing out.

Smithie was behind the bar, glaring at me.

"Am I fired?" I asked.

Smithie snatched the apron away and said, "You're a pain in my fuckin' ass, that's what you are." He shoved the apron under the bar and shoved my stuff at me. "I'll cash you out. I'll have your tips ready for you on Friday."

Guess I wasn't fired.

Then I noticed, down the bar, Lee was standing and talking to Vance.

Shit *and* damn.

My night was now complete.

What was Lee doing here?

"Hey Lee," I called, trying to be cool.

He looked up, his eyes flicked behind me, he grinned broad and he looked back at me.

"Jet," he replied.

I smiled at Vance who was also grinning, his eyes giving my body a sweep, then his grin broadened to a breathtaking, white smile when his gaze caught mine. Then he looked behind me and I felt a hand curl around my upper arm.

"Let's go," Eddie said in my ear.

I stiffened and turned. Obviously, the ignoring thing didn't work.

I tried another evasive tactic.

"Lenny's taking me home," I said.

That didn't work either. Eddie steered me toward the front door.

"No one's takin' you home. You're comin' to my place."

Eek!

I dug in my heels and pulled my arm out of his hand.

"I can't. I have to get home," I told him.

"You aren't going home," he returned.

I stared at him. "I *have* to go home."

"You aren't safe at home. You'll be safe with me and that's where you're stayin'."

At his words, panic filled me.

"You think Slick will go to my apartment?" I asked.

"I think Slick'll do just about anything to get his thirty K," Eddie answered.

My stomach rolled and I leaned forward.

"But, my Mom's there. She can't..." I stopped talking and then, not meaning to, I gave him the girlie "please" look that worked on Smithie, "Eddie, I have to go home."

He looked at me for several seconds, then he muttered, "Fuck." He grabbed my hand and pulled me forward. "I'll take you home."

Relief flooded through me as he pushed through the front doors. "Thanks Eddie."

My relief was short-lived.

"We'll stop by my place on the way. I'll pick up a change of clothes."

Eek, eek and *eek!*

"What?" I shouted.

Eddie stopped us by his truck. "You don't stay at my place, then I'm stayin' at yours."

No.

No, no, no.

"I'm sure I'll be all right," I assured him.

"I'm sure too, mainly because I'll be there to make sure," Eddie said, opening the passenger side door.

"We don't have a lot of room," I told him as he helped me into his truck.

He stood in the opened door, looking at me.

"You got a couch?" he asked.

"Yes," I said, and wished I didn't. "But it isn't very comfortable."

"You sleep on it?" he asked.

"No," I answered

"Your Mom sleep on it?" Eddie kept it up.

This wasn't getting any better.

"No," I answered.

"Then you have room."

"Eddie——" I said to the slamming door.

Eddie swung in behind the wheel and my mind whirled, trying to find some excuse, any excuse, for Eddie not to come to my house, spend the night on the couch, protecting me from men with knives.

I couldn't find one.

He started the truck and off we went... to my doom.

Chapter 6

It Was Time to Take Things in My Own Hands

The alarm went off and I stared at it.

Five twenty.

I hated my life.

I hit snooze.

My alarm went again.

Five twenty-seven.

I *really* hated my life.

I hit snooze again.

My alarm went again.

Five thirty-four.

Seriously, my life sucked.

I turned off the alarm, rolled out of bed, and, still half asleep, shuffled out the door, through the living room and into the kitchen. I opened the coffee filter to make sure Mom had set it up last night with coffee. She did, so I flipped the switch. I shuffled back through the living room and down the short hall, yawning and pulling my hair away from my face with one of my hands.

I knocked on Mom's bedroom door, and when I heard her call I opened it and leaned against the doorjamb. I didn't have the energy to hold my body upright.

"Mornin', Mama," I said across the room.

"Mornin', dollface," Mom replied sleepily.

"You getting up?" I lifted both my hands to pull my hair off my neck and bundle it on the top of my head and I left my hands there.

Mom tried to get up with me in the mornings. That way I could get her sorted before I went to work. She could sleep while I worked, not to mention she could go to bed early.

"Sure, I'll have breakfast with you," Mom said.

"You wanna try it alone today? Or do you want me to help?" I asked.

Mom was walking around a bit. Depending on her energy levels, she could get herself in and out of her chair, to the bathroom, around the apartment, even stand at the kitchen counter for a while. She was also doing a lot better at getting herself dressed, which was exhausting one-handed. The PT and OT told her she'd get used to it, get stronger, and it would eventually be a walk in the park (literally). Even though progress was slow, it was happening.

Mornings were good. Evenings were not so good. Ada came over at night to watch TV with Mom because Ada wanted the company, but also to be close to Mom in case something happened. Ada was too old to do transfers or pick Mom up if she fell, but she could make a phone call or go down the hall to one of the more able-bodied neighbors.

"I'm gonna try it alone," Mom told me, ever the trooper.

"Okeydoke." I said, pulling the door to, but keeping it slightly ajar so she could have privacy, but I could hear if she called. I turned away, my hands going back to holding up my hair, my eyes to the floor. I walked a step and then stopped dead.

I saw two bare feet, their heels and ankles covered with the hems of some faded jeans. My eyes traveled up the jeans, hit a set of well-defined abdominal muscles covered in luscious olive skin. The abs gave way to a very nice chest and shoulders, and on top of it all was Eddie's head, complete with sexy-sleepy eyes and messy hair.

I froze and stared.

I totally forgot about Eddie.

"Where's your bathroom?" he asked, his voice slightly gruff from sleep.

I didn't have the capacity to speak, so I just took one of my hands from my hair and pointed at a door.

He walked the three steps to me, stopped, put his hand to my jaw and brushed his lips against mine. A thrill of electricity tore through my body, rooting me to the spot, and then he walked into the bathroom and closed the door.

I stood there a second then whirled and ran to Mom's bedroom, suddenly full of energy. I threw her door open and charged in then closed it behind me.

Mom had the light on and was sitting on the side of the bed. Her head shot around and she looked at me, her eyes bright and wide awake. "Was that a man's voice I heard?" she asked.

I didn't answer.

What could I say? I was in a tizzy.

I ran to her bathroom, throwing on the light and staring at myself in the mirror. Thank God, I didn't look a fright. Face free of makeup and I didn't have a bedhead. In fact, Trixie's new 'do seemed the ultimate. It looked good all the time, even after I'd slept on it.

When I turned around, Mom was standing, leaning against the doorjamb to the bathroom. "What's happening?" she asked.

"I forgot to tell you, Eddie's here," I answered.

Her eyes got wide. "You brought a man home last night?"

"I'm sorry," I replied. "It isn't what you—"

"That's great!" she cried.

I closed my eyes.

My mother.

I opened my eyes.

"Mom, it isn't what you think. It's a long story, I'll tell you later."

"You have a lot of long stories lately. None, incidentally, that you've actually told me," Mom returned.

I didn't have time for this. It was morning and Eddie was there.

"Mom," I whined, sounding like a six year old. "Eddie's here!"

Mom looked at me for a second, nodded and turned, all business. "Right. I need to use the bathroom, then you can help me get my bra on and I'll get dressed."

We took care of Mom first and I left her to the dressing bit. I used her bathroom and her face soap and tore her brush through my hair. I stared at myself in her mirror. I was wearing the LA Dodgers nightshirt that my sister sent me. It was huge and shapeless and came down to about mid-thigh. Eddie had already seen me in it, which wasn't exactly devastating, but I wished I'd been wearing some cute, girlie pajamas or a nightie.

I didn't know what to do. If I got all dolled up before appearing in the common areas of the apartment, I'd look like I was trying too hard. But the Dodgers nightshirt lacked panache.

Who was I kidding? It was me who lacked panache. I'd just have to go with it.

By the time I was out of her bathroom, Mom was no longer in her room, so I went into the hallway and the main bathroom door was open. I ducked in quickly, brushed my teeth and came out, hearing voices coming from the kitchen.

I took a calming breath, squared my shoulders and forged ahead.

I walked in the kitchen, trying to look cool and casual, as if I had guys over all the time and didn't feel like an idiot in my Dodgers nightshirt.

Eddie was sitting at the table. He'd topped the jeans with a tight, red t-shirt and had a mug of coffee in front of him. He looked up at me when I walked in. His eyes moved the length of me and I could see the dimple come out. I didn't know what to make of that, but decided to consider it a good thing.

Mom spoke and my attention swung to her.

"Hey dollface. Don't worry, Eddie and me introduced ourselves. I'm making him eggs." She threw one of her gorgeous smiles at Eddie then her eyes turned back to me. "You want coffee?"

Mom was standing at the counter, her wheelchair positioned by the table. She'd put on a lilac t-shirt dress that had peach flowers embroidered on the v-neck. It was essentially a modern-day muumuu. It was easy to put on because, if she stood up, gravity did a lot of the work, and it was stretchy so she could shove her bum arm through. It was simple and inelegant, but with her coloring, it looked smashing on her.

"Thanks, Mom. In a second."

My brain was beginning to kick in and worry was starting to envelope me.

I turned to Eddie and asked, "Can I talk to you a minute?"

I didn't wait for him to answer, just turned around and walked into the living room. I heard him follow me.

I needed somewhere private to talk and looked around. The living room was no good; Mom could hear (and she'd be listening, for certain). The dining room was part of the living room, and I couldn't take him to Mom's bedroom.

I sighed huge and took him to my room.

My room was boring. My old apartment was part of a big Victorian mansion that had been sliced up into apartments decades ago. It had all sorts of wonky rooms, wood floors, and I'd made the most of it with fun little knick-knacks, Christmas lights covered in flowers, that kind of stuff. I hadn't had time to make this new space fun, not only my room but also the entire apartment. All my old stuff was still in boxes in the corners. The space was boring and depressing, and looking at it through what I imagined were Eddie's eyes, kind of embarrassing.

He followed me into the room and didn't even look around. He was watching me.

"Can you close the door please?" I asked.

He did as I asked, and when he turned back to me, I launched in.

"Listen, Eddie, Mom doesn't know Dad's in town, and I don't want her to know. They don't get along and it'll just upset her. In fact, I don't want her to know any of what's been going on. She had a stroke eight months ago and I don't want her troubled with this. If she knew about all this stuff, she'd be worried sick, her blood pressure would get out-of-control, and I don't even want to think...." I paused, not wanting to get upset, took a breath and finished, "So you can't say anything."

I waited to argue, for him to tell me I was wrong, or being unfair, or that I should warn her, or for him to disagree with me in some way, but instead he said, "All right."

I blinked at him.

"All right?" I asked.

"Yeah, all right," he repeated.

I stared.

He was far more awake. His hair was still messy, but it suited him (in a big way) and he was watching me closely.

"That's it?" I asked.

"Nope," he answered.

I knew it. Here we go.

"Okay then, what?"

He took a step toward me, pulled me into his arms and kissed me. It was a serious kiss, including tongue; no brush on the lips this time, and there was absolutely no need for a do-over.

It was delicious.

When he ended the kiss and started to lift his head, I pressed my fingers in his hair at the same time I went up on tiptoe, my mouth following his. I didn't care if it seemed needy or greedy. All I knew was I wanted more.

He made a noise that sounded an awful lot like a groan and he kissed me again, walking me backwards, his mouth on mine. He shifted us and we were falling onto the bed, him on his back and me on top of him. We bounced, our lips disengaged and I was about to say something, trying to cut through my Eddie Daze, when he flipped me on my back and rolled over on top of me.

He wasn't messing around. It wasn't play. This was serious stuff. We were full-on necking and groping, mouths, tongues and hands everywhere. It was unbelievably fantastic. All of this was leading somewhere and I wanted to go there. I wanted it *bad*.

All of a sudden, he pulled his mouth away and tucked my face in his throat.

"Eddie?" I whispered against his skin, confused at the quick change and not liking it (at all).

"Your Mom. My eggs," was all he said.

Damn! I totally and completely forgot.

Furthermore, if I kept this up, I'd be late again for Indy.

I was the worst daughter in the world and the worst employee in the universe. If I didn't sort all of this out soon, I'd be out of two jobs, and Mom and I would be living on the street eating cat food out of tins with our fingers.

I jerked away, jumping off the bed but Eddie grabbed a handful of my nightshirt and yanked me back.

"Hang on there, *chiquita*," he said and I came off my feet and landed in his lap.

I looked at him and muttered semi-hysterically, "I have to get going. I have to take a shower. I have to go to work and, after work, I gotta find Dad and sort this mess out."

I was pushing against him to get up and we got in kind of a slapping match with our hands (well, I was slapping, Eddie was more in control and defend mode). Finally he grabbed my wrists and held them between our bodies.

"Jet, calm down."

"I can't calm down. I have things to do, I can't just——"

He interrupted, "Have a life?"

"Exactly!" I was so relieved he understood I sagged against him.

His eyes got weird and he shook his head. "Jet, you are *not* going to find your Dad. If your Dad gets in touch with you, you phone me."

I glared at him.

I *did not* think so.

It was time for me to take things in my own hands.

"I have to figure this out, Eddie. If I don't, I could lose my job at Smithie's, and I need that job. Smithie is a good guy, but there are limits to the times cops can come and shut him down because of me."

Then, like an idiot, I forged ahead, planning my day verbally, "I'll work late for Indy, make up the hours, go out tonight, hit the spots where Dad hangs out when he's in Denver—"

"Aren't you forgetting something?" he cut in.

I stared at him, confused.

"We have a date tonight," he reminded me.

Damn, I forgot that too.

He looked at my face and his jaw tensed. "Christ, you're killer on a guy's self-confidence."

I was *such* an idiot. No, I was beyond idiot, though I didn't know what beyond idiot was.

"I'm so sorry," I said, leaning into him a little.

He let go of my wrists and his arms went around my waist. He tucked his face into my neck and right below my ear he said, "If you're really sorry, you can make it up to me tonight."

Eek!

"Eggs," I said, trying to stay focused, even as a shiver ran through me.

He pulled his head from my neck and smiled at me, dimple and all.

I was pretty certain he felt the shiver.

Then the dimple disappeared and he looked at me. "I'll take you to work, but I have to ask you not to go anywhere without someone with you. It's not safe. Can you promise me that?"

I thought about it. I thought about lying about it. I decided I could and said, "Sure."

He watched me for a beat.

"Mom," I reminded him, thinking to change the subject and coming off his lap.

I grabbed his hand and pulled him from my bed.

It was not a picture I'd soon forget, Eddie sitting on my bed. In fact, I hoped it was burned into my memory forever.

He didn't resist, but the minute he stood, his hands came up and rested on either side of my neck, right where it met my shoulders.

"You wouldn't lie to me, would you?" he asked, watching me closely.

"About?" I tried wide-eyed and innocent.

He wasn't biting.

"Anything," he replied.

I took a deep breath and decided to be honest. "Maybe, but only if it was important."

"Like your Dad being in deep shit, that kind of important?"

I bit my lip.

He sighed. "You have my card?"

I nodded.

"Program me into your cell," he ordered. "Call me if you need anything, and do not do anything stupid."

I could do the first two. The last one I wasn't so sure about.

⬧⬧⬧

Eddie dropped me off in front of Fortnum's, and I walked in five minutes after opening time.

The line at the espresso counter was five deep, but the minute Tex saw me, he pointed the portafilter at me and boomed, "We got rules around here, Loopy Loo!"

I'd been working there for over three months and the only rule there seemed to be was that nothing but country or rock 'n' roll could be played on the CD player. I didn't even want to remember the day I put in my Coldplay CD. Ally went berserk.

I figured Tex wasn't happy with me doing a no-show the day before and I felt like a total heel. I started to say something when Tex continued.

"Next time you get in a bar brawl or wrestle with some guy holding a knife, you call me."

All five customers turned around and stared at me.

I stared at Tex.

"What?" I asked.

"I'm Fortnum's designated bodyguard," Tex told me.

I looked at Duke, who was working behind the espresso counter with Tex.

"He kinda is," Duke confirmed.

I had to say, I was a bit alarmed that Fortnum's needed a designated body-guard. I didn't have time to think about it because Indy came up behind me, grabbed my hand and pulled me behind the book counter.

"I guess Lee told you," I said to her when we stopped and I caught a look at her serious face.

"Yeah, he told me. Are you okay?" she asked.

"Sure," I said, trying to make it sound like I had it all together.

She didn't buy it, and her eyes narrowed.

"Jet?"

"No, really, I'm fine."

She moved closer to me and squeezed my hand. Then she said in a quiet voice, "I know you think you're pulling the wool over everyone's eyes, but we all know that everything isn't fine with you. Talk to me, Jet. Maybe I can help."

I didn't know what it was, maybe the hand squeeze, maybe the quiet voice, maybe because she'd always been so nice to me. Whatever it was, I took a breath, trying to think of some way to evade her question and then, instead, it all came pouring out. Everything. Dad leaving us, Mom breaking down, Lottie going to LA, Mom's stroke, us making do, and the current situation with Dad.

I finished with, "And if all that isn't bad enough, I've got a date tonight with Eddie and I have absolutely no clue what to wear."

Throughout my story, she looked concerned, sometimes mad, sometimes like she was going to interrupt but, at my final comment, she smiled. "That last bit, I can help you with. The rest of it, Lee can help you with."

I knew Lee was a private detective. I also knew that he was really good at what he did, and I knew that he was really expensive. He drove a fancy car, had a fancier motorcycle, had a huge workforce and had some kind of plush offices in Lower Downtown Denver. I couldn't afford Lee, and I couldn't afford to owe anyone else a favor.

"I can't ask Lee——" I started.

"You *can* ask Lee, but you don't have to. I will," Indy assured me.

"Indy, I'd really like to take care of this on my own."

"Lee says it's dangerous."

I laughed. "Did you *not* hear my story? I can take care of myself, and everyone else. I've had a lot of practice."

Indy looked at me. "I don't know. I've had a run-in with the criminal underworld of Denver, and it wasn't much fun."

I was curious but didn't ask.

"I'll be safe and I'll be smart, I promise," I assured her, wishing I was just as sure, and knowing I was anything but.

"What're you gonna do?" she asked.

I shrugged. "I don't know. Find Dad first. Find out what this is all about. Then take it from there."

Immediately she replied, "I'll go with you."

No.

No, no, no.

I couldn't have Indy coming with me. If something happened to her, both Lee and Eddie would be pissed at me, not to mention Duke, Tex and the entirety of the Denver Police Department (Indy's Dad was a cop, as were Lee's Dad *and* his brother, Hank).

"I don't think——" I started to say, but then Tex was there.

"I'm comin' too," he announced.

I closed my eyes. This was spiraling out-of-control.

I opened them again. "Please listen to me——"

"No way, Loopy Loo. You aren't hoardin' all the action." He turned to Indy, "You're drivin' because we can all fit in your silly-ass car. When we see a break in the coffee action, I'll go home and get my shotgun."

My mouth dropped open and I was pretty sure my eyes bugged out of my head.

"Don't worry, Jet. Just as long as we don't get into any situations that require grenades, we'll be fine." Indy said this like she wasn't joking.

Tex looked at Indy for a beat. "I'll pack a few, just in case," he said. Then Tex lumbered away and I stared at him, mouth still open.

Indy looked at me and, bizarrely (I thought), she laughed.

⌁

We left Duke and Jane in command of the bookstore after the post-lunch caffeine rush and we all climbed into Indy's dark blue VW Beetle.

We swung by the hotel where Dad stayed, but they hadn't seen him. We also swung by a couple of bars Dad went to when he was in town and asked around. No one at the bars had seen him either. Then we headed out to Lakewood, a suburb to the west of Denver, to visit my Dad's friend, Bear.

Bear was nicknamed Bear for obvious reasons. He was nearly as big as Tex, who was incredibly tall, and hairier than Tex, who looked like a demented, gray-blond Santa Claus with a russet beard. Bear looked like he'd been asleep for one hundred years and hadn't had a shave when he woke up. Both were built to last, as in solid.

Bear was a sometimes-plumber but most-of-the-time-bum. He was just as fun and crazy as Dad but had more staying power. He'd been married for over thirty years to the long-suffering Lavonne.

Lavonne, on the other hand, didn't have staying power.

She left Bear at least once a year. However, for reasons known only to Lavonne, she always came back.

I hadn't seen Bear in over a year, back when times were better, and he and Lavonne had come to a big picnic in Washington Park that I had for Lottie when she came to visit.

Tex, Indy and I walked up to Bear's house, which was a one-story, cracker box house that had yellow aluminum siding and a mess of kid's toys in the front yard. This was telling, because Bear and Lavonne's two kids were the same age as me and Lottie and had moved out of the house nearly a decade before.

I knocked on the door and Bear answered. His eyes got big, then they got panicked, then they settled on cagey.

Not good.

"Jet! Shit! Haven't seen you in ages, girl. How're you keepin'?" Bear greeted.

"Hey Bear."

He pulled me into (you guessed it) a bear hug and then let me go. His eyes moved to Indy briefly and then stayed on Tex.

I introduced everyone. Throughout the introductions, Bear pretended to be cordial, but he was anything but relaxed.

"What brings you out here?" he asked, not taking his eyes off Tex and not moving from the door.

"Dad's in town," I said.

Bear's eyes finally came to me.

"Is he?" Bear lied. He totally knew Dad was in town.

"He's in trouble, Bear. Can we come in for second and talk?" I asked.

Bear didn't move from his body blockade of the door. "Wish you could, girl, but Lavonne's workin' nights and she gets a little cranky when her beauty sleep's disturbed."

At last, Bear spoke the truth. Lavonne got cranky when the sun rose, when it set and when the earth revolved around it. Then again, Lavonne had been supporting a ne'er-do-well for thirty years, albeit a lovable one. That would make me cranky too.

"Do you know anything about Dad?" I asked.

"Un-unh, haven't heard from Ray in ages," Bear answered.

Back to lying.

Damn.

I sighed then ran down my latest adventures with Dad, Slick and Slick's knife.

It was then Bear looked angry.

"What're you doin' workin' at a titty bar?" he demanded to know.

Wonderful.

"That isn't the point," I told him.

"It is the point," Bear returned. "You need money?"

Like Bear had money.

Before I could answer, Tex boomed, "Let's stay focused here, people."

Bear tensed, still angry, and he glared at Tex.

I moved into Bear's line of sight. I didn't need two big, hairy men wrestling amongst a bunch of rusty tricycles. I had to find Dad, and then find a Killer Eddie Date Outfit and make sure my legs had a clean, close shave. I didn't have time to go off target.

"Bear, I really need to find Dad."

Bear looked at me.

"I haven't heard from Ray. All right? If I do, I'll call you. And I won't tell Lavonne you're workin' at a titty bar. She'd have a shit hemorrhage."

With that, we had no choice but to say good-bye. Then we trooped back to Indy's Beetle. We sat in it, me in the back, Indy driving, Tex in the front passenger seat.

We stared at the house.

"Do you think your Dad's in there?" Indy asked me.

"No, but I think Bear knows where he is," I answered.

"Maybe we should drive around the corner and hang out for a while, watch the house," Indy suggested.

"Fuck that. I don't do stakeouts. I need food. I missed lunch. Let's roll," Tex said in a voice you didn't want to argue with.

Indy took us to the Einstein's Bagels on Alameda. Tex got an onion bagel with turkey, sprouts and cream cheese, a bag of chips, a huge cookie and a Rice Krispie treat. Indy and I got Diet Cokes. We sat at a table so Tex could eat.

"You got any more ideas?" Tex asked me, his mouth full.

I shook my head.

He turned to Indy. "You were more fun."

I'd heard snatches of conversation about Indy's drama, but never the full story. Since I'd shared my life story, I thought it would only be fair to ask hers. The time was right. Tex had a mountain of food to get through, so I asked.

She didn't hesitate. She didn't have anything to hide. She told me the whole thing, with Tex interjecting every once in a while. He'd been more than a bit player in her drama. He'd gotten himself shot while protecting her, which explained the sling he'd worn when I first met him.

They'd only known each other a few weeks longer than I'd known them, which was surprising. I thought they'd known each other for years.

After she was done, I didn't know what to say. Her story made Slick and his knife seem tame. Then again, she had Lee and his army of hotties backing her up.

Tex wiped his mouth with a paper napkin and threw it on the table. "I gotta go home, play with the cats."

Tex was a kind of nutcase Renaissance man: by day a coffee genius, by night a cat sitter. Apparently, he always had dozens of cats coming and going at his house. According to him, sometimes, if he didn't like the feel of the cat's owner, he wouldn't let them have it back. I didn't find this surprising. Not a lot of people would argue with Tex, even if he was essentially stealing your cat.

We all got up when I noticed Tex tense and look behind me.

I turned and saw two men I'd never seen in my life standing there. They looked like they'd seen the movie *Reservoir Dogs* and decided to base their wardrobe on it. Both slim, both dark-headed, wearing black suits, thin black ties and white shirts.

"You lookin' for Ray McAlister?" The taller of the two asked Tex.

Oh no.

This just got worse and worse.

Who were *these* guys?

"What's it to you?" Tex answered, obviously not feeling the need to be gracious and polite.

They looked at each other.

I was closest to them and Tex grabbed hold of my t-shirt and pulled me backwards and to the side and put himself between the bad guys and me.

"There's no need to get testy, we just asked you a question," the shorter of the two said to Tex, trying diplomacy.

"Yeah, we're lookin' for him. These two are Girl Scouts and he owes them cookie money," Tex returned, not feeling diplomatic.

They looked at each other again.

"I'm not sure we like your attitude," the taller man noted.

Tex stared at him. "What's the deal with you? You got two bodies and one brain?"

It was like Tex *wanted* them to get angry.

If that's what he wanted, he got it.

The taller guy stepped closer. "Fuck you."

Uh-oh.

"Fuck you back," Tex replied.

Eek!

"Tex," Indy said, sidling over to me and pulling me away, "let's go."

The *Reservoir Dogs* men weren't done with us.

"You find McAlister, tell him Louie and Vince want to talk to him," the shorter one said.

"You find him, you tell him Tex wants to talk to him, but first, Lee Nightingale wants to talk to him," Tex retorted.

They looked at each other again then they looked at Indy.

"Thought I recognized you," the taller one said.

"Get your fuckin' eyes off her." Tex got in between them and Indy and me, which put him dangerously close to the taller guy.

"Back off, old man. And tell Nightingale to keep his fuckin' nose out of this. Those friends of his too, the wetback cop and the fuckin' dealer."

Looking back, perhaps I should maybe have counted to ten.

Then again, until recently, I'd been mild-mannered and boring, so who would have ever guessed I would have lost my mind like I did. Though, words like the "N-word", "raghead", "wetback" and the like always set my teeth on edge. So I guess my reaction to them calling Eddie one of those words wasn't *that* surprising.

I launched myself at the tall guy. I must have taken him off-guard because he staggered back and we both went down amongst the tables at Einstein's.

I landed on top of him. He went, "Oof!" and I'm pretty sure I knocked the wind out of him. This was to my good fortune, because in any other circumstance he could have probably kicked my ass.

I took advantage, and we were rolling around, a tangle of limbs. I heard shouting, and we rolled into and upset a bunch of tables. I think Tex got into it with the shorter guy because I heard a scuffle but couldn't pay that much attention, because my guy got his wind back and began to kick my ass.

I heard Indy shout, "Knee him in the nuts!"

This sounded like a good plan. I found my opening and pulled my knee up with all my strength and connected, solidly.

My guy made a noise that made even me feel sorry for him. I was lifted up by my waist, set on my feet and then I heard Tex shout, "*Run!*"

We hightailed it to the Beetle and Indy peeled out of the parking lot, but we could see a cop car, sirens blaring, approaching the light at the corner of Alameda and Logan.

Indy didn't even slow down.

We went back to Fortnum's, which was only a few blocks away. Without a word, we all got out of the car and walked in the store.

Duke and Jane both looked up when we walked in. Duke's eyes narrowed. Jane started to smile.

"If anyone asks, we've been here all day," Indy said immediately.

Duke dropped his head in his hand.

"If you want to go with that story, you might want to brush the potato chips out of Jet's hair," Jane remarked.

My hand flew to my hair. I'd lost my ponytail holder and so I ran my hands through it. Chips flew out everywhere.

"I'll get the broom," Indy muttered.

"You might also want to wipe that... is it cream cheese... off your shirt too," Jane suggested.

I stared down at my shirt.

Tex's hand settled on my head. "Now that's more like it, Loopy Loo."

Dear Lord.

Chapter 7

My Date with Eddie

When it seemed the coast was clear and Fortnum's wasn't going to be raided by a SWAT team in search of the perps who trashed an Einstein's Bagels, Indy took me to her house.

She'd given me a grilling about my wardrobe and decided nothing I had would do. She called Ally into the Killer Eddie Date Outfit Search. Ally bagged up some of her clothes and accessories and we all descended on Indy's duplex.

I tried on one hundred thousand outfits before we settled on something. Nice, but not too nice. Sexy, but not obvious. Cool, but not trying to be cool.

It included Ally's green, wraparound top that showed a bit of cleavage, was super tight *everywhere,* and the sleeves were way long and had a little hole in them that hooked on your thumb. This topped a pair of Indy's jeans that were faded enough not to look like I was being dressy but also not too grungy. We added a bunch of Indy's silver bangles on my wrist, worn over the fabric of the top and some big, dangly earrings of Ally's. The kicker was a pair of strappy green sandals that were so sexy, Smithie would have let me break the color code for shoes at work. These were borrowed from Indy's next door neighbor, who was Denver's top drag queen. Luckily, he had small feet; or I liked to think that way. Not that my feet were large.

Ally took me home and, as usual, I was running late. I'd need a decade to prepare myself to be a suitable date to Eddie's lusciousness. I needed an hour just to get ready for Smithie's. I had forty-five minutes to get ready for Eddie.

I was in my room, finishing my hair, when the buzzer sounded and panic seized me.

"I'll get it," Mom shouted.

At the thought of Mom letting Eddie in, panic dissolved into nearly uncontrolled hysteria.

"Tell him I'm running late," I shouted back.

"Good girl, keep him waiting," Mom encouraged.

My mother.

I rushed through the final touches, nearly forgot the bangles, and went into a mini-freak out when I couldn't find a suitable purse. I had a full mental conversation convincing myself that guys didn't notice purses when a knock sounded at my door.

"Eddie's waiting," Mom shouted through the door, obviously thinking that Eddie had waited long enough.

"Coming!" I yelled back.

I got over the purse trauma, grabbed the one I normally used, and rushed to the door, when I heard the buzzer go again.

"I'll get it," Mom shouted, outside my door.

Who in *the hell?*

I walked out and Eddie was lounging in the living room. Jeans had been a good call. He looked no different than normal. Long-sleeved, black, thermal tee, worn jeans, black cowboy boots and a black belt with a silver buckle.

No matter how casual he was dressed, he could have been in a magazine.

His eyes changed when he saw me and he came out of his chair.

"Hi," I said, and just stopped myself from slapping my forehead as it came out breathy, like I'd just run a race.

He didn't say anything, he just smiled.

My insides curled.

"Look who's here!" Mom called, wheeling in using her foot with Trixie behind her, carrying an overnight bag.

I stared.

Then Trixie started speaking. "I thought to myself, 'Self? What are you gonna do on a boring Thursday night?' And I answered myself, 'You're gonna have a sleepover with your good friend Nancy.' So here I am," Trixie announced, as if she had sleepovers with Mom all the time (which she did not). "You must be Eddie." She dropped the bag and smiled at Eddie.

Could they *be* more obvious?

Eddie's smile didn't falter.

"Eddie, this is my Mom's best friend Trixie. Trixie, this is, um… Eddie," I introduced.

I kind of wished Slick would've broken in at that moment and knifed me, such was my desire for someone to kill me and put me out of my misery.

Eddie greeted Trixie and before it could get any more out of hand, I nearly ran across the room and grabbed Eddie's hand.

"I was running late so we have to go," I said.

I tugged Eddie's hand, and luckily he moved with me towards the front door.

"Don't worry about us, we'll be just fine." Trixie followed us to the front door.

I threw a look over my shoulder which should have turned her to stone. She just smiled at me.

"Stay out as long as you like," Mom shouted from the living room.

"Thanks Mom," I shouted back, stopped at the door and looked at Trixie. "You'll take care of her?" I asked quietly.

"Do you need to ask?" Trixie was just as quiet.

"I can hear you!" Mom shouted.

I was pretty certain I heard Eddie chuckle.

Wonderful.

I kissed Trixie's cheek, shouted good-bye to Mom and pulled Eddie down the hall.

We were out the front door of the building when Eddie remarked, "That was fun."

I didn't answer and I slowed from my onward charge. Now that I got him away from Mom and Trixie, I wanted to drag my feet.

Eddie took over and guided me toward his truck. At the passenger door, instead of opening it, he turned to me but he didn't say anything.

I waited.

Then I asked, "What?"

He pushed me against the truck, his body came up against mine, and he kissed me, full-on tongue. When he lifted his head, he had an arm wrapped around the middle of my back, his fingertips resting nearly at the side of my breast and the other hand resting on my hip.

"What was that?" Dammit, I was breathy again.

"Just wanted to say I like what you're wearing."

"You could have just said it," I pointed out.

"Preferred to show it."

I had to admit, I preferred it, too.

He let me go, pulled me aside, opened the door and helped me in.

It took me some time to pull myself together as we drove the streets of Denver.

Finally, I said, "Sorry to say this, but I should be home early. Slick's out there, and Mom and Trixie are all by themselves."

"I pulled in a favor. A squad car is going to do a regular round of drive-bys," Eddie replied.

Something about Eddie doing that made me feel pleasantly strange. It wasn't a feeling I'd ever had before, but it was nice.

"How will they know if something's wrong?" I asked.

"They're gonna make an excuse and buzz up," Eddie answered.

"They won't say—" I started to worry.

"Relax, Jet. I told them to be cool."

I didn't know what to say. So I settled on simple, "Thank you."

Eddie didn't respond.

The next thing I knew, we were pulling into his alley. Eddie hit the button on a garage door opener that was attached to his sun visor and we pulled into the garage at the back of his house.

"Did you forget something?" I asked.

"Nope," Eddie answered, setting the brake and turning off the truck.

I sat perfectly still in my seat.

"What are we doing here?" I asked.

"We're havin' dinner," he said, angling out of the truck.

I watched him walk around the front and come to my side.

Having dinner?

At Eddie's house?

I didn't know how to process this. Dates usually didn't take place at someone's house. Well, not first dates. I'd known Eddie awhile, and he'd been in a fight for me, spent the night at my house, we'd made out a couple of times and I'd slept in his bed, but this was still a first date.

I threw open my door and jumped down.

When I cleared it, Eddie pushed my door shut, grabbed my hand and tugged me along behind him.

"Are you going to make dinner for me?" I asked his back.

"No."

"Are we ordering pizza?"

He opened the backdoor and we went into the kitchen.

"My Mom cooked for you," he informed me.

I stood just inside the door and stared at him.

"Your Mom... cooked... for me?" I stammered.

He pulled me into the room, closed the door and maneuvered me so my hips were against the counter; his hands were on them and he was close.

"Yeah. She called today. She wanted me to come over tonight and I told her I had plans. She asked about you, I told her, and she decided to cook dinner for you."

I blinked at him. "What did you tell her about me?"

He came closer. So much closer that I had to tilt my head way back to look up at him. He bent his neck so his face was close to mine.

"I told her you were a pretty blonde with a great smile who's workin' two jobs and takin' care of her disabled mother at the same time."

My body got tense. I had an uncomfortable feeling that this was a pity dinner, maybe in more ways than one.

He felt me tense. "Steady there, *chiquita*. *Mamá* just knows you're workin' hard and you need a quiet night. After followin' you around for a couple of days, I need a quiet night too. That's all this is. She was tryin' to be nice."

"I don't like people knowing about me," I told him, my body still stiff as a board.

"I already got that."

We were at a standoff and just staring at each other.

Then I smelled him and I started to slip into an Eddie Daze. My body began to relax and then it began to tingle.

"I'm hungry," I told him, trying to shake the "Daze".

His hand came to my jaw and his eyes got warm.

"Me too."

He wasn't talking about food, and my belly began to feel funny.

"We should eat," I said.

His lips turned up at the corners and his eyes dropped to my mouth.

"Yeah, we should eat." His voice was low and kind of hoarse, and I wondered what he was thinking about eating.

I slid out from in front of him and took a mental deep breath.

"What can I do to help?" I asked, trying to sound bright and cheery.

He smiled at me. He knew exactly how he affected me, and I found it perversely attractive and annoying.

He opened the wine and told me where the plates were.

His Mom had cooked homemade tamales, Spanish rice, refried beans and made a salad. The rice and beans were in a divided crock pot, the salad in the fridge and the tamales staying warm in the oven.

We piled up our plates and went to the dining room.

Eddie lived in a one-story bungalow in Platte Park. I hadn't taken much in the last time I was there, and the night before I'd waited (more like dozed) in the truck while he packed a bag.

When he flipped the light switch I saw it was living room up front with a gorgeous tiled fireplace, and a couch and armchair, both built less for decoration and more for roominess, comfort and durability. To the left were two bedrooms, separated by a bath and a small hall. The floors were hardwood and looked like they'd recently been redone. The walls were painted a warm sage. There were no decorative touches, pictures on the wall or fancy furniture. Just a thick rug in front of the couch with a coffee table on it.

The living room led into a dining area with a beat-up wood table and ladder-back chairs, a bay window and a built-in hutch with mirrored back and glass-fronted doors. There was nothing in the hutch.

I stared at the dining room table.

Eddie did, too, and then he said something in Spanish that sounded half annoyed, half amused.

It had been laid with place mats, silverware, napkins and candles. I didn't think Eddie was the type of guy who owned cloth napkins or candles, and I began to wonder about the "pity" part of his Mom's dinner. I started to wonder more if Eddie's Mom was kind of like mine.

We sat down and Eddie didn't bother lighting the candles.

I began to get nervous, wondering what we'd talk about.

I didn't have to worry. Eddie asked questions that were not too demanding, and I answered, telling him a little about Lottie, but mostly about Mom.

I asked questions and found out Eddie had bought the house as a wreck about three years ago and was slowly doing it up. He had three sisters, two brothers. He was the second born and his father had died of a heart attack a little over a year ago. The family was close. They all still lived in Denver, and the loss of their father was a blow. I also found out he'd known Lee since the third grade, and with Lee came Indy, Hank and Ally.

Then we were finished eating and I realized I'd been lulled into a false sense of security.

Dear Lord, what were we going to do now?

I didn't want to think what we *could* do, so I jumped up and grabbed the plates.

"I'll do the dishes," I announced, deciding that was a good plan. Then I hustled into the kitchen.

I was rinsing the plates when I heard Eddie come in behind me.

"Leave them," he said to the back of my head.

I didn't turn around.

"No, there's not a lot. I'll just do these and wrap up the food." And anything else I could think up to avoid him while we were in his house. I wasn't beneath cleaning his bathroom if I had to.

Eddie came up behind me. His hips pressed mine into the sink, an arm came around my middle and his other hand moved my hair away from my neck. Then his mouth was where my hair used to be.

"Leave them," he said against my neck in a voice that clearly stated his words were not a suggestion.

I did a full body shiver, and between my legs, my doo-da quivered.

His mouth moved up my neck to behind my ear.

Then the doorbell rang.

His arm tightened and his mouth went away.

"Jesus Christ," he muttered, and even though I couldn't see him, I was pretty sure it was muttered through gritted teeth.

Eddie walked out of the kitchen.

I rinsed the dishes, put them in the dishwasher and heard my cell phone ring. I wiped my hands on a dishtowel, grabbed my purse and just missed the last ring. I looked to see who it was, worried it was Mom, but it was Indy.

I heard voices talking in Spanish, so I put the phone on the counter, deciding to text Indy later, and I walked into the other room. I saw Eddie standing in front of a tiny, Mexican woman with shiny black hair and a near-perfectly round body. She was carrying a small baker's box, the kind in which you pack birthday cakes.

She turned to me and looked me up and down. Then her face split in a smile.

"Hello," I greeted.

She came toward me. "*Hola*. I'm Blanca, Eddie's Mom."

Uh... wow.

Kristen Ashley

This was a surprise.

I glanced at Eddie and his hands were on his hips, his head was tilted back, looking at the ceiling. This was not a happy posture.

For some reason (probably residual hysteria), I found this amusing.

I smiled at Blanca.

"I'm Jet," I told her.

Then the front door opened and two women and a man walked in. It wasn't difficult to see they were related to Eddie. One of the women was tall, and so was the man. The other woman was tiny, like Blanca. They were all glamorously good-looking, just like Eddie.

They all looked at me.

Eddie glared at them, then dropped his head and ran his hand through his hair and muttered words in Spanish and English, none of them nice.

I looked at the newcomers.

"Hey," I said to them.

There were general greetings and small waves and lots and lots of white teeth against dark skin.

"These are my kids, Carlos, Rosa and Elena," Blanca said. Elena was the short one.

"I'm Jet," I repeated, still smiling and beginning to think this whole thing was hilarious.

"Are we having a reunion?" Eddie asked.

Carlos laughed. Rosa and Elena looked at each other and grinned. Blanca gave Eddie a death glare and spat something at him in Spanish. Then she turned back to me, all smiles again.

Yep, Eddie's Mom was just like mine.

"I forgot the dessert so I brought you Napoleons from Pasquini's," Blanca told me.

She did not forget dessert. She deliberately delayed delivery of dessert so she could check out Eddie's date. I wondered if it was me, or if this happened to Eddie all the time. I couldn't imagine Eddie would put up with this all the time so it had to be me. I didn't know what to make of that so I pushed it aside.

I came forward and took the box from her. "That sounds lovely. Dinner was delicious, by the way. Thank you."

"*De nada*," she said, graciously inclining her head.

106

Everyone stood around, smiling at each other. That was, everyone but Eddie.

Finally, I broke the silence. "Did you get enough for everyone? Should I serve these?" I asked Blanca.

"No!" Eddie finally snapped and I couldn't help myself, I turned my smile to him.

He glared at me.

His family watched us.

Eddie looked at his mother and said something in Spanish. It didn't take an interpreter to translate she was being ousted.

"All right, all right. We're going," she told her son and turned to me. "Eddie told me about *tu madre*. How is she?"

I was still smiling, too amused to be annoyed she knew about Mom.

"She's fine," I assured her.

"She need company tonight? Maybe we could swing around..." Blanca offered.

I couldn't help myself, I started laughing.

Eddie didn't think it was funny and started talking, more Spanish, this rapid-fire, beyond annoyed and vaguely threatening.

"*Ay Dios mio, mi niño*, you're wound up tonight," Blanca said to Eddie, and Carlos burst out laughing. Blanca turned back to me. "He's a little bit hot-blooded, just like his Papa."

No kidding. I'd already figured that out.

"I'll bear that in mind," I told her, trying to keep a straight face

She came closer to me and looked me in the eyes. Then she nodded to herself and touched my arm. I didn't know what to make of this either, and decided to think about all of it later.

Then she walked toward Eddie, reached up and touched his shoulder. He bent low to give her a kiss on the cheek and murmured something that was still annoyed but also sounded loving. The sight and sound of it made me feel pleasantly strange again, and I had to force myself to look away.

There were good-byes and more small waves and they were gone.

Eddie stalked toward me, grabbed the box and then stalked into the kitchen.

I walked to the doorway of the kitchen and stood there.

"That was fun," I told him.

He put the box down and started stalking again. This time his eyes were dark and his intentions were clear.

Eek!

I retreated, slammed up against a wall and he positioned his body close to mine.

I was looking up, my head tilted way back, and his face was less than an inch away.

"One thing good about that. I've never seen you smile so much, and I don't think I've ever heard you laugh."

"Your mother's funny," I told him, beginning to find it difficult to breathe.

He came even closer, and difficulty breathing was no longer my main concern because the oxygen in my lungs started burning.

"My mother's meddling, and nosy, and hell-bent on having dozens of grandchildren, the sooner the better."

I gave a little nod in the room I had to work with. I was trying not to think of giving Blanca grandchildren, but more, trying not to think of how I'd go about doing that.

"That sounds familiar," I replied.

His hands came up to my jaw, holding my face tilted. His eyes went liquid and he muttered something in Spanish. I caught the words *cariño* and *hermosa*, I began to lift up on my toes when my cell started ringing.

"Ignore it," Eddie said against my mouth.

I wanted to, I really did, but I couldn't.

"I can't," I whispered. "It might be Mom."

He immediately let me go and stepped away.

I walked to the kitchen and picked up the phone, which had stopped ringing.

I looked to see who'd called, and it was again Indy. I thought this was weird, considering she knew I was on a date with Eddie. She couldn't want a progress report this soon.

"Indy's called twice," I said as Eddie put the Napoleons on plates.

He handed one to me. "If she needs to speak to you, she'll phone back."

He grabbed the wine and walked into the living room. I followed him. He set the wine and his plate on the coffee table, went to get our glasses, put them on the table and sat down. He grabbed the remote and turned on a baseball game.

I stood next to the couch and stared at the TV.

"Um... what are we doing?" I asked.

Eddie retrieved his pastry and put his feet up on the coffee table. "I have another brother, a sister and five dozen cousins. I'm not starting anything again until visiting hours are over."

Goodie. A reprieve.

I sat down on the opposite side of the couch, putting my phone on the coffee table, and I ate my Napoleon, my eyes on the game. I wasn't a big sports fan. If pressed I'd go to games, mainly for the atmosphere, but I wasn't fond of watching them on television.

The minute I consumed the last bite of my pastry and put my plate down, Eddie's feet came off the table. He leaned down, grabbed my ankles and pulled them in his lap. Then he started to work on the straps of my shoes.

"Eddie..." I began, trying to pull my legs away.

His hands wrapped around my ankles. "Quiet, *chiquita*. You're going to relax."

He tossed my shoes several feet away and then he pulled off his boots. I settled into my corner, as far away from him as I could get, thinking this was slightly anti-climactic. I didn't have high hopes for my date with Eddie, but I expected it would be me who screwed things up in some way, or bored him to death. I didn't expect to spend the night watching a baseball game.

His hand shot out and he grabbed me, dragging me across the couch, as he put his feet back on the table. He tucked me into his side so my shoulder was wedged under his armpit and my cheek was against his chest. He wrapped his arm around my waist, his hand resting on my hip.

Dear Lord.

I wasn't bored anymore. I felt nice. As in, *real* nice.

I put my feet up on the couch and curled into him, keeping my eyes on the game and daydreaming about doing this with Eddie again, maybe every night for the rest of our lives.

The next thing I knew, my cell phone was ringing. I could also hear Eddie's.

I'd fallen into a doze and somehow my arm got wrapped across Eddie's waist. I came up, pulling my hair away from my face and grabbed my phone. Eddie leaned forward and pulled his phone out of his back pocket.

My phone said "Indy calling". I flipped it open and said, "Hello?" at the same time I heard Eddie say, "Yeah?"

"Jet? Are you with Eddie?" Indy asked by way of greeting, her voice sounding funny and not in a good way.

"Yes. Is something wrong?" I asked.

She hesitated then asked, "Is he on the phone?"

I looked over at him. He was listening, then his face got tight and his eyes moved to me.

"Yeah," I said to Indy.

"He's talking to Lee. I tried to stop him. I promise I did everything I could think of."

I felt a chill run up my spine.

"What's happening?" I asked.

"Listen, our adventure at Einstein's got out and—"

I didn't hear her say anything else as the phone was pulled from my hand and flipped closed.

My head snapped around to Eddie. "Hey! I was talking to Indy."

"I know."

He slid our phones onto the table, looked at me, his eyes serious and maybe a little pissed off.

"What's going on?" I asked, moving away from him.

"You've had a busy day," he replied.

Uh-oh.

I thought, at that juncture, it might be wise to keep my mouth shut.

"Went lookin' for your Dad like I asked you not to do and found some trouble at a bagel place," he remarked.

I forgot about keeping my mouth shut.

"Eddie, it's none of your—"

His eyes narrowed. "*Chiquita*, if you tell me it's none of my business, I swear to God, I'll shoot you."

I jumped up from the couch and put my hands to my hips.

"Well it isn't!"

He angled off the couch and took a step toward me so he was towering over me.

I really wished I had my shoes back, but I held my ground.

"It fucking well is," he returned in his scary quiet voice.

I glared at him.

"How do you figure that?" I asked.

He threw his arms out and looked around. "What the fuck do you think is happening here?"

"I don't know!" I yelled at him and, actually, I didn't.

He looked away from me, tore his hand through his hair and muttered in Spanish. Then he turned back to me.

"Witnesses state that a blonde woman of your description was seen rolling around on the floor at Einstein's on Alameda with a guy who fits the description of Vince Fratelli."

I decided, again, to be silent.

"Jet, Vince Fratelli is a bad guy," Eddie told me. "Not just a bad guy, a scary bad guy. He's muscle for a very scary bad guy. Who knows what he's done? Likely broken knees, cut off fingers, killed people. And you attacked him in fucking Einstein's Bagels."

Not good. Really not good. Vince *did* sound like a scary bad guy.

I went into defense mode. "Well I didn't know!" I yelled.

Eddie's quiet voice went away and he shouted, "*What the fuck were you thinking?*"

"He called you a wetback!" I shouted right back.

Yeesh.

Eddie stood stock-still and stared at me.

"I'm sorry?" he asked.

"I didn't think. He said it and I just flipped out and the next thing I knew we were rolling around on the floor. Indy yelled at me to knee him in the nuts. I did. Tex grabbed me and we took off. The whole thing lasted less than ten minutes."

He shook his head. "I don't know whether to kiss you or shake some sense into you."

I knew which one I would pick, but I was too angry to make the suggestion.

I backed away and rounded the coffee table, retrieved my shoes and turned to Eddie.

"I want to go home," I demanded.

"You aren't goin' home. We're not done talkin'."

I turned and walked toward the kitchen.

We were *so* done talking.

I nearly made it when he caught my hand, gave it a yank and I whirled around. He twisted my arm around my back and pulled my body up against his.

"I'm fuckin' sick and tired of watching you walk away from me," he growled.

My heart stopped.

This would probably be part of that hot-blooded thing Blanca was talking about.

"Eddie—"

He didn't let me start. "You've dated Mexican-Americans before. People say shit. It's their problem, you ignore it."

"Eddie—" I tried again.

He continued, "I already told you that you were my business, but it's pretty fuckin' clear you didn't understand. I've been tryin' to get your attention for months, but you're so busy and exhausted and whatever the hell else you are it hasn't worked. So I'll say, straight out, so there's no confusion. I want to spend time with you, I want to get to know you, and I want to sleep with you and it doesn't have to be in that order."

I didn't even try to speak. I couldn't. His words robbed me of the ability of speech.

"While that's happenin' and however long it lasts, you're my business and I'll explain that too. I keep you safe and I keep your Mom safe, however that has to come about. And no one hustles you, not even your fuckin' father, or they answer to me."

I was not only speechless, my belly was beginning to feel funny and that strange pleasant feeling was back.

Eddie went on, "I know you have a problem with that, you've made it loud and clear, but I don't give a fuck. I'm gonna keep coming at you until I wear you down. Do you understand me?"

He paused and glared at me and I realized he expected an answer.

Since I was incapable of a verbal response, I just nodded.

"Good. Now, because it's likely you not only have Slick after you, but also Louie and Vince, you've got two choices. Either I take you home and I stay there with you, or I make a call and plant someone at your apartment building and you sleep here with me."

"Trixie's at home. There's nowhere for you to sleep," I reminded him.

"I sleep with you."

Dear Lord.

"I'll sleep here," I decided.

"I sleep with you here too."

Eek!

"I'll sleep on the couch," I offered.

"You sleep in my bed."

"Then, will you sleep on the couch?" I asked.

"I'll sleep in my bed with you."

"Eddie—" I started to object but he interrupted me again.

"Nothing's going to happen. Not tonight. I'm too tired and too pissed off."

I tried to decide if I could sleep with a tired and pissed off Eddie.

I decided I couldn't sleep with a tired and pissed off Eddie.

"Those two choices aren't choices at all," I pointed out. "They're the same thing in different places."

"They're all you've got," he told me.

"I don't like it."

"I don't care. I told you not to go after your Dad. You did and you bought yourself a fuckload of trouble to add to the shitload you already had. If I gotta keep you safe, I'll do it how I need to do it and I want you close."

"But... sleep with me?" I asked.

"You don't get it," he said, his brows drawing together.

"I think I do." I was beginning to go from freaked out to angry.

He let go of my wrist but tightened both arms around me. "Slick's known for using that blade, and not in good ways. I already told you what Vince is capable of. They come after you, I want them to get me first."

Okay, so at that, the anger started to melt into that weird feeling again.

"You can't do that for me," I whispered.

"I'm not doin' it for you. I'm doin' it for me. I won't get what I want out of you if your throat's been cut."

Putting it that way, it almost made sense. But only almost.

"This is going too fast, it's—"

Again, he didn't let me finish.

He interrupted me by laughing. If you can believe, he actually *laughed*.

His hands moved up my back and his head tilted toward me.

"Since I'm bein' honest with you, *chiquita*, I'll tell you I usually play with what I want until I feel the time is right to move in. The time was right with you a long fuckin' time ago, but you've been so focused on your own shit you gave me no opening. This hasn't been fast. You want to see fast, we'll go into the bedroom and I'll show you fast, but I'll show it to you slow."

Oh... dear... Lord.

My stomach curled, and that was a pleasant feeling, too.

Regardless, for self-preservation, immediately I said, "I don't want to see fast."

His arms separated, one stayed up my back, the other one went low on my waist.

His mouth came to mine and I quit breathing.

With his lips against mine he said, "You've got one night's reprieve. To-morrow, I start movin' in."

What did I do with that? I mean, I pretty much thought he was already "movin' in".

He didn't give me a chance to do anything.

"I gotta make a call and then we're goin' to bed," he announced.

Eek!

Chapter 8
Eddie Fixes One of My Problems

The alarm went off and, as it didn't sound like mine, I knew immediately where I was.

I took stock of my surroundings and realized the warm coziness I felt had a lot to do with being tangled up in Eddie Chavez.

My body tensed and I started to move away.

Eddie's arms, which were wrapped around me, tightened. One of his thighs, incidentally, was wedged between my legs, and my thigh was hooked over his hip. Not to mention one of my hands was pressed against his chest, the other arm wrapped around his waist, um... *eek!*

"You need to turn off the alarm," I said instead of "good morning".

"Turnin' off the alarm would mean lettin' you go," he replied, his voice sexy-rough.

I decided to ignore his sexy, rough voice.

"And?" I asked.

"I'm not gonna do that," he answered, and snuggled closer, though I wouldn't have thought that possible.

I listened to the blaring noise. It was annoying.

"You have to turn it off," I said.

"I'm not turnin' it off."

"Someone has to turn it off. You're closer. I don't know what button to press."

He didn't answer.

I listened to the noise. I tried to pull away.

This time, Eddie's arms and thigh tightened.

I was stuck.

"Oh for goodness sake," I snapped and then pushed into him, rolled him on his back and reached over. This meant I was sprawled on top of him, and I decided to hate Eddie instead of love him and want to give Blanca grandbabies.

There were at least seven dozen buttons at the top, so I just ran my fingers down all of them in hopes one of them would turn off the alarm. Instead, the buzzing went away and an old Big Head Todd and the Monsters tune came on.

It wasn't just a good song, it was a great song, but it was also a sexy song. Wonderful.

I pushed against Eddie's chest and peered closer at the alarm to see which button would turn off the music and saw it was also a CD player. Just when I was about to push "stop", he pressed into me and rolled me on my back, him on top.

Not good.

Last night, after Eddie announced we were going to bed, he was good to his word.

He planted a lookout in the parking lot of my apartment building. I called Mom to tell her I wasn't coming home, to her everlasting glee, which amounted to a piercing scream of joy which I could swear Eddie heard from across the room. He'd given me a t-shirt that was faded black, had been washed a million times and was soft and comfy. Then we'd gone to bed and slept, no hanky panky, nothing.

I wasn't going to press my luck.

I decided to go for belligerence. I needed to get up, get dressed and get the hell out of there as fast as humanly possible, and I figured being a bitch was the way to go.

"Get off me. I need to turn off the music," I told him, looking into dark eyes that were still drowsy and doing weird things to my peace of mind.

"I like this song," he informed me.

His face disappeared into my neck and I could feel his lips there.

Guess belligerence wasn't going to work.

"What are you doing?" I pretended not to like his lips on my neck.

"It's tomorrow," he answered, and then I had to pretend not to like his sleepy gruff voice vibrating on my neck.

"So?"

His lips glided up my neck; his teeth nipped my earlobe and he said, "Your reprieve is over."

Damn. I was afraid of that.

"Eddie…" I started to say, but he kissed me.

Really, it was too much to take. His warm body on me, his warm bed under me, his mouth on mine, his tongue in my mouth, his hands *everywhere*—I couldn't withstand it.

So, I didn't try.

I kissed him back and, just like in my daydreams, I ran my hands over his chest, his belly, his back. He felt nice, hard, sleek and warm.

One of his hands went up my shirt, cupped my breast, and he rubbed the pad of his thumb across my nipple.

It felt so good, my mouth disengaged from his, I closed my eyes and sucked in breath.

His head came up and I opened my eyes to look in his.

They were liquid.

His finger joined his thumb and they did a roll on my nipple. Electricity shot straight to my doo-da. My neck arched, I bit my lip and I think my nails dug into his back.

He watched the whole show, his face changed, looking somehow hungry, and that look sent a shiver through me.

His other hand came up the shirt, it was whisked over my head and then it was gone.

His mouth was on mine then it traveled lower, until his lips locked around my nipple. My hands went into his hair, holding his head while he used tongue, teeth and suction until I couldn't stand it and I moaned.

He came back over me, his mouth on mine, and I was kissing him with everything I had when his hand cupped me between my legs over my panties, his fingers pressing in.

His head came up barely an inch.

"Christ, *cariño*, you're already ready for me." His voice was hoarse and sounded approving.

Regardless, at his words, I froze. Then I moved my hand down to circle his wrist and pulled it away.

"No," I said.

I mean, it was too humiliating.

In the throes of delicious sexual activity, I could forget.

I could forget that I was Just Jet and there would be a time when he'd realize that. When Damsel in Distress Jet was saved and there was nothing interesting about her anymore. I could forget that he was Hot Handsome Eddie and it'd never last because he'd eventually realize he was out of my league. I could forget knowing that other people would look at us and think, "What is *he* doing with *her?*"

I could forget for a moment. But the truth was all that was there.

He was with a gorgeous blonde just two months ago.

I hadn't had an orgasm in eight months and hadn't slept with anyone since Oscar.

He was the most popular boy at school and I was the girl with glasses, braces and a funny wardrobe.

It just wasn't ever going to work.

His hand twisted, dislodging mine from his wrist and his fingers laced in mine.

"Un-unh, Jet. You can't switch off on me just like that," he said, and looked at me closely.

"I have to go to work," I told him.

"Talk to me," he returned.

With my other hand I pushed at his shoulder, using my body to push at him too.

He didn't budge.

We were full-frontal, skin-to-skin, it felt good and, all of a sudden, I wanted to cry.

"I have to go," I said, a little desperately.

He lifted my hand and held it between our bodies.

"Talk to me," he repeated, quietly this time.

I glared at him.

"I have to go," I repeated, a lot louder this time.

He lifted our hands up to his mouth and touched his lips to them, his eyes never leaving mine. Then he held them to his chest, and I had to remind myself to breathe.

"Did someone hurt you?" he asked softly. His eyes had gone funny, gentle and something else, something I couldn't read.

I blinked, confused.

"Pardon?" I asked.

"Hurt you, touched you in a way you didn't want?" he explained.

I blinked again then my breath caught in my throat.

"Do you mean rape?" I asked.

He didn't answer, he just looked at me.

"Why would you think that?" I went on.

"One second, you're running hot, the next, ice cold and near tears. It would certainly explain why you're so guarded. *Cariño*, I'd like to understand," he said it like he meant it, and that pleasant feeling hit me again, but this time it was so powerful it knocked the wind out of me.

"I haven't been raped." I spoke quietly.

"You'd tell me?" he asked.

"I'd tell you," I answered.

I didn't realize how tense his body was until I answered him and he re-laxed against me.

"Then tell me what it is," he urged.

"It wasn't that," I replied.

"Then what is it?"

"It's nothing."

"Jet."

"Really, Eddie, it's nothing."

His brows came together when it dawned on him I wasn't a wounded soul, but instead, just an idiot.

"It's not nothing. If it was nothing, right now, instead of talkin', we'd be in about the same position but your legs would be wrapped around my back. It's something."

My stomach curled. I ignored it.

"It's nothing."

"Goddammit, Jet," he said through clenched teeth, losing patience.

"Eddie, I have to go to work."

"No, you have to talk to me. You don't talk to me, I'm cuffin' you to the bed until you do talk to me."

I stared at him. "You wouldn't do that."

"Fuckin' try me."

Oh... dear... Lord.

I stared at him again trying to figure out if he would do it.

The look on his face said he would.

"Get off!" I bucked against him, to no avail.

"Talk!" he clipped.

"I haven't had an orgasm in eight months! Okay?" I yelled. "Now get off!"

Yeesh.

The lengths a girl had to go to were ridiculous *and* embarrassing.

He stared at me.

"You're joking," he said.

"Would I joke about something like that?" I asked.

"*I* wouldn't joke about something like that."

I gave him a look.

He grinned.

"It isn't funny," I snapped, feeling immensely stupid.

"No, you're right, it isn't. I'm just glad there's finally a problem of yours I can fix."

Uh-oh.

"I don't think..." I started but he kissed me again. It was a great kiss and then it was all hands, mouth, teeth, tongue, both his and mine. It was delicious. It was almost even beautiful.

When his hand went between my legs again, he didn't mess around with my underwear. He just dipped right in, his fingers pressing, hitting the perfect spot and they began moving.

It didn't take long. As I said, it'd been a long time, but he had talented fingers, strong and creative. I was breathing heavy against his mouth. I was holding onto him tight, and then it happened.

And it was glorious. Fucking unbelievable, and trust me, it was definitely worth the f-word. It was worth a thousand f-words.

After I finished, I opened my eyes and saw him watching me with a look that was both soft and satisfied, even though he'd gotten nothing out of it.

I didn't have time to be embarrassed. He rolled over me and pulled me off the bed so we were standing at the side. His arms came around me and he pressed me deep into his body.

"Now, I'll take you to work," he stated and he bent his head and touched his lips to mine. Then he let me go, turned and walked away.

I stood and watched him go. He had a great behind. I'd been spending months appreciating it through his jeans, but now I could see that fact, especially as he was only wearing a pair of blue and white striped boxers.

By the way, Big Head Todd and the Monsters were still playing on the CD.

Eddie parked behind Fortnum's and I got out of the truck. He did, too, so I hurried forward but my sexy green sandals slowed me down. He caught up to me and grabbed my hand so we walked into the store, fingers laced together.

Indy, Ally and Tex were all behind the espresso counter and their heads came up when we entered. Indy and Ally took one look at Eddie and me and smiled. Tex scowled.

There was a line of customers ten deep, ready to give their orders.

"The cavalry arrives!" Tex boomed. "These two ain't worth shit behind the counter. Get back here, Loopy Loo."

I started to walk forward but Eddie's hand tightened in mine and I turned around.

"I have to get to work," I said for, like, the millionth time that day.

He closed in on me and replied, "Okay, but first, promise me you won't go lookin' for your Dad."

I thought about it then nodded. I decided that if I didn't make my answer verbal then maybe it wasn't a full-blown lie. More like half a lie or even a third of a lie, which wasn't as bad. Was it?

He looked at me for a beat then turned toward the books and dragged me along behind him. He walked in two rows, turned left and stopped halfway down the aisle.

"Eddie, I have to help out. Did you see how many people were in line?"

He dropped my hand but then both of his went to where my shoulders met my neck.

"I've got something else to explain to you."

Oh no, not this again.

I braced for impact.

"This morning, things changed," he announced.

I stared at him.

"What things?" I asked.

"Before, I was makin' you my business. Things are different once I sleep with a woman, make her come and intend to do it again. Now you just *are* my business."

Dear Lord.

My knees went weak and I grabbed onto his t-shirt to stay standing.

One of his thumbs started stroking my neck.

"You still got a bouncer takin' you to Smithie's?" he asked.

I nodded.

"Get Tex or Duke to take you home from Fortnum's and walk you up to your apartment," Eddie continued. "I'll pick you up from work tonight."

"Oh… kay," I replied slowly.

He smiled, dimple and all, and bent his head to kiss me deep. He let my neck go but tucked my hair behind my ear. Then he was gone.

I wandered out of the books, still half in an Eddie Daze. The minute I exited the shelves, Indy and Ally descended on me. I saw that Duke had arrived and was working the espresso counter with Tex.

"How'd it go?" Indy asked.

"You have to ask? She's still in her clothes from last night. Fuckin' cool!" Ally cried.

Both of them stared at me.

I stared back.

"Well!" Indy nearly shouted.

I gave them an abbreviated version of the Eddie Date.

They looked at each other then turned to me.

"More," Ally demanded.

I sighed and gave them the longer version, including Mom and Trixie, Blanca and Eddie's siblings, details on Eddie's "Sleep with You/Keep You Safe/Wear You Down" Speech and maybe got a little carried away and shared a bit much about that morning's activities.

When I was done, both of their mouths were open and their eyes were glazed over, just like I expected I looked when I was in an Eddie Daze.

I nodded in understanding at their reaction.

"I know," I breathed.

"If you hens are finished pecking over Eddie's carcass, we could use a hand back here," Duke yelled.

Obviously, it was time to get to work.

So we got to work.

The morning was a crush. Ally chose a Nickelback CD for the occasion and played it loud.

Normally, "work" at Fortnum's didn't seem like work. It was more like hanging out with your friends all day, which was sometimes interrupted by something that felt kind of like work.

Just after noon, the crowd significantly died down and Tex turned to me.

"Let's go, Loopy Loo. I got a plan to get your Dad's friend talking." He turned to Ally. "We'll take the 'stang. You're drivin'."

I gave him a look.

"Does this plan involve your shotgun?" I asked.

"Nope," he said and I felt some relief. Then he went on, "At least Plan A doesn't."

Uh-oh.

"What about Plan B?" I pressed.

He started walking toward the door. "Let's just hope Plan A works."

Wonderful.

We all got into Ally's brand-new Mustang convertible, Indy, Tex, Ally and me, and rolled out to Lakewood. Ally parked outside Bear's house and we barely cleared the Mustang when Bear appeared at the door, turned and carefully closed it. He met us halfway down the walk.

"I haven't seen your Dad," Bear said by way of greeting.

Not good.

"Bear..." I started but then the door opened and Lavonne appeared.

Lavonne dyed her bobbed hair an ultra-fake-looking black. Her roots were steel-gray, she was two inches shorter than me and at least thirty pounds lighter, if not more. She was petite, wiry and had a two pack a day smoker's voice.

"What's goin' on out here?" she demanded to know then, "Jet! Ohmigod! Look at your hair. It looks great!"

She rushed forward, always a bundle of energy, and gave me a tight hug.

"It's been too long," she said and then her pleasure at seeing me started to dissolve as she looked around, took in Indy, Ally and especially Tex. Everyone stared at Tex. Tex was a sight to see.

Then her gaze settled on Bear.

"What's goin' on?" she asked again, reading the situation like only a mother, or the wife of Bear, would.

"Nothin'," Bear muttered.

"I'm lookin' for Dad," I said at the same time.

Lavonne looked at me. "Your Dad was here just this morning. Hasn't he been to see you?"

I looked at Indy. Indy looked at Ally. Ally looked at Tex. Tex looked at me.

"What's goin' on?" Lavonne asked for the third time.

"Can we come inside?" I asked.

Lavonne's mouth tightened, she turned and we all followed her inside.

The inside of Lavonne and Bear's house could not have been more different from the outside. Lavonne had strict rules about what was a woman's domain and what was a man's. The man tended the yard, garbage and car. The woman tended the house, food and laundry.

Lavonne's living room was neat and tidy, and overly decorated in hearts. There were bent twig hearts on the walls tucked with dried flowers, heart wreaths, little painted-wooden hearts, heart toss pillows on the couch, heart frames filled with pictures of her kids.

I did a round of introductions. Bear sat on the sofa. Indy and Ally took armchairs, and I stayed standing. Tex positioned himself close to me, like a guard. Lavonne stood by Bear and lit a cigarette.

Everyone listened to my latest tale of woe.

Then Lavonne's hand streaked out and she flicked Bear upside the head using her middle finger propelled by her thumb.

"Yo, woman!" Bear yelled, arching away from her.

Lavonne turned to me. "Ray's been stayin' here the last two nights. I didn't know any of this was goin' on."

Lavonne's tone said she was pretty unhappy.

Then Lavonne's hand came out and she flicked Bear again.

"I said yo!" Bear shouted.

She had one hand on her hip, the other one holding the cigarette aloft and the glare she directed toward Bear was evil.

"What's this all about, Bear? And I'm warnin' you, you spill or this time I ain't leavin'. This time, I'm packin' *your* bags."

This was clearly not an idle threat because, without any delay, Bear started talking.

"Gambling." Bear looked up at me. "Your Dad's been gambling. Got himself in a financial situation, so he went to Slick, who's a loan shark."

I sank down on the arm of one of the armchairs next to Ally, hoping to get my heart started again.

"He had a windfall a couple days ago, bought himself into another game to make back the money he owes Slick. Instead, he lost and now he owes Marcus."

Tex, Ally and Indy looked at each other.

I didn't know what their look meant, but I'd worry about that later. I already had too much to worry about.

The windfall Dad had was my hard-earned five hundred bucks.

I felt like crying.

"How much does he owe this Marcus?" I asked.

"Fifteen grand."

Ally's hand came out and grabbed mine.

Fifteen grand? How did five hundred in pocket money become a debt of fifteen grand? That was forty-five thousand dollars in total. Even if I started stripping, sold everything I owned and sold my plasma every month for a year, I couldn't come up with forty-five thousand dollars.

Lavonne flicked Bear again.

"Why didn't you tell her this yesterday? And where's Ray now?" she snapped.

"Ray asked me to keep it quiet and he's out tryin' to fix it." Bear's eyes swung to me. "I swear, Jet, he's tryin' to fix it."

I stood up and shouted, "How? Gambling? Stealing? He's sure as hell not going to get a job waiting tables at Bennigan's and make that kind of cabbage!"

Bear stood up too. "He's tryin' to do right!"

Lavonne reached high and flicked him.

"Don't yell at Jet," she snapped.

Everyone looked at Bear and Bear's face got red and he exploded, "Why is everyone mad at me? I didn't get forty-five K in the hole playin' poker. It ain't my fault." Then he decided the smart way forward was to deflect attention from himself. "Anyway, Jet's workin' at a titty bar."

Damn.

Everyone held their breath as Lavonne's wide, angry eyes turned to me. "Excuse me?"

"Lavonne——" I started but she interrupted me.

"You're workin' at *a titty bar?*"

Wonderful.

"I'm not dancing, just waiting tables," I assured her.

Lavonne didn't feel assured. "A titty bar's a titty bar. You're not the type of girl who works at a titty bar. I know your mama didn't raise you like that," she retorted.

I pulled my back up.

Firstly, there was nothing wrong with working at a titty bar. It was good, honest work and good, honest people worked there (okay, maybe Richie, one of the bouncers, was a bit of a jerk). Secondly, on her dresser, Mom had a framed picture of Lottie sprawled across the top of a Corvette with her naked boobs pressed against the hood and her ass in a glorified thong pointed skyward.

Mom totally raised us like that.

"There's nothing wrong with working at a titty bar," I defended myself.

Lavonne deftly sidestepped my defense of titty bars.

"Your mother know about this?" Lavonne asked.

I nodded.

"What's she say?" Lavonne pushed.

I hesitated, sighed and sat back down on the armchair. Then I gave Lavonne the rest of the story.

When I was done, she walked to a little desk in the corner (which had hearts carved into it) and took out a piece of paper and handed it to me. Then she went back to the desk, popped her smoke between her lips and spoke with the cigarette bobbing precariously.

"You write down your address and phone number on that sheet. Girl, I *cannot* believe you did not tell me Nancy had a stroke eight months ago. What must Nancy think, none of her friends poppin' 'round?" She was digging through her desk and grabbed something and started writing. "Always took too much on yourself, even as a little kid. Never sharin' the burden. Lettin' people get away with murder. That father of yours takin' advantage, Lottie off enjoyin' herself without a care in the fuckin' world while you mopped the kitchen floor. You're fuckin' Cinderella, is what you are." She ripped a check out of a checkbook and handed it to me, taking the cigarette from her mouth and letting out an enormous plume of smoke. "'Cept Cinderella didn't have a choice. You do."

I took the check and looked at it. It was for five hundred dollars.

"Lavonne! I can't take this!" I exclaimed.

Lavonne smashed the cigarette out in a heart-shaped ashtray and crossed her arms on her flat chest. "You can, you will. You'll cash it and you'll use it."

I stared at the check then I stared at her.

"I know you don't have this kind of money," I informed her.

"Yes I do," she retorted. "It's my Christmas Club. Been savin' up all year to buy this moron a flat screen TV. After today, he ain't gettin' no flat screen TV."

Bear collapsed on the sofa and put his hand to his forehead.

Lavonne nodded to me. "Merry Christmas."

I tried to hand the check back to her. "Really, I can't."

"Your Mama know Ray's in town and all that's happenin' to you?" she asked.

Uh-oh.

I shook my head slowly.

"She'll go on not knowin' if I see that check's been cashed," Lavonne stated.

Wow. Lavonne was *good*.

"I don't know what to say," I told her.

Her face softened the tiniest bit and her lips turned up. "Say thank you and keep yourself safe. If we see or hear from Ray, we'll call you."

"You too?" Tex boomed and everyone jumped. Surprisingly, I'd forgotten he was in the room. He was looking at Bear, his brows were knit and his eyes were narrowed.

"What?" Bear asked.

"You see her Dad or hear from him, you call her. Yeah?" Tex asked.

Bear waved his hand, still coping with the loss of his flat screen TV. "Yeah," he said.

I wrote down my address and phone number and gave it to Lavonne, and she walked us to the door.

"I'll pop by and see Nancy soon as I can," Lavonne told me.

I turned and smiled at her. "She'll like that."

Lavonne and I hugged, everyone said good-bye, and we got in the Mustang.

"I think I want to be her when I grow up," Ally said. "Except, without the good-for-nothin' husband."

I smiled at Ally and my cell phone rang. I pulled it out of my purse and looked at the display.

It said, "Unknown number". I flipped it open anyway, hoping it was Dad.

Before I could say a word, I heard, "Where are you right now?"

This was said by Eddie, or, I should say, a not very happy Eddie.

I panicked and to buy time, I mumbled, "Um." But I drew it out as long as I could.

Indy was sitting next to me in the backseat, passenger side. There came a knock on her window and everyone jumped.

My head swiveled around and so did everyone else's. Through the window, I saw a pair of narrow hips wearing jeans. My heart stopped, thinking it was Eddie, then Lee leaned over, looked through the window and crooked a finger at Indy.

Lee looked about as happy as Eddie sounded on the phone.

Damn.

Damn, damn, damn.

"Holy shit," Indy whispered.

She was right. It was a holy shit moment. Not to mention, obviously Lee saw us and called Eddie. This was not good. At least, it appeared not good for Indy.

Well, the good news was (for me), Eddie was on the phone instead of with Lee.

Then there came a knock at my window.

Everyone's head swung around and, through my window, I saw a pair of narrow hips wearing jeans and a familiar silver belt buckle.

"Get out of the car, Jet," Eddie said into my ear and then there was a disconnect.

My heart stopped. Unfortunately, I'm afraid, "holy shit" didn't cover it.

Chapter 9

For Me, If It Can Get Worse, It Will

"How's it hangin' boys?" Tex asked when he swung out of the car.

Ally got out, too, and left the driver's side open. Her seat was pulled forward, a man's hand came in and grabbed mine, and I was "helped" out of the car.

I no sooner got my sandals on the sidewalk when I was tugged forward by a fast walking, pissed off Eddie Chavez.

I passed a good-looking black guy, lean, tall, with twists in his hair, looking at me with a grin on his face that went from ear to ear. I didn't get time to say hello as Eddie kept pulling me along.

I looked over my shoulder. I didn't know why, maybe to shout "help", and I saw that Lee was pulling Indy in the opposite direction.

Wonderful. Now I'd got Indy in trouble.

Eddie stopped a couple houses down, turned, and pulled me around so his back was to everyone and he was in my way.

"What are you doing here?" we asked in unison.

Eddie took a step closer, eyes glittering.

"Me first," he said, looking down on me.

"I was visiting some friends," I answered and it wasn't entirely a lie.

Eddie's eyes narrowed.

"So, this doesn't have anything to do with the fact that your Dad's been spending the night here?" Eddie asked.

Dear Lord, how did he know that?

I decided not to ask and not to answer. Instead I thought maybe I should try being vague. I hadn't tried that tactic before.

"Um…" I mumbled.

I saw his jaw clench and I was pretty sure he was about to yell.

Count vague out.

"It's my Dad, Eddie," I said quietly.

Then (I swear I couldn't help it), tears filled my eyes.

Maybe I could have controlled myself, but Eddie's hand wrapped around the back of my head and he pulled my face into his chest.

He smelled good, he felt hard and strong and, being held against his chest like that, I could pretend he was the only thing in the world. I felt safe, maybe for the first time in my life. Definitely for the first time since I was fourteen. So I grabbed onto the material of his t-shirt at his sides and let the tears flow.

"I take it you know about Marcus and the extra fifteen K?" Eddie asked.

I didn't know how he knew about that either but I was crying so hard I didn't have the voice to ask, so I nodded my head.

He said something in Spanish and his other arm wrapped around me, but he kept his hand in my hair, my head held to his chest.

When I got myself somewhat together, I announced, "My life sucks."

His arm around me tightened.

"I have to agree with that, *chiquita*," he murmured.

"I... I... don't think I can fix this, Eddie," I stammered against his chest, admitting out loud what I'd been thinking for days, burrowing closer and wrapping my arms around him. "I keep trying to think of a way out, but I can't."

"Let me handle it," Eddie stated.

My head came back and I looked up at him. "How're you gonna do that?"

Then I looked around me and realized he hadn't answered my previous question, so I pulled back a bit and Eddie's hand fell away from my hair to wrap around my back.

"What are you doing here?" I asked.

"I was lookin' for Ray."

Not good.

"Why?" I pushed.

"A variety of reasons," he answered.

Now Eddie was being vague.

"Those would be?" I prompted.

He lifted his hand and placed it on my cheek, his thumb wiping my tears away. Then he ran his knuckles down my other cheek on the same errand. He watched his hand work and then his eyes came to mine.

"There's this girl. See, I wanna get to know her, not to mention do other things with her. Until this mess is sorted out, gettin' what I want is more of a challenge than I normally like. So, I'm gonna sort it out."

I felt a thrill race through my belly.

"But, don't you have a job?"

"They let me go my own way."

The Denver Police Department didn't let Eddie go his own way. Indy told me that Eddie just went his own way and then put up with the consequences.

"Let me do this for you, *chiquita*." His voice was soft.

"It's a family problem, I can't ask you…" I stopped as it hit me. "What's Lee doing here?"

We both looked over Eddie's shoulder. Lee and Indy were two houses down on the other side of Bear and Lavonne's, both with hands on their hips, and it didn't look like a loving conversation.

Eddie looked back at me. "Lee's workin' a connected job for some clients. I pulled him in the Ray search."

My eyes bugged out. "I can't afford Lee!"

"You don't have to afford Lee. He's *mi hermano,* and Indy's your friend and his woman. This is a freebie."

"I can't—"

"Would you stop saying 'I can't'?" he asked.

"Well, I can't," I pointed out.

"You can, Jet. These are your friends. Do you think they're out here for thrills?"

I looked back over Eddie's shoulder and took in Ally and Tex. Ally and the black guy were leaning on the Mustang and talking. Tex was obviously impatient and scowling back and forth between Indy and Lee and Eddie and me like he was watching an annoying tennis match.

My heart clenched and I got that strange pleasant feeling, like the one that kept coming at me during my Eddie Date.

"I think they're *partially* out here for thrills," I tried to cover up how moved I was by this show of support.

When I looked at Eddie again I saw the dimple was out.

"I expect you'd be right about that."

I decided to change the subject. "Who's the black guy?"

"*Mi otro hermano.* Darius. We all grew up together."

"He doesn't come into Fortnum's. Is he a cop too?"

Everyone in Eddie, Lee and Indy's circle were cops, private investigators or crazy people. Darius didn't look crazy, so I took a wild guess.

"Drug dealer," Eddie said like he would say "shoe salesman".

I stared at him.

"Really?" I breathed.

He nodded.

"Why don't you bust him?" I asked.

The dimple was back, this time with a full-fledged smile.

"I don't *bust him* because he's my brother." Eddie's arms tightened around me and his head dipped down, "It's a long story. I'll tell you sometime when we're not yellin' at each other, sleepin' or fending off our nutcase families."

My belly curled.

"Okay," was all I could think to say.

He watched me for a beat. "Can I trust you not to go after your Dad?" he asked.

I nodded.

"Does that nod mean I can trust you or you'd rather not lie out loud?"

I couldn't help it. He figured me out, so I smiled at him.

His eyes warmed.

"I could fall in love with that smile," he murmured as if he was talking to himself and I wasn't even there.

My entire body froze.

He felt it, his lips turned up at the corners, and then he touched them to mine.

Then he said, "One thing at a time."

☙❧

"How did your date go with Eddie?"

Mom had heard the key in the lock and was standing in the middle of the hallway waiting for me after Duke brought me home.

"It was a little... weird," I said and walked by her and into the house. "I met his Mom."

"You met his Mom! Oh... my... God. That's great!" Mom cried.

I dropped my purse on the couch and decided to change the subject, and not tell her I'd also met most of his family too. She'd start calling florists and churches.

"What are you doing out of your chair?" I asked.

She walked in, her left arm dangling useless, her gait unsteady, but she looked all right, even though it was getting late in the day.

"I'm feelin' good. I also did two loads of laundry and cleared the dishwasher."

I smiled. I couldn't help it. This was great news.

She smiled back. She knew it was great news.

"Did the mechanic call about my car?" I asked.

"Nope," she answered then continued. "But you would not believe what happened last night. We had some excitement. The police called up and said there was a flasher in the building. They wanted to know if Trixie and I saw him. We didn't, but we sure as hell went lookin' for him."

I started laughing, knowing this was the buzz-up that Eddie arranged, and I began to feel a little less stressed out.

I had nearly a thousand dollars in my purse from tips, Smithie's generosity and Lavonne's check. Not to mention, it was payday from both Smithie's and Fortnum's. Mom was getting around better and I had friends looking out for me. Eddie was going to figure out what to do about Dad and I'd had some good sleep this week. I was beginning to feel I could take on the world. Or, at least the next week. Usually, I was barely able to cope with the next hour.

I lay down for a while, took a shower, and Lenny phoned, telling me he was my ride.

I swung into Smithie's on time for the second time in a week.

"Once is a miracle, twice means pigs are flyin'," Smithie remarked when he saw me. "You got your shit sorted out?" he asked, putting my apron on the bar with another envelope of tips.

"Not yet but I'm working on it." I gave him my coat and purse.

Smithie looked at Lenny. "She's not five feet away from you the whole night. Got me?"

Lenny nodded.

"Good, now get to work," Smithie finished.

It was Friday, and Fridays were always packed at Smithie's, seeing as they were payday. Payday also meant the boys felt generous, which meant decent tips.

With two good nights this week and a shift on Saturday, if my car didn't cost me a fortune to fix, I might even be getting ahead.

Half an hour before closing, I felt a hand on my shoulder and then Lenny materialized by my side.

"No hands, big man," Lenny warned.

I heard Tex's booming laugh and turned around, dislodging the beefy hand. "He thinks he can take me." Tex's voice was amused.

"It's okay, Lenny. He's a friend." Lenny drifted away, his eyes still on us, and I turned to Tex. "What're you doin' here?"

"I'm gonna be speakin' to Indy, get you girls some uniforms just like that for Fortnum's. We'd all retire in a year."

Wonderful. At this rate, everyone was going to see me in my Smithie's uniform.

I pretended I was going to bat him with the tray and he pretended to cower.

Then he answered me, "Chavez called. He's caught up in something that sounds like jen-you-ine police work. He asked me to pick you up. Said he'd see you tomorrow."

I felt an immediate sense of disappointment. Then I felt the need to pretend I didn't feel disappointed. I smiled brightly at Tex.

"It'll be a while," I told him.

"Not like there's nothin' to do," he replied and wandered toward the bar, his eyes on the stage.

I worked the end of the shift and helped set up for the next day. I didn't realize how relieved I was that nothing happened until I handed my cashed out apron to Smithie.

"I must be goin' fuckin' crazy. I'm actually *disappointed* that my joint didn't descend into pandemonium because of your shit," Smithie said to me.

"Maybe tomorrow," I retorted.

Smithie gave me a barely there smile. "Get outta here."

Tex was waiting at the door and he escorted me to his bronze El Camino. When we were in and buckled up, Tex took off like a rocket and I felt the g-forces pulling me back against the seat. George Thorogood was blaring from the eight track.

"What happened to your car?" he yelled over the music, somehow calmly, as if he wasn't propelling us at a million miles an hour to our doom with "Bad to the Bone" as our soundtrack.

I pried my body from the seat.

"It's at the mechanics," I yelled back.

Tex was silent a beat, then he shouted, "I got some money stashed away. If you need it——"

I interrupted him, "No, Tex, I'm fine."

"Not from where I'm sittin', woman."

"Really," I said, a little more quietly but loud enough to be heard. "I'll be okay."

He made a noise that sounded like a snort. "If you need it, it's there. That's all I'm sayin'."

I felt the warm feeling in my belly again.

He parked in a disabled spot at my apartment building and got out to escort me.

I was at the doors to the building, keying in the security code, feeling Tex standing behind me when I heard a noise and a scuffle. I turned to see Tex go down, hitting the ground with a thud akin to a giant redwood tree falling.

I looked up to see Louie and Vince, still wearing their *Reservoir Dogs* outfits and staring at me. Louie's face was blank. Vince looked like he wanted to break me in half.

Louie came forward, grabbed my arm and stated, "Let's go. Marcus wants to talk to you."

Damn.

Damn, damn, damn and double damn.

I should have remembered to keep worrying, because, for me, if it could get worse, it would.

⌐◼⌐

They took me south, to the fancy section of Englewood with the big estates and multi-million dollar homes.

We turned right, drove down a secluded lane and pulled to a stop at a house that looked less of a house and more of a castle. They guided me up the walk, Louie on my left, Vince on my right, and we went over a bridge that went over what looked like moat.

Normally, I would find it funny, a castle with a moat in Denver.

Nothing was funny at that particular moment, however.

We walked in the front door and they walked me down a long, wide hallway that was made of stone with a plush, red carpet runner down the middle of it. Every once in a while, on the wall, there was a light fashioned to look like a torch. There were also two full sets of armor and a bunch of crests and crossed swords on the wall.

We turned right into a big room, then right again into what looked like a den, then left into what was a study. There was more of the medieval castle décor there with a big, heavily carved desk, leather upholstered chairs and pennants flying from brass rods at the ceiling.

A man stood there. He was younger than I expected the king of the castle to be, and very good-looking. If I saw him on the street, I'd give him a second glance. Tall, dark, with serious blue eyes that were somehow frightening, like he'd seen it all, done it all and wasn't scared of any of it.

His eyes moved the length of me and something flickered in them when he took in my Smithie's uniform. He hid it quickly.

"Take a seat," he invited.

I immediately did as I was told and sat in one of the chairs facing the desk. Louie and Vince stood behind me. The man sat across from me.

"You Jet McAlister?" he asked.

I nodded.

"Ray's daughter?" he went on.

I nodded again. Even though I knew this had to be about Dad, I still felt my heart die a little bit knowing he was the cause of yet another disaster for me.

"I'm looking for Ray," he told me.

I nodded, not sure what to say and too scared to speak anyway.

"You seen him?" he queried.

I shook my head.

His eyes moved from me to Louie and Vince then back to me.

"It's important I find him. Do you know where he'd be?" he asked.

"I..." There was a frog in my throat so I cleared it and said, "I'm looking for him too. He's not real good at sticking around when things get... difficult."

His face tightened at that, and the scary part of his eyes escalated to such a point where I was pretty certain I was going to pee my pants.

I'd never met anyone like him before. His menace vibrated off him like a physical touch.

I wanted to run, but I felt rooted to the spot. I had the feeling that this man was going to hurt me, or he was going to let Vince hurt me, and I didn't want either of those things to happen.

"Honey Bunch? What're you doin' up so... oh my, we have company."

I turned at this new voice, a female voice with a deep country twang. My mouth dropped open at what I saw.

Dolly Parton, or a fair impersonation of her, was standing in the doorway. Big blonde hair, tiny body, enormous knockers, wearing a pink negligee set, complete with marabou feathers, even on the high-heeled slippers she wore. I realized she wasn't Dolly because she had to be my age, or maybe a year or two older.

I didn't know what propelled me out of the chair but I stood and turned toward her.

She peeked around Louie and her blue eyes got huge. Then she looked at the man behind the desk and they narrowed.

"What're you doin' with a Smithie's girl?" she asked, hand on hip, hip jutting out and attitude hitting the room like a body blow.

"Daisy, honey, this is business," the man behind the desk said.

"With a Smithie's girl? In the middle of the night? I don't *think so*." Her voice rose on the last two words.

"It's not what you think," the man replied.

"Anything I think it better not be, Marcus, darlin'."

Louie, Vince and I were watching this discussion, our heads swinging back and forth between the participants.

Marcus looked at us and then ordered, "Get out." I started to follow Louie and Vince but Marcus said, "Jet, you stay."

I didn't know whether to be happy or sad that I was left with Marcus and Daisy, who were in the throes of a domestic situation. Though I didn't expect any time I spent with Vince would be a good time.

Daisy moved aside just enough to let them pass and then she closed the door and walked into the room.

Her eyes trained on me. "Jet, is it?"

I nodded, scared to death of her, even though she had to be three inches shorter than me, even wearing high heels.

She looked at Marcus. "What's this about?"

Marcus leaned back in his chair. "Her father owes me fifteen large. Poker."

Some of the tension eased out of Daisy and she glanced at me again.

"You close with your Daddy, Sugar?" she asked.

As it seemed some of the attitude had seeped out of the room, I dug deep and found my voice. "He left us when I was fourteen, but he comes back every once in a while. Some people wouldn't call that close but... he's my Dad."

Daisy nodded as if she understood perfectly.

She turned back to Marcus. "Tell me again why Jet's here?"

"Her Dad's a hard man to find," Marcus explained.

The attitude came back.

"You see what she's wearin'?" Daisy asked.

Marcus sighed. "I see it."

"No one fucks with a Smithie's girl. Not even you. Comprende?" Then she turned to me, "I worked at Smithie's. I danced a pole. Marcus met me there, so it's kinda our special place. How is Smithie? I haven't been back in *ages*."

Her tone had gone from seriously pissed off to sweet girl talk in a flash.

I tried to keep up.

"I drive him kind of nuts," I told her, taking advantage of what I hoped would be a turn of luck for me.

She laughed. It sounded like pretty, tinkling bells.

"Everyone drives Smithie nuts." Her voice was nostalgic.

"He says I'm a pain in his ass," I carried on.

"I used to be a pain in his ass. Then I married Marcus. Now, as you can see, I'm a pain in *his* ass." She smiled at me, huge and dazzling. Her teeth were so white they could light up the dark.

I felt it safe to smile back at her. Anyway, she was kind of funny, and seemed sweet when she wasn't being scary.

"If you girls are finished reminiscing, maybe I can ask Jet a few more questions?" Marcus butted in.

Marcus was saved the edge of Daisy's tongue when a knock came at the door and Louie stuck his head in. "Nightingale's here."

Thank you, God.

I did a mental sigh of relief.

Marcus closed his eyes in frustration.

Daisy clapped her hands.

"Lee's here! I haven't seen him in *ages*."

The door opened all the way and Lee walked in.

His eyes hit me in a way that told me he was surveying both my physical and mental well-being. He seemed okay with what he saw, which assured me I did not look nearly as freaked out as I really was. Then he looked at Daisy.

"Daisy," he murmured.

"Lee, Sugar Bunch, lookin' good, as usual." She winked at him.

His lips twitched.

"Let me guess," Marcus said to Lee, "this one has your protection too. What? Are you building a harem?"

Lee shook his head. "I'm running this errand for Eddie."

Marcus, who seemed to have accepted his fate, went scary tense again. I had the feeling he didn't like Eddie.

"What's it got to do with Chavez?" he asked Lee.

"Jet," Lee replied, and he wasn't talking to me. He was talking to Marcus. My name was the answer to Marcus's question.

"Shit," Marcus muttered and looked at me like *I* was now a pain in his ass. His eyes swung back to Lee. "You tell Chavez I want my fifteen grand."

"Take it up with McAlister. And some advice, Marcus, keep Jet out of it. It took a lot to talk Eddie from comin' here himself with a couple of uniforms. You don't want that kind of trouble."

"I got trouble with you over this?" Marcus asked and the tenseness was still there.

"Keep Vince under control and your focus on McAlister. If he makes good, keep him away from your tables. You do that, you have no trouble with me," Lee answered.

I looked at Daisy. Daisy was watching this like a hawk.

She caught me looking at her and she came forward and hooked her arm through mine. "I'll walk you to the door, Sugar," she said and propelled me out of the room.

"I'm sorry you got woken up in the middle of the night," I apologized as we walked from the big room down the hall.

She waved her hand. "Happens all the time."

Um... eek!

Then she went on, "You must've just come off shift and, no doubt, dead on your feet."

I nodded.

She stopped at the front door and her face got serious. "No harm will come to you, I'll see to that. But your Dad better get his shit together. I'm not sayin' this to scare you, Sugar, I'm tellin' you like it is. Comprende?"

I nodded again.

"Maybe I'll pop by Smithie's sometime," she said in another quick change of mood.

"I'm working tomorrow night."

Now, why did I tell her that? I didn't want to become friends with Scary Marcus's wife. Did I?

"Sounds good to me," Daisy replied and her eyes slid sideways as Lee joined us.

"Don't be a stranger," she called after us when we left, and I didn't know if she meant Lee or me.

Lee put me in his silver Crossfire and I buckled up.

After he got in, I turned to him. "They knocked Tex out just outside my building."

"Stun gun. He came to and called me. He's fine."

I nodded and began a delayed reaction shiver as Lee turned onto University Boulevard.

"You okay?" he asked.

I shook my head, and then, realizing that he couldn't see me because he was driving, I said, "No."

"Did Vince——?" Lee started.

I interrupted, "No, they just dropped Tex, grabbed me, put me in a car and took me to Marcus. I didn't fight or anything."

I didn't know if that was the right thing to do or not until Lee murmured, "Smart."

Lee pulled up to my building. The El Camino was still there, as was Eddie's red truck with Eddie leaned up against it, arms and ankles crossed. The casual posture belied the look I caught on his face when the lights of Lee's Crossfire hit him.

Tex was standing beside him.

Lee stopped a few yards away from Eddie's truck and he turned to me as I unbuckled my seatbelt, stopping me from getting out with a hand on my arm.

"It's unlikely that Marcus will do anything to you. It isn't his style. He stays focused, doesn't like mess and his problem isn't with you. If you have to have criminals then you want the kind like Marcus. He took you so it'd get back to your Dad, and if your Dad thought you were in the line of fire, it would smoke him out."

I felt added relief with his assurance and Daisy's. At least, relief for me. Dad was another story.

Someone opened my door, but Lee wasn't finished so I didn't turn away.

"Vince is another story. He's lookin' for an excuse at payback for Einstein's. Vince isn't the kind of guy who'll take a blow like that to his reputation without gettin' even."

My relief was instantly swept away.

"Stay careful," Lee went on, "close to Eddie, and if you can't be close to Eddie, then call Tex or Duke. If you're stuck, phone me and I'll send one of my guys. Yeah?"

I nodded.

He stared at me.

"I'm being serious," he said and he sounded serious.

I nodded again.

I was serious too. Serious as a heart attack, which I understood was very serious, considering I'd nearly had one every day for a week.

He let me go and nodded behind me. A hand curled around my arm and I turned to see Eddie leaned into my door. He helped me out, closed the door and Lee took off.

Tex made it to us and put his big hand on my head.

"Shit, woman," he said, then repeated himself, shaking his head, "Shit."

I realized he was concerned, and I felt tears crawl up my throat.

"I'm okay, Tex. They didn't hurt me," I told him.

His eyes turned to Eddie. "I fucked up, Chavez. Swear to Christ, it won't happen again."

Eddie nodded.

"Get home," he said to Tex.

Tex took another look at me and then lumbered off to his El Camino.

I turned to Eddie and opened my mouth but didn't get a word out.

141

"I'm spendin' the night with you, in your bed, and I'm not arguin' about it," he declared.

I felt relief sweep through me again.

I didn't want to be alone tonight, no way, no how.

"Okay," was all I said.

Chapter 10
Eddie Thought I Was Worth It

I could swear I heard a knock at my door. All warmth left me. My bed moved, there was the sound of clothes rustling and then I heard the door open.

"Eddie!" Mom gasped.

I burrowed deeper into the pillows, trying to find dreamland again. I wanted to go where life was safe, normal and mundane. Where people didn't hold knives to your throats, whisk you away against your will, or hot guys didn't pursue you against all the laws of nature.

"Jet's sleepin' in today," Eddie said quietly.

There was a hesitation while I was sure my mother mentally designed my bridesmaid dresses.

"Tell her Lavonne popped by for a surprise visit and she's taking me to breakfast," Mom whispered. "I won't be back for *hours*," she added meaningfully.

My mother.

I burrowed deeper into the pillows.

Eddie didn't answer verbally, but the door closed. There was more rustling of clothes, the bed moved and the warmth came back in the form of Eddie's partially naked body fitting itself to my back.

"Was she in her chair?" I asked, my voice muffled by the pillow.

His arms tightened around me. "She was standing. Go back to sleep."

I started to push up. "She needs to take her chair. I'll have to show Lavonne how to fold it, just in case."

Eddie pulled me back down. "They'll figure it out. Sleep."

"What time is it?" I asked. "I have to get to the bank, the grocery store—"

Eddie's hand came up and curved around my breast. "If you're awake..."

Electricity shot straight to my doo-da.

"I could sleep," I lied, settling back down, already two-thirds of the way to completely turned on.

His hand stayed where it was, but it didn't move with intent and he pulled me deeper into him.

Surprisingly, after a few minutes, I slept.

I woke up, happy and warm.

For about two seconds. Then I catapulted straight to freaked out.

I was curled around Eddie, who was on his back. He had one arm wrapped around me and the other hand resting in the middle of his chest, very close to where my face was.

I looked up to see if he was awake, my cheek sliding on his chest and I saw he was asleep, eyes closed, face relaxed.

I'd never seen him looking like that.

He was a cool, badass guy when awake, always exuding a certain somewhat dangerous magnetic energy. In sleep, he was somehow even more hot, more attractive, more magnetic and definitely more dangerous.

It totally freaked me out and I had thought I was already totally freaked out.

I started to move away. His arm tightened and he rolled into me and half on me. His head came up, his eyes opened and he looked at me.

"Hey," I said, for lack of anything else to say.

His eyes were sleepy but his lips formed a half smile.

He didn't answer my "hey". Instead, his hand came up and he ran his fingers through the hair at my temple, his eyes watching his hand move through my hair. Then it curled and his knuckles ran along my jaw.

"Payback time," he murmured, his hand cupping my jaw, his thumb running along my bottom lip, his eyes still watching his movements.

"Pardon?" I asked, out of my freak out and firmly established in an Eddie Daze.

His face disappeared into my neck.

"Yesterday, I took care of you. Today, we both get what we want," he said against my ear. Then he pressed his hips against me and I knew exactly what it was *he* wanted, because I felt it against my leg.

My heart skipped a couple of times and stuttered to a halt.

I felt his tongue touch below my ear and I shivered.

Okay, well, whatever. So, I was going to sleep with Eddie. So, he'd probably break my heart. Worse things had happened to me, right?

I ran my hands up his back, hooked my leg around his thigh and turned my head to give him more access to my neck.

Then I saw the time on my alarm clock and froze.

"Holy shit!" I cried.

I tried to knife up but Eddie's weight was on me, so instead I hit my forehead against his jaw, as he'd felt me tense and lifted his head to look at me.

"Fucking hell," he muttered, looking down. "What's the matter?"

"Have you heard Mom come back?" I asked him.

"No."

"Get off, get off, getoffgetoffgetoff," I demanded pushing at him.

"Jet," Eddie took my hands by the wrists and pulled them over my head, "calm down."

"I can't calm down! It's eleven o'clock. Mom left hours ago. What if something happened? Where's my cell?" I was looking wildly around.

"It's on the nightstand. Jet, relax. She's a big girl. She'll call if anything happened."

I glared at him. "I have to get to the bank, the store, call the fucking mechanic and find out what's wrong with my fucking car. I can't sleep in on a fucking Saturday like *normal* people! I've got things to do!"

Okay, so maybe it wasn't an f-word moment, as such. But I'd almost allowed the Eddie Daze to destroy my life. I was in a super-double-extra freak out.

He grinned. "I thought you *were* normal people, just your average, everyday..."

I would probably regret it, but I growled.

His grin turned into a smile and he let go of my wrists.

"*Chiquita*, you are too adorable."

"Get off."

His face dropped and he nuzzled my neck. "When I'm ready."

"Eddie! The Credit Union closes in an hour! Get off!"

His head came up again and he framed my face with his hands.

"No."

I glared.

He was still grinning and he looked almost... playful.

This was not good.

"I'll make you a deal, *cariño*. If you can throw me off, I'll get off. If you can't, we spend the morning my way."

My eyes bugged out.

"That isn't fair. You're stronger than me," I objected.

"You could try being creative."

My mouth dropped open.

I could create a knee to his nuts but that might put the hurt on Blanca's dreams of dozens of grandchildren, and I was pretty sure I liked Blanca.

I tried the girlie "please" look.

His head bent and he kissed it off my face. When he was done, I wasn't thinking of anything, especially not throwing him off. I liked him exactly where he was.

His lips slid along my cheek to my ear. He nipped my earlobe with his teeth and his hands went up my nightshirt. He lifted his head and then, *woosh*, the nightshirt was gone.

Wow. He wasn't messing around, and he wasn't wasting any time. Guess Eddie had cottoned on to the Jet Freak Out and wasn't going to take any chances.

"This really isn't fair. I can't throw you off half naked," I muttered.

"You couldn't do it before, but it'll be more fun this way if you try," he said against my lips, his hand curling around my breast, his thumb rubbing along the nipple. I closed my eyes and gave a repeat performance of the day before. When I opened them again, the playful look was gone and the hungry look was there, and I realized I'd given him exactly what I wanted.

"I don't think I like you," I told him even as my arms wrapped around him (of their own volition, I swear).

He smiled against my mouth.

"You like me," he said and he kissed me again.

When he lifted his head, I shook mine.

"No, I don't like you. In fact, I *really* don't like you."

All of a sudden, his hand moved down my belly and dipped in my underwear and my eyes widened even as my back arched when his fingers pressed in.

"You like me." His voice had gone gruff and I knew he had his proof.

Just as quickly as it came, his hand was gone and he grabbed my hand and pulled it between us, pressing it in his boxers and wrapping my fingers around him, and I had some proof too.

"And I like you, and just about now, I can say I'd like to be inside you," he whispered.

Just about now, I could say I'd like that too.

I moved my hand against him, rolling my thumb over the tip. He made a sound in his throat that vibrated in my doo-da, and he kissed me with an intensity I'd never felt before in all my not-so-vast experience.

It was far more hot, far more devastating to my mental health, and definitely wild.

He rolled onto his back, taking me with him, his hand on my bottom in my underwear, my hand still wrapped around him and stroking.

"You could get up now," he said against my ear as I ran my lips along his neck, smelling Eddie and knowing I'd never forget that smell or the feel of him in my hand, not for the rest of my life.

"I've changed my mind." I told him.

"About fuckin' time." he muttered, his hand moved from my bottom to wrap around my wrist, pulling it away from him. He knifed up and I straddled him, my head bent down, his tilted back, and then I was kissing him, my hands going in his hair, both his hands pushing my underwear down my bottom.

"Anyone home?" my mother yelled.

We both froze, mouth-to-mouth, his hands in my pants, mine in his hair.

"You've got to be fuckin' kidding me," Eddie said through clenched teeth.

"I don't understand, Jet never sleeps this late and Eddie's truck is still down there. Lavonne, you put the coffee on, I'll just check."

Eddie pulled up my panties, his hands went to my waist and he half moved, half threw me to the side.

He angled off the bed and grabbed his jeans as we heard Lavonne's scratchy voice saying, "Sure thing, Nancy."

I rolled over, got out of bed, snatched up my nightshirt and tugged it on as a knock came at the door.

"Jet, dollface? You in there?"

"Yeah, Mom! Coming!" I shouted.

I was standing at one side of the bed, Eddie on the other wearing his jeans, three of the five buttons done up. His face looked like thunder.

"Is Eddie in there?" Mom called.

Eddie's head swung to me and he looked about ready to commit homicide.

I stifled a giggle and was smiling flat out.

I mean, really. It was too much. We were like school kids getting caught on the couch.

"Yeah. We're both coming out!" I yelled.

"Okay, sweetheart." Then I heard Mom limp away.

Eddie turned to me, his eyes glittering.

"You better be worth it," he growled, and I knew he meant it as a joke, but what he said wiped the smile from my face and I became perfectly serious.

"I'm not," I told him honestly.

I watched as his face changed, the incredulous glitter faded from his eyes and something else took its place. Something I couldn't read, and didn't want to read.

Before he could reply, I pulled my hair back out of my face and walked out of the room.

⇥⇤

I took the fastest shower in the history of womankind, pulled on a pair of jeans, a black, button-front shirt that was too fitted and, as such, showed cleavage (another gift from Lottie) and a pair of black, high-heeled boots, because Eddie was still there and I had to make some effort. I pulled my hair back in a ponytail and spritzed with my fanciest perfume. I didn't bother with makeup because there was no time and headed out of my room.

Eddie was dressed, sitting drinking coffee and shooting the breeze with Mom and Lavonne in the kitchen like this was a normal, everyday occurrence. Not like he'd just been interrupted by my Mom with his tongue in my mouth and his hands pushing my panties half down my ass.

I didn't have time for niceties, nor did I have time to freak out at Eddie hanging out in my kitchen with my Mom and Lavonne, nor did I have time to freak out generally at all that was my life.

"Hey there, Jet. Lookin' good," Lavonne called.

"Hey Lavonne." I smiled a greeting at Lavonne and turned to Eddie. "I have ten minutes to get to the bank. Will you take me?" I asked him, not wanting to, but having no choice.

I *really* had to find out what was happening to my car.

As an answer, Eddie stood which I guessed meant "yes".

"You haven't had coffee," Mom pointed out.

I poured some milk and coffee into a travel mug and turned to Eddie. "Let's go."

Eddie walked with long strides and I hustled in my high-heeled boots to the truck. Without a word, we got in. He started the truck and we took off.

We were halfway there, with only minutes to spare, when I nearly shouted, "Can't you go any faster?"

"Relax, *chiquita*, I'm already going ten miles over the speed limit."

I gave his profile a look that said, "So?"

Luckily, he missed the look.

"Don't you have one of those flashy-lighty things like Kojak?" I asked.

"Yeah, but I'm not allowed to use it for trips to the Credit Union. Just beer runs during half-time."

See? My luck sucked.

He'd barely parked in the Credit Union parking lot when I had my door open and I jumped out of the truck.

Amy was locking the doors when I ran up. I'd worked with Amy for years. We were friends and used to hang out together, go to movies, spend time drinking margaritas and ripping apart Amy's (many) ex-boyfriends. She was sweet, funny and I missed her. I only saw her now when I made a deposit.

As I walked to the doors, I put my hands into a prayer position, mouthing the word "Please".

Amy opened the doors. "Jet! I haven't seen you all week."

"Car problems," I explained, sliding in beside her. "I've got a week's worth of tips that need depositing."

"No problemo, I haven't counted my drawer yet," she told me.

"Thanks, you're an absolute gem," I said.

I looked across the room, smiled and nodded to Jody. Jody had close-cropped, straw-blonde hair and glasses. Jody had been at Arapahoe Credit Union since time began. As far as I knew, Jody had smiled once in her entire life and that was when a long disliked customer had his car repo'ed.

Her eyes were at the door and Amy's eyes moved to the door too.

"We're closed," Jody said, all guard-dog-at-the-gate.

"I'll do him," Amy breathed, too enthralled to realize her wording was not exactly tactful.

I didn't have to look to know that Eddie had walked in behind me.

"I'm with Jet," I heard him say.

Both Amy and Jody stared at me like I'd just won the three hundred bazillion dollar lottery.

See what I mean? People were going to wonder what Eddie was doing with me. Even my friends and acquaintances stared at me with wonder.

I snatched a deposit slip and walked up to Amy's station. Jody left her drawer, partially to lock us in the building but mostly to lock everyone else out.

I pulled out my wads of cash and Lavonne's check and began counting expertly, my mind on my task, my hands sifting through the bills quickly, automatically placing the money in piles of hundreds. Eddie positioned himself beside me, his elbow on the counter, his eyes watching my hands.

"How's your Mom?" Amy asked, picking up a pile and counting it to double check.

"She did a couple loads of laundry and emptied the dishwasher yesterday, and she's walking around a lot more." I lifted my head and Amy and I smiled at each other. I'd been giving her a bi-weekly update on Mom for months. We both knew how important this was.

Then I went back to counting.

"When she gets back on her feet, are you gonna come back to work for us? It hasn't been the same since you've been gone," Amy told me.

It took superhuman effort to keep my eyes off Eddie.

He didn't know anything about my past life, and I didn't want him to.

Some way, somehow, by the end of the day, I was going to have to let Eddie know where I stood, which was far away from him once this all blew over.

I hadn't figured out how to do that yet, but I'd find a way.

I'd decided in the shower that what happened that morning couldn't happen again. *Ever* again. It all had to stop, and soon, or I'd likely lose my mind, not to mention my heart.

"Maybe," I said to Amy. The answer was more like "probably". As much as it would hurt to leave Fortnum's, Fortnum's meant running into Eddie, and that I couldn't do.

Amy turned to Eddie and smiled. "Jet was a hoot to work with. Not so much here. Can't really have much fun here. But..." She turned to me and her smile broadened. "Remember that time when we went to visit Donna's kid when he was getting chemo and you got all the kids on the ward together and pretended to have a shootout in the elevator bays using your hands as guns? That was hysterical." She turned back to Eddie. "Jet even did a tuck and roll on the floor and accidentally knocked over a male nurse. I nearly peed my pants laughing."

Her face flushed as she realized she'd just told a hot guy she'd nearly peed her pants.

My face flushed as I realized Amy had just told Eddie about my tuck and roll in the hospital corridor. It was not a crowning moment of glory for me.

I stopped counting and stared at her in horror. It was definitely not the time for a trip down memory lane.

Eddie smiled at Amy. The effect was mesmerizing (even for me, and the smile wasn't pointed in my direction), and it was all the encouragement Amy needed.

She forged ahead, turning to me, bright-eyed and firmly in the throes of a mini Eddie Daze.

"And when we played that practical joke on David when he had that new girlfriend?" Amy looked back to Eddie. "She was a screaming bitch, by the way. She *totally* deserved it."

"That was a good one," Jody chimed in, licking her finger and counting bills.

"Amy——" I started but Amy was warming to her theme.

"He was having dinner with her at Wazee Supper Club and Jet walked in wearing curlers in her hair, ratty slippers and an old bath robe and started shouting at him about going out with his floozies while she was at home with their six kids."

"I'll never forget it," Jody said. "We all went down to watch. That was worth missing the Broncos on Monday Night Football."

Amy went on, "Now he's married to Lisa and we all *like* her."

I closed my eyes and silently asked the Good Lord if he was busy and maybe could he help me out.

"And remember when——" Amy started.

The Good Lord asked me to leave a message.

"Amy, Eddie doesn't want to hear this stuff," I interrupted.

"Yes I do," Eddie said.

Wonderful.

Jody's head came up and she looked closely at me.

"See, he does," Amy went on, oblivious, and she made to start talking again but Jody came away from her drawer and into Amy's station.

"I'll help you count, Jet. I'm sure you've got a lot to do, what with your Mom and all," Jody said.

I felt the tension ease out of my body, and I would have kissed her if I didn't think she'd bitch-slap me for even trying.

"Thanks Jody," I replied.

"I'm so sorry, Jet. I didn't think," Amy mumbled and smiled tentatively at Eddie, then started to concentrate on my deposit.

I guess the Good Lord got to his messages quickly and sent an angel in the form of Jody as his stand-in.

Whatever. It worked for me.

We walked out of the Credit Union, I threw myself into Eddie's truck and snatched my travel mug out of the drink holder, taking my first sip of caffeine for the day. I needed it. I actually needed it laced with Jack Daniels, but I'd take it as it came.

Eddie got in and turned to me. "So, you used to work there."

I avoided his eyes, looked out the windscreen and sipped more coffee.

"Yeah," I answered.

"You'll have to teach me the tuck and roll. Maybe I can use it during a shootout."

Where were freak flashes of lightning when you needed them? At that point, I didn't care if it took out me, or Eddie, or both of us.

I turned to him. "Do you get in shootouts often?"

"Not really."

"Then you'll be safe."

He grinned.

"How's the kid?" he asked.

I stared at him, confused. "What kid?"

"The one you had the shootout with in the hospital," he answered.

Out of nowhere, I felt the tears hit the backs of my eyes and I sucked in a breath to try and control them.

It was Eddie's turn to stare at me.

"Shit," he muttered.

"Yeah," I whispered.

Devin was a good kid, and Donna was a good friend. She and her husband moved to Montana after he died, couldn't face the memories and wanted a fresh start. If her last letter was anything to go by, the tactic wasn't working.

I got myself under control and said, "You can take me home now."

"I thought we were going to the grocery store."

I looked away and sipped coffee.

"If Lavonne's still at home, I'll ask her to take me. Lavonne may be small and she can be nice but mostly she's mean as a snake. No one will mess with her. You can go and do... whatever it is you do on a Saturday."

He started the truck. "This Saturday, I'm taking you to the grocery store."

Wonderful.

⚜

He took me to the giganto King Soopers on Colorado Boulevard.

I grabbed a cart and hit the store at my usual pace, which was otherwise known as the I-don't-have-time-for-this-I-had-to-be-out-of-here-twenty-minutes-ago pace.

I threw things in the cart on the trot and Eddie wandered. I lost him in the produce section and he caught up with me while I was price checking canned chili. I made my choice and started the dash but he caught my arm.

"Are we in a race?" he asked.

I looked at his hand on my arm and then at him. Then I lifted my hand and counted things off on my fingers.

"I have to get home and eat. Then I have to help Mom with her exercises. Then I have to pay bills and balance my checkbook. Then I have to make dinner because Mom and I try to have a sit down dinner on Saturday night no matter what. Then I have to..."

He moved in so close, my breath caught.

"Am I invited to dinner?" he asked.

Damn.

I walked right into that one.

"Don't you have better things to do? Baseball games to watch? Criminals to bring to justice?"

He shook his head.

What could I say? No?

Okay, maybe I could say no, but that'd be rude.

"Oh, I guess," I sighed (as if *that* wasn't rude).

For some reason, he looked amused.

Then we both heard, "*Mi hijo!*"

I turned to see Blanca headed our way, pushing a cart that was loaded down with enough food to feed the Denver Broncos, the Colorado Rockies and the staff at NORAD. She was trailed by another short, female Eddie relative who had a look on her face that was very similar to the one Eddie was wearing.

Eddie bent low and kissed his Mom on the cheek. Then Blanca walked to me, reached up and grabbed both sides of my face and hauled me down for a big, old smackaroo right on the mouth.

When she let me go, she turned to the girl behind her.

"This is Jet, Eddie's girl," Blanca declared then turned back to me. "This is my youngest daughter, Gloria."

We greeted each other. I didn't bother telling her I wasn't Eddie's anything (or, at least, trying not to be), and I noticed Gloria had a dimple just like Eddie's.

"You two are grocery shopping," Gloria noted, and it was obvious this fact was borderline hilarious to her.

Blanca nodded her head with approval, as if they'd caught us at Dillard's filling out our wedding list. Then Blanca's eyes lit. "You'll come to my house for dinner tonight," she announced.

No.

No, no, no.

"We're having dinner at Jet's, with her Mom," Eddie answered and I felt a wave of relief wash over me.

For about a nanosecond.

Blanca's eyes widened then narrowed. Then she burst out in a flood of Spanish and I caught the words, *madre de ella*, *primera*, and *comida* and I knew I was in trouble. Blanca ended on, "Then you come to my house tomorrow."

No!

No, no, no, a thousand times no.

I opened my mouth to say something, but Eddie got there first.

"We'll be there at six."

My mouth stayed open.

This was going to put a *major* crimp in my plans to keep Eddie at arm's length (that would be Gulliver's arm if I was Lilliputian).

"Bring your mother, *chiquita*. I can't wait to meet her," Blanca said.

How come everyone was after me but no one could kill me or maim me? It would make my life so much easier.

"Mom would love that," I told her, and she would. It would be a meeting of the minds. A meeting in hell.

Gloria was smiling, full-on.

"Maybe we should invite the cousins," she suggested.

I turned and glared at Eddie, thinking maybe he'd help, but instead he wrapped his arm around my neck and pulled me into his side.

Blanca stared at us with an expression that could only be described as blissful.

Then she snapped out of it.

"Gloria, get another cart," Blanca ordered. "We'll have to go back through. *Hasta mañana*," she called and she was off, on such a mission she went without any kisses good-bye.

I turned to Eddie and, as his arm was around my neck, this put us full-frontal so I tilted my head back.

"You could have done something about that," I snapped.

"Like what?" he answered, his face a lot closer than was comfortable.

I tried to pull back but it didn't work. "I don't know. Politely declined somehow."

"I'm having dinner with your mother before you have dinner with mine. Come hell or high water, *Mamá* is gonna one-up your mother somehow. Trust me, sooner is better than later. It gives her less time to plan."

Without thinking, I stated, "My life sucks."

Eddie tensed. "It's dinner with my mother. It isn't the end of the world."

It was for me.

"That's not what I meant."

It was, in a way, but not in the bad way Eddie took it.

His eyes got serious.

"We need to have another chat," he said.

"No!" I nearly shouted, panic stricken. "No more chats."

His brows drew together.

I tried to calm down and said, "At least, not until I figure out what *I* have to say."

"How long is that gonna take?" he asked.

About four lifetimes.

Of course, I was going to have to speed it up.

I needed my life to get back to its normal, everyday boringness.

But first, I needed to go to the liquor store and buy a bottle of Jack. I didn't drink Jack but I thought now was a very good time to take up bourbon.

Instead of imparting any of this information on Eddie, I answered, "I don't know."

Then he told me, "You've got until tomorrow."

My mouth dropped open, then I snapped it shut and I asked, "You're giving me a deadline?"

He loosened his arm, but held me around the neck and pushed the cart with his other hand, moving us forward.

"You aren't exactly a fast mover, and any time I give you, you'll use to retreat. That's not gonna happen. So yeah, I'm giving you a deadline."

I decided it was a good time to stop talking.

We made it through the rest of the shopping ordeal without incident until we hit the checkout line. I wasn't paying attention and before I knew it, Eddie slid his credit card into the card machine.

"What are you doing?" I asked.

"Paying for your groceries," he answered.

I stared. Then I glared. "You can't pay for my groceries," I said.

"Why not?"

I didn't know.

"I don't know." Then it hit me. "They aren't your groceries," I finished.

"I'm eating some of them, aren't I?"

This was true, he was.

He turned from me, back to the cashier.

Guess that conversation was over.

I bent over and pounded my head on the little check writing desk.

"I'd let *him* pay for *my* groceries," the cashier decided to throw in.

I didn't respond.

I walked to the end of the checkout, commandeered the cart the minute the bag boy put my last bag in it and, without looking back, motored out the door.

⌐╬═

I saw Mr. Greasy Coveralls pulling my car into the lot of the apartment building just before Eddie and I swung in.

I felt a moment of elation. My car was not only running, it looked waxed and happy-shiny, like it had a new lease on life.

Eddie parked. I threw open the door to the truck and walked to Mr. Greasy Coveralls.

"It's fixed!" I cried.

"Yeah, it had a blah, blah, blah, with its blahdity, blah, blah. Then there was the blah, blah blah."

Of course, he used words for the "blah blahs", but I didn't understand a single one of them.

"How much?" I asked, looking happily at my car, which represented freedom, independence and no more borrowed rides or bus and taxi fares.

"Seven hundred and fifty dollars."

My breath caught, my heart seized and I was sure I was going to throw up.

I looked at Mr. Greasy Coveralls.

"Why didn't you call me before doing anything?" I asked.

Mechanics were supposed to call, tell you what it was going to cost before sucking away your lifeblood. That's how it worked. I thought it was the law.

"That's the charge *before* detailing it, the oil change, putting in a new filter and plugs and changing the wipers. Oh, and you had a brake light out," he shared....

I started hyperventilating.

Mr. Greasy Coveralls watched me like I was a particularly inept performance artist. Then he looked at Eddie.

Then back at me when I yelled, "I don't have that kind of money! The car isn't even *worth* that kind of money!"

He looked back at Eddie as Eddie's hand slid against the small of my back.

"It's taken care of," Mr. Greasy Coveralls said at the exact same time that Eddie muttered, "Jet."

"Taken..." I started to say and then it hit me. Mom, Ada and me watching through the window as Eddie talked to Mr. Greasy Coveralls.

I turned and stared at Eddie. "You didn't."

A car swung in. Mr. Greasy Coveralls handed Eddie my car keys and got in the other car and took off. I didn't take my eyes off Eddie the whole time.

"Tell me you didn't," I demanded.

He watched me closely.

"I did," he replied.

I considered scratching his eyes out. Then I thought that probably wasn't very nice. I mean, he just spent, like, a thousand dollars on my piece of shit car.

Then I considered screaming. But I decided to reserve my energy. Who knew what was going to happen next, and I needed to be prepared.

So, instead, I stomped to the truck. I wrenched open the door to get the grocery bags but I was pulled out of the way and the door was shut by Eddie.

That was it, I could take no more, and I whirled around to face him.

"I'll pay you back, every penny. The minute we get upstairs, I'll write you a check."

It would almost break the bank but I was going to do it.

"I'm not gonna take your money," he replied.

"You are. I don't like to be indebted to anyone."

Especially not you, I thought but did not say.

His hand went to my belly and he pushed me gently against the truck. "That's the point. I *want* you indebted to me."

He *what?*

"You *what?*" I yelled.

He closed in and I had nowhere to retreat. Anyway, I was too freaked out to retreat.

"If you're indebted to me, you're connected to me. Whatever makes you take care of your Mom, your Dad, kids getting chemo and friends who make bad decisions on who to date is gonna make you stay connected to me because you owe me. You aren't connected to me, the minute this is all over with your Dad, you're gone. I'm makin' certain that doesn't happen."

I didn't know what to say. He'd totally figured me out.

How did *that* happen?

Nevertheless, I tried to speak. "I... you—"

He cut me off, bent his head closer and started talking. I could smell him and I could feel his heat and I had to admit, it was getting to me.

"Whatever your next disaster, I'm gonna be there. Buying your groceries, fixin' your car, dealin' with your Dad, I don't give a fuck. I want you to owe me. It gives me the upper hand, and I'm gonna need the upper hand to wear you down. And Jet…"

He stopped, he was looking into my eyes, and he had that look he had this morning, after Mom and Lavonne came home and before I walked out of my room. The look made my belly feel funny and my knees get weak.

"What?" I asked. Honestly the suspense was killing me.

"There's one thing today proved."

He moved in even closer, his body was brushing mine and his face was an inch away.

"*What?*" I kind of shouted.

What could I say? It'd been a rough day. I was close to losing it.

"Whatever happens, you're worth it and I don't want to hear you say again that you're not. Get me?"

I felt that warm strangeness hit me and I had no choice but to nod.

Chapter 11

Dinner at My Place

"I'll get it!" Mom yelled.

I was in the kitchen, finishing dinner, freaking out and I knew Eddie was at the door. He'd left after helping me bring up the groceries, saying he had things to do. I was glad for the break. He was getting to me, wearing me down like he said he would, and I needed to regroup.

I'd done my chores and then got ready for Smithie's, so I was in my slut makeup but wearing my day outfit. I'd change into my Smithie's uniform at the very last minute.

Mom had gone weirdly quiet, sensing my mood, but also, I thought, because she was up to something. I couldn't worry about it. I had enough worries to last a lifetime.

Mom wheeled into the door of the kitchen. She'd overtaxed herself that day and I could see the exhaustion in her face. Nonetheless, she wasn't missing tonight, no way, no how. When I told her Eddie was coming to dinner, she'd put both her hands to her cheeks, her mouth dropped open and tears filled her eyes. Such was the reaction of Moms with big dreams for their daughters when hot guys with good jobs and fancy trucks came over to dinner.

I decided to wait to tell her we were going to Blanca's tomorrow. She was already residing on cloud nine, it was too soon for a promotion to cloud ten.

"Eddie's here," she told me unnecessarily as I could feel his presence in the house with senses honed from months of Eddie Torture.

"Great, dinner's ready. Everyone at the table," I ordered abruptly.

I had planned the evening closely. We had an hour and a half to eat dinner and in that time I also had to change and get to work. It was enough time not to seem rude (or, at least, not *too* rude) but not enough time for true disaster to fall.

Or so I thought.

"But…" Mom started, "shouldn't we offer him a drink? Maybe sit and have a chat?"

I did not *think* so. No chats. Eddie could drink at the table while forking food in his mouth.

"No time, supper's done and I'm about to mash the potatoes. Go, go, go!"

Mom wheeled out, defying my order and intent on being both meddling and polite. "I'm asking him what he wants to drink."

"Just do it in a hurry," I called after her, knowing Eddie probably could hear. "We don't want cold potatoes."

I hid in the kitchen, fiddling over the final touches. I knew this was the act of a supreme wuss, but I didn't care. Mom came in, made Eddie an iced tea, then Mom went out.

I put food in serving dishes and started to head to the table. I'd made chicken fried steak, an enormous mound of mashed potatoes, peppered white gravy and green beans. Mom forced me into frying all eight beef cutlets I bought, rather than just four, telling me Eddie was a man and men were big eaters. I'd never known anyone who could eat two huge chicken fried steaks, much less five, but who cared. I didn't have the energy to fight her.

Maybe he could.

Maybe he would, just to be nice, and then he'd lapse into a food coma. I was focusing on the next hour and a half and hoping I'd survive it. An Eddie Food Coma would just be a bonus.

"Let's eat," I announced, walking into the living room and heading toward the dining table. I was balancing two bowls and a platter and nearly dropped them when Eddie looked at me.

The minute he saw me, his eyes got funny, kind of lazy, amused and assessing all at the same time. His eyelids came down just a bit, the corners of his lips turned up and his dimple came out.

"I'll go get the gravy," Mom said and wheeled away, guiding herself with her foot.

I set the food on the table, busy, busy, busy. I was just noticing the table Mom laid was set for five rather than three when I felt Eddie come up behind me.

"Take a seat," I said, not turning to look at him and not caring if I seemed impolite.

I was back to my Bitch Strategy. I was counting on the fact that no one really wanted to be around a bitch, not even Eddie.

His hands went low on my hips, I felt pressure there and he turned me around. His hands slid around me, still low on my hips so they settled at the top of my behind and he pressed me close.

I looked up, the lazy look was still on his face but he was smiling full now.

I took a mental deep breath.

"Food's gonna get cold," I warned.

"What's the matter now?" he asked.

I blinked.

"What do you mean? Nothing's the matter."

He watched me and then something lit in his eyes. I didn't know what that something was, but by the look of it, it was something that made Eddie very happy.

"You're scared of me," he murmured, pulling me closer.

I blinked again and my body got stiff. "I'm not scared of you," I lied.

The smile was there, but now it, too, turned lazy and somehow... satisfied.

"Yeah, you are."

"Am not," I denied.

"You are and you should be."

My eyes got round. "Why?"

"Because, you don't give it, I'm gonna take it and you know it."

"Give what?"

"Anything," he said, and his mouth came to mine. "Everything."

Dear Lord.

My breath caught. My doo-da quivered. I grabbed onto his biceps and he kissed me. I slipped firmly into the Eddie Daze and, I'm afraid to say, kissed him back. When he lifted his head, it took a few seconds for me to open my eyes.

"*Chiquita*, you're too adorable," he muttered, watching me, the lazy look gone, the hungry look in its place.

The buzzer went and I jumped.

"I'll get it!" Mom yelled and immediately exited the kitchen, her snail's pace fetching of the gravy explained. I knew she was giving Eddie and me a moment and probably eavesdropping at the same time. If her fast advance from the kitchen was anything to go by, she'd positioned herself right at the door.

My life sucked.

"I really don't like you," I declared, taking it out on Eddie.

He just smiled.

He let go but stayed close and I turned.

Ada walked in, Mom following, still carrying the gravy.

That explained place setting number four, and Mom making me prepare enough food for an army. I had a sneaking suspicion as to who was going to be at number five, and my eyes narrowed on my mother. She ignored me.

"Jet, you look pretty," Ada said, and I bent to give her a kiss.

Only Ada would describe my slut makeup as pretty.

"Hey Ada," I greeted her.

She looked at Eddie and her eyes lit. "And you're Eddie."

She offered her hand, Eddie took it and smiled at her.

Ada turned her bright gaze to me. "He's a looker."

She wasn't wrong.

"Food's gonna get cold," I repeated, beginning to feel both panicked and ticked off, neither of which I could let loose at that particular moment.

"But Trixie hasn't arrived yet," Mom said as everyone started to take their places at the round table.

"She'll have to catch up," I replied, scooting as both Mom and Ada bumped me around like I was the ball in a pinball machine, adeptly forcing me to sit next to Eddie.

Damn.

Damn, damn, *damn*.

"Jet tells me you're an officer of the law," Ada commented as we started to pass food around, Mom shakily pouring iced tea for everyone. I knew better than to take it away from her. She was challenging herself, like the therapists told her to do, showing off in front of Eddie. Though I wished she wouldn't do it while dealing with liquids.

"Yeah," Eddie replied, taking a chicken fried steak and then handing the platter to me.

"Have you ever been in a high speed chase?" Ada asked, passing Eddie the green beans.

"Once or twice," Eddie answered, taking beans.

Ada's eyes got round, handing over the potatoes. "Did anyone crash?"

"No."

She looked disappointed then she rallied, "Ever been in a shootout?"

Eddie mounded potatoes on his plate, his eyes sliding to me, then back to Ada. "Yeah."

My heart skipped a beat at the thought of Eddie in a shootout. He'd joked about it this morning and it never crossed my mind how dangerous his job really was.

"Ever been shot?" Ada asked, excitedly.

I held my breath and my body tensed.

"No," Eddie answered.

I felt my body relax.

Thank God.

Ada's lips pursed; denied the gory details.

"Ever shot anyone?" she pressed, relentless, handing him the gravy.

"Yeah."

Ada's face brightened.

My breath stuck at the thought of Eddie shooting someone. He always seemed like a dangerous, badass guy, but shooting someone took it to a new level.

I looked at him out of the corners of my eyes and could see he was being polite, but didn't want to talk about it. Then again, who'd want to talk about shooting someone, even a bad someone, even if you were a dangerous, badass guy?

Ada opened her mouth to say something else and I interrupted her, "Ada, honey, maybe you and Eddie can talk about shooting people after we eat."

Her mouth snapped shut in frustration. Eddie's hand went under the table and he ran his fingers up the side of my thigh. I guessed that was his way of saying a silent thank you.

I had to admit, I liked it.

Ada tried a different tact, "Do the police still do those ride-alongs, you know, where they take civilians on patrol?"

Eddie looked at me again then he started to cut into his steak. "Sure," he answered.

Ada bumped into Mom on cloud nine, and then she went for the gold. "Do they take senior citizens? I'm eighty-one, but, I swear, I have the reflexes of a sixty year old."

I stopped with a fork full of steak, potatoes and gravy halfway to my mouth, wanting to see how Eddie got out of this, and not about to help him this time.

"Probably not," he replied honestly, not pausing in his eating.

He chewed and swallowed.

Ha ha! He was stymied and buying time.

"But I'll arrange for you to have a tour of the station if you want," he finished.

Ada's face broke into a smile.

"Do you think they would fingerprint me?" she asked. "You know, just for the heck of it?"

"No problem," Eddie told her.

Ada looked like she'd died and gone to heaven. Cloud nine a distant memory, she was on cloud twelve and sitting next to God. "That would be grand," she breathed.

Wonderful.

Now Eddie was doing favors for my friends. I'd never be able to pay him back and get him out of my life.

"Ada's addicted to those cop shows," Mom explained.

Eddie smiled just as the buzzer rang.

"I'll get it," I said, because Mom was transfixed watching Eddie smile.

Trixie was at the door. "Hey Jet. Sorry I'm late."

I was just relieved there was no overnight bag.

"We've already started eating," I told her.

She wasn't listening. She was walking into the dining area and beaming at Eddie.

"Eddie! Great to see you again. Hey Ada." She sat down, poured herself some iced tea and, without further ado, started to pile food on her plate.

"Eddie's going to arrange a tour of a police station for me," Ada announced. "They're gonna take my prints and everything!"

"That's fantastic," Trixie replied, then turned to Mom, "Have you packed?"

I looked from one to the other as Mom nodded.

"Packed?" I asked.

Trixie looked at me. "Yeah, your Mom's spending the night with me."

I closed my eyes and silently asked God, *Why me?*

God had no reply.

The table was created for four, five was a tight fit. Eddie's arm slid along the back of my chair even as he continued to eat. I looked at him and realized he was having the time of his life.

He met my gaze.

"I *really* don't like you," I whispered.

His dimple came out.

"What was that?" Mom asked.

"Nothing," I muttered and started to shovel food into my mouth.

"Jet, this meal is wonderful," Trixie said, digging in. Then she looked at Eddie. "Jet's an excellent cook."

"The best," Mom chimed in.

"You should taste her meatloaf. Never had meatloaf as good as Jet's," Ada added.

Dear Lord.

Meatloaf was meatloaf.

Yeesh.

"And she makes lemon meringue pie, from scratch, even the crust. Her crusts are light and flaky. You've never tasted anything so good," Trixie said.

"Always been a good cook. She's got the gift," Mom put in.

I wondered how rude it would be if I got up and started walking, and didn't stop until I hit Vancouver.

"She's a great kid," Trixie went on, winking at me.

"Couldn't have asked for better. Got great grades, never got into trouble. Even when her Dad left, Jet kicked in... took care of everyone," Mom said.

I froze.

This particular conversation was not going to happen, not now, not ever.

"Mom..." I warned, giving her a killing glance.

"What? You did." Mom looked at Eddie. "She was fourteen, got herself a job to help me with grocery money—"

"Mom..." I repeated, a lot louder this time.

"What?" Mom asked, a lot louder too. "You did. I'm not embarrassed to admit I fell apart when your Dad left. Especially not considering I'd raised a daughter who kept the family together." She turned to Eddie and smiled her dazzling majorette smile. "I take full credit."

I leaned into her, what I thought was threateningly.

"Stop talking," I demanded, still in the throes of the Bitch Strategy.

I guess I wasn't very threatening.

"You should be proud of yourself," Mom said to me, using her "don't argue with your mother" voice.

I ignored The Voice.

"Why? Anyone would do it," I returned.

"Lottie didn't," Trixie pointed out.

This was true. Lottie didn't, mainly because I didn't want her to. I wanted her to be able to be a kid, and that's what she was.

"Let's change the subject," I suggested.

"Eddie," Ada said, forging into the breach. "What do you think of Jet's new hair-do? Isn't it pretty?"

I gave up trying to eat and leaned back in my seat.

"Somebody, please kill me," I asked the ceiling.

Eddie's hand curled around my neck and his thumb stroked me there.

Electricity shot from my neck, straight to my nipples.

Bad idea, leaning back in my seat. I forgot about Eddie's arm.

I leaned forward immediately.

"What's for dessert?" Trixie asked, her eyes dancing. She'd caught the hand action. "I hope it's lemon meringue pie."

I could have shot myself.

I'd made chocolate sheet cake. Trixie loved my chocolate sheet cake, demanded that I make it for her birthday every year. I should have bought something Sara Lee.

"Chocolate sheet cake," Mom announced.

Trixie's eyes got huge and she turned to Eddie. "You'll ask her to marry you after you taste her chocolate sheet cake."

I threw my chair back, got up and grabbed my plate. "I'm done. Anyone else done?"

Mom looked up at me. "Jet, sit down. No one else is done."

"Then I'll go make more iced tea." And I ran.

My fucking mother.

And yes, it was definitely an f-word moment.

I hid in the kitchen, making more iced tea and getting the coffee ready for dessert. I also got out the dessert plates and forks, cleaned the pots, rinsed my plate and cutlery, put them in the dishwasher and wiped down the counters.

Then Trixie came in, bearing used dishes.

She glared at me. "That was rude."

I didn't care if it was rude. Rude was good. I was embracing rude with everything I had.

"You don't understand what's going on," I told her.

"So explain it to me," she shot back.

Since I didn't understand what was going on either, I couldn't.

"Just trust me, this is not what it seems," I shared.

"Mm-hmm," she said, all pissed off and not believing me, not even a little bit. She put the dishes in the sink and then a hand to her hip.

I was surrounded by women who could pull off the attitudinal hand on hip. Again, I had to ask, why me?

She went on, "From where *I* sat, it seemed like he was very interested in every word that was said. From where *I* sat, he seemed very interested in watching you the whole time we talked. From what *I* can see, he seems like a nice guy."

"How can you tell? You haven't let him get a word in edgewise," I pointed out.

She started to look uncomfortable then hid it. "Maybe we were laying it on a bit thick."

"A bit?" I snapped.

Her hand came away from her hip, her face changed and she grabbed my arms.

"Jet, honey, who made the rule that you weren't allowed to be happy?"

"No one. I'll be happy... someday. Just not with Eddie."

"Why not with Eddie?"

"Have you *looked* at Eddie?" I asked.

Her eyes got kind of dreamy.

She'd looked at Eddie.

"Enough said," I finished.

She stared at me, coming back into the room.

"What's the way Eddie looks got to do with the price of tea in China?" she enquired.

How to explain?

See, the thing was, good things didn't happen to me. It wasn't as if I had a sorry, sad life. My life wasn't better or worse than anyone else's. I'd had ups, I'd had downs.

Okay, so there were a lot of downs, but there were also a lot of good times, too.

I just knew I wasn't lucky. I also knew my limitations. And finally, I knew that dreams didn't come true, not your Mom's dreams for you, not your Mom's best friend's dreams for you and certainly not your own. Life was finding your piece of happiness, even working for it if you had to, and settling in.

I knew I'd find my piece of happiness, but even if Eddie truly did have some weird attraction to me, I'd never, not in a million years, settle in with him. I'd always be wondering when he'd figure it out or find something better. And I didn't want a life like that.

That was why good-looking people were with good-looking people, and plain folk were with plain folk. You didn't court that kind of unhappiness.

Trixie had been married twice and was currently on the market. She had taste in men like my Mom and Lavonne, but enough confidence to get them to take a hike when she was done carrying them. She'd find someone else, I knew it. She always did. She was that kind of woman. When she was done being alone, she wouldn't be alone. She'd never understand.

"Never mind," I said.

She stared at me. "Next time I see Ray, I'm gonna kill him."

She'd have to stand in line.

"Why?" I asked.

"Never mind," she replied.

We rinsed the dishes and put them in the dishwasher. Trixie carried out the sheet cake and I trailed with ice cream and plates. Trixie served up while I did coffee. The whole time, I avoided looking at Eddie.

"I'll come around at five thirty to pick you up tomorrow," Eddie said, finishing his cake and looking at Mom.

Uh-oh.

I still hadn't told Mom about Blanca's dinner.

"Pardon?" Mom asked, looking between Eddie and me.

"I forgot to tell you, we're going to Eddie's Mom's for dinner tomorrow," I told her.

Trixie smiled. Mom beamed. Ada actually clapped.

I sat back in my chair and closed my eyes.

"You ladies can come if you like, Mom's having a party," Eddie told Trixie and Ada.

I leaned forward in my chair and opened my eyes, turned to Eddie and glared. "What do you mean, a party?"

"She's asked the cousins, Indy and Lee, all of the Nightingales and Indy's Dad," Eddie explained.

No.

No, no, no.

This was *not* happening.

"I'd love to come," Trixie accepted.

"I'd be delighted. I never go anywhere," Ada said.

Wonderful.

"I'll come by at five thirty, I'll take Ada and we'll follow you," Trixie planned, talking to Eddie, and Eddie nodded.

I got out of my chair again. This time, I had a valid excuse.

"I need to get ready for work."

Without waiting for a reply, I walked to my room.

I was in my Smithie's uniform, sitting on the bed and slipping on a pair of black pumps when a knock came at my door.

"Come in," I called, thinking it was Mom or Trixie to give me another lecture.

Eddie walked in and closed the door.

Damn.

"I'm almost ready," I told him.

I stood and grabbed my jeans jacket, pulling it on.

Eddie watched me, shoulders against the door, arms crossed on his chest, eyes on my uniform. For the first time that night he looked unhappy.

"What?" I asked.

"I don't like you working there," he said.

I grabbed my purse, but he wasn't done.

"And I *really* don't like that outfit."

I sighed.

"I don't have much of a choice," I stated, walking toward him. "Anyway, it doesn't much matter if you like it or you don't, it doesn't have anything to do with you."

He was standing against the door and not moving.

"Can you get out of the way?" I asked, looking up at him.

I should have looked sooner. His eyes were glittery which meant he'd gone from unhappy to pissed off.

"I thought we'd been through this," he commented, his voice scary quiet.

171

Uh-oh.

I decided to ignore it.

"I can't be late for work."

"I can see my plan isn't working," he replied, changing the subject.

"What plan?" I asked, staying as far away from him as I could without retreating or looking like I was staying as far away from him as I could. I was beginning to feel a thrill of fear working up my spine.

"Honesty, being a nice guy, doing good deeds, getting you indebted to me."

I stared at him, scared of what he'd say next.

"So?" I asked.

Okay, so I had to know, even though I didn't want to know.

"So, I'll have to try a new plan."

If his old plan was honesty, being nice and doing good things, I didn't want to know what his new plan would be.

He told me anyway.

"The way I see it, the minute I got my hand in your pants and made you come, that bought me nearly an entire day of you bein' nice to me. You didn't yell at me once, you cried in my arms and fell asleep in them too. So, I'm guessin' that's the way to keep you sweet."

Oh... dear... Lord.

I just stared. I mean, what did you say to that?

He kept going, "I'll take you to work, I'll pick you up and you're spendin' the night at my house."

Eek!

I finally found my voice. "I don't like your plan."

"Then quit behavin' like a bitch, it isn't you and doesn't suit you."

My mouth dropped open. I knew I was being a bitch, but I never expected him to call me on it.

My eyes narrowed and I put a hand on my hip. I'd been doing that a lot lately. I didn't think I was the kind of woman to put a hand on her hip, but there you go.

"Pardon?"

"Your Mom and her friends love you and they're proud of you. Tonight, you embarrassed your mother."

"It isn't about her," I snapped, "It's about you."

"I know it's about me. It doesn't matter, you still embarrassed her."

"She'll get over it."

"Can I expect more of this tomorrow night, with my mother?" he asked.

See, I wasn't wrong with what I told him. Trixie, Ada and Mom would get over it and I knew that.

There was no way I'd be bitchy to Blanca. Blanca was a nice lady.

Eddie didn't need to know that. For now, if I was going to be a bitch, then I was going to have to go all the way. I leaned forward a couple of inches and kind of lied, "Maybe."

He pushed away from the door and came at me. "Then I'll have to make sure you're sweet."

Eek! Eek! *Eek!*

I put my hands up to ward him off.

"You could just back off and leave me alone," I tried.

His chest came up against my hands and then pushed them backward until they were pressed between our bodies.

"That's not gonna happen."

I looked up at him.

He looked down at me.

We had a staring contest.

I lost the staring contest, let out a big sigh and relaxed against him.

"Oh, all right. I'll stop being a bitch," I gave in.

The scary glitter went out of his eyes and warmth seeped into them. "I knew you couldn't keep it up."

This was true.

I still gave him a look.

He wrapped his arm around my neck and guided me to the door. "Let's get you to work.

Chapter 12

Enough Was Enough

Eddie walked into the club with me.

Smithie took one look at us and shouted, "I got new furniture on order and I don't wanna hafta buy more! Get that motherfucker outta here!"

Eddie's hand was at my back and at Smithie's words it slid around to my hip. I thought this was a dangerous sign, so I looked up at him to gauge the danger level. There was no smile, but the dimple was out and I took this as an indication I could relax.

I put my jacket and purse on the bar and slid my cell into the apron Smithie gave me.

"He's just dropping me off."

Smithie was glaring at Eddie, who'd casually put his forearm on the bar like he was going to stay all night. At my words, Smithie's eyes slid to me.

"I take it since you got a fuckin' escort, you ain't got your shit sorted out yet," he said.

"No," I admitted.

"Richie!" Smithie hollered and I jumped.

Richie, the jerk bouncer, trotted up, checking out Eddie and me as he came (more me, if you want the God's honest truth). He was blond, blue-eyed, about two inches taller than me and fifty pounds heavier, all of it muscle.

"You're pullin' Jet Duty tonight. You ain't five feet away from her all night, got that?" Smithie ordered.

Richie nodded.

Eddie sized Richie up and I could tell by his jaw tightening that he didn't like what he saw but he kept it to himself.

Smithie looked at me. "You're a pain in my fuckin' ass. Get to work."

I walked away from the bar, tying my apron around my waist. Eddie came with me and I stopped and looked up at him.

"You better go. You stay any longer, Smithie's going to have an aneurysm."

Eddie looked down at me then his hand went through my hair at the temple. He watched it go and then his eyes locked on mine, his hand settling in the crook of my neck.

"I have to go anyway, got things to do. Don't get into any trouble. If Slick comes by and pulls a knife, don't be a hero. You run, then you call me." He waited a beat to see if this sank in. I nodded, somewhat curious at what things he had to do. I didn't ask, because I probably didn't want to know. "I'll pick you up when you're done," he finished.

I had no choice about accepting the ride. Lee told me to stick with Eddie, or someone, and I was scared enough to comply. Since the idea of calling Duke or Tex to come and get me at three o'clock in the morning didn't appeal, nor did asking a favor of one of Lee's boys, I was stuck. I'd have to carry through my plan to avoid Eddie some other time.

Then Eddie said, "You're spendin' the night with me."

It wasn't a question.

I decided to treat it as one. Needless to say that some other time to avoid Eddie included not spending the night with him.

"I'd rather go home."

"No offense, but my bed's more comfortable."

"I meant alone," I clarified.

He grinned as if what I said was amusing, leaned down and touched his lips to mine.

Then he walked away.

I sighed, watched him go and I had to admit, I enjoyed the show.

Guess I was spending the night with Eddie.

"Not your fuckin' boyfriend, right?" Smithie yelled at me.

Wonderful.

The night started out good, busy but quiet. No bachelor parties, no brawls, no men with knives.

This luck didn't last long.

"Jet!"

I was at the waitress station when I whirled at my name to see Indy, Ally and two men, one slim, the other Hispanic, standing behind me.

"I fucking *love* that outfit," Ally said, her eyes huge and approving.

"I do too," the slim man agreed. "Can I borrow it? It would be *divine* with 'She Works Hard for the Money', don't you think?" He turned to Indy but he didn't wait for an answer and glanced around. "No... wait... is there a gift shop here that sells those tops?"

This must be Indy's neighbor, Tod, and Tod's partner, Stevie.

"I borrowed your shoes," I said to him. "Thank you. I still have them. I'll get them back to you tomorrow."

"Keep 'em," he invited, waving his hand. "The dress they went with ripped. Irreparable. It was traumatic. I loved that dress. The shoes are just an ugly memory now."

"But..." I stammered, sort of in shock at his generosity. "Those are great shoes."

He shrugged. "Just think of me as the shoe fairy." Then he acted like he was bonking me on the head with an imaginary magic wand. "Make your own good memories in those shoes."

I gaped for a second, and then he winked at me. I couldn't help it, so I smiled at him and then turned to Indy. She did belated introductions and I asked, "What are you doing here?"

"Came to see your other life. You don't mind, do you?" Indy answered.

I shook my head and, for some reason, I didn't. It was way too late in the day, my secret was out and nearly everyone had seen my Smithie's uniform anyway.

"Be sure you're in my station," I pointed at some tables. "I'll take care of you."

"Hey, you!" Smithie shouted, lumbering down the bar toward us, pointing at Ally. "Or you." He pointed at Indy. "You friends of Jet's?"

Both Indy and Ally nodded.

"Either of you dance?" he asked when he made it to the waitress station.

Uh-oh.

Not good.

"Smithie..." I started.

"Quiet, Jet, I'm fuckin' recruitin'," Smithie shushed me.

At his words, Indy, Ally, Tod and Stevie all looked to the stage. Then they looked back at Smithie.

"Not *that* kind of dance," Ally said.

"Trust me, you'd make a fuckin' fortune," Smithie informed her.

"Can you spell 'yikes'?" Tod whispered loudly to Stevie.

Smithie ignored him.

"Think about it, get my number from Jet, call me. You'd be drivin' a Porsche in a month," he promised.

"You told me I'd be driving a Porsche in a month," I cut in.

"Well, *you* got a fuckin' uptight, fuckin' cop boyfriend who don't want you onstage and I'm still a fuckin' dancer down. I'm scoutin' and these girls are talent."

"Um... thank you?" Indy said, or more like, asked.

"You're fuckin' welcome," Smithie replied then turned to me and raised his brows. "Hello? This ain't a social club for hot chicks and gay guys. Get to work."

Then he lumbered back down the bar.

Tod turned to Stevie. "See, I told you it would be interesting."

Stevie gave him a look. "Anyone sees us here, we're getting kicked out of the Gay Club."

"Pul-leese," Tod took off toward my station, "who's gonna see us here?"

Indy and Ally waved as they went and settled at a table.

⇥⇤

An hour and a half later, I was just finishing serving Indy and Company's fourth round of drinks when I turned, again at my name.

"Well, hey there, Sugar Bunch."

It was Daisy. She was wearing a pair of platform go-aheads (toeless mules that were backless, and thus, when wearing them, you had to "go-ahead") and a spangly dress with so many beads and sequins it glittered like a disco ball. The hem was cut at a wide slant starting at her upper thigh on one side and going down to mid-calf on the other, the entire hem sporting a beaded fringe. She had so much cleavage bursting forth that I feared one of her breasts would pop out at the slightest movement. Completing this ensemble, her hair was two sizes larger than last night and seemed, at first glance, to take up most of the room.

"Daisy!" I greeted her.

She gave me a brief hug, like we'd been friends for years instead of just meeting once under supremely scary circumstances.

She let me go and said, "After meeting you last night, I got nostalgic. Thought I'd stop by, see how the old gang was doin'." She looked at the stage. "But I don't know any of these girls."

I looked at the stage too, thinking that, in most cases, stripping wasn't a long-term job prospect. JoJo and Mandy were the only ones who had been there since I started. Most of the others were new, and some had come and gone in the eight months I'd been around. In fact, not including Tanya, I was the most veteran cocktail waitress on staff. Smithie had a huge employee turnaround.

"I don't mean to be nasty, but these girls need to get some moves," Daisy noted. "When I drove in, I didn't see a Porsche or Corvette in the parking lot. That's just sad."

"Did you drive a Porsche when you worked here?" I asked.

"Sure, Sugar. I bought one the second month."

Wow.

I looked at Indy's table. They were all staring at Daisy with awestruck faces.

"Daisy, I want you to meet my friends." Daisy turned and planted a mega-watt smile on the table at large and the awe in Tod's face turned to reverence. "This is Indy Savage, Ally Nightingale and um… Tod and Stevie," I finished, not knowing their last names.

Now Daisy's eyes were wide. "Indy Savage and Ally Nightingale! I heard about you two. I know Lee."

Indy and Ally looked at each other.

"I'm married to Marcus," Daisy explained.

Understanding hit them and they nodded. Marcus had been involved in Indy's drama but obviously they hadn't met Daisy.

Indy smiled. "Do you want to join us for a drink?"

"Best offer I've had all night, Sugar," Daisy accepted and Stevie immediately got up and grabbed a chair for her. He held it while she planted her narrow ass in it. "Well, aren't you sweet?" she said to Stevie, with another dazzling smile and a little tinkly-bell giggle.

"I'll get you a drink," Stevie said, and if he wasn't gay, I would have sworn he'd fallen in love.

"It's my job to get drinks," I told him, putting my hand on his arm and giving him a grin, then I turned to Daisy. "What'll it be?"

I brought her a drink and Smithie caught me at the waitress station while I was putting in another table's orders.

"You got Daisy at your friends' table," he said. "Treat her like a queen. She's a fuckin' VIP. She used to work here and once a Smithie's Girl, always a

Smithie's Girl. Even more so now she's married to the biggest, badass mother-fucker in Denver."

"I know Daisy. I know Marcus too," I said to him.

He stared at me. "How do you fuckin' know Marcus?"

I thought about lying and decided against it. Don't ask me why, it was a stupid decision. "He kinda kidnapped me last night after work, that's how I met Daisy. She kinda saved me."

I realized immediately I should have lied

Smithie stared at me some more, his eyes going a little wild. Then he shook his head, and I didn't know if it was to clear it or if it was because he knew my life was a complete mess.

Finally, he spoke. "Of course she'd fuckin' save you, you're a Smithie's Girl."

"That's what she said."

Smithie gave me an unhappy look. "Steer clear of Marcus. He's fuckin' bad news with a capital Fuck."

I nodded. I had every intention of steering clear of Marcus.

I started to put my drinks on the tray but Smithie caught my wrist.

"Got a friend, a brother, owes me a favor. I ask, he'd keep you safe and outta sight until your trouble clears and he's the kinda guy no one messes with. If Marcus is involved in this fuckin' shit, I'm ready to pull that favor. I'm guessin' your cop boyfriend has you covered. The minute I think he's fallin' down on the job, you're takin' a fuckin' vacation."

I felt that strange warmth again as I looked at Smithie. "Thanks Smithie, but I can't go away. I have Mom to worry about."

"Your Mom will go to LaTeesha's."

LaTeesha was one of Smithie's women. I'd met her on a several occasions and liked her. She was a nurse's aide at an old folks home. By all reports, she loved her job and the oldies loved her. This was proved with her regular wage enhancements when the oldies would die and put a little sum for her in their wills.

"Smithie…" I started.

His hand went up.

"No fuckin' discussion. I'm keepin' an eye on you." Then he dropped my wrist and moved away.

Wonderful.

The night stayed busy and as peaceful as a night could be at a strip joint. Indy, Ally, Daisy, Tod and Stevie called in a steady round of drinks, were nearing three sheets to the wind and frequent bursts of laughter could be heard from their table. They were more entertainment for the customers. Even fully clothed, Indy, Ally and Daisy weren't hard to look at.

It was nearing closing when I dropped a round of drinks on a table at the farthest edge of the stage.

I'd never liked that corner, even when my life wasn't chaos. It was shadowy and always seemed somehow disconnected from the club.

I turned and nearly ran right into Vince Fratelli.

I froze, my heart stopped and I looked up at him.

"I been watchin', know you have a bodyguard and I know you have Chavez's protection," he said, his eyes hard. "There'll be a time when you aren't protected and I want you to know, come that time, I'll be there."

My heart started pounding and my eyes flew beyond his shoulder. Richie was close but he wasn't paying attention, he was watching Indy's table.

"Look at me when I'm talkin' to you, bitch."

My eyes went back to Vince and fear closed my throat at his tone.

He kept going. "Been spendin' my time thinkin' about what to do to you. You think you're safe. Chavez's piece. You should know, Marcus and Chavez, they hate each other. Marcus'll give me a bonus, I fuck with you, no matter what Daisy says. Anything to stick it to Chavez. Anything. Even war with Nightingale."

I was rooted to the spot.

I wanted to run, to scream, but my body wasn't functioning.

My mind had totally shut down.

"All fours," he said, leaning into me. "I'm gonna do you doggie-style and you're gonna beg for it, even if I have to put a gun to your head."

I thought, for a second, I would faint, but then he was gone. Just as quickly as he came, he melted into the crowd and disappeared. I leaned against the wall, hugged my tray to my chest and took deep breaths to try to calm down.

This was now officially out of hand.

I wanted to tell someone, I wanted someone to protect me, to make me safe.

I didn't know Eddie that well, but I was getting to know him real quick. I had a feeling that if I told him that hot-blooded streak would come out and he'd lose his ever-lovin' mind. If I told Smithie, I'd be going on "vacation", and I couldn't afford vacation. If I told Indy, she'd tell Lee and he'd tell Eddie and war would break out. I wasn't sure I knew what war meant, but war was war and I didn't want Eddie or Lee involved in any type of war, especially not because of me.

Even in a packed strip club I'd never felt so alone and scared. Never in my whole life.

My mind re-engaged when I saw Tanya, walking funny, with a man I'd never seen close to her back. She was heading toward the dancer's hall where their dressing room was. The waitresses rarely went back there during shift and the customers *never* went back there.

I looked closely and saw he had a gun held to her back.

Oh... dear... Lord.

What now?

For some reason, I didn't think. I just acted. I didn't want to bring attention to Tanya and the guy and I didn't want to waste any time. I had to admit I hoped Richie would follow me. It was his job, even though he'd never been really good at it.

As quickly as I could, I followed them, straight to the dancer's dressing room.

I heard the guy say, "Out." And before I entered the room, the dancers were hustling out, faces pale, jostling me.

"Tell Smithie," I whispered to JoJo as she passed. She nodded.

I entered the room, trying to be calm and casual.

"Hey Tanya, what's up? Table ten is asking for drinks."

Tanya's face was a mask of terror and my stomach lurched at the sight.

The guy's head turned to her. "Tanya?" he asked. "I thought you were Jet."

Fuck.

Fuck, fuck, fuck.

And it was a multi f-word moment, let me tell you.

I said, "I'm Jet." At the same time Tanya yelled, "Don't!"

The guy turned to me. He was white, tall, brown-haired and had an ugly scar running from the corner of his mouth down to his jaw. My heart was hammering in my chest but it tripped and faltered when he turned the gun to me.

"Leavin' a message for Ray," he said to me. "Steal from me, somebody pays. That'd be you."

Then, without hesitation, he fired.

My luck took a turn and he missed. I dove to the side, my tray flying in the opposite direction.

Tanya pulled free and dove to the side too.

I did my tuck and roll as shots rang out. Then I stood, my mind a blur except for the fact that I was pissed, right the hell, off.

I mean, really.

Enough was enough.

I charged him, bent double and hit him in the belly with my shoulder. We both went down, me grappling for the gun.

Another shot was fired and I vaguely sensed activity in the room.

Soon, I was joined by others, wrestling, a pack of arms and legs and lots and lots of nails.

JoJo had joined the tangle, wearing nothing but a g-string, the pasties long gone. Tanya was there too, obviously feeling the need to get hers back. A couple of other strippers jumped into the fray, the gun was wrenched free and we ended up with me straddling the guy's stomach, my hands pushing down his shoulders. JoJo had her knees on one of his wrists, Tanya holding down the other arm with both hands and Meena, another stripper, was lying flat out on both of his thighs.

We didn't have to hold him down. Indy was there and had gotten hold of the gun and was pointing it at him, looking seriously badass and like she knew her way around a gun.

"Don't fucking move," Indy clipped.

I turned from Indy to the guy.

"What the fuck!" I shouted in his face.

He spat at me. Luckily, this too missed and the spittle just went up in the air and then landed right on his cheek.

"Talk or I swear to God I'll strangle you to death. What's this all about?" I snapped.

I was not a woman on the edge. I was a woman who'd been pushed off the edge and was in free fall.

I moved my hands in order to wrap them around his neck when I was hauled off him. I fought it, kicking and growling as Richie and another couple of bouncers picked him up and shoved him with a thud, face first against the wall, kicking his legs out wide and patting him down.

"Cool it," Smithie said in my ear, his arm around my belly, pulling me out the door.

I saw Ally, Daisy, Tod and Stevie. They were all standing close to the door and staring at me. Tod and Stevie with world-weary but concerned expressions. Daisy and Ally looked nearly as pissed off as me.

Smithie firmly but gently pushed me against the wall in the dancers' hallway and got up close. I was still struggling to get back to the bad guy.

"Settle, child, it's over," he said in a gentle voice.

His gentle voice hit me and I stopped struggling. The fight just left me.

"Smithie! What the hell was that? I thought your girls had protection." Daisy was there, hands on hips, attitude crackling, Indy and Ally flanking her like honor guards.

I saw a bartender escorting two police officers down the hall, one of them Ally's boyfriend Carl, and all of them were moving at a jog. They went into the dressing room.

Smithie ignored Daisy and turned to me. "You're officially on vacation."

"What's goin' on here? Do I need to call Marcus?" Daisy, not used to being ignored, threatened.

"Fuck no," Smithie said. "It's taken care of. Tonight, Jet's goin' on vacation."

"What kind of trouble do you have?" Daisy asked me.

I closed my eyes and leaned my head against the wall.

When I opened them, I looked at Indy. "He said Dad stole from him."

Indy's eyes flared.

Daisy was on a roll and when she started speaking, my eyes went to her.

"No one fucks with a Smithie's Girl. No one. This is outrageous. Sugar, I'm talkin' to Marcus. We're just goin' to see about *this*."

"Please, no," I begged. "Don't talk to Marcus."

Marcus meant Vince. I didn't want anything to do with either one of them and I certainly didn't want to owe one a favor while the other one was planning to rape me.

Something changed in the air, something stronger and even scarier than Daisy's attitude. I looked to my left and saw Eddie coming toward us.

Serious uh-oh.

He held his body in a way that was controlled but clearly hostile. His eyes were glittery and he'd gone so past pissed off that he had rocketed straight into fury. Before he could open his mouth to say a word, though, Smithie moved.

For a big man, he was lightning-quick.

Richie had walked into the hall. In the blink of an eye, Smithie had Richie by the arm and he slammed him against the wall, his hand leaving Richie's arm and he planted it at his throat.

"I thought I fuckin' told you, not five feet away from her!" he shouted in Richie's face.

Richie stared up at Smithie and opened his mouth to speak. Smithie didn't let him.

"You pay more attention to what's happenin' on the fuckin' stage and not to their protection. The girls on the floor ain't job satisfaction eye-candy, motherfucker. You're there to keep 'em safe. You're fuckin' fired. I don't want to see your sorry ass anywhere near my place again. You got me?" Smithie warned.

Richie looked at me, eyes full of angry blame. Then he nodded to Smithie.

Wonderful. Another enemy.

I opened my mouth to protest and defend, not because Richie was a good bouncer, he wasn't. Smithie was right, he was there for the jollies, being a big man bouncer at a titty bar and ogling the girls. But I didn't want someone else after me.

I didn't get to say anything because Eddie stepped in.

"Look at me," he demanded to Richie, forcing Smithie out and getting smack into Richie's space.

Eddie didn't need to hold him where he was physically, his wrath was enough to keep Richie pinned to the wall.

When Richie's eyes turned to him, Eddie said, "Don't even fuckin' think about it."

Richie stared at Eddie, his face changed and if he'd wet his pants, I wouldn't have been surprised. Then again, Richie had been there the night Eddie took care of Bachelor Number One and Eddie wasn't nearly as furious then as he was now.

Eddie turned to me as I noticed Lee and Carl materialize behind Indy and Ally. I didn't have a chance to react as Eddie's hand curled around my arm.

"Let's go," he said.

"No way." Smithie stepped in our way. "Jet's takin' a vacation. She ain't safe and you ain't keepin' her safe so she's gonna disappear until this shit blows over."

Eddie, already tense, froze rock-solid.

"I'm sorry?" he asked in his quiet voice. "I thought she got shot at on your watch."

An uncomfortable look crossed Smithie's face.

Eddie kept talking. "Find another waitress. This was Jet's last night."

It was my turn to freeze rock-solid.

"What?" I asked Eddie.

Eddie didn't answer me.

"Let's go," he repeated.

"I don't *think* so!" I yelled. "I need this job."

"You'll be taken care of," Eddie replied, like it was as easy as that, and began to pull me away.

I yanked my arm out of his hold.

"Yeah? Is that so? You gonna pay for Mom's therapy? The rent on a dis-abled-accessible apartment? Her follow-up MRI? You don't have any fucking clue, do you? This isn't as easy as a couple bags of groceries and fixing a stupid car. This shit is relentless. This shit is *my life!*" I shouted.

Everyone was staring at me and I didn't care. I turned to Smithie.

"Am I fired?" I asked for the millionth time.

He shook his head. His face still held anger but it was softening.

"You ain't fired, child, but you ain't comin' back either. You're not safe here. I'll hold your job open until you can come back and not get shot at."

My world, already spinning out-of-control, tilted and I could swear I was going to fall off. There was absolutely nothing to hold on to.

So I held on to the only thing I ever had.

I squared my shoulders.

I hadn't been in worse spots than this, it was true, but I had also always made my own way.

I'd do it again.

Somehow.

"Fine," I snapped and walked away from Eddie, right by Smithie and through Daisy, Indy, Ally, Lee, Carl, Tod and Stevie and a dozen dancers, bouncers and waitresses.

Fuck it.

Fuck it all.

I walked into the club and behind the bar, grabbed my purse and coat, pulled my cell out of my apron and handed the apron to the bartender.

"I'll come back for my tips," I said to him and walked to the front door.

Eddie was standing there. I didn't look at him.

I had no idea where to go or what to do. The only thing I knew I wasn't going to do was cry, even though I wanted to, really, *really* badly.

I hesitated when I got outside and Eddie grabbed my hand and pulled me to his truck. We got in, took off and rode to his house in complete silence. I should have protested but I didn't have it in me. I was struggling for control of my emotions. I had a man with a knife after me, another man was planning on raping me and another man had shot at me. I had to pick my battles.

Eddie walked me into his kitchen and I slammed my purse on the counter then stood in the middle of the room while he closed the door.

He came at me but I skirted around him, walked back to the door and threw it open.

I leaned over and took off one of my stiletto-heeled pumps and threw it in the backyard and did the same with the other one. I closed the door and turned to Eddie.

He was staring at me, residual hostility still glittering in his eyes.

"I *hate* those shoes," I pointed out the obvious.

I walked through the kitchen and into his bedroom and started to open and shut drawers. Or, more like yanking open drawers and slamming them shut, looking for a t-shirt.

Eddie came in, gently tugged me away from my assault on his innocent dresser and started to pull me in his arms.

"No!" I wrenched free. "I need to go to bed. I need a t-shirt."

I turned to the drawers. He pulled me back and into his arms, this time less gently and with more determination.

"Don't, Eddie. I'm hanging on by a thread here," I told his throat.

If he held me, I'd lose it, I knew it.

"Why?" Eddie asked.

My eyes lifted and I noticed his were guarded, but the hostility was gone.

"Why what?"

"Why are you hangin' on?"

I stared at him.

"I can't let go," I told him, thinking it was obvious.

"Jet, everyone has to let go."

"Not me," I replied.

His arms tightened and I tensed and pushed away. It didn't get me far, but I concentrated on the act anyway.

"Why not you?" he asked.

I didn't answer. Eddie shook me.

"Why not you?" he repeated.

The tears hit the back of my throat and I gulped them down.

"Jet," he prompted.

I shook my head but answered, "I can't because there's no one to catch me when I fall."

His guard went down and his eyes warmed. He'd looked at me with warm eyes before, but never like this. They came complete with a look so tender it made my breath catch.

"Everyone's got their hands out waitin' for you to take one. *Cariño*, you gotta learn when to take someone's hand *before* you fall."

I couldn't help it, I couldn't take anymore. I put my forehead to his chest, slid my arms around his middle and relaxed into him. Then, I felt the tears roll down my cheeks.

He stood there, holding me and stroking my back for a while. I had to admit, it felt good. Super good.

We both heard the doorbell go and Eddie said quietly, "That'll be Jimmy." He pulled a little away and looked down on me. "You gonna be okay?"

I wiped the tears away and nodded. He kissed my forehead and that felt good too.

We walked into the living room and Eddie let in Detective Marker. He greeted me, his eyes soft with concern. A handsome black man and a young-looking white guy, both in uniform, came in with Detective Marker. Eddie introduced them as Sergeant Willie Moses and Officer Brian Bond.

"Sorry, we have to ask you a few questions, while it's fresh. It won't take long," Detective Marker explained.

I sat down on the couch and answered questions. Eddie stood by the couch for a while, then I saw him motion with his chin to Willie, the black officer, and they both disappeared into the kitchen.

I kept answering questions, but glanced into the kitchen every once in a while.

Eddie and Willie were out of sight, but once Eddie paced into the doorway, his cell to his ear, his other hand at his hip, then he went out of sight again.

"I think we're done," Detective Marker said. "You still got my card from last time?"

I nodded and so did he.

"Call me if you remember anything or something else happens," he went on and I nodded again. "Chavez! I'm done," Detective Marker called.

Eddie and Willie came in. I stood and Eddie saw them out the door. I watched out the window as Detective Marker drove off, and Eddie, Willie and Brian stood on the sidewalk next to the squad car. Eddie was talking, Willie and Brian listening. Willie looked up to the house and said something to Eddie, and Eddie looked too. I stayed at the window and kept watching. He disengaged from them with a low wave. I remained where I was as he came back in.

His eyes locked on mine after he closed and secured the door.

"Let's find you a t-shirt," he said quietly.

I didn't move.

"What was that all about?" I jerked my head to the window. I had my arms crossed and I was trying not to look as exhausted as I felt.

Eddie came up to me, flung an arm around my neck and took me into the bedroom. He let me go, opened a drawer and handed me a white t-shirt.

I took it and stared at him.

"What was that about?" I repeated.

He turned square to me, but didn't touch me.

"You've been branded."

I blinked.

That didn't sound good.

"Pardon?" I asked.

"Told Willie, called Lee and Darius. Word goes out tonight that you belong to me. Anyone fucks with you, they fuck with me, the DPD, all the boys at Nightingale Investigations and Darius Tucker. I'm callin' in all my markers. I'm not takin' any more chances with this shit. Now you got an army of protection, whether you want it or not."

I kept staring at him as that strange sensation took hold of my belly in a vice-like grip.

"But…" I whispered. "Why?"

It was then he walked to me, put his hands to my neck and gently pulled me toward him until our bodies were touching. He looked down at me and his eyes changed. The warm, tender look was there but so was something else. Something I couldn't read.

"Because you make a fucking great chocolate sheet cake."

Chapter 13
Out, Coffee and Breakfast

I woke up alone in Eddie's bed.

I pulled myself up and looked at his side of the bed. He'd gone to bed with me, held me full-frontal, his arms tight around me until I fell asleep. Now he was gone. The only thing on his side was a note on the pillow, next to it, a new toothbrush in its wrapper.

I grabbed the note.

Out, coffee and breakfast, was all it said.

I got out of bed and went to Eddie's bathroom. It had a claw-footed tub, a pedestal sink and new tile, but needed to be painted. I searched in the medicine cabinet and found his toothpaste, brushed my teeth and washed away the scary remnants of my makeup with hand soap. My face immediately cried out for moisturizer. It was going to have to wait.

I went into the kitchen to grab my phone and call Mom and heard my phone beeping inside my bag. I dragged my cell out of my purse and saw I had three texts and four phone messages.

I stared at the phone. I'd never been that popular.

Text one was Indy: *Text back, let me know you're okay.*

Text two; Tod and Stevie: *This is Tod and Stevie, thanks for an exciting evening. Come over for cocktails, leave all gunmen behind, kisses.*

Text three; Ally: *Next time don't go alone. Remember, we got your back.*

Tears filled my eyes after reading Ally's text, but I practiced deep breathing and forced them down.

Next, I took on the phone messages.

First message was Tex: "What the fuck, Loopy Loo! I thought I told you I was designated bodyguard! I mess up once and I'm out of the loop?" Disconnect.

In an abrupt change of mood, Tex's message made me a laugh out loud.

Second message was Daisy: "Indy gave me your number. She thought it'd be okay. I'm not tellin' Marcus, Sugar, 'cause you asked me not to, but I think we need to talk. We girls need to stick together. Call me," and she left her number.

Thoughtful and sweet, but still scary.

Third message was Indy: "Lee told me Eddie's taking care of you. Call me, honey. I want to know you're okay."

Fourth message was Duke. He was already talking before the beep so I missed the first couple of words: "This kind of shit, girl. Dolores says to bring your Mom and stay with us in Evergreen. We live remote and Tex can set some booby traps. Think about it." Disconnect, again.

I leaned my hip against the kitchen counter. That weird warmth I kept feeling didn't feel so weird anymore. I knew it was those hands that Eddie said people were holding out to me.

I took a deep breath because I was about to take an entirely different kind of serious plunge and programmed some new numbers into my phone. Then I texted a general "I'm okay" to Indy, Ally, Daisy, Tod and Stevie (and yes, even Daisy). Neither Duke nor Tex had cell phones.

The backdoor opened and Eddie came in. He was wearing a tight, gray, long-sleeved tee, seriously faded jeans, no belt this time and running shoes instead of cowboy boots.

It was the first time I'd seen him without cowboy boots and it affected me in a strange way, as if he'd taken off some kind of mask and was showing me a different Eddie, an Eddie no one else saw.

He was carrying two coffees and a white bag. Before either of us could say a word, my phone rang.

It was Indy.

Eddie's brows came up and I said, "Indy," then flipped open my phone.

"Hey," I said.

"Hey. You okay?" she answered.

"Yeah," I replied.

Eddie handed me a coffee and upended the bag on the counter. Two enormous blueberry muffins fell out.

"Where are you?" Indy asked as I took a sip of coffee. Cappuccino, no sugar, just like I took it.

Eddie knew how I liked my coffee.

Um… eek!

Eddie leaned a hip against the counter less than a foot away from me, tore off the muffin paper and took a bite, sliding the other muffin to me.

"Eddie's," I answered Indy and looked fully at him.

His eyes were on me and my face began to burn. Something about this was bizarrely intimate and I wasn't ready for it. I'd had too many emotional traumas to stand around in Eddie's kitchen calmly eating muffins like I did it every Sunday.

I dropped my head and put my coffee on the counter. I tried to take the paper off my muffin one-handed and felt a new appreciation for my mother's disability.

"Lee tells me Eddie's branded you," Indy shared. "Never heard it called that before, but Lee did it with me during my ordeal. Beat the shit out of the guy who hit me, spreading a message. It's a good thing, Jet." she was obviously trying to talk me into trusting Eddie and not going into a full-fledged freak out.

Too late. I was way past freak out. I'd look back on my endless freak outs with happy nostalgia. Nope, I was in "Pissed Off Female with a Score to Settle" mode.

Except, of course, when it came to eating muffins in Eddie's kitchen.

"Eddie explained it last night. I'm okay with it," I told Indy.

I'd managed to get the muffin cup off and tore the bottom of the muffin free. I took a bite and Eddie's hand came into my vision.

I looked up at him just as he cupped my jaw.

"Say good-bye," Eddie ordered, his eyes warm.

My stomach clenched and I gulped down my bite.

"Is that Eddie?" Indy asked. "Tell him hello."

"Indy says hello," I said to Eddie.

Eddie's head came down.

"Good-bye," he muttered against my mouth.

I turned my head to escape his mouth.

"Eddie says hello too," I told Indy, feeling like an idiot, but keeping her on the line as if my life depended on it.

Eddie's mouth detoured to my neck, and tingles spread from my neck south.

Indy laughed. "I heard what he said. I'll let you go. See you tonight."

"No!" I cried desperately, but she disconnected.

I took the phone away from my ear and flipped it shut. One of Eddie's arms wrapped around me and he pulled me tight to him. I felt his tongue touch below my ear and the tingles intensified.

My phone rang again.

His head lifted and just before I could flip it open and embark on a very, very long conversation with whoever called me, he pulled it out of my hand, looked at it and then opened it with his thumb and put it at his ear.

"Yeah?" he said then he waited. "She's fine. Call back later." Then he flipped it shut without even saying good-bye.

I glared at him as he slid the phone onto the counter.

"Who was that?" I asked and both his arms came around me.

"Ally, checkin' in."

"I would have liked to talk to her," I said to him, my voice filled with attitude. An attitude I never knew I had before.

"I know, *chiquita*, you're so scared of me, you'd talk to Ted Bundy if you thought he'd keep you out of my bed."

"That's not true!" I lied.

It was *so* true. Ted Bundy was gross, but he'd be interesting to talk to and I was in a serious Eek Moment at the thought of being back in Eddie's bed, especially with Eddie in it.

"It's true and it's not gonna happen. I finally got almost an entire day where you don't have to run around like a crazy woman, chargin' through grocery stores or beggin' bank tellers to stay open for you. And you don't have to work. You're mine all day and I have plans."

Dear Lord.

Eddie had plans.

I felt my doo-da quiver.

"Eddie, I have to call my Mom," I told him. "Then I have to go get some flowers for *your* Mom. Then I have to make something, I don't know, cookies, or a pie, so we don't go to Blanca's empty-handed. My Mom would just die if we went to your Mom's without some sort of baked good. Then I have to..."

He picked up my phone and handed it to me then his arm went back around me.

"You have five minutes to call your mother," he allowed.

My mouth dropped open. "Five minutes! What? Are you going to time me?"

"Yep," he replied.

All right. So I'd programmed new friends in my phone and went ahead with this branding business without a fight. There was only so much a girl could take.

Maybe there was something between Eddie and me, and maybe I'd be stupid not to explore it. But I had bad guys to track down. First and foremost, my fucking father. I couldn't spend the day in Eddie's bed.

At least, that was what I was telling myself was my excuse. Not that I was scared shitless of being bad in bed and disappointing him. Or worse, being truly happy for the first time in my life and having it not last.

I pulled out the glare again. It wasn't working but I'd keep trying.

"You can't make me go to bed with you," I declared.

The dimple came out and one of his hands dipped down and went under my t-shirt, making a bee-line for my breast while he returned, "*Chiquita*, I won't have to make you."

He cupped my breast and my lips parted when his warm hand held its weight.

Damn.

Damn, damn, damn.

"I really don't like you," I told him.

"Call your Mom," he said, his hand leaving my breast and trailing down my side to my back.

I called Trixie and shoved the entire bottom of the muffin in my mouth. Eddie didn't let me go, but I heard him chuckle.

I continued with The Glare. It might not work, but it made me feel better.

"Hello?" Trixie answered.

"Trixie?" I said through a mouth of muffin.

"Jet? Is that you?"

I swallowed, painfully. "Yeah, how's everything?"

"Groovy tunes. Your Mom and I just got back from IHOP and we're thinking about hitting Target. You need anything?"

I tried to think of a list of things I needed. Not one thing came to mind.

"No," I replied, dejected.

"You home?" Trixie asked.

I looked at Eddie. He was watching my mouth move.

"I'm with Eddie."

"Good. Have a *great* day. We'll see you at five thirty."

"Right," I said. "Can I talk to Mom?" But she'd already disconnected.

Damn!

Everyone was conspiring against me.

I flipped the phone shut. It rang again immediately but Eddie plucked it out of my hand.

"Stop doing that," I snapped.

He tossed it in my purse and then turned me so my back was to the door and started walking forward, forcing me to walk back.

"They'll leave a message," he said. One of his hands was still up my shirt, his other hand went low and up the shirt as well. They met, then separated, one going up my back, the other one cupping my behind. The whole time, he walked me backwards.

His mouth came to mine and he brushed his lips there, and then they trailed down my neck. We cleared the kitchen door and he was moving toward the bedroom.

I thought wildly of how to delay.

"I've decided what I want to say," I announced, even though I hadn't, but if he stopped, I'd wing it.

"Later," he murmured against my neck, his hand on my bottom coming up and then dipping in my undies to cup me skin to skin.

It felt good.

Jet, focus, I told myself.

"It's important," I said out loud.

He pushed me into the hall, his mouth coming to mine.

"*This* is important, that'll wait until later," he said against my mouth and kissed me, his tongue sliding into my mouth.

Next thing I knew, my nipples were tingling, my doo-da was quivering, I was kissing him back and my legs hit the bed.

The minute they did, he stopped, his hands swept away the t-shirt and he tossed it aside.

"Eddie…" I was half in a daze, half in denial.

He pushed me back a bit and looked down at me

"I haven't even seen you properly, *cariño,*" he muttered. He took a long look and then his hands went to the middle of my back and gently pushed up, arching it. He was murmuring in Spanish, and I was thinking my last thoughts of escape before his head bent and his mouth found my nipple.

"Yes," I whispered, my mouth not controlled by my brain.

His mouth moved on me and I lost all thoughts of escape. Instead, I pulled his t-shirt free of his jeans and slid my hands under it, taking a moment to explore the muscles and skin on his back as his mouth moved to my other breast.

Then I was done with exploring his back, and even though it dislodged his head, I pulled the tee up. Eddie came up with it, and I yanked it free. His mouth came down on mine, but it was me who kissed him and that was, well... *that*.

It all went totally out-of-control, mouths, hands and tongues, everywhere. Eventually I managed to undo three of the buttons on his jeans, then gave up with impatience and slid my hand down his crotch outside the jeans. Feeling him rock hard, I decided I wasn't happy with the jeans in my way so I went inside the jeans and wrapped my hand around him.

He was going commando.

Um... *yum*.

He growled into my mouth, his hand went around my wrist and pulled it away. I made a sound of protest that was lost when he pushed me back. I fell onto the bed and started to come up, but instead, watched him flip off his shoes and pull down his jeans. I had the barest second to catch a glimpse of him, and, in that second, feel a hint of panic at his size. Then he reached forward and tore my panties down my legs, tossing them aside.

I was so stunned and turned on, all thoughts of his size flew out of my head.

He put a knee to the bed, spread my legs and moved over me, his warm body settling on me, pressing against me, *everywhere*.

"Please tell me you're on the pill," he muttered in my ear.

I suffered terrible cramps and hemorrhaging during my periods. I'd been on the pill since I was seventeen to control it.

Of course, I didn't tell him this.

"I'm on the pill," I said.

Immediately, he slid inside me.

His mouth had moved and was against mine, and the minute he moved inside me, mine opened in a silent groan. He was big, he filled me deep and it felt beautiful.

He moved, not slow, not gentle, not leading into anything and not messing around.

It was fast, it was hard and it was rough.

I wrapped my legs around his hips, my arms under his pits, hands holding onto his shoulders. I just managed to whisper the word "harder" into his ear before it overwhelmed me and I came.

Not quiet, not delicate, but a full-on, neck arching, limbs tensing, "ohmigod-ohmigod" moaning orgasm.

⌦⌫

"Now you can tell me what you have to say," Eddie said.

It was well after, heart rates and breathing had slowed, and we were on our sides, front-to-front. Eddie had hooked my knee around his hip and tucked my face in his throat.

Normally, I would have been in a freak out, both at being naked next to a naked Eddie after just having sex *and* him calling me on my earlier lie. But I'd come too hard. His solid body felt too good, he smelled great and I was just too tired of worrying about it all.

"I forget," I lied.

He was stroking a hand along my spine and he stopped, lifted his head and, in my ear, he whispered, "*Mi pequeña mentirosa.*"

My head came up and nearly hit his. I pulled out The Glare, which was getting a lot of use that day, and snapped, "I'm not a liar."

He grinned at me, eyes warm and satisfied, and looking at them made my belly feel funnier than ever, but in a good way.

"Yes you are," he returned, cupping the back of my head and pressing it into his throat again. "You have no idea what you want to say."

"Do too," I grumbled against his throat.

"Then say it."

Damn.

Damn, damn, damn.

"Well…" I drew the word out long until I felt his body shake, and I had the feeling he was laughing.

My head came back up.

"Are you laughing?"

He wasn't only laughing; he was smiling, white teeth, dark skin, dimple and all.

"*Chiquita*, you're adorable."

"I'm *not* adorable," I snapped.

He shook his head and rolled over, taking me with him so I was on top. I pulled up with my forearms on either side of him.

"You are," he said when I was looking down on him. "You're the only woman I know who can come that hard and start arguing five minutes later."

"I didn't come 'that hard'," I lied.

His face changed, the satisfaction deepened and I held my breath.

"You did. I watched."

Wonderful.

"Okay. You want to know what I have to say?" I asked, deciding I'd *much* rather be on this subject than on the subject of how hard I climaxed.

His brows went up. "You remember?"

My eyes narrowed. "Don't be a jerk."

He rolled again, this time, me on my back, Eddie up on his forearm, half his body on mine.

"Okay, *chiquita*, I'm listening."

And he was.

Shit *and* damn.

I looked at the ceiling. "Fine, then. You and me. We're not going to work."

He didn't say anything so I looked at him.

He was watching me, his eyes hard to read. I just stared at him.

Then he spoke. "That's it?"

I nodded. "That's it."

"Let me get this straight." He didn't move, just watched me. "You're lyin' naked in my bed and you're breaking up with me?"

I didn't know there was something to break, but I nodded anyway.

"Why?" he asked.

I was afraid he'd ask that. Mainly because I didn't have an answer. At least not one that I'd share with him, or even one I fully understood myself anymore.

In the end, I did the only thing I could think to do. I grasped at straws.

"I know you have a thing for Indy."

Um...

Uh-oh.

I should have left it where it was.

His face wasn't hard to read anymore, at all. His eyes were glittery and his jaw was clenched. He said some stuff in Spanish then reverted to English.

"You're a piece of work. You'll say anything to protect yourself, even when you don't know what you're protectin' yourself from."

"So, you're saying you don't have a thing for Indy?"

There was another jaw clench, but he spoke through it, and through his teeth too. "No, I'm not sayin' that. What I'm sayin' is what I felt for Indy disappeared the minute you dropped those fuckin' cups."

My mouth fell open and I stared.

He went on, "It was obvious to everyone who watched our idiot dance. The only one it wasn't obvious to was *you*."

I didn't have anything to say to that because he was right. It *wasn't* obvious to me. In fact, it was news to me, news I didn't know how to cope with.

"Christ!" He tore his hand through his hair and then fell to his back. "I even know you're worth it and I'm wondering if you're worth it," he muttered and it was his turn to address the ceiling.

I lay there a moment and then, mindlessly, I got up and grabbed the t-shirt I slept in. I didn't know where to go from there. I pulled it over my head and just got my arms through when I was tagged around the waist and pulled back into bed.

"What are you doin'?" he asked, again looming over me with me on my back.

"Getting up."

"Why?"

I blinked. "You're angry at me. I thought I'd go."

His eyes narrowed. "Is this your new tactic, piss me off and I'll let you go?"

It wasn't, but it was a good tactic. I wished I'd thought of it. It was kind of the essence of the Bitch Strategy, but that was more to make him think I wasn't worth the effort. Now that he thought he knew I was and he knew I couldn't hold on to the Bitch Strategy for more than an hour and a half, I was looking for new ways to go.

He watched my face move with my thoughts and then he rolled over me. His hands went in the shirt and swept it off faster than it took me to put it on. He arched up and tossed it, far, far away from the bed. Definitely not in arms reach.

Then he came back to me, opened my legs and pulled them around his back.

Dear Lord.

"Eddie," I said.

"I thought I wanted to hear what you had to say, but I prefer you bein' secretive. Your friends and family will tell me all I need to know, and it'll be the truth."

"Eddie," I tried again.

"*Chiquita*, you come complete with bad guys after you with guns and knives, an asshole father that takes you for a ride and puts you in harm's way, a Mom you have to take care of a lot less than you think you do and a sense of self-preservation that's nearly impenetrable."

"Eddie," I tried to interrupt him but he was on a roll.

"You also have the prettiest smile I've ever seen and you're the sweetest piece of ass I've ever had. I don't know if that balances out, but right now, I don't give a shit. *You* aren't goin' *anywhere*."

"*Eddie!*" I yelled.

"*What?*" he yelled back.

"Okay! I'll stay. We'll see how it works out."

The minute the words left my mouth, my eyes grew huge.

What was I thinking? Had I lost my mind?

No.

No, no, no.

I had to find a way to go back.

He watched my face again and shook his head.

"Un-unh, *cariño*, no retreat. You're mine."

Then, he kissed me, his tongue slid inside my mouth at the same time he slid inside of me.

He started moving. His mouth went to my ear, and into his I said, "I can't do this, Eddie. I have things to do. I have to find another job... I have to—"

"Jet. Quiet," he said, moving inside me. "We'll figure it out."

My arms went around him and my hips started moving with his.

"You don't understand," I whispered.

"We'll figure it out," he repeated.

"I can't ask you to—" I started to say but his hand went between our bodies. His fingers pressed against me and my mouth stayed open, but no sounds came out as electricity shot through me.

His mouth came to mine, and against it he said, "We'll figure it out."

Chapter 14

Blanca's Party

"Isn't *this* exciting?"

Ada was sitting between Eddie and me in the truck and we were on the way to Blanca's. Mom and Trixie were following. It was easier for Mom to get in and out of Trixie's car and her wheelchair was already safe in the trunk. Ada wanted to ride in the "fancy truck", and no one had the heart to refuse her. It took us three goes to shove her bony behind into the cab, but we got her in and we all headed out.

So, there we were, a mini-convoy on the way to my doom.

I'd spent most of the day in Eddie's bed. Eddie spent most of the day in me.

Around three o'clock, I caught sight of the clock and panicked.

I pulled Eddie out of bed and nagged at him to shower.

Then I paced and texted Daisy as a response to her second phone message (the one left after the call Eddie didn't let me answer), setting a meeting with her the next day while he showered and dressed. He wore what I considered (in my limited experience) an Eddie dress-up outfit; black, light-weight, v-neck sweater over a white t-shirt, jeans that were seriously faded (the only kind I think he owned) and his signature black cowboy boots and silver-buckled belt.

Then I dragged him to Fresh & Wild so I could buy flowers for Blanca. I even wore my Smithie's uniform, ignoring all the stares as I tramped through a swank Cherry Creek grocery store in my slut outfit.

Then we went to my house. I took a shower and began my herculean preparations. At the same time I made peanut butter cookies and smushed a big, old square of Hershey's chocolate in them after they came out, hot and puffy, from the oven. I ran back and forth between the bathroom and the kitchen like a woman on fire.

Eddie hung out through all this activity, alternately watching a football game and watching me.

At one point he strolled into the kitchen and grabbed one of the cookies when I wasn't paying attention and ate it in one bite, then immediately reached for another one.

I smacked his hand. "Those are for your mother."

His arm wrapped around my waist and he pulled me to him. "Trixie was wrong. Chocolate sheet cake bought you protection. Make these for me and I'll put a ring on your finger."

Dear Lord.

Trixie and Mom came home, thankfully both already done up in new outfits they reported they'd picked up that day at TJ Maxx, hair and makeup at the ready.

I wasted precious time trying on seven hundred and fifty outfits for them while my ear was to the cell phone, describing every outfit to Ally for her opinion.

We settled on the green dress Trixie bought me for my birthday the year before. It had cap sleeves, a square neckline, a square cut at the back exposing my shoulder blades and the skirt came to a respectable brush-the-knee hem. Problem was, it was skintight. That was a con. The pro was, it went with Tod's sexy green sandals. I had nothing else suitable, and Mom, Trixie and Ally all approved so I went with it.

Trixie did my hair while I did my makeup, saving time multitasking. I put some big, gold hoops at my ears, some clackety, thick, carved-wood bracelets on my wrists, spritzed with my swish perfume and tore out of the bedroom.

We had five minutes to get to Blanca's.

"Let's motor," I ordered and shoved the cookies at Trixie, the flowers at Mom and herded everyone out, standing at the front door and motioning everyone through with a wide sweep of my arm.

Eddie stopped at the door and called into the hall where Mom and Trixie were knocking on Ada's door. "We'll be out in a minute."

He closed the door and pushed me against it.

"Eddie!" I protested. "We have to go. We're going to be late."

He didn't respond, he pressed his body into mine and he kissed me.

Not a light touch on the mouth but a full-on make-out session.

I was stuck in an Eddie Daze when he disengaged from my lips, but rested his forehead against mine and ran his hands down my sides.

"I like your dress," he said.

I was getting that.

His fingers trailed the zip at my side.

"I like it, but I'm gonna like takin' it off more."

Eek!

∗∗∗

Eddie idled at the curb outside Blanca's bungalow in the Highlands area while we all unloaded.

The street was packed with cars and you could hear a party in full swing.

Mom took my arm and Trixie took off to look for a parking spot, Eddie trailing her.

I watched them go and then asked Mom, "Don't you want your chair?"

She shook her head.

"Nancy, is that wise?" Ada queried softly, looking at Mom closely and carrying both the cookies and the flowers.

"I'm going to walk in there," Mom declared.

It wasn't that she was in the mood to show off and challenge herself again. This was a pride thing. But she'd already had a long day and this concerned me.

I knew better than to argue, and luckily Mom had me to hold on to before she fell. And hold on to me she did. She had my arm in a death grip.

We walked slowly to the house and I saw Rosa, Eddie's sister, coming around the side.

"*Hola!*" she called, smiling. "Thought I heard Eddie's truck. We're around the back, this way."

She led us to the back and into a yard that was one of the most magical things I'd ever seen. Late summer blooms were still in the garden, bushes held bunches of Christmas lights, colorful lanterns were strung up high and lit lumieres were down low.

It looked like every chair and card table in the neighborhood had been set up, most of them full of food, and there were more people there than in the parking lot doing tailgates at Mile High Stadium before a Broncos game. I saw Indy, Lee, Ally, Hank, their parents and Indy's Dad hanging around. I gave them a wave.

Soft, Mexican guitar music played in the background.

I realized immediately that I should have made more cookies.

I was impressed that Blanca could pull this off in less than forty-eight hours.

I was terrified that all of this was for Eddie and me.

I couldn't have asked for a better wedding reception.

"Jet!" Blanca disengaged from a bunch of people and rushed forward. The bunch of people she was with turned and stared at me openly.

I smelled Eddie before I felt his hand at the small of my back, and Trixie came around the other side of Ada. I didn't have the chance to greet them as Blanca was there.

"How are you?" she asked, her eyes smiling with the sheer delight of a mother intent on ending her days spoiling her grandchildren into unruly brats, and seeing that time looming brightly just ahead of her.

"*Bien. Y tú?*" I replied.

She grabbed my cheeks, pulled me down to her and gave me a big kiss on the lips.

"*Bien, mi hija,*" she said softly, letting my face go.

Uh-oh.

In less than a week, and with Eddie and I only having one (weird) date, I'd graduated to her *hija*. That meant daughter.

Eek.

I pushed down the panic and made the introductions. "Blanca, I'd like you to meet my Mom, Nancy, and our friends, Trixie and Ada."

Mom's fingernails were digging into my arm, but she let go, balanced and held her hand out to Blanca. Blanca took it into both of hers.

"Welcome to my home," Blanca said.

Mom smiled her majorette smile and I saw Blanca's eyes become dazzled.

Then Mom grabbed onto my arm again, and we nearly both went to the ground as I staggered slightly with the weight she transferred to me. Blanca's eyes moved to Mom's hand on my arm and then to me. They were questioning. I shook my head in the barest hint of "no" and she immediately turned her attention to Trixie and Ada while I steadied Mom and myself.

"Jet made you cookies!" Ada announced and shoved the cookies at Blanca.

I turned to Eddie, leaning away from Mom as best as I could while still holding her up.

I got up on tiptoe, put my free hand on Eddie's bicep and said into his ear, "Mom needs a chair, like, now."

Our eyes caught, he nodded then he touched his lips to mine.

I could swear I heard a collective sigh from our audience.

Wonderful.

"Nancy, do you want a drink?" Eddie asked as he pried her hand loose from my arm and guided her away.

I watched them go, Mom leaning heavily into Eddie's body.

Okay, so, I could love that guy.

There you go, I admitted it.

Shit *and* damn.

~*~

I spent the next two hours shuffled between Blanca, Elena and Rosa, being introduced to Eddie's family; aunts, uncles and cousins.

And there were *a lot* of them.

In this time, Eddie semi-disappeared. He was there, but wasn't. I saw him with Lee. I saw him with Hank. I saw him with Lee's Dad, Malcolm, and Indy's Dad, Tom. I saw him with some of his male cousins (needless to say, there was definitely a male/female divide).

I did not see him anywhere near me.

I also had more food shoved at me than I'd eaten in a week, all of which I consumed so I wouldn't appear rude, and I seemed to be carrying a mystical bottomless margarita glass.

Bottom line, no matter how full I was, I was also quite drunk.

I kind of needed to be drunk because I found out the reason behind the big bash that included Christmas lights and tables groaning with food.

In Eddie's thirty-three years (yes, I learned that too), I was only the second woman he'd ever brought to meet "the family".

Worse than that eek-worthy fact, I was the only one Blanca liked.

I also found out a lot about Eddie. Maybe too much.

See, there's a reason Eddie seemed dangerous. Eddie had a checkered past. In fact, everyone, all the way down to the cousins, were still saying rosaries in grateful thanks to the Holy Trinity that Eddie chose to enter the Police Academy rather than embark on a life of crime.

Though, from the many, *many* accounts of his escapades, he would have been pretty good at a life of crime.

I was listening in a drunken stupor-esque glaze of horror to one of Eddie's aunties talking about one particular time (there were several) when Eddie stole a car, when a hand wrapped around my arm.

I turned, then looked down to see Eddie's sister, Gloria.

She said something in Spanish to the auntie and then led me away.

I looked over my shoulder.

The auntie seemed somewhat perturbed to be interrupted while scaring the bejeezus out of me, so I turned back to Gloria.

"I think that might have been rude," I said.

"You should thank me. I'm saving you," Gloria replied. "They're trying to scare you. See if you got grit. Any girl of Eddie's has to have grit. You looked ready to bolt."

She wasn't wrong. I was ready to bolt.

"You need another margarita," Gloria decided.

That was the only thing I *didn't* need.

"I'm already two sips away from blotto," I shared.

In fact, I was finding it difficult to walk straight and could no longer feel my tongue.

Gloria laughed. "You need to be two drinks into blotto to deal with *my* family."

I was thinking she wasn't wrong about that either.

She led me to Indy and Ally and I collapsed in an unoccupied chair. Gloria whisked away my margarita glass and headed toward the nearest full pitcher.

"You okay?" Indy asked. She was smiling.

Drunk or not, I didn't find anything amusing. "My life sucks."

She laughed.

"This is the new definition of trial by fire," Ally remarked, glancing around.

"You got *that* right, sister," I agreed, Gloria handed me a fresh drink and sat down with us. "I'd rather be shot at," I finished.

"The night's still young," Ally said.

I wished she wasn't speaking the truth.

A peal of female cackles tore through the crowd and I looked over to where Mom, Trixie and Ada were sitting with Ally's Mom, Kitty Sue, Blanca and some of Eddie's aunties.

"Your Mom's having a good time," Indy noted.

"You meet her?" I asked.

"Yeah, she's sweet," Indy replied.

"She's the devil," I said.

It was our turn to dissolve in peals of female cackles.

It was when I stopped giggling and was brushing a tear of hysterical hilarity from the corner of my eye when I noticed Eddie's gaze locked on me. He was standing with his brother, Carlos, and Lee and Hank, and he had a beer in his hand.

He looked hot.

"Eddie's hot," I said to no one in particular.

Everyone looked at Eddie, his lips twitched and he turned away.

"You got *that* right, sister," Ally said.

I sighed a dreamy sigh. "He's *so* out of my league. What am I doing?" I asked, again, to no one in particular.

Everyone looked at me.

"You're joking, right?" Gloria asked.

I shook my head, crossed my legs and belted back half my margarita.

"We had sex today. *A lot* of sex. It was fucking amazing, definitely worth the f-word." I realized who was in our circle and turned to Gloria. "Sorry."

"Don't mind me," she mumbled, grinning at Indy.

"I'm seriously screwed, in more ways than one." Then I giggled to myself and luckily, everyone giggled with me.

"Maybe that margarita wasn't a good idea," Gloria remarked.

My purse was lying in my lap and it started ringing. I handed my margarita to Indy and dug out my cell.

"Probably Tex, he's pissed at me that he missed the shootout," I told them.

Gloria's eyebrows rose to her hairline and I flipped open my phone.

"Hel-lo?" I sing-songed.

"Nice dress," a male voice I knew too well because the memory of it was burned in my brain, said in my ear.

I sobered immediately and my entire body stilled.

"Maybe I'll make you wear it when I do you," Vince said.

Chills raced down my spine, bile came up my throat and my voice went on vacation.

How he got my phone number, I'd never know. I didn't even want to know.

"I'll shove it up around your hips..." He paused. "Oh, now, that's sweet. Here comes your wetback boyfriend."

My head came up and I saw Eddie walking my way.

Dear Lord.

Vince could see us.

I stood on shaky legs and looked around in a panic, trying to find where Vince was hiding. The yard backed up to an alley and had houses on either side. There were people everywhere. The shakes in my legs hit my torso and I wrapped my arm around my stomach.

"Yeah. I'm watchin' you bitch. Waitin' for my moment. I don't give a fuck what protect—"

The phone was ripped away from me and Eddie was there. He put the phone to his ear and listened for a minute.

Obviously, Vince wasn't done talking.

Eddie's faced changed to an expression I'd never seen before. It was beyond what he wore last night. It was beyond anything. It was indescribable.

He flipped the phone shut and stared at the ground for a second, his jaw working.

I held my breath.

Then he turned and, with a vicious sidearm throw, he threw my phone across the yard. It slammed into the margarita pitcher with such force, the glass pitcher exploded, and so did my phone. Bits of it went through the glass and skipped across the table and most of the yard.

Everyone went silent and turned to look.

I stared in the direction of my phone.

"Eddie." That was Lee, standing close, his voice low, his eyes serious.

I realized my mouth was dry and I swallowed.

Eddie's eyes went to Lee.

"Fratelli," was all he said.

A muscle moved in Lee's cheek.

"*Mi hijo.*" Blanca was there and speaking quietly in Spanish to Eddie. He responded in Spanish and his mother's startled eyes came to me. "*Sí*," she said.

Eddie turned to me. "Your mother stays here tonight, tomorrow she moves to Tex."

It wasn't the time for discussion and certainly not the time to argue. Eddie was beyond angry. I was scared speechless. Trixie and Ada arrived, Mom leaning on Trixie, all of them looking worried.

I nodded.

"You're with me," Eddie went on.

I nodded again.

"The party's over," he finished.

Chapter 15

Whacked

Once Eddie announced the party was over, I learned how Blanca could pull off such an extravaganza so quickly.

Eddie's sisters and aunties went into action, clearing, cleaning and tidying while the interested parties moved to Blanca's living room: Me, Eddie, Mom, Trixie, Ada, Blanca and, for moral support, Indy and Ally.

Hank and Lee came with us and stayed for a bit, then, when Tom brought in my mother's chair and handed Trixie's keys to her, they all went into the hall and formed a male huddle with Malcolm, talking in quiet voices with tight faces.

Hank and Lee peeled off and disappeared. Malcolm and Tom hooked up with Kitty Sue and left.

I noticed this and didn't, mainly because I was busy trying to tell Mom about the mess I was in without giving her another stroke. I sat on my knees on the floor in front of her. She was sitting on the couch, and Eddie was standing beside me.

I told her the story of my week.

Mom's face got pale.

Then her eyes got hard.

When I was done she said, "Your *fucking* father."

Wow.

I didn't think I'd *ever* heard Mom say the f-word.

"Mom, stay calm," I urged.

"I'm calm. I'm calm enough to say when they put me away for murdering your father, they'll know it's premeditated. One-armed or not, I'm gonna kill that jackass." She looked up at Eddie. "Sorry Eddie."

He cocked his head slightly, indicating he wasn't going to cuff her just yet.

Mom's eyes turned back to me. "Why didn't you say anything?"

"I didn't—" I started but she interrupted me.

"I know what you didn't," she snapped in a mother-talking-to-idiot-daughter voice. "You didn't want me to get sick again. Jet, for goodness sake,

I'm not made of glass. You can't handle me for the rest of my life like I'm going to shatter."

"Easy for you to say," I whispered and stared at her.

She didn't see herself in the hospital bed after it had happened, her whole left side limp and slack, even her face, her voice slurred and her eyes unfocused. It was horrible.

I wasn't going to say it but I didn't have to.

Her hand went to my cheek.

"Thank you, dollface," she said quietly, and I pressed my cheek into her hand as tears filled my throat.

Then she said, "But from this point on, you're off-duty."

My eyes flew to hers but she was looking at Eddie.

"I'm moving in with Trixie," she announced.

I gasped.

Eddie spoke.

"You're stayin' with my mother tonight. Tomorrow you're movin' in with a friend who can keep you safe. I don't know what's gonna go down next and I'm not takin' any chances. When it's over, you can move in with Trixie," Eddie declared in a voice not to be trifled with.

"Okay," Mom replied immediately, deciding not to trifle.

"But—" I started, feeling the somewhat desperate need to trifle.

Eddie pulled me up by my arm and talked over me. "Trixie, you come back with us, pack a bag for Nancy, enough for a week." He turned to me. "You pack a bag too."

I opened my mouth to speak, but Eddie kept on issuing orders, looking at Trixie.

"You can bring Nancy's bag back, but I don't want you two to go anywhere unless you arrange to have someone with you. Do you understand what I'm sayin'?"

Trixie nodded, eyes wide as saucers.

Eddie kept issuing orders. "Indy, stop by to see Tex. Tell him he's gonna have company."

Indy nodded too.

Eddie started to drag me toward the door.

"Let's go," he said.

I looked at Blanca.

"I'm so sorry," I said to her, on the trot because Eddie was still dragging me.

"I'll take care of *tu mama*," she promised.

⌒◄►

We took off in our mini-convoy and went back to my apartment, Ada riding with Trixie. Before going into her apartment, Ada gave me tight hug.

"You're a good girl," she said, her eyes glistening. She nodded to Eddie, probably too scared of him at that juncture to give him a hug, and went through her door.

I told myself not to cry, and luckily my self listened.

Trixie packed for Mom and gave me another tight hug.

She looked at Eddie then looked at me. "It'll all be okay," she said.

I wished I could believe her.

Trixie took off, I packed and Eddie and I went to his place.

We didn't talk. Eddie was in a mood.

Truth be told, I was in a mood, too, but I was keeping my mood to myself.

And my mood revolved around my *fucking* father.

Where was he?

It didn't matter. I was going to find him and tell him exactly what I thought.

Something else. I was never again going to be as scared as I was that night. Never.

I didn't know how I was going to get control of my life, but I was going to do it, one way or another.

No one made my Mom say the f-word.

Eddie carried my bag into his house and dropped it on the floor in the bedroom. Then he went around the house, closing all the blinds and making sure all the doors were secure. I stood in the middle of the living room, turning in slow circles, watching him move.

His face was hard and I could tell he was barely hanging onto his control.

Once he was done closing us away from prying eyes and locking us in tight, he grabbed my hand and dragged me to the bedroom. There, he dropped my hand and turned away, pulling off his sweater.

"Eddie," I called.

He glanced at me as he sat on the side of the bed, tugging off his boots.

"I have something to tell you, and you have to promise not to get mad," I shared.

Or, more like, *more* mad.

His eyes flickered and something fluttered in my belly.

He dropped his second boot, stood and moved in close.

"What?" His voice was as tight as his face.

I took a breath. "I saw Vince last night, at Smithie's, right before I saw the guy with the gun. He made his threat then. I didn't tell you 'cause, well, the guy with the gun kinda took precedence."

Okay, so I was being semi-honest. It wasn't the time to tell Eddie that I never intended to tell Eddie. It was the time to make sure Eddie had every piece of information Eddie needed to do... whatever Eddie had to do.

"He said if he fucked with me, Marcus would give him a bonus because of you. He said you and Marcus hate each other. He said Marcus would even go to war with Lee to get at you. Whatever that means."

Eddie's jaw worked.

Then he asked, "He say anything else?"

I shook my head, but looked away and said, "Just stuff about what he was gonna do to me."

"Yeah," Eddie replied and my eyes moved back to him. "He told me that too."

It was clear that none of this did anything for Eddie's mood.

"I'm sorry about all of this. You can't..." I stopped, my eyes dropping, not knowing what to say and I took a step away, but he caught me by the waist and pulled me back.

"Jet, look at me."

I looked at him.

"He isn't gonna touch you."

He said it in a way that made me believe it.

His hand went up my side and then pulled down my zipper.

"No one touches you," he went on and pulled my skirt up my hips, bunching the dress at my waist and then up, yanking it off. "No one... but me," he concluded.

His eyes weren't warm and liquid. They were hard and glittery.

I had the feeling this was more than just about Vince. This was about any-one, anywhere. This was about me being branded in an entirely different way.

The breath in my lungs started to burn.

"Oh... kay," I said and that one word shook.

He pulled off his t-shirt and his hands came around me and unhooked my bra. He slid the straps down my arms and tossed it aside. I wanted to cover myself but I didn't figure that was a good move.

"Are you angry?" I asked.

He was looking at my body, but his eyes came to mine.

"Yeah," he answered. "I'm angry."

His hands pushed down my panties until they fell to the floor

He lifted me up by my bottom and I had no choice but to wrap my arms and legs around him. He twisted and put a knee to the bed, planting me on it and then settling on top of me.

"Maybe we should talk," I whispered.

"Now she wants to talk," he muttered into my neck, his hand between us, working the buttons at his fly.

I felt a different kind of flutter in my belly.

His mouth came to my ear, his fingers touched me between my legs and I caught my breath.

"In a minute, I'm gonna fuck you so hard, neither of us are gonna think about this, and after, we're gonna be so exhausted, we'll sleep. Tomorrow, we'll talk. Does that work for you?"

I bit my lip and nodded my head.

It *so* worked for me.

"Good," he murmured.

Then he did what he promised.

I woke. It was still dark, and I knew something wasn't right.

Eddie wasn't in bed with me and I heard voices in the other room.

I threw my legs out of bed, felt on the floor for anything to put on and my hand found Eddie's sweater. I pulled it over my head and walked to the door.

It was closed.

It hadn't been closed when we went to sleep.

I started to open it; it came ajar an inch, and then I stopped and listened when I heard Eddie talking.

"... this shit," he finished.

There was a pause.

"I can take care of this for you," another man said.

There was no answer.

"Give the word, Ed. I'll take care of Fratelli."

My breath stuck.

"Darius, you're not going to whack Vince Fratelli for my girlfriend."

Eek!

Eddie called me his girlfriend!

"No, I'll have Fratelli whacked because he's an asshole. I'll be happy to give the order. I'll be beside myself with fucking glee."

Oh... dear... Lord.

I knew what "whacked" meant. I watched TV (or I used to).

It meant "killed".

There was another pause and I could feel the negative waves pounding against the door.

"You forget, *mi hermano*," Eddie said softly, an edge of warning in his voice, "I'm a cop."

Silence and more negative waves.

Darius finally spoke. "The offer's on the table."

"That's where it's gonna stay," Eddie replied.

More silence while I imagined Darius shrugging.

"Don't tell Smithie any of this shit. He's told you he's ready to call in his marker for Jet. I don't want him to take that offer you just gave me," Eddie ordered.

You could have blown me over with a feather.

Darius was the "brother" that owed Smithie a favor.

How small *was* Denver? And if it was that small, why couldn't I find my Dad?

Then Eddie asked the same question.

"Any hint of McAlister?"

"The guy's slippery. I know he was at a table the other night; did well. Not well enough to pay off Marcus, but he paid him all the same. I'm guessin' with whatever he stole from King."

King?

Who the heck was King?

He had to be the guy who shot at me.

"What'd he get from King?" Eddie enquired.

"The cops don't know?" Darius sounded surprised.

"He's shut tight. Not sayin' anything. Asked for an attorney immediately."

"Not smart, shootin' at a cop's girlfriend," Darius remarked.

Yes, it was the guy who shot at me.

And there it was again, someone calling me Eddie's girlfriend.

Dear Lord.

"Whatever it was, it was worth twenty large. That's all I know," Darius told Eddie.

Twenty large?

Holy cow.

I'd probably shoot someone if they stole something from me that was worth twenty thousand dollars.

Well, probably not, but I'd consider it.

"Slick still in the picture?" Eddie went on.

"Slick's taken to ground. Slick's got the DPD and Nightingale Investigations all over his ass. Slick ain't showin' his face for a good, long time. Thirty K or no."

Finally, a piece of good news.

"Where does Marcus stand in this?" Eddie continued.

"He's cut Vince loose. Either that, or lose Daisy. Ain't no way he's losin' Daisy," Darius answered.

I was shocked.

What happened to war?

Not, of course, that I *wanted* war.

"Vince is renegade?" Eddie asked, sounding incredulous.

"Vince is on a mission and Vince is on his own."

I didn't take this as good news.

"That's too bad, I wanted Marcus tied to this," Eddie said.

Eddie didn't take it as good news either, but for a far scarier reason.

Darius laughed. "You'll have to nail him some other way, Ed. Word is Daisy likes Jet, and Marcus wants Daisy happy. You know how it is."

No answer and a long moment of silence.

"She worth this?" Darius asked quietly.

"Jet?" Eddie asked in return.

"Yeah," Darius replied.

I opened the door and did it as loudly as I could, then walked to the bathroom.

I didn't want to hear Eddie's answer and I didn't think I could close the door without them knowing I was listening.

It was while in the bathroom that I realized I had no underwear on.

Wonderful.

I made noise in the bathroom, banging stuff around and turning on the sink. I went back to the bedroom, my eyes avoiding the living room. I stood there wondering what to do, then I dug in my bag, grabbed a pair of jeans and yanked them on.

I walked out into the living room, pulling my hair out of my face.

I looked to Eddie, then to Darius. Both of them were standing in the living room, both of them were watching me.

"Everything okay?" I asked.

I stopped next to Eddie. His arm went around my neck and he pulled me into his side.

"We wake you?" he asked softly, looking down at me, his arm still wrapped around my neck.

I shook my head and then stopped and stared at him. He must have worked out his anger earlier, his eyes were back to warm and tender.

I slipped into a mini-daze and murmured, "Felt you gone."

His eyelids lowered a bit and his mouth relaxed.

"Go back to bed. I'll be there in a minute," he replied.

I gave a nod, put my hand to his stomach to push away but Darius broke in, "I'm outta here. Be in touch."

I looked at him. He was talking to Eddie but looking at me, his face blank but his eyes were assessing.

Eddie told me he was a drug dealer and he talked casually about ordering people's deaths. I felt something very sad about that because I had this weird feeling he was a nice guy. I had a feeling that this wasn't who he was, but who he had to be.

Darius left, doing some kind of hand gesture to Eddie and not saying a word to me.

Eddie locked up after him and he and I walked back into the bedroom. He'd put on his t-shirt and jeans to talk to Darius. He took them off in the dark.

I took off my jeans, left on the sweater and got into bed.

Eddie joined me, his hands coming under the sweater and whipping it off.

"I'm cold," I said to him.

He tucked me into him, front-to-front. "You won't be for long."

He held me awhile and he was right.

I was nearly asleep. Don't ask me how. Probably the warmth from Eddie's body and something to do with his arms wrapped around me.

Then Eddie spoke and made me jerk awake.

"How much did you hear?"

Damn.

Caught.

"I don't know," I admitted, "A lot?"

Eddie didn't say anything.

"It was wrong to listen," I said by way of apology.

"I would have listened," he told me.

I couldn't help it. I smiled against his neck.

"You're going to have to explain to me about Darius," I whispered.

Eddie didn't hesitate.

"When we were kids, we were close. He was a good guy. A little wild, less wild than Lee and me."

From what I learned that night, I thought it would be difficult to be *more* wild than Eddie.

Eddie kept talking. "His Dad was murdered and he and his family had it rough. He took a road that seemed easy at the time, quick money and a way to work out his shit. That road became harder, but he'd chosen the path, and now refuses to look back."

"That sounds very sad," I noted.

And it did.

Eddie made no comment. Being Darius's friend through it all, he knew just how sad it was.

"Why was he here in the middle of the night?" I asked.

Eddie paused, as if wondering whether it was safe to share. Then he spoke. "We work together sometimes, when it's mutually beneficial, but we keep it

221

quiet. The Department wants him taken out and they aren't too happy with our relationship. I'm Vice and not tremendously popular with the brothers."

"It's not safe," I concluded.

"No. It's not safe."

"For either of you?"

"No."

"But you're working together now?"

He didn't answer.

"For me?" I pushed.

He didn't answer.

"I think you might be a little scary," I told him.

He turned to his back and pulled me into his side. "Don't listen to my aunts. I'm not nearly as scary as they want me to be."

He was wrong.

He was terrifying.

Chapter 16
Coffeemaker

The alarm went off, Eddie touched a button and rolled out of bed.

I snuggled into the pillow.

He wrapped a hand around my wrist and pulled me out of bed.

"What are you doing?" I asked, half asleep, half pissed off and halfway across the room.

"Time to shower, then time to find bad guys," Eddie replied.

Shower?

I was still waking up when he picked me up and put me under the hot water. I looked up at him in disbelief, blinking as the water came down on me when he joined me and pulled the shower curtain around us.

"Something to learn about me," I told him. "I'm a Snooze Button Girl."

He smiled down at me, reached around and grabbed the soap.

What he didn't do was respond.

I turned my back on him, the best way to hide my naked body.

Why were men so okay with nudity? It wasn't fair.

Of course, Eddie had a great body. He certainly had nothing to hide. If I had Eddie's body, I'd probably wander around naked all the time. Not that I had a bad body. I had curves in all the right places. They were curvier a few months ago, when I had time to eat.

"I really don't like you," I said to the showerhead.

His soapy hands came around my middle, he pressed his body against my back and his mouth found my neck. "Something I *have* learned about you, you're grouchy in the morning."

"I'm not grouchy in the morning," I grouched.

His hands at my middle separated. One went to cup my breast, the other to cup between my legs.

"No, you're grouchy all the time," he said this like it was amusing.

I was only half paying attention. I was more interested in what his hands were doing. His fingers on one hand did a roll on my nipple as his other fingers pressed deep.

It felt nice.

My head fell back on his shoulder.

"I've also learned how to make you sweet," he murmured against my cheek.

I had to admit, he'd *definitely* learned that.

I turned my head and ran my tongue down his neck.

I tasted water and Eddie, and I didn't feel grouchy anymore.

⊰⊱

After our somewhat prolonged and unbelievably enjoyable shower, I brushed my teeth, pulled on some underwear and one of Eddie's clean t-shirts and wandered into the kitchen to make coffee.

I couldn't find his coffeemaker. In fact, I couldn't find much of anything.

I went back to the bathroom, knocked on a door that was already opened and entered at Eddie's call. He was standing at the sink, wearing jeans and nothing else, shaving.

"I can't find your coffeemaker," I said.

His eyes slid to me. "I don't have one."

I stared.

Everyone had a coffeemaker. This was America.

Even more, Eddie was a cop. Everyone knew cops drank lots of coffee and ate donuts.

I looked at Eddie's rock-hard abs.

Okay, so maybe Eddie didn't eat donuts.

I shook off my surprise.

"I can't find your kettle or any instant," I tried.

"I don't have a kettle or instant coffee."

I kept staring. "What do you do for coffee?"

His eyes went back to the mirror. "I go to Fortnum's."

"Well then, what do *I* do for coffee, like, right now?" I asked.

"Get ready for work?" he suggested.

I put on The Glare.

"You need a woman," I told him, trying to be uppity and throw some attitude.

It wasn't a smart thing to do.

His eyes came back to me and his expression turned my bones to water. Eek!

I left the bathroom.

I slapped on minimal makeup, put on jeans and a v-necked, scarlet-red, long-sleeved t-shirt that Mom bought me, and yes, you guessed it, it was skin-tight. I blew my hair dry and pulled it back in a ponytail holder. Because I felt in the mood, I put on a pair of kick-butt, high-heeled, tan boots and a belt so wide it strained the limits of my belt loops.

Eddie pulled on a long-sleeved, white, thermal t-shirt, his jeans, boots and belt, took his gun and cuffs from the drawer in the bedside table and clipped them to the belt on his jeans. His final touch was to grab his badge from the dresser and hook it on his belt.

I picked up my purse and we rolled out the backdoor.

We were halfway across the yard when I noticed Eddie scanning. My stomach clenched and I started scanning too, looking for heads peering over Eddie's tall fence. He unlocked the garage and then we were in the truck, waiting for the garage door to open, Eddie watching it through his rearview mirror, all the while fishing in his pocket. Then he held out a set of keys to me.

"Keys to the house," was all he said.

I took them. My stomach clenched again and he started the truck. He was about to put the truck in gear when I put my hand on his forearm. He didn't move his hand, but his eyes came to mine.

There were a lot of things to say.

"Thank you," being the biggest one on the list, but the words weren't good enough.

"I'm sorry to be a pain in the ass" was another one that was way up there.

I knew I should say something, anything, but I didn't know what to say.

"I don't know what to say," I said.

His eyebrows came up.

I took my hand from his arm and looked away.

"*Chiquita*, is this about the keys?" he asked.

"It's about everything," I told the window.

Silence.

"Hey," he called quietly and I looked at him.

His eyes were serious.

"I'm guessin' you feel you owe me big just about now."

225

I nodded.

He smiled slowly. First the dimple, then his lips curved, then his white teeth came out.

I narrowed my eyes at him, turned away, did my seatbelt and crossed my arms on my chest. "I *really* don't like you," I said.

He laughed.

"I'm not joking," I told him.

"You're so full of shit," he replied, but he said it like it was a good thing.

Wonderful.

⌐▞▞⌐

We walked into Fortnum's together. It was a few minutes before opening, but there were already two people waiting to get in. I let them in and left the door open.

Jane and Tex were behind the coffee counter. They both looked up when we arrived and Tex opened his mouth to boom, but I got there first.

"Eddie doesn't have a coffeemaker. Coffee! Now! No lip!" I snapped.

I went directly behind the counter and stared at Tex as he banged around the espresso machine, making me a strong Americano at the same time he made Eddie a cappuccino. The whole time, he was grinning.

I handed Eddie the cappuccino that Tex gave me, sloshed milk into my Americano and took a sip without stirring it.

I looked at Tex. He was still grinning.

"What's funny?" I asked.

"You, Loopy Loo." His eyes moved to Eddie. "Sorry Chavez, but she's a lot more fun when people are shootin' at her."

"You're a nut," I told him.

"That I am, darlin'," he replied, unperturbed, and turned to the first customer.

Eddie backed me into the counter behind the espresso machine.

"Gotta go," he said, his arms sliding around me, one hand still holding the cup.

My hands were between us and it was either wind them around him or spill coffee over both of us. As coffee was a life force at that moment, I wound my arms around him.

His eyes had that warm and tender look.

"After work, we'll go shoppin' for a coffeemaker," he told me.

Dear Lord.

Shopping with Eddie for a coffeemaker.

How did *this* happen?

I just stopped myself from checking to see if my hair and eyebrows had burned off, considering our relationship was progressing at the speed of light.

He watched me and then his face came closer to mine. "I hate to say this, but part of me likes that you're forced in a corner. That way you can't retreat and I can see you really want to."

It was my turn to watch him. "What happens when I'm out of that corner and I don't need you to rescue me anymore?"

It was the six million dollar question, and I held my breath waiting for the answer.

"One thing at a time," he said.

Not the right answer.

"No, I really want to know. What happens when I'm not getting shot at and I'm not interesting anymore?"

His eyes changed and he looked at me as if I'd asked him if I could spend the afternoon painting his house in shades of Pepto-Bismol and adorning the front yard with plastic flamingos.

Then he told me, "You think I'm a little scary? I think you're a little crazy."

Okay, so it was time to let it all hang out.

"I'm not crazy. I'm anything but crazy. I'm so not crazy that I'm anti-crazy. Eddie, I hate to tell you this, but I'm boring."

He waited a beat, watching me, and then burst out laughing.

My mouth fell open.

Then his head dropped and he nuzzled my neck.

"Definitely crazy," he muttered against my neck and then lifted his head and looked at me. "And totally full of shit. You couldn't be boring if you tried. And if this is your next tactic to try to get me to give up, go for it. It'll be amusing to watch *you* try to be boring. Almost as amusing as it was to watch you pretend to be normal."

Well, what could you say to that?

Except, I'm *so... very... sure.*

227

He didn't read my look of supreme unhappiness, or more likely, ignored it. Instead, he touched his lips to mine and he was gone.

Yeesh.

Even the truth didn't work.

⇥⇤

Mid-morning, Indy swung through the door.

"How're you doing?" she asked when she got to me, her eyes concerned.

"After work, Eddie and I are going shopping... for a *coffeemaker*," I answered, thinking she'd understand my plight.

She blinked. "No, I mean with the guy who's threatening to rape you."

I waved my hand and went back to steaming milk.

"Oh that. I'm over that," I said.

Her mouth dropped open.

She snapped it shut and said, "Last night, with that phone to your ear, you looked like you were going to have a coronary."

"That was last night. I was taken off-guard. Now I feel like throwin' down, kickin' butt and takin' names and... whatever," I petered out, not having any more macho-speak at the ready. "I'm done with being scared."

"Right on, Loopy Loo!" Tex encouraged, pulling a portafilter off the espresso machine with brute force, even though he didn't need to, and slamming the grounds out of it.

"What are you going to do?" Indy asked.

I looked at her. "I have no idea, but I'll think of something. The only thing I know I'm *not* going to do is nothing."

She looked at me for a beat, and then she smiled.

⇥⇤

It was close to noon when the bell went over the door and Mom and Blanca walked in.

"Great, Tex, here she is," I said to Tex. "Now you can meet my Mom."

Tex looked up and across the store.

Then his face froze. "Un-unh," he muttered.

"Hey, dollface," Mom called.

I smiled and waved at Mom and Blanca, but turned to Tex.

"What do you mean, 'un-unh'?" I whispered frantically.

Tex was still frozen.

Mom made it to the coffee counter and she gave him her majorette smile. "You must be Tex," she said.

He made a kind of guttural noise, grabbed my arm and marched me out from behind the counter. He then frog-legged me to Indy, who he also grabbed by the arm, and he shoved us down the aisle of books turning into fiction, the M-N-O section. Then he stopped and glared at me.

"You didn't tell me she was pretty," he accused.

I looked at Indy. Indy looked at me.

"Give me your phone, woman," Tex said to Indy.

She handed over her phone. He flipped it open, started to push buttons at random and it started beeping alarmingly.

Indy snatched the phone out of his hand.

"Who do you want to call?" she asked.

"Chavez. Get me Chavez."

Indy scrolled down her phone book and hit Eddie's number. Tex seized the phone from her hand and put it to her ear.

"Chavez?" Pause. "We got a problem."

He walked down the aisle and muttered something.

I looked to Indy. She was smiling. I smiled back.

"Uh-huh," he said, nodding. "Uh-huh," he said again, still nodding. There was a pause, "Fuck no!" This was an explosion and I jumped. Then, "Right." Then he threw the phone back at Indy who caught it and flipped it shut.

He looked at me. "All right, Loopy Loo. Let's go meet your mother."

We walked back to the front of the store, and I couldn't help it. I was near to laughing.

Tex thought my Mom was pretty.

Mom and Blanca were looking concerned.

"Let's try this again," I said when we approached them. "Tex, Nancy and Blanca. Nancy and Blanca, Tex."

"You like cats?" Tex boomed to my mother.

Mom jumped, stared up at Tex and nodded.

Anyone would nod, even if they hated cats.

"Then this'll work," Tex declared. "I'm goin' home at one, can you wait that long?"

"Sure?" Mom asked and answered, not certain which way to go.

Everyone stood around and looked at each other.

"Maybe you can make them a coffee?" I suggested to Tex.

Tex turned to me, blank-faced.

I felt a little sorry for him. I mean, I knew how he felt.

"What'll it be?" Indy asked. "Tex is the best barista in the Rocky Mountains. Whatever you want, it'll be fantastic."

"Latte?" Mom asked.

"Just coffee for me," Blanca said.

Tex lumbered behind the counter.

"He's a little strange, isn't he?" Mom leaned in and whispered to me.

"He'll lay down his life for you, or, more to the point, for Jet," Indy answered in a voice that said she meant it.

Mom and Blanca looked at each other.

That was enough for them.

<hr/>

Twenty minutes later, Ally and Kitty Sue walked in.

"Blanca! *Qué pasa?* How's it going, Nancy?" Kitty Sue peeled off and went to sit with them and Ally came to me.

She handed me a shiny, new, very expensive, cellular phone.

"Mom and I got you that. I already programmed everyone's numbers in it and it's charged. You should text everyone so they'll have your number," Ally said.

I looked at the phone. I looked at her. I opened my mouth to speak but she got there ahead of me.

"Think of it as a Christmas present," she said, waylaying my denial.

"It's October," I told her.

She shrugged.

"I don't know what to say," I said quietly.

"How about, 'thank you'?" Mom yelled from across the room, using The Voice.

Tex let out a guffaw of laughter then snapped his mouth shut and I could swear his cheeks got a little pink.

I looked at Ally and swallowed.

"Thank you," I whispered.

Crinkles came to the corners of Ally's eyes. "My pleasure."

I texted everyone Ally had programmed into my phone, including Indy, Ally, Tod, Stevie, Daisy and yes, even Eddie, with my new number.

Kitty Sue left, and so did Blanca. Tex loaded Mom's chair and bag in the back of the El Camino, loaded Mom in the front, and roared off with Carlos Santana's "Winning" blaring from the eight-track.

Duke showed up just before Tex left, and fifteen minutes after, the bell over the door went and Vance walked in.

I held my breath. Any girl who sees Vance holds her breath, be she five or one hundred and five.

He was just that fine.

He was wearing a pair of army green cargo pants that had seen a lot of wear, a skintight burgundy t-shirt that looked in danger of cutting off his circulation at his muscular biceps and a pair of dusty brown cowboy boots that looked like they'd actually been put into a pair of stirrups (more than once). His shiny black hair was pulled back into a ponytail, and his dark eyes were fringed with a set of lashes so lush you could almost call them girlie, if you had a death wish.

"Good! You came!" Indy cried immediately and I looked at her.

She grabbed my arm and pulled me toward Vance.

He shook his head when we arrived at him.

"Thought I'd tell you to your face, this isn't gonna happen," Vance said to Indy.

Indy narrowed her eyes.

"What isn't going to happen?" I asked.

Vance turned to me. "When we talked about you at the staff meeting, I voted to lock you in the safe room."

My mouth dropped open.

Kristen Ashley

I didn't even know what the safe room was, but I knew I didn't want anything to do with it. And I didn't want to think about being an agenda item at a Nightingale Investigations staff meeting at all.

"Pardon?" I asked.

"Eddie'd have a shit fit, you wanderin' around the office during day hours, hangin' with the guys. Lee thought you'd be a distraction. The guys voted with me." His eyes did a body scan and the look in them changed to something that made me feel like swaying toward him, like he had a powerful sexual tractor beam reeling me in.

"Sometimes, distractions are good," he said softly. "In your case, it'd be job satisfaction."

Dear Lord.

My mouth went dry.

What the hell was *this* about?

"Lee vetoed," Vance finished and the tractor beam disconnected.

Thank God.

I pulled myself together.

"You don't help us, we'll go alone," Indy threatened, completely ignoring the strange, sexually-charged byplay.

"You try to go alone, I grab her and take her to the office. Eddie can pick her up there. Lee'll deal with you," Vance returned.

Eek!

That didn't sound good. I didn't want Vance grabbing me (at least not *that* way... what was I saying, I was sleeping with Eddie, not *any* way) and I certainly didn't want Lee "dealing with" Indy. Lee was Scary with a capital S.

"What are you two talking about?" I cut in.

Indy turned to me. "You want to find your Dad. Vance is really, really good at finding people. I asked him to help."

I looked to Vance.

Vance was watching Indy talk, but when I spoke, he looked to me.

"It'd be nice if you could help," I said, not really wanting to, but also wanting to find my father enough to ask. "I'll pay you," I added. I also couldn't pay him, but maybe he'd take installments.

His body turned fully to me and the tractor beam switched on again. "I'll find your father, but you aren't gonna help and you aren't gonna pay me. Though it won't be free. You'll owe me."

232

Dear Lord.

In debt to another hot guy. I didn't know if I could hack it.

No, I *knew* I couldn't hack it.

I looked him in the eye and had to wonder what form his favor would come in.

It didn't take a mind reader to get the gist.

While he waited for my answer, his eyes went weird, as in *sexy* weird.

"Mild mannered coffee girl by day," he muttered. "But I've seen you in your Smithie's uniform."

Sweet Jesus.

That fucking Smithie's uniform.

It was like Superman's leotard. No one paid attention to Superman when he was Clark Kent. Put on the leotard and all the women were falling at his feet. Smithie's uniform had the same power.

"I'm not working at Smithie's anymore," I told him.

His eyes dropped to my scarlet-red tee. "That's a shame."

I forced myself to breathe and looked to Indy.

She was bugging her eyes out at me like we were in fifth grade and the cutest boy in school came up to me during recess.

I looked back to Vance.

"I think I'll go it alone," I said.

He stared at me a second, then said, "Can't let you do that either."

Um... what?

"What?" I asked.

"You don't know what you're dealin' with and you don't know what you're doin'," he answered.

Okay, so I was getting a little fed up with guys telling me what I could and couldn't do. Even hot guys.

"I'm not sure you have a choice," I informed him.

I was proud of myself. It came out with attitude and conviction. Enough to make his dark eyes flare. I thought he was angry for a second, then he got over it and his lips twitched.

"Chavez is fucked."

I didn't know what that meant and I didn't ask.

Vance looked at Indy. "We're goin' to Zip's."

Immediately, Indy clapped and cried, "Yippee!"

"Zip's?" I asked.

"It's a gun shop," Indy explained.

"*What?*" I kind of yelled.

Why on earth did we need a gun shop?

Vance answered my unasked question. "I'm not gonna help, but I'm not lettin' you two loose in Denver without protection. We're goin' to get you some gear." He turned to Indy. "You take your car. Jet's on the Harley with me."

Harley?

As in, Harley Davidson motorcycle?

With Vance?

No.

No, no, no and really, *no.*

"I'll go with Indy," I said.

"You aren't out of sight on my watch," Vance announced in a Tough Guy Therefore No Discussion Voice.

Wonderful.

⌐▨▷¬

I'd never ridden on the back of a motorcycle in my life, much less a Harley.

I had to admit, I liked it.

I liked it *a lot.*

I found out that Zip didn't only sell guns. Ole Zip sold a lot of different kinds of guns; handguns, shotguns, rifles. He also sold knives, ammo, stun guns, Tasers, mace, pepper spray and calendars with my sister's picture on the front. I pointed this out to Indy while Vance wasn't paying attention.

"Nice," she drawled, looking at Lottie wearing a barely there bikini, her body completely wet, her hair surprisingly dry and balancing precariously on a BMW motorcycle.

Vance outfitted us with stun guns, Tasers and pepper spray. He explained how to use them, he gave instruction on how to be safe and he tried to pay.

I argued.

He gave me a Tough Guy Look.

I pulled out The Glare.

While all this was going on, Indy paid.

That was okay with me. I could owe Indy. I didn't expect her favor had anything to do with my Smithie's uniform.

We were on our way back to Fortnum's, our bag of goodies in Indy's Beetle, Indy following us. We didn't have a lot of time before we had to meet Daisy at the Oxford Hotel for a drink and I was getting fidgety. I didn't want to keep Daisy waiting. She could be scary.

We were stopped at a light on Colfax and I was pressed against Vance, my crotch to his ass, my chest to his back, my chin kind of resting on his shoulder. He drove fast and hard. I tried holding onto his waist and keeping a distance but I nearly went ass over head off the back of the bike when he shot from the curb.

It was a wrap-your-arms-around-and-hold-on-for-dear-life kind of ride.

A car rolled to a stop at the light and I automatically looked to my right.

My eyes widened at what I saw and I think I screamed a little inside my helmet. Sitting in the driver's seat was Eddie. He was looking out the window, his mirrored shades directed at me, the rest of his face wearing a murderous expression.

I had on a helmet, but I was also wearing a distinctive scarlet-red t-shirt, my hair was coming out the back of the helmet because I had to take out my ponytail holder, I was with Vance and Indy's car was right behind us. It wouldn't take a police detective to figure out it was me, but Eddie *was* a police detective and from the expression on Eddie's face, he'd figured it out.

Damn.

Damn, damn, damn.

There was a toot on the horn behind us, Vance looked in his mirror and I looked behind. Indy was gesturing to her side and to Eddie. I looked at the car pulled up next to her.

Eddie was being trailed by a Crossfire; Lee's Crossfire, with Lee behind the wheel.

Fuck.

Fuck, fuck, fuck.

Vance looked right. Not wearing a helmet, he made a hand gesture salute to Eddie, two fingers straight out and a flick of the wrist. Mr. Cool.

We all drove together to Fortnum's, Vance and I leading the new definition of My Convoy of Doom. The entire time I tried to come up with a plausible explanation; in other words, a believable lie.

Vance pulled in up front. Indy and Lee parked in the back. Eddie parked behind us. I was off the bike and had the helmet off when Eddie arrived.

"What the fuck?" Eddie asked, looking at Vance and using his scary quiet voice.

Vance had come off the bike and was smiling, flat out. I didn't think this was good. I thought it was kind of in your face. Even though it was not helping the situation, I had to say, I admired Vance for having the balls to pull it off.

I decided to neutralize the situation.

"Eddie, I can explain," I said.

His eyes turned to me. He had his arms crossed on his chest, his legs planted wide and I wished I'd let him take his anger out on Vance. Vance was a badass too. At least it would be a fair fight.

"Yeah?" Eddie asked, his voice dripping with disbelief.

Okay, I'd used the ride home to try to come up with a believable lie. The problem was I didn't succeed.

"Well…" I started, drawing out the word to buy time.

All of a sudden, Eddie grabbed my arm, yanked the helmet out of my hand, tossed it to Vance and pulled me away about five feet.

Guess he didn't feel like giving me time to come up with a believable lie.

When we stopped, he opened his mouth to speak, but I got there first.

"I can see you're angry, I don't know why but—"

He interrupted me.

"You don't know why?" he asked.

"No, you see—" I began again.

"No?" he interrupted again, still using his scary quiet voice.

"Well no, what I was going to say was—"

"I'm drivin' down the road and, stopped at a light, I see the woman who's sharin' my house, *my bed*, wrapped around another guy. You're that woman and you don't know why I'm angry?"

It didn't sound good when he said it that way.

"Eddie—"

He got close, his eyes were glittery and his voice was still scary soft.

"Don't fucking 'Eddie' me. Seems I gotta spell everything out for you, so listen good, *chiquita*. Last night, when I said no one touches you but me, that means *you* don't touch *anyone but me* either."

I put a hand to my hip.

I mean really, did he think I was stepping out on him?

"It wasn't what you obviously think. Vance was just taking us to Zip's!" I informed him.

Uh-oh.

I immediately saw my mistake. I should have told him we were out to lunch, visiting the dog pound to play with sheltered puppies, buying crack, anything but going to Zip's.

"What were you doing at Zip's?" Somehow, the low, scary voice got lower and scarier.

I decided not to lie, not because I thought it was a good way to go. More like I couldn't come up with another story quick enough.

"Vance was outfitting us with gear."

"What kind of gear?" Eddie asked.

I decided to be vague. "A few bits and pieces."

"What kind of bits and pieces?" I shouldn't have tried vague. I'd already learned that Eddie wasn't fond of vague.

"Stun guns, Tasers, pepper spray," I said.

"Why?"

I took a deep breath and, since I was being honest, I went whole hog. "I'm going to look for Dad."

His eyes narrowed, his mouth tightened and my stomach lurched, but I tried not to let on that he was kind of flipping me out.

"Show me," he said.

I stared at him. I thought of ignoring his request, but decided against it. He'd push it and I'd end up doing it anyway.

Indy had the stun guns and Tasers in her car. The only thing I had was the pepper spray in my purse. I opened my bag and barely got it out when Eddie's hand came out and smacked against mine, sending the pepper spray skittering down the sidewalk.

"Hey!" I snapped, my head coming up and I pulled out a genuine glare.

"What do you do now?" he asked and came in close.

I was getting mad. He was making me look like a fool. I knew he was doing it to make a point, but still.

No, wait. Doing a quick emotional scan I realized I was already mad.

"Well?" he bit out, leaning in.

Kristen Ashley

I wrapped the strap of my bag over my shoulder and planted *both* my hands on my hips, a Double Diva Threat.

"That wasn't fair. You're Eddie. I wasn't ready——"

"You aren't gonna be ready when this shit goes down either."

I leaned into him too. "I've been doing all right so far."

"You've been lucky so far."

All right, enough.

I threw my hands out, getting nose-to-nose, and I yelled in his face.

"Yeah? Well, finally! For the first fucking time in my fucking life I've been lucky and I'm gonna ride that wave. What I'm not gonna do is fucking sit in a house with the fucking blinds pulled and the fucking doors locked and wait for other people to solve my fucking problems, the whole time scared out of my fucking mind!"

Yeesh.

That was a lot of f-words but the moment warranted it.

"You need to be smart," he said, not moving out of the space I invaded.

"I need to get control of my life and I'm going to get it and I don't care how. You might not like it, but that's the way it is."

"You put yourself out there, I can't keep you safe."

I stared.

Then, I swear I couldn't help it, I laughed. And something else I couldn't help. Since I was so close to Eddie, I leaned into him, and when I did I wrapped my arms around his middle and put my forehead to his chest. It was either that or fall over with the hilarity of it all.

"This shit isn't fuckin' funny," Eddie said to the top of my head. His hands were on his hips, he wasn't touching me and he wasn't happy.

I looked up at him, my arms still wrapped around him, my body pressed against his.

"Eddie, don't you get it?" I asked softly, still smiling. "I've never felt safe in my whole life. Never. Until now."

Something flickered in his eyes but he didn't move.

I pressed closer and tilted my head back further. "Three months ago, if this happened to me, I'd have sat in a house with the blinds closed, the doors locked and been scared out of my mind."

He hesitated a moment then I felt his body relax and his hand came up to my jaw, the pad of his thumb against my cheekbone.

238

"You're so full of shit, *chiquita*," he said quietly, but the scary had gone out of the quiet. He was looking in my eyes, the glitter in his melting and I knew I'd won.

Finally, I'd won an argument with Eddie.

I felt like dancing around. Instead I gave him a squeeze.

"Am not," I said.

"You would have been as hell-bent to risk your neck and solve your Dad's problems. You just wouldn't have had some crazy Rock Chick to get you in trouble while she's tryin' to watch your back."

"Indy's not a crazy Rock Chick."

"And Indy isn't the only one watchin' your back."

I smiled at him. I knew what he meant, because that warm feeling was in my belly again, but, I decided, and for the life of me I didn't know why, to tease him and maybe, just a little bit, flirt.

So I cocked my head and said, "I know. Ally's watching it too."

Wow. Flirting worked.

His eyes went liquid. My belly fluttered, his other arm went around me and his thumb came under my chin and tilted my head back even further.

"Ally *is* a crazy Rock Chick," he said.

I couldn't help it. I let out a little giggle.

He watched me for a beat then his face got serious. "I don't like what you're doin', I don't agree with it and if I can, I'll stop it."

Wonderful.

I didn't like that he didn't like it, but I nodded anyway.

We were at an impasse and we both knew it.

"This your way of tryin' to prove to me you're boring?" Eddie asked. "If it is, I should warn you, it really isn't workin'."

I shook my head then tried again to use the truth and said, "Eddie, trust me, I *am* boring."

The dimple came out. "You're crazy."

"I'm not."

"What are you doin' now?"

"Indy and I are meeting Daisy at the Cruise Room for a drink."

His eyes flared. "You *are* crazy."

"I'm *not*."

We stared at each other again. I was preparing for another battle, but to my surprise, he gave in again.

"For Christ's sake, *chiquita*, be careful," he said.

I snuggled deeper into his body. I didn't have a choice since his arm went super-tight around me, and I said, "Okay."

Chapter 17

Daisy, Indy and Me—The Unholy Trinity

We met Daisy in the ultra-cool, art deco Cruise Room of the Oxford Hotel.

Daisy was already sitting in a booth, waiting for us. She was decked out in second-skin denim and rhinestones, the two-buttoned jacket exposing acres of cleavage. The purply-pink neon that had been giving cool-ass atmosphere to the Cruise Room for nearly one hundred years was shining in platinum-blonde hair that was so teased and sprayed I figured environmental watch groups had campaigns dedicated to stopping her single-handed destruction of the ozone layer.

We ordered dirty martinis and settled in.

Daisy turned cornflower-blue eyes to me. "All right, Sugar, tell Auntie Daisy all about it."

I didn't hesitate. She knew some of it anyway after my Smithie's meltdown, so I told her the story of my life, reciting it for the millionth time that week. Any hopes I held of quietly going it alone were long since gone.

Halfway through my story, she took my hand and didn't let go.

When I was done, she squeezed my hand.

For some reason, she asked, "Jet, darlin', you seen *Steel Magnolias?*"

I nodded.

"That's my favorite movie of all time," she told me.

This wasn't a surprise.

She leaned into me. "You and me, Sugar, we're Steel Magnolias." Then she let go of my hand, and without further ado, she launched into her story.

It was a whole hell of a lot more sad and scary than mine.

Halfway through her story I grabbed her hand and didn't let go. When I did, tears filled the bottoms of her eyes, but she didn't let them fall.

This wasn't a surprise either. If her story was anything to go by, Daisy hadn't been touched by kindness a whole lot in her life, either physically or emotionally. In fact, Marcus and Smithie were the only two men she'd known that treated her right.

When she was done, I squeezed her hand.

"Now I'm with Marcus, and don't get me wrong, I'm mostly happy," she told me. "But a girl has to have girlfriends, comprende?" Indy and I both nodded, we comprende'ed. "And, I'm here to tell you, the snooty society bitches of Denver just *do not* get me. I don't have a single friend in the whole world who isn't laughing behind my back or scared to death of Marcus."

I looked at Indy.

"I think it's time for another martini," Indy said and gestured to a waiter.

Daisy went on after we'd received our second round.

"I ain't ashamed to say, I haven't had as much fun as I had with you and your friends at Smithie's in *ages*. That is, of course, before you got shot at," she said to me.

"Of course," I replied.

We all let this sink in while we took a sip of the second round.

"Do you think I have to worry about Vince?" I asked.

She winced. "Vince is a mean, dirty motherfucker, if you'll excuse my French. I wouldn't have thought he'd go against Marcus, but the jackass is entirely unable to take a blow to his manhood, in this case, literally."

Then she gave a little tinkly-bell giggle.

I wasn't certain I thought it was funny.

She caught the look on my face and the laughter went out of hers. "I'll ask Marcus to keep an eye out for him."

Um, I didn't think that was a good idea. I wasn't sure Eddie wanted Marcus to be a member of my Protection Posse.

"Daisy—"

She shook her purple-tinged head, wagged a finger at me and I was quiet. I wasn't quiet because I didn't have an argument. I was mesmerized by her fingernail, which was super-long, filed in a lethal curve and had little fake diamonds imbedded into it in the shape a four-leaf clover.

She dropped her finger and we all took another sip of the second round.

Then Daisy said, "What're you gonna do about your Daddy?"

I took a deep breath and shared, "I've been thinking. He's playing poker, right?" Indy and Daisy nodded, "So, I've decided. I need to get into a game and ask some questions. Maybe someone knows where he is."

Daisy stared at me like I'd just announced my intention to invade Nicaragua.

"You play poker?" she asked.

"No."

"Those games are serious, girl," she told me. "First off, they don't know you and probably won't let you in. Second, they ain't fond of women sittin' a table. Third, you don't sit a table unless you know what you're doin'."

I'd figured that.

"I have a plan," I said, and I did. It was kind of a stupid plan, but it was all I had.

"We're all ears," Indy urged when I didn't go on.

"Well. I thought I'd wear a modified Smithie's uniform. The uniform has a weird power over men, so if I wore something like that maybe they'd let me in. Then, before I did it, I'd read a book about poker and then..." I hesitated, "I guess then I'd just wing it."

Daisy laughed her tinkly bell laugh again.

"Ain't you sweet?" she said when she was done laughing.

Um, guess my plan wasn't going to work.

Then her eyes got serious. "I play poker. I'll sit a game, no one'll say boo to me. You and Indy come with and I'll ask the questions. Those boys know me and they'll talk, thinkin' I'm askin' for Marcus. We'll find out where your Daddy is and we'll sort this all out."

I wasn't sure that was a good idea. "Maybe I should try to do this myself, you and Indy——"

Daisy shook her head, and with what I was noticing was her customary brutal honesty, she said, "I can't have babies, Sugar. Marcus and me been tryin' for two years. But I got a motherin' instinct, believe you me, and this Mama Bear ain't lettin' her new cub get eaten by the big, bad lions, comprende?"

I wasn't sure all that went together but I wasn't going to say anything.

"It'll be fun," she stated in a swift change of mood, though being eaten by big, bad lions didn't sound fun. "We'll get dressed up, make a night of it. You two got somethin' spangly to wear?" Her purply blonde head swung from Indy to me.

I shook my head, thinking this may be our way out, but Indy said, "You remember Tod?" Daisy nodded. "Well, he's a drag queen and generous with his wardrobe."

Wonderful.

These two had an answer for everything.

Daisy sucked back half of her martini. My throat burned in sympathy.

When she was done, she decided, "Perfect. We'll do it tonight."

I choked on my martini.

Tonight?

"I think I have a problem with that," I told her.

Indy and Daisy turned to me.

"Eddie isn't thrilled about me going after Dad, and I'm kind of living with him," I shared. "We're going shopping for coffeemakers tonight, and then I don't know what we're doing. I'm not sure I'll be able to get away."

"Oowee, coffeemakers. Sounds like this Eddie is serious," Daisy said.

I gave her a look and she giggled.

Indy sat back. "This is where I come in. I used to get grounded all the time. I might be a little rusty, but I was the queen of the escape plan. Leave it to me."

Daisy's laugh tinkled again. "This is soundin' better by the minute."

Not to me.

To me it was sounding scarier by the minute, but I had no choice. If I didn't want to get raped (eventually), shot at anymore and owe a posse of new friends for saving my life and my somewhat-tainted virtue, I had to kick in.

So we lifted the dregs of our second martini and toasted our plan; Daisy with a giggle, Indy with a grin and me with a belly clutch.

⌦⌫

It was an hour later and we were slowly nursing our fourth martini (because two was enough, four was just plain crazy) when Daisy's eyes locked on something over my shoulder and she sucked in breath.

"Oh sweet Lord, if I didn't have Marcus, I'd get me some of *that*."

I looked over my shoulder and saw Eddie scanning the room. His eyes hit me and he started coming our way.

My belly curled in a happy way.

I ignored my belly, turned back and told Daisy, "That's Eddie."

Daisy's eyes dropped to the badge Eddie wore on his belt.

"Eddie, as in Eddie Chavez?" she asked, her eyes getting wide.

I nodded.

"Seein' as my baby's in the business he's in, I don't normally like cops, but this time, I'm makin' an exception," she declared.

I felt a hand curve around the back of my neck and I tilted my head to look up. Eddie bent low and his mouth touched mine. My happy belly curl went into overdrive, then he straightened and took in Indy and Daisy.

"Ladies," he greeted.

I introduced Daisy. She put her hand in his and said, straight out, "Sugar Bunch, you are *fine*."

Eddie smiled, but didn't say anything. Then again, what *could* you say?

His eyes turned to me. "We've got an errand to run," he reminded me, like I'd forget.

I got up and waved to the girls.

"I'll call you later," Indy said, giving me a look.

I nodded to Indy as Eddie steered me out of the room. It took a lot of steering. I had a serious buzz on.

When I wandered into him, Eddie looked down at me and his hand at my back slid around my side and he pulled me to him but kept walking.

"You drunk?" he asked, sounding amused.

"Maybe just a little bit," I admitted. "I think I should have stopped at the third martini."

We'd cleared the bar and were standing by Eddie's truck, parked at the curb. He pushed me into it with a hand at my belly and got close.

"So, you're saying you *didn't* stop at the third martini?"

I shook my head.

"And you're maybe just a *little bit* drunk?" he went on.

I nodded my head.

He got in closer.

"Boring, my ass," he muttered.

This time, I cocked my head and pulled out The Glare. Maybe it was the third martini, maybe it was the second sip into the fourth, but I went all attitude.

"Mark my words, Eddie Chavez, and don't say I didn't warn you. When this is all over you'll wonder what the hell you're doing with me. I'm boring, boring, boring... b-o-r-i-n-g." I was pretty pleased, considering I was seriously tipsy, that I could spell boring.

His head dipped low and came close to mine. "How bad do you need coffee in the morning?" he asked.

I blinked, not keeping up with the conversation.

"Why?"

"I'm thinkin', in your condition, I might try and see how boring you are naked."

Eek.

"I need coffee really bad in the morning," I told him.

He grinned. "Right."

We got in the truck and Eddie pulled out.

"What was with the look?" Eddie asked when we were headed out of Downtown.

"What look?" I tried innocence. Of course, Eddie would have noticed Indy's look.

"Indy's look," he answered.

See what I mean?

"There wasn't a look," I lied.

"You are so full of shit," he muttered.

This time, he wasn't wrong.

We went to Best Buy on Colorado Boulevard and Eddie directed us toward the coffeemakers. I stood in the aisle, swaying a little bit, not only because of the martinis but also because I was in Best Buy with a hot guy shopping for coffeemakers. I stared at the plethora of machines on display as if one was going to grow teeth and bite me.

"What do you want?" Eddie asked.

"A coffeemaker," I replied.

"Yeah," he grinned at me, "but which one?"

I stared at them, did a quick price check and pointed at the cheapest one.

Eddie shook his head, the grin still in place. He walked past the one I pointed to and grabbed an upper mid-range, programmable, 14-cup KitchenAid. It wasn't the mother of all coffeemakers, but it wasn't anything to turn your nose up at either. He tucked it under one arm, took my hand and pulled me down the aisle.

"Anything else you need to make you less grouchy in the morning? A blender? A toaster?" he asked.

I came to a dead halt and stared at him.

"You don't have a toaster?" I asked, horrified.

He changed directions and headed to the toasters.

We swung by my apartment and grabbed some provisions (most especially coffee) and then went to Eddie's house.

He unloaded the new appliances while I unpacked the groceries. Then I called Famous and ordered a large pizza, one half with everything for Eddie, the other half triple cheese and mushroom for me. Eddie heard me order while plugging in the coffeemaker and his brows went up.

"It's all about the cheese," I explained.

His eyes drifted down my body and his lips twitched as he flipped open the instruction book to the coffeemaker. I wasn't certain what that meant, but I was certain I wasn't going to ask.

I left him to deal with things with cords. I went into the living room, sat on the sofa and phoned Mom.

"Hey Mom," I said when she answered.

"Hey dollface," she replied.

"How are you getting on?" I asked.

Eddie wandered in, sat down and turned on the TV. The remote went into hyperdrive as he flipped through channels.

"Tex and me are drinking hooch," Mom answered.

I was leaning back, but I shot bolt upright when I heard her answer.

"You can't drink hooch on your meds!" I yelled.

Eddie's eyes came to me.

"Just a little drinkie poo," Mom said.

"Stop drinking," I ordered.

Her voice came to me, ignoring my order, and she was whispering, "I think Tex kinda likes me." Then she giggled.

Dear Lord.

"Tex is a nut," I told her.

"He's sweet."

Tex?

Sweet?

"You think Tex is sweet? How much hooch have you had?" I asked.

"Oh! Gotta go, Tex found his laser lights and we're gonna play with the kitties. Love you." Then she disconnected.

I flipped the phone shut and stared at it.

"I think Tex and Mom are on the weirdest date in the history of the world."

Eddie put down the remote, took the phone out of my hand, and slid it onto the coffee table next to the remote. He then put his hands under my pits and dragged me across the couch, twisting me so I was pulled over his lap. He pushed me back and slid out from under me, to his side and came up on his elbow. He rolled me to my side, back to his front, and at the same time he leaned forward, pressing into me. He grabbed the remote; his eyes went back to the TV, and with his arm still around me he started flipping through channels again.

It was a complicated maneuver, but he pulled it off effortlessly and completely ignored my comment.

I twisted my head around to look at him. "Eddie, did you hear me? I think something's happening between Mom and Tex."

Eddie's eyes didn't move from the TV. "Good. Gettin' some would improve Tex's disposition, and I figure it's been a while for your Mom too."

Eek!

"You *did not* just say that," I said.

Eddie found a baseball game and tossed the remote onto the table. He looked down at me. "She's a woman, she's pretty. He's a man, he's gonna notice."

"He's not a man. He's a crazy person. He's got a shotgun, and I think he has grenades."

"From what I hear, tear gas too." Eddie's eyes went back to the TV.

That was it.

I pushed away and got up. "That's it, we're going over... *oof!*"

Eddie tagged me around the middle, pulled me back on the sofa and rolled over me.

"You got enough to worry about, *chiquita*. You don't have to make shit up."

My eyes widened. "I'm not making shit up!"

His eyes got warm, his eyelids lowered, his hands started roaming and I had other things to worry about. His mouth started roaming with his hands and I stopped worrying altogether.

"This works out, Tex'll be your stepdad," Eddie said against my neck, his hand going under my shirt.

I thought about that. It actually wasn't a bad thought. Tex was a nut, but he was a good guy.

"He'd be a good stepdad," I said into Eddie's ear and I slid my hands in his shirt.

Eddie looked down at me.

"Shit works out in weird ways." He touched his lips to mine, then he lifted his head and said, "Two months ago, I couldn't get you to look at me. Now you're livin' with me."

"Temporarily," I said.

"Whatever. Just as long as I get to make you sweet on a routine basis, I don't give a fuck."

My breath caught.

The doorbell rang.

"Pizza time!" I said a little loudly, considering his face was less than an inch away.

Eddie's eyes lit; he smiled and then he kissed me, the smile still on his face (I could feel it), making the pizza guy wait. Then he angled up and left me panting on the couch, and thinking that just as long as Eddie kissed me like that on a routine basis I didn't want anything to do with temporarily.

✄

We both took off our boots and settled in for the night.

We ate the pizza. Eddie drank a couple of beers, and, as I'd already had over my alcohol quota for the day (and had to be prepared for whatever the evening would bring), I drank Diet Coke. We watched a game for a while, me up against Eddie's side with my bare feet tucked under me on the couch. Eddie's feet were on the table.

It felt good. It felt nice. It felt so good and so nice that I could get used to it. I knew I shouldn't, but I decided just to go with it... for now.

It was when Eddie was clearing away the pizza box that my mobile rang.

It was Indy.

"Don't talk, just listen," she ordered.

Oh no. Here we go.

"Okay," I replied.

"At around ten, Ally's gonna come to the door. Eddie'll answer. You be in the bedroom. Leave a note for Eddie and crawl out the bedroom window. You don't need anything, just your purse and you. We've got everything else covered."

Dear Lord. This did *not* sound like a good escape plan.

In fact, it sounded like a terrible, amateur escape plan that Eddie would totally figure out.

I heard Eddie walk back in the room.

I looked at the time on the DVD player. It was just after nine.

"Do you understand?" Indy asked.

"Yep," I answered.

"Ten o'clock, bedroom window. See you then."

"Sure," I said.

She disconnected. I flipped the phone shut and put it on the coffee table.

"Everything okay?" Eddie asked.

"Yeah," I lied, trying not to hyperventilate.

"You sure?" Eddie was standing by the couch.

I looked up and gave him a bright, false smile.

"Sure I'm sure," I lied again.

He took one look at my face, his brows drew together and I was pretty certain he was going to tell me I was full of shit again.

I needed a reason to be in the bedroom in less than an hour.

I'd always been a good girl. I'd never been grounded. I'd never had a reason to be sneaky. I wasn't out of practice. I'd never been *in* practice.

I stood up and did the best I could.

"I'm going to bed," I announced.

Eddie looked toward the bedroom, then back to me, and his eyes narrowed under his drawn brows.

"'Night," I said and walked right by him into the bedroom.

I yanked my pajamas out of my bag. They had a stretchy, peach eyelet camisole and lightweight cotton drawstring pants. They were cute. I bought them for myself for Christmas last year, but hardly ever wore them. I figured they were thin enough that I could put my clothes back on over them in a flash.

I was focusing on my pajamas and practicing deep breathing when Eddie walked in.

I headed to the bathroom.

"You don't have to come to bed, you can finish watching the game," I told him, making to walk by him, but he grabbed my pajamas and threw them so they landed on my bag.

I stopped and watched them fall.

"I was going to put those on," I pointed out.

His arms slid around me. His face was closed and he was watching me.

I held my breath.

Finally, he said, "Bed sounds good."

Damn.

He walked me backwards, his hands coming under my t-shirt, and then up and then it was gone.

Hmm, this didn't seem to be going to plan. If I couldn't pull off the first part of it, how was I going to manage the last?

I threw a shot out in the dark, "Eddie, I'm tired. Exhausted. Long nights, you know?"

He pulled his tee off and threw it in the direction of mine.

I sucked in breath.

He had a great chest, what could I say?

"Don't worry, *chiquita*, I'll do all the work."

Eek!

He undid the belt at my jeans and shoved me back so I fell on the bed. It was gentle, but it was also macho, and I felt my heart begin to pound as my doo-da quivered.

His hands went to his belt. I heard the clink as it came undone and he began to work on the buttons of his jeans. I rolled and started to crawl across the bed.

"I've changed my mind, I think I want to see the end of the game," I lied, beginning to panic.

"Hang on there, *chiquita*," he said. He caught my calves and pulled me back, whipping me over. Then, before I could protest, he was on me, his mouth on mine. Ally, Indy, Daisy and our plans for the evening flew right out of my head.

He unzipped my jeans, still kissing me and his hand went inside, between my legs. I pressed against him and slid my hands into his jeans at the back, hold-

251

ing on to his world-class behind. He had *the best* behind, or at least the best I'd ever had.

His fingers pushed in deeper. I bucked against his hand, breathing heavy against his mouth, and all of a sudden his finger slid inside me.

The oxygen started burning in my lungs.

"Dear Lord," I breathed, my lips against his.

"You wanna tell me what's goin' on tonight?" he asked.

My eyes were closed. At his question, they flew open and I looked in his. They were liquid but they were determined and I knew he'd totally figured me out.

Shit and damn.

I told the truth. "No."

His finger moved. It felt nice.

I bit my lip.

"I need to cuff you to the bed?" he asked.

"No," I whispered, though he probably did.

His finger moved out and then back in. That felt so nice it was off the scales nice.

"You and Indy plannin' on doing something stupid?"

I pressed my face into his neck and touched my tongue there, partially to buy time, but mainly because I wanted to.

I stuck with honesty. I was too turned on to try anything else.

"Maybe," I said.

His finger went away but only to go and do a swirl somewhere better.

"Am I gonna be able to talk you out of it?" he asked.

One of my hands went from his ass to his crotch. He was hard. I took this as a promising sign.

"Probably not."

The promise didn't pan out, he pulled his hips and his hand from me and he started to move away.

Um, no.

No, no and definitely no.

I rolled with him, pushed him back at his shoulders and got on top, straddling him. He knifed up and nearly dislodged me, but I held on tight. He was sitting on the edge of the bed and I was sitting astride his lap. I looked down at him and I could tell he was pissed.

I felt my heart squeeze.

I knew I had to do something about his anger. Not only because I needed Eddie to finish what he started, but also because I *really* didn't like the idea that he was pissed at me.

I didn't know what to do so I decided just to ask.

"I have to do this and I want you to understand," I whispered. "Please, don't be mad at me."

Then I went for broke, put my hands on either side of his face, bent my head and kissed him. I think it was the first time I'd full-on kissed him, without it being in the heat of passion (well, okay, there was heat), but more simply just to kiss him.

The kiss was a good idea

After a beat his arms came around me. One hand went into my jeans at my bottom, the other one undid my bra. He slid it off my shoulders, pressed into the middle of my back, broke from my kiss and took my nipple in his mouth.

It felt so good my back arched and my fingers slid into his hair.

He cupped my other breast and tilted his head back to look up at me. "How much time do we have?"

His eyes weren't pissed off anymore and I smiled at him. Because I was happy, because he was a good guy and because I was going to get some.

"Ally's knocking on the door at ten, then I'm supposed to climb out the window."

He shook his head at our stupidity, flipped me onto my back, pulled my jeans down my legs and tossed them aside.

I felt like jumping for joy, but that would require me getting up and there was no way in hell I was going to do *that*.

"When I'm done with you, you can call Indy and tell her to come to the front door with Ally."

To show my appreciation, I ran my tongue up his jaw and at his ear I said, "Thanks Eddie."

"I'm sure you can find more creative ways to show your gratitude."

Dear Lord.

I pushed off with my foot and rolled him on to his back. My hair fell around us when I lifted my head.

"I can do that," I told him, and I was pretty certain I could, or at the very least, I could try.

I started to work my way down his chest.

"You better be here in the morning," he murmured when my mouth was at his abs.

I ran my tongue along the waistband of his jeans and he ran a hand through my hair.

"I'll make the coffee," I promised.

"I don't give a shit about coffee. I'm thinkin' about the shower."

Chapter 18

Poker and Stun Guns

We got ready at Ally's, and upon arrival I found that Indy recruited Tod and Stevie for the dress-up portion of the evening.

I walked in the front door, and without saying a word of greeting Tod looked me up and down and said, "I've got *just* the thing."

Then he rifled through a bunch of dresses, tossing aside shoes and whisking away feather boas. He threw what appeared to be a swatch of navy blue material at me. I caught it and shook out the dress. It was tiny, stretchy, had spaghetti straps and was stitched with a bazillion little blue plastic disks.

"Shoes!" Tod shouted, snapping his fingers at Stevie who gave Tod a glare that had to be in contention for The Glare of All Time, such was its magnificence. Still throwing The Glare, Stevie came forward with matching slingbacks that had a pencil-thin heel, a scary pointed toe and a row of the same blue plastic disks that were on the dress were stitched across the toe.

"Tod found the shoes first, then he made the dress," Stevie informed me.

"I can't wear this dress," I whispered to Stevie. "It's been made for a small child."

"It's stretchy," Stevie whispered back.

"It's gonna have to be," I told him.

It was. It covered everything it was supposed to cover (barely) and even came down to mid-thigh if I pulled it hard enough.

Tod did my makeup on a level one half notch down from full-on drag and Daisy did my hair in the only way she knew how. When I looked at myself, I had four times as much hair as I normally had. I didn't look like me. I looked like eye candy in an 80's rock video.

"How did you do that to my hair?" I asked Daisy.

"Magic, Sugar," she answered.

Ally and Indy were in the same get-ups. Indy was in green Lycra with a slashed neckline that gave more than a hint of cleavage (*much* more). Ally was wearing her own red knit dress with a turtle neck but no sleeves, a teardrop cut out at her cleavage, and it was so short she wouldn't be able to bend over for fear of an inadvertent moon.

"My babies! I'm so proud. You look like the Burgundy-ettes," Tod cooed, throwing his arms out to encompass us all and then hugging us in turn. His drag name was Burgundy Rose and he looked in danger of proposing a road show.

"We better get going," Indy said quickly before Tod could produce a Tina Turner CD and make us practice doing backup for "Proud Mary".

Stevie stood at the door.

"All right girls." He handed out bags as we trooped through. "I've checked. Stun guns and Tasers are charged, pepper sprays are readily available. Knock 'em dead."

Dear Lord.

I took my bag, gave Stevie a kiss on the cheek and we rolled out to the Mustang. We almost couldn't fit all of our hair into the car, but luckily we were wearing fewer clothes so it balanced out.

"Jet?" Indy called, turning in the front passenger seat to look at me when Ally started to follow the directions Daisy gave her.

"Yeah?" I answered.

"What'd you mean about the Smithie's uniform having a weird power over men?" she asked.

I shrugged then I realized my hair hid my shoulders.

"You heard Vance," I said by way of explanation.

She kept turned and I could feel her stare in the dark.

"At Blanca's party you said Eddie was out of your league. What's that all about?" Ally asked from the driver's seat.

Daisy was sitting next to me and I heard the fabric of her dress (ice blue, skintight, ultra-miniskirt with a v-neck that showed most of her ample cleavage) slide against her seat when she looked at me.

"You think that, Sugar?" she queried.

"Well," I said, feeling uncomfortable. "Yeah."

Daisy burst out laughing.

I looked in the direction of her hair.

"He's a cutie pie, that's for *certain*," she noted. "But make no mistake, you two look great together. Phenomenal. He's all tall, dark and handsome and you're all blonde, sweet and pretty. The perfect match. Comprende?"

I looked out the window.

"It's just 'cause you all like me," I mumbled.

I wasn't saying it to fish for compliments. In fact, I didn't want to be on the subject at all.

Daisy's hand took mine in a tight grip. "Sugar, it's true. I like you, but ain't no way I'd lead a girlfriend of mine into a world of hurt if she got herself caught up with some dickhead with his head up his ass."

Boy, Daisy didn't mince words.

"You're gorgeous," Indy threw in.

"Please, let's not talk about this," I begged.

Indy ignored me. "Eddie thinks you are."

"Eddie wants to rescue me," I explained.

Daisy emitted a tinkly laugh before she said, "Eddie wants a lot more than that. No man buys a coffeemaker with a woman he wants to rescue. No way, no how. He buys a coffeemaker with a woman he wants to fuck. A lot. And for a good long time, and I don't mean the fuckin', I just mean time. Comprende?"

Dear Lord.

How could I *not* "comprende"?

"Vance thinks you're hot," Indy put in.

"Vance has seen me in my Smithie's uniform," I reminded her.

"Hank hasn't seen you in your Smithie's uniform and he thinks you're hot," Ally told me.

My mouth dropped open and I saw Indy's hair turned to Ally.

"He tell you that?" Indy asked.

"Heard him talking to Lee," Ally answered.

"Holy cow," I said, in a state of, like, *total* shock. "Really?"

"Yeah, um, I don't get it. Do you *not* look in the mirror?" Ally enquired.

"That's what my sister says," I told her.

"Sugar, I hope you don't mind me sayin'. Your Daddy left you 'cause your Daddy's a jackass, not because you ain't all that, 'cause I'm here to tell you, you are. Smithie won't have a girl work for him who isn't all that, and that's the God's honest truth," Daisy declared.

This was true. Every girl who worked at Smithie's was hot. It was a job requirement.

"I thought Smithie felt sorry for me because of Mom."

Daisy let go of my hand and made a snorting noise with her nose. "Smithie'd give you fifty dollars and tell you to take a hike. He wouldn't put you in heels and a skimpy outfit and have you traipse around his bar. The point is, *all* his girls gotta give the guys hard-ons and make 'em want to hang around longer, order drinks and enjoy the show. He ain't gonna make no money if he's got some plain-ass bitch draggin' around."

I saw Indy's hair nod.

So, all this was making sense to me, but it still made me uncomfortable.

"Okay. Can we stop talking about how hot I am and giving guys hard-ons?" I asked.

"Sure, Sugar," Daisy gave in as if it was all the same to her. "Let's talk about your Eddie and his hard-ons. Do tell, does the promise of what I saw in those jeans hold true? Please tell me it does. It would be *so* disappointing if he stuffed a sock down there or somethin'."

I laughed. If Eddie used a sock his crotch would enter the room before he did.

"He doesn't use a sock and he's so *not* disappointing it's kind of scary," I shared.

"How scary?" Ally asked.

"Mind-bogglingly scary," I answered.

"I've always wanted to know if Eddie was even close to the promise of Eddie, 'cause the promise of Eddie is seriously shit-hot." Ally noted.

I thought about Eddie. I thought about Mom leaning against Eddie. I thought about Eddie getting so angry on my behalf he'd punch out Bachelor Number One and throw a phone into a margarita pitcher. I thought about Eddie's hands and mouth on me. I thought about Eddie moving inside me. I thought about Eddie in the shower. I thought about being tucked up against Eddie on the couch.

I sighed, deep and huge.

Indy turned back in her seat. "I think that's enough said."

"You got *that* right, sister," Ally agreed.

＊＊＊

We arrived at the poker table, which was somewhere I didn't know and somewhere I never wanted to go again. I just knew it was in the back of a seriously not trendy bar and up some barely lit stairs that didn't smell good. Daisy knocked on a closed door and when the big guy opened it, he didn't look happy to see her. Then he hid it and was all smiles.

"Daisy!" he greeted.

"Got a game goin', Butch?" she asked.

"Sure, Daisy," Butch replied.

"Room for me?" she went on.

"Always room for you, Daisy." Then his eyes came to Indy, Ally and I and I wondered why he ended everything he said with "Daisy".

"Those are just my girls," Daisy explained. "They're not gonna play, just watch."

He shuffled his feet. "I'm not sure about that, Daisy," he said.

"Where I go, my girls go." She pushed in and I had to admire her even though she scared the shit out of me.

He was twice her size, which put him much taller than all of us. I didn't know about pushing into a room where I wasn't wanted, but Daisy was in and we had no choice but to follow.

We all traipsed in (at this point the Daisy-ettes) and sweet, Tinkly-Bell Laugh Daisy was all gone. This was Serious Kick-Butt Daisy.

"Boys," she murmured, scanning the table.

The men at the table stared at her.

Then they stared at us.

They weren't happy.

It wasn't exactly Brad Pitt teaching wannabe megastars how to play poker in *Ocean's Eleven*. It was dirty, smoky, smelled of sweat, and I didn't like the idea of my Dad hanging out in such places, night after night. The thought of it was just plain sad.

They finished their game, found a chair and Daisy sat, Butch giving her chips when she gave him a roll of cash. My eyes bugged out when I saw the roll of cash, but she turned to me and I saw her hair move in a "no" and I just stopped myself from giving out a little scream.

Indy, Ally and I stood quiet several feet away from the table. No one talked. It was all about the cards. Daisy folded her first hand. She got beat on a bluff her second. She won huge on her third.

While they were dealing the fourth, she spoke to the man at her side.

"Where's Ray tonight?" she asked, calm as you please, like Dad was a frequent guest at dinner parties.

"Don't know," he mumbled, not looking at her.

"Marcus is lookin' for him," she said and the guy shrunk into himself.

"Thought he'd taken care of his thing with Marcus," another guy remarked.

"This is a new thing," Daisy replied.

"Ray's a dumb fuck," a different man said.

Now, I might have been mad at my Dad, but I didn't like hearing someone call him a dumb fuck. I tensed, visualizing my stun gun in my hand, and Daisy, in mother bear mode, slid her eyes to me and her hair did another negative shake.

Daisy turned to Dumb Fuck Guy. "You know where he is tonight?"

"If he was smart, he'd be in Argentina. Since he's not, he's sittin' a table somewhere." His eyes met Daisy's. "And no, I don't know where."

Daisy folded the next hand and lost huge (and I think on purpose) on the next. Then she got up, motioned to us and cashed out with Butch. We left the room and none of us said good-bye. They didn't mind us being impolite.

We bellied up to the bar down below, ordered drinks and stood there trying to ignore the stares we were getting.

"Can I just say, you are *the shit*," Ally said to Daisy.

Indy and I nodded.

Tinkly-Bell Laugh Daisy was back.

"Thanks, Sugar," she giggled.

"Did you lose that last hand on purpose?" I asked.

She nodded. "Not good form to go out a big winner, not if I don't want to make trouble for my Marcus."

I had to admit, it was true. She was the shit. She knew everything.

"We still don't know where Jet's Dad is," Indy pointed out.

Okay, maybe not everything.

Daisy knocked back her vodka rocks. "We ain't done yet, neither."

Off we trooped to the Mustang and Daisy gave Ally more directions. We hit a bar on Colfax, deep on Colfax, in a zone I'd never been to before.

We walked in and I noticed it had a reverse mix race majority, some white faces, predominately black. Regardless of the fact that we weren't the only white people there, we *were* the only white people there wearing skintight Lycra and enough hair spray to supply the Denver Broncos Cheerleaders for an entire season. This caused somewhat of a sensation and I felt that sensation lifting the hairs on the back of my neck.

Daisy charged through the bar like she owned the joint. She went down a back hall and rapped on a closed door.

An enormous black woman with an afro even bigger than Daisy's hair (needless to say, it was *huge*), opened the door, her face like a storm cloud. I sucked in breath and pulled my purse closer, the better to reach my pepper spray. Then the cloud cleared and the woman's face broke into a bright smile.

"Daisy-girl!" she cried and came into the hall with us, closing the door and enveloping little Daisy in a big hug.

"Shirleen. How's tricks?" Daisy asked when Shirleen let her go.

"Shit. They're always shit. You know that," Shirleen replied, the smile never leaving her face, which I thought was strange considering "tricks" were shit.

"Let me introduce my girls," Daisy said and performed the introductions.

"Oowee! Looks like you all are paintin' the town pink to-nite!" Shirleen declared and looked us all over with approving tawny brown eyes. I had the feeling Shirleen had Ada's rose-tinted glasses on, or she was prematurely blinding.

"Only way a town should be," Ally said.

"You got *that* right, sister," Shirleen noted and we all grinned.

Daisy got down to business. "We're lookin' for Ray McAlister. He in there?"

"Ray? Haven't seen Ray in a coupla days. He got trouble, you know what I mean?" Shirleen replied.

Daisy's hair nodded, so did mine, Ally's and Indy's. We knew what she meant.

"This is his little girl," Daisy pointed at me.

"Shee-it!" Shirleen squealed and her eyes turned to me, wide, bright and happy. "Been wantin' to meet you. Everyone's talkin' 'bout you. Heard you kneed Fratelli in the balls at a bagel place. Wish I'da been there. You coulda sold tickets to that."

"It was kind of a spur of the moment thing. He called my boyfriend a wetback," I explained.

Damn.

Now *I* was calling Eddie my boyfriend.

Shirleen's grin faded and her eyes narrowed.

"Fuckin' dick," she said. "Fratelli's not a big fan of the brothers either." She turned to Daisy. "Marcus, now, he's a good man, respects the brothers. 'Bout time he cut Fratelli loose."

Daisy's hair nodded again.

"You see Ray, you call me, would you do that Shirleen?" Daisy asked.

"You got it." She put her hand on the doorknob. "Gotta get back. Go to the bar, tell 'em Shirleen said to set you up."

"You're a peach," Daisy replied.

Shirleen disappeared behind the door. We went to the bar and told the bartender Shirleen set us up. He didn't quibble and used a heavy hand.

"What now?" Ally asked, sipping her Designated Driver Diet Coke.

"I know of another table, but ain't no way they'd let me sit it and ain't no way I'd try. Marcus would have a conniption," Daisy answered.

This was not good news. This meant the night was a bust.

No Dad, no control of my life, no end to my nightmare.

All dressed up and nothing to show for it.

Damn.

I glanced across the room and then froze solid when I saw Darius.

He saw me at the same time and did an eye-sweep taking in Indy and Ally. Then, without hesitation, his hand went to the back pocket of his jeans and he pulled out his cell.

"Shit!" I hissed, turning to the bar.

"What?" Indy asked.

"Darius is here. He saw us. He's calling Eddie." I looked at her. "Or Lee."

Indy looked across the room, obviously saw Darius and then turned around.

"Shit!" she hissed.

"I'm gonna go say hi," Ally announced.

Indy grabbed her. "Don't say hi! We're in Darius Domain. He doesn't want some white woman in red knit with her ass hanging out walking up to him to say hi."

"He's Darius," Ally returned as if that explained everything.

Something to know about Ally, apparently, she wasn't scared of anything.

Daisy was looking across the bar, bold as brass, staring right at Darius.

"You girls know him?" she asked.

We nodded.

She turned to us, Serious Kick-Butt Daisy firmly in place. "You don't know him right now."

Ally stared at her.

"Gotcha," Indy said, pulling Ally back to the bar.

Luckily, that was that.

We sucked down vodka, mine and Indy's cut with cranberry juice, Daisy's cut with ice.

So much for the big, dangerous night out with the girls.

"Yo, bitch!"

We all turned to see who the bitch was.

To my surprise, the bitch appeared to be Indy.

A small, round black woman with ringlets invaded Indy's space.

"Remember me?"

Indy blinked at her.

"Um…" Indy mumbled.

The woman looked at me.

"She don't remember me," she said.

I stared.

Guess I was wrong about the big, dangerous night out with the girls.

She turned back to Indy. "Few months ago, you stun-gunned me."

Daisy, Ally and I looked at Indy. Indy's face registered recognition.

"Uh-oh," Ally mumbled.

"Uh-oh is right, bee-atch," the woman said, not taking her eyes off Indy.

The negative power force enveloping us ratcheted up a notch.

"Who you callin' a bee-atch?" Ally asked, hand going to hip.

Okay, so we'd reached ground zero in a serious Holy Shit Situation.

The woman moved into Ally's space. "I'm calling you a bee-atch, bee-atch."

I was thinking that wasn't the right answer.

"Why don't I get you a drink?" I put in, trying to defuse the Holy Shit Situation.

"Don't want a drink," she answered, not looking at me. "Ain't no one disrespectin' *me*. You hear what I'm sayin'?" Her ringlets were bouncing around while she was shaking her head and I didn't take this as a good sign.

"I'm not the one who charged over here, getting into people's faces. *That's* disrespect. *You* hear what *I'm* sayin'?" Ally flashed back, hair bobbing around her head and somehow the Holy Shit Situation escalated.

"Ladies," I tried to cut in just as the woman's fist came forward in a jab.

I ducked. She missed me and hit Daisy right in the eye.

I rose up and stared.

Daisy staggered back a step on her rhinestone encrusted, ice blue, platform go-aheads.

Then she steadied herself.

"Uh-oh," Indy, Ally and I said in unison.

Then Daisy pounced.

It was fair to say at that juncture that mayhem ensued.

Ally jumped on the pile of arms and legs on the floor, which consisted of a rolling Daisy and the black lady. The black lady's friend came up and shoved Indy and they got in a tussle. Other people either watched or thought it might be fun to join in and started shoving and punching each other. I stood in the middle of it all, opened my purse, pulled out my stun gun and switched it on. It started crackling and hissing which I figured meant it was ready to roll.

I wasn't wrong.

I leaned over and touched it to black lady number one. She let out a squeak and went slack. Then I touched it to black lady number two, with the same result, except she was standing and she hit the ground like a dead weight.

I looked at the stun gun then looked at Indy.

"Rock 'n' roll!" Indy shouted, putting her arms up, forefinger and pinkie extended in the famous rock 'n' roll double devil's horns.

I switched off the gun, shoved it in my bag and then I helped up Daisy and Ally. I grabbed Indy's arm, turned tail, and ran, dragging Indy along with me.

I chanced a glance backward at the growing brawl to see Ally wave at Darius.

He was grinning.

We got in the Mustang and Ally burned rubber.

We were a couple of miles away when Indy said, "I think I tore Tod's dress. He's gonna have a shit fit."

"That ain't nothin', Sugar, I think I might get a black eye, and worse, I broke a nail," Daisy replied.

There was a beat of silence.

"That was righteous," Ally said quietly.

"You got *that* right, sister," Indy agreed.

***

We dropped Daisy first then Ally took me to Eddie's.

We idled at the curb, me in the front seat, all of us looking at Eddie's house. The lights were on.

"Damn, shit, fuck," I whispered.

It was definitely a multi-curse word moment.

The outside light went on, the front door opened then the security door opened. Eddie stood inside the opened door wearing jeans and a plaid flannel shirt, feet bare, shirt unbuttoned, chest and abs partially exposed, hair a sexy mess, face unreadable.

"Holy crap," Indy breathed from the backseat.

"Fuck, shit, damn," I whispered.

I was wrong. *This* was a multi-curse word moment.

"I don't know whether to feel sorry for you or to stun gun you and take your place," Ally remarked.

"I think he's going to cuff me to bed the next time," I said.

"Lee tried that with me. It doesn't work," Indy offered.

Um… eek!

"I think you best mosey on up there, pa'dner. He doesn't look like he's gonna wait much longer and I'm not sure you want to know what he'll do when he's done waiting," Ally suggested.

I got out of the front seat and Indy got out of the back and our hair was forced to get out with us.

I hugged Indy.

"Thanks," I said into her ear.

"It was a blast," she said into mine.

I leaned over, my dress rode up. I pulled it down just before disaster struck and waved at Ally. She blew me a kiss.

Then I walked up to Eddie.

He stood aside and let me enter.

"Hey," I said as I walked by, surprising myself by sounding cool instead of freaked out.

His eyes did a full body scan. Then, slowly, he shook his head.

Okay, I was done with being cool.

I made a beeline for the bathroom, leaving him to lock the door.

I washed my face and tore a brush through my hair. With effort it went from Freaky Diva to Charlie's Angels.

The house was dark when I opened the bathroom door, a dim light coming from the bedroom.

Eddie was in bed, on his side, covers up to his waist, chest bare, head in his hand, eyes on me, face still unreadable.

Eek!

I turned off the light, slid off my shoes, tore off the dress and pulled on the camisole that was still lying on my bag. I left the bottoms for another day.

I crawled into bed and settled, my back to him.

Eddie didn't move.

"Thanks for letting me in," I said to the wall, attempting to gauge his mood.

No response.

"Goodnight," I tried.

He moved, settling in, obviously on his back, not touching me and not speaking either.

Hmm.

There were a few of problems with this. First, I was wide-awake and coasting on a serious wave of adrenalin, adrenalin that needed to be worked out somehow, and I knew how I'd prefer it to be worked out. Second, I was too freaking shy to do anything about it. I definitely wasn't able to make the first move. Last, I was pretty certain Eddie was ticked off, so even if I *wasn't* too shy, he clearly wasn't in the mood.

Instead, I fidgeted, I moved, I turned and I tried to count sheep.

I was rearranging my pillows for the third time when Eddie's arm came out and hauled me across the bed, tucking me into his side.

Finally.

"Jazzed?" he asked.

"Um… yeah."

"Stun-gunning angry black women in bars on Colfax'll do that to you."

Wonderful.

Darius told on me.

"Darius," I said.

Eddie didn't answer.

"I tried to be a mediator, I swear. I even offered to buy her a drink. But apparently Indy stun-gunned her a few months ago. Then she called Ally a bee-atch, which Ally didn't like. Then she punched Daisy in the eye. Then Daisy jumped her, and Ally jumped them, and they started rolling around on the floor. *Then* some other woman shoved Indy and—"

Eddie interrupted me, "You can stop talking now."

I closed my mouth and laid there a second, pressed up against his warm, hard body.

Then (I swear, I couldn't help it, it was the adrenalin, and maybe a little of my newfound coolness) I ran my hand down his chest, across his abs, then back over his chest and my fingernail might have somewhat purposefully snagged his nipple.

He grabbed my wrist and held my hand where it was.

"You tired?" I whispered.

"It's after one in the morning," he replied, but didn't answer my question.

I thought about this and came up with a solution.

"I'll do all the work," I said quietly.

He didn't respond and he didn't move.

Damn.

Finally, he said, "Please tell me you didn't have the chance to bend over in that dress."

I did a mental replay of the night.

I hadn't.

Except for when I bent over to use the stun gun of course.

I didn't share that with Eddie.

"I didn't even sit down, unless I was in the Mustang."

He didn't say anything.

I squirmed next to him.

"Um…" I dragged it out, "about me doing all the work?"

He pulled me over his body. His hands slid down my bottom, the backs of my thighs and hooked at my knees, pulling them up so I was straddling him.

My mouth found his in the dark.

"Can I take that as a yes?" I asked.

He didn't answer, but he pulled off my camisole.

I was guessing that was a yes.

I went with my guess, and I was right.

Chapter 19

Lottie

The alarm went off. Eddie touched a button and rolled out of bed.

I slid the covers over my head. Maybe, if I hid, he wouldn't remember I was there.

He yanked the covers off me, grabbed my hand and pulled me out of bed.

"Did you *not* hear what I said about the snooze button?" I asked as he marched me across the room.

"It's a good thing you're so damn pretty, *chiquita*, because mostly, you're a pain in the ass."

⟫⟪

I didn't have to make the coffee. Eddie had programmed it the night before, and when I wandered into the kitchen the pot was full to the brim. Fourteen whole cups of hot, fresh java.

Heaven.

I had two cups while getting ready and I made Eddie one.

I poured us both travel mugs. We loaded ourselves in the truck and Eddie took me to Fortnum's. He kissed me, deep but brief, while we sat in the truck in front of the store. He idled at the curb, watching while I walked in. I gave him a wave when I unlocked the door and went inside. He lifted his chin, slid on his shades and took off.

Then I looked behind the espresso counter. Duke and Jane, no Tex.

My heart skittered then stopped.

"Where's Tex?" I asked.

The first customer came in behind me.

"Not here," Duke answered.

"What do you mean, not here?" I asked.

Duke looked around. "I mean, not... here."

"He's always here," I told him.

"Well he's not now," Duke replied.

"Fuck!" I shouted, and the customer turned to stare at me. "Sorry," I muttered. I set my travel mug on the book counter and hauled out my cell.

I called Mom's cell and got her voicemail.

I left a message. "Call me the minute you get this."

Then I hung up, scrolled down my phonebook and called Tex.

He didn't have an answering machine so it rang about twenty times before I hung up.

Then I called him again.

On the seventh ring, he answered.

"What?" his boom was muted.

"Tex? Where are you?" I asked.

"Hungover," he answered.

"Mom's not answering her cell. Where is she? Is she okay?"

"She's fine."

Then he disconnected.

I stared at the phone.

"Tex just hung up on me," I told Duke and Jane.

They just looked at me.

"He says he's hungover," I said to them as the second customer walked in.

"Maybe he is," Jane offered.

I scrolled down to Eddie's number and pushed the green button.

"Yeah?" he answered.

"Hey, it's me," I said.

"Yeah?" Eddie repeated.

"Jet," I told him, making sure that he knew who he was talking to.

Silence for a beat then he said, "*Chiquita*, I know who it is."

I could hear his smile in his voice, which made my belly curl, even though I was in borderline freak out mode.

I ignored the belly curl.

"We have a crisis," I informed him.

Silence for another beat then he asked, "Didn't I drop you off about five minutes ago?"

"Yes."

"How do we have a crisis in five minutes?"

"Tex isn't at work. He says he's hungover," I told him.

"So maybe he's hungover," Eddie replied.

"He can't be hungover and protect Mom! He's falling down on the job. Mom has to move in with us."

More silence.

Then, "Your mother isn't movin' in with us."

There was no smile in his voice on that comment.

"Then we have to move to my place," I stated.

"Last time I stayed the night at your place, your Mom knocked on the door when my hands were in your pants. We're not movin' to your place and your Mom isn't movin' to mine."

"Eddie!" I cried.

"Jet, my plan has two goals. One is to keep you and your Mom safe. Two is for us to have some privacy and time to get to know each other. Your Mom moves in, my second goal is in the toilet."

"We can get to know each other when Mom's around."

"Not the way I want us to get to know each other."

My belly curled again and I felt spasms in three different places. I took a breath and shook it off.

"I bet you'd hit the snooze button if Mom was with us," I said.

"Yeah, but then we wouldn't have time for a long shower."

Dear Lord.

I had to admit, I liked long showers. At least, I liked long showers with Eddie.

I didn't tell Eddie that.

Instead, I said, "I'm pretty certain I don't like you."

To which he replied, "You're so full of shit."

The smile was back in his voice.

I sighed and flipped my phone shut.

What else could I do?

Indy strolled in mid-morning. "How'd it go with Eddie?" she asked when she dumped her bag in the locked drawer behind the book counter.

"Darius told on me," I answered.

She nodded. "He told on me too."

"How did Lee take it?" I asked.

"Lee's used to me doing crazy shit. What I want to know is, how'd Eddie take it?"

"He didn't like it, but he got over it."

For some reason, this made me happy and I grinned at her.

She grinned back.

⁂

Half an hour later Vance walked in with another one of Lee's boys, a guy named Mace. Mace didn't come around very often. According to Indy, he was more of a nighttime person. Mace had to be six foot three, had the prerequisite Nightingale Investigation Team killer bod; black hair, jade eyes and a jaw so square, it could be used in math class.

Indy reported that Mace had some native Hawaiian in him and was supposedly a top-notch surfer. This wasn't surprising. Even for a big guy, Mace had the grace of a top-notch athlete who knew how to use his body. He gave up the surfing game when he discovered snowboarding. Then he lost the boarder Zen when some shit hit with his sister and he gave up *that* game to go recreational in his spare time. Now, in his not so spare time, he hunted people for Lee and cracked heads together when the mood struck (which was a lot).

Indy didn't know what the shit that hit with his sister was about, except it was seriously not good and it put Mace in a perpetual bad mood.

One more thing: Mace was hot. All Lee's guys were hot in one way or another but Mace was a little different. Mace was *broody* hot.

Ten minutes after Mace and Vance settled in to the comfy seating area with coffees, Lee and another of his guys, Matt, walked in.

"Powwow," Duke muttered, eyeing the boys, and Indy, Jane and I watched as Matt peeled off to sit with Vance and Mace. Lee came over and ordered coffee.

Sometimes Lee would hold powwows in Fortnum's. I didn't know why. I didn't ask and when they did, I steered clear.

The powwow's significance magnified when Hank arrived and didn't even bother buying a coffee. Hank was a cop, not one of the boys, and his presence made things official.

It also put the hotness quotient of Fortnum's seating area into uncharted levels.

"Yikes," Indy said.

She could say that again, but only in a good way.

The bell went over the door and I looked up.

Tex was wheeling Mom in.

"Hey dollface," Mom called.

"I'm not talking to you," I called back loud enough that the Hot Crew quieted and looked at me. I ignored them. "And especially not you," I said to Tex.

"What'd I do?" Mom asked, eyes round.

"Don't give me no shit, Loopy Loo," Tex boomed, but quietly (don't ask me how, but he managed it). "I'm in no mood."

"You got my Mom drunk!" I shouted, hand on hip (where I was getting this hand on hip business I did *not* know, but I was digging it).

Tex winced. "Stop yelling."

"I'm not yelling!" I yelled.

They made it to me. Mom grabbed my hand, totally ignored my outburst and said, "Tex is going to teach me how to make espressos, cappuccinos, lattes, everything. He says there are at least a dozen syrup flavors, even burnt marshmallow! Isn't that right, Tex?"

Her eyes were shining.

Dear Lord.

"That's right, Nance," Tex replied and wheeled Mom around where I stood in the middle of the front of the store and took her behind the espresso counter.

"Nance?" I asked, turning in a half circle to follow their progress.

Mom threw me her majorette smile.

Tex glowered.

"Don't you have shit to do?" he asked.

I opened my mouth to say something. I didn't know what, but it was going to be *something*, when the bell over the door went again. I looked in that direction and Smithie was walking in.

My glare transferred to Smithie.

"I'm not talking to you!" I yelled.

"Shee-it, bitch. What's your problem?" Smithie shot back.

"You fired me!" I shouted.

His hands went out at his sides. "I didn't fire you. I just put you on unscheduled, unpaid vacation."

"Yeah, you fired me!" I snapped back.

"I'm guessin' from the attitude you don't have your shit sorted out yet," Smithie remarked..

"No, I don't. I'm working on it, okay?" I retorted.

He walked up to me and handed me an envelope. "Your tips from Saturday."

The wind went out of my sails. It was a nice thing to do, coming all the way down to Fortnum's to give me my tips.

I took them.

"Thanks," I muttered.

"There's extra in there from the girls and the bouncers. They did a collection, knew you needed it," he said.

Damn.

Trust my luck, after twenty-eight years, to find my attitude and toss it around when folks were doing something nice for me.

I felt the tears crawl up the back of my throat and I swallowed them down.

"I don't know what to say," I mumbled as I shoved the envelope in my back pocket.

"Maybe 'thank you'?" Mom snapped from behind the espresso counter, again, using The Voice. "Yeesh, you'd think I didn't raise her right," she said to Tex.

"That your Mom?" Smithie asked.

I didn't have the chance to answer when the bell went over the door again.

I turned and saw my sister, Lottie, standing there.

She was wearing skinny, black jeans and a black tank top with the Audi circles straining across her D-cup boobs. She had a knockout tan and her blonde hair was flopping around the back of her head in a loose bunch designed to look sexy and messy. It worked.

"Eyeeeeee!" I squealed, thrilled to see her, forgetting everyone; Tex, Duke, Smithie, Jane, Indy, Mom and the So Fine Commando Wild Bunch. I ran and threw myself at her.

Lottie squealed too and we hugged, swinging each other back and forth and laughing out loud.

Mom wheeled up and pulled herself out of her chair for her own Lottie hug. Lottie helped her sit back down then turned and shot a bleached teeth, LA smile at me.

"What're you doing here?" I asked, still smiling.

"Gotta call from Lavonne, then from Trixie, then Lavonne again and finally Mom," Lottie said.

My smile died, and with it, my excitement at seeing Lottie.

"What'd they say?" I asked.

Lottie's smile died too. "They told me what's been going on."

Wonderful.

My hand went back to my hip. "They shouldn't have done that."

Her hand went to her hip. "Why not? No, wait, why didn't *you* tell me?" she asked.

"I was handling it."

She shoved my shoulder.

My entire body froze.

"You weren't handling it, you crazy bitch," she said.

"That's what I'm sayin'," Smithie put in.

Lottie didn't even know who he was and she nodded at him.

I pulled out the Double Diva Threat and put both my hands on my hips. "*I'm handling it.*"

She shoved my shoulder again.

"Don't shove me," I snapped, shoving her back.

"Girls," Mom warned.

As we had our entire lives, we ignored her.

"You're crazy," Lottie told me. "All this shit going down with Dad, and you, workin' in a titty bar!"

I shoved her again. "Nothin' wrong with working in a titty bar," I retorted.

"No, you're right, there isn't anything wrong with working in a titty bar, except *you* working in a titty bar. You aren't the kind of girl who works in a titty bar."

She shoved me and then she yanked my hair.

"What's that supposed to mean? And don't you yank my hair!" I yanked hers back.

"Girls," Mom repeated, realizing from lots of experience that the hair yank was a significant escalation in hostilities.

"I'll yank your hair if I wanna yank your hair!" She yanked it again and I shoved her. She ignored my shove and kept talking, "Always taking it all on your shoulders, not calling, telling me you needed money, taking two jobs. You're an idiot."

"I'm not an idiot!" I yelled.

"You are, you should have called," she yelled back.

"I didn't want to worry you. I wanted you to live your life," I told her.

"You and Mom *are* my life, stupid." Then she shoved me again. "I'm moving back to Denver."

I shoved *both* her shoulders.

"Are not!" I shouted.

She grabbed onto my hair, yanked and didn't let go.

"Am too!" she yelled.

Then we went down, mostly yanking each other's hair and yelling, "Let go!" but we also rolled around, she bit my shoulder and I elbowed her in the ribs. It was nothing we hadn't done before, though, the last time we did it we were in junior high.

All of a sudden, we were soaking wet. We froze and looked up and Mom was holding an empty plastic pitcher. Then we looked down at ourselves. We were wet through. Lottie was okay. She was already wearing a skintight black tank top. Though her mascara was running down her cheeks.

I was wearing a white, long-sleeved, scoop-necked t-shirt, which had been rendered virtually see-through with the water. I was also wearing my laciest bra. You could see it, but thank God it was holding up and not exposing the *whole* show.

"My two girls, rolling around on the floor of a coffee house. Goodness gracious, *get up*," Mom snapped, standing and utilizing the Diva Threat pose much better than I could do it, even with one arm.

We got up.

I turned to Lottie.

"Are you really moving to Denver?" I asked.

"Yeah," she answered.

"But you love LA," I said.

"Johnny and I split up. LA's shit without Johnny and I miss the mountains. I'm comin' home."

She smiled at me.

She didn't miss the mountains, she missed her family.

I smiled back.

I had to admit, it would be nice having Lottie home.

"You wanna job?" Smithie, suddenly, was there.

Dear Lord.

I performed the introductions sopping wet and not giving a damn. "Smithie's my boss at the strip club. Smithie, this is my sister, Lottie."

"I know who the fuck she is. She's Lottie Mac, Queen of the Corvette Calendar," he said to me and turned to Lottie. "You dance at my club, I'll give you a fuckin' marquee. I'll give you a spotlight. I'll clear the stage for your dances. I'll have to buy a fuckin' velvet rope and hire new bouncers. Shee-it, you'll be drivin' a Porsche in a week."

Lottie looked at him.

"That works for me," she said, as if that was that.

"What?" I yelled.

Smithie turned to me. "You make it a sister act, I'll take you off un-planned vacation and fuckin' put you in my will."

"I'm *not* dancin' a pole!" I shouted.

"All right, calm down. Fuck," Smithie said.

It was then I felt something not unpleasant, but somewhat scary, slide across my skin, and I looked up to see the gang of hotties all standing, watching and every last one of them flashing a grin.

"What are *you* lookin' at?" I snapped, not to any one of them in particular, but in their general direction.

Don't ask me why I didn't run and hide in the books, I just didn't. I guess that wasn't me anymore.

"Babe, you just made me a regular," Mace replied.

I glared and his grin deepened into a smile. I'd never seen Mace smile. I'd never even seen Mace grin and I felt my nipples go hard.

Lottie finally noticed the boys and her mouth dropped open.

"Good Christ," she whispered.

"Don't mind them," I said. "They're here all the time."

Slowly, Lottie turned to look at me.

"You were holding out on me," she replied. "I should have bit you harder."

Indy took us to her duplex to get us some dry clothes. Unfortunately, my mascara was running down my cheeks, too, so we also did a quick makeup fix.

Tod came over, announced there was a sale at King Soopers and Stevie had bought a year's worth of shaved turkey, so we all went over to their side of the duplex to have turkey and Swiss sandwiches.

We walked in the backdoor to the kitchen and were confronted with a chow dog, small for her breed, with an enormous ruff around her neck, but her bottom was almost completely shaved. She looked like a miniature, beige lion with attitude. She barked twice, her front feet coming off the floor, her claws clicking on the tiles when she landed. Then she ran to each of us in turn, head-butting our shins.

I knelt down to give her cuddles and she panted in my face and allowed it as if she was prizing me with a sacred treasure. Then she pranced out of the kitchen, fluffy tail fur bouncing on her bald ass.

"That's our dog, Chowleena." Tod smiled down at me. "She likes you."

⚞⚟

We were sitting around the dining room table, Lottie, Indy and Tod comparing lash-lengthening strategies, when my phone rang.

It said, "Daisy calling."

I flipped it open. "Hey, Daisy."

"Hey Sugar, what're you up to?" she asked.

"Well, I think my Mom is on the longest date in history with a crazy, ex-con, Vietnam vet who has a shotgun, grenades, tear gas and twenty-five cats. And I got in a wet t-shirt, knockdown, drag out fight on the floor in Fortnum's with my sister who's just in from LA. Oh, and we did it in front of most of the boys on Lee Nightingale's payroll," I shared.

Silence.

"Darlin', you know how to live," Daisy finally said.

"Normally, I'm really boring," I told her.

She laughed her tinkly-bell laugh. She didn't believe me either.

"What's up with you?" I asked.

"Got a call from Shirleen. Rumor has it Ray's hittin' her table tonight."

I looked up at Indy, Tod and Lottie and my eyes grew wide.

"You girls ready to ride again?" I heard Daisy say in my ear.

"Just a second. Indy's right here, let me ask."

I relayed the story to everyone. Indy and Tod smiled. Lottie looked angry.

"Dad's a shithead," Lottie said.

"You guys in?" I asked.

Tod and Lottie nodded.

"Ally's got a shift at Brother's tonight but I'm in," Indy replied.

Ally was a bartender at My Brother's Bar. It'd be a bummer that she couldn't come but I figured with Lottie and Tod in the mix, we could almost equal her attitude.

"Ally's working but Tod wants to come and so does my sister, is that okay?" I told Daisy.

"Peachy, darlin'. Can't wait to meet your sister," Daisy answered.

"You might know her, she's Lottie Mac, Queen of the Corvette Calendar."

"No shit? 'Course I know her, Sugar, she's a celebrity."

I grinned at my sister.

"Yeah," I said, feeling proud. Then I hesitated. "Do you mind if we wear our own clothes?" I asked.

More of the giggle. "Sure, just as long as you got a little sparkle on."

I figured I could do *a little* sparkle.

"Tell her we'll meet here," Tod cut in.

"Tod says to meet at his place." I gave her directions, signed off and flipped my phone shut.

"You ready for this?" I asked Lottie.

"Ready to kick Dad's ass? Fuck yeah," Lottie replied.

I rolled my eyes.

Indy and Tod grinned at each other.

Guess Lottie had the seal of approval.

My phone rang again.

It said, "Eddie calling."

"Uh-oh," I muttered when I saw it.

"Eddie?" Indy asked immediately.

"Is that your new boyfriend?" Lottie asked.

Tod nodded for me.

I still wasn't ready to fully commit to the boyfriend thing, I'd said it once and once was enough.

"Who told on me now?" I asked, flipping open the phone.

"Half a dozen you could choose from," Indy answered.

My life sucked.

"Hello?" I said into the phone.

My opening was greeted with silence.

"Eddie?" I called when the silence went prolonged.

"You sure you want to stick with this boring tactic? Gotta tell you, *chiquita*, it *seriously* isn't workin'."

Wonderful.

"Lee phoned you," I guessed.

"Lee, Hank, Duke not to mention Mace and half a dozen cops who heard it on the grapevine and wanted to determine the commitment level of our relationship."

I blinked at the table. "Pardon?" I asked.

"For the record, I made it clear our commitment level is in the red zone," he told me.

Dear Lord.

"We've only had one date," I replied.

Silence.

Then some muttering in Spanish and finally, "We gotta have another chat?"

No!

No more chats.

"I think I got it," I told him.

"I hope so *chiquita*, if you don't, you will," he said quietly.

Eek!

"I got it."

"Shit, you're killin' me," he sounded frustrated.

I felt bad for him but I didn't know how to help. Helping him would be putting myself out there and I felt plenty out there already.

I decided to change the subject, "My sister's in town."

"Yeah, heard that too. I'd like to meet her, but I'm caught up in something and need to work late tonight. I'll pick you up from Tex's."

I looked around the table. Everyone was staring at me. "Actually, I'm going out tonight with Indy, Tod, Lottie and Daisy. I'll probably be out late."

That's all I shared, he could guess the rest.

More silence.

More Spanish.

He guessed the rest.

"Eddie—"

Finally, he said, "I'll ask Lee to tail you."

"No!" I protested. "We think we have a lock on Dad and Lee'll scare him off."

Lee would scare anyone off. One look at us with Lee in charge, word would spread like wildfire and Dad would be gone.

"It'll be okay," Eddie assured me.

"Anyone sees him with us..."

Eddie laughed softly but it was a serious laugh. "If Lee tails you, *no one* will see him, not even you."

Somehow, that scared me more.

"I don't think—" I started.

"Trust me, *chiquita*."

"I'm not sure—" I tried again.

"I want you to trust me and I'm askin' you to do this for me. It'll give me peace of mind. I might have some shit goin' down tonight. I don't need to be worried about you."

My breath froze in my lungs.

This was a lot, trusting Eddie, doing something for Eddie and worrying about Eddie all at the same time.

I made a split-second decision.

"Call Lee," I gave in.

He talked in Spanish again, his voice now soft, I knew some of the words, and they were sweet.

Then he said, "When you're done, you're comin' to my place."

He wasn't asking.

"Yeah," I said, feeling the warmth curling in my belly. I couldn't say anything else. I was in an Eddie Daze.

"Leave your sister with Tex," he ordered.

"Okay." I was still in The Daze.

"Be careful."

"You too," I said quietly, meaning both words and meaning them a lot.

He was silent for a beat and then he said, "This is the part that makes you worth it."

I blinked again, not keeping up with him.

"Pardon?"

"You got two kinds of sweet and I like both of 'em."

Then he disconnected.

Dear Lord.

Chapter 20

War

The afternoon passed in a whir.

We went back to Fortnum's, then Duke took me to the bank (my second ride on a Harley) so I could deposit my tips and the (very generous) collection from the folks at Smithie's.

While I was gone, Lottie trailed Mom and Tex home in her rental in order to visit with Mom and get settled at Tex's.

Tex seemed surprisingly content with his house filling up with women. Indy explained Tex had been a loner and kind of hermit for years before he met her, so she figured he was making up for lost time.

Duke and I went back to Fortnum's. I helped close and then Lee and Indy took me to my apartment to find something sparkly to wear. I'd packed for Eddie's during a mammoth flip out and thus didn't do it very well. I was going to use the opportunity to pack more (a girl's gotta have options).

Lee made Indy and I stand in the front hall while he did a walkthrough of the apartment. I felt kind of stupid standing there, not to mention uncomfortable. The favors people were doing for me were spreading far and wide. So far and so wide, I'd never be in a position of payback.

"All clear," Lee said with a chin jerk.

Indy followed me into my bedroom while Lee hung out in the living room and flipped open his cell. Before going into my room, I glanced at him as he moved around my living room and a thrill went up my spine. He was just talking on the phone but he'd somehow completely claimed the space. In fact, his presence filled the entire apartment with a kind of dangerous, badass magnetism.

"He kinda scares me," I admitted to Indy when we'd entered my room.

She threw herself on my bed to watch me pack.

"He's kinda scary," she told me.

I stopped digging through my closet and stared at her.

"How do you get over it?" I asked, then immediately started digging again. It was a nosy question and really wasn't my business.

Then, I couldn't help myself, I had to, I decided to share.

"I'm only asking because Eddie kinda scares me too. He's a cop. He says something's 'going down' tonight. I don't know what, but it doesn't sound good. It flips me out. How do you take the worry?"

Clearly not thinking I was nosy, she shrugged. "I love him."

Simple as that.

Though, I guess that would do it.

We went to Eddie's to dump my bag, Lee doing the walkthrough/all clear thing again.

I pulled out what I was going to wear that night and then we went to Indy and Lee's.

Indy and I got dolled up together in their bedroom. Lee silently brought us a spiced rum and Diet Coke then disappeared. The way he did it, I was beginning to realize why she loved him, other than the fact he was hot. Not because he got her a drink (which was nice), but the way he got her a drink. He didn't ask, he didn't make a big deal about it, and it was a sweet thing to do. It was tremendously cool, and, deep down inside, I hoped for something like that for myself one day. A lot closer to the surface, I liked Indy and I was glad she already had it.

While we got ready, we talked and giggled and I swear, it felt like I was back in high school getting ready to go to a dance in the gym.

I didn't have anything sparkly, so Indy loaned me some glitter dust to put on my collarbone and some cream that made my cheekbones glisten. It wasn't a lot of sparkle, but it would have to do.

I wore a silky, deep-purply-gray tunic with a low slash at the throat, which if I turned right could give a hint of cleavage. Other than that, it was kind of demure (I bought it myself), with long sleeves that got fuller down the length. The thing that made it kind of demure, rather than totally demure, was that it had two slits at the sides which were about two inches higher than they really needed to be, and therefore, they showed some skin.

This topped jeans and black flats (just in case I had to make a run for it). I went heavy on the makeup; not exactly Smithie's, but not my everyday look, either, and I did the deep part, sultry-thing with my hair.

I thought I looked all right, though nothing to write home about. I felt safe in the jeans and hoped Daisy wouldn't quibble.

See, jeans were multi-purpose in Denver. An invitation could say "semi-formal" and there would be people at the party wearing jeans. It was just the way of the Rockies. A true Denverite would wear jeans to meet the Queen of England and somehow pull it off.

Once we exited the bedroom, we found that Lee had not only disappeared, Lee had *disappeared*, leaving a note. So we headed over to Tod and Stevie's. Daisy was already there, having a cocktail, playing with Chowleena. You could only, just barely, see the black eye under her concealer.

More proof that Daisy was the shit. I'd never be able to conceal a black eye and still look as good as she did.

Stevie and Tod were both flight attendants, and Stevie was out on a flight and not due back until the wee hours which meant Tod was stag.

When I walked in, Tod's eyes got huge. "Girlie, you are Queen Chameleon. Every time I see you, you look different."

I smiled. "Is that good?"

"Fuck yeah, it's good," he replied. "You are *workin'* that shirt, and you're only in my living room. The world will stop when you walk out the door."

Daisy smiled at me. "See?" she asked, as if Tod's approval proved a point.

"He's gay," I said.

Tod looked between me and Daisy.

"What's my sexuality got to do with anything?" Tod asked.

Daisy turned to him. "She doesn't think she's all that. Thinks she's plain Jane and boring."

Tod swung his wide eyes to me. "Good. You're workin' that too and you don't even *know* you're workin' it."

Daisy's tinkly-bell laugh sounded. "Damn straight, Sugar!"

Then they high-fived.

Dear Lord.

"Who's designated driver?" Indy asked.

"I've only had one rum and coke, it can be me." I said.

"I don't *think* so," Daisy returned. "You need liquid courage for a face-down with your Daddy. This'll be my last one, I'll drive."

Lottie showed up. We introduced her to Daisy and Daisy and Lottie formed a deep bond in five minutes while sharing breast enhancement surgery stories.

We ordered Chinese. We ate Chinese. We drank and we waited.

We didn't want to show up at the scene of our last crime too early, and Shirleen told Daisy that Dad wasn't normally early to the table.

At eleven thirty, we started to roll out, but then Tod stopped dead in the kitchen.

"Un-unh. I tried. I really tried, but can't do it. Be back." Then he ran up the stairs.

We all stood in the kitchen staring at each other. He came down with a pair of burnished silver stilettos with a pointed toe and a thin ankle strap that crossed at the back as well as a matching belt. He handed the belt to me and then knelt at my feet.

"What are you doing?" I asked when he lifted a foot, took off my black flat and threw it into the living room.

Chowleena was standing in the door to the kitchen. She watched my shoe fly over her head, gave a bark, then settled on her ass.

Tod slipped the pump on in its place.

"I do *not* worship at the altar of Sarah Jessica Parker and all things *Sex and the City* to go out with a hot-lookin' girlie in black flats. You wear black flats when you're eight and ninety-eight, not anytime in between."

"Tod—"

"Huh!" he snapped, giving me The Hand.

I knew better than to argue with The Hand.

So, if something went down and I couldn't run, at least I'd die dressed to the nines from top-to-toe.

⋈

We went straight to the bar when we got there and I scanned the crowd for any sign of Darius or angry black women.

Luckily, the coast was clear.

The bartender came right up to us. "Shirleen said to wait until she gives you the high sign," he told Daisy and Daisy nodded.

Then she turned to me. "You ready for this, Sugar?"

No. I wasn't ready for it. I had a lot of things to say to Dad, but had no idea how to say them. And what would it matter anyway? Vince was still going to be after me. I was just going to have to go with the moment.

"Ready as I'll ever be," I told her

She squeezed my arm. "That's my girl."

The troop turned to the bar to order drinks and I stood just outside the clutch.

"Buy you a drink?" I heard a man ask and I turned to look. My eyes hit a well-defined collarbone and muscular throat above a navy Henley, so I looked up.

Mace was standing there.

"Say yes and then look like you're flirting with me," he ordered in a soft voice.

My stomach clutched and I ignored his instructions because I was in sort of a mini-freak out. Mace could put any girl in a mini-freak out, *especially* telling her to flirt with him and *most especially* using a soft voice.

"What?" I asked, sounding stupid.

His eyes shifted and he lifted a chin to the bartender. "Two beers," he said.

I shook off the freak out and leaned into him.

"What are you doing here?" I whispered.

He circled me, getting close, cutting me off from my posse and forcing my back to the room. He leaned against the bar, looking for all the world like a guy on the prowl with me being the prowlee.

"Lee got word shit's goin' down tonight. He put together a team."

No.

No, no, no.

No shit going down and no team.

I could just about handle my friends offering moral support when they were having fun while they were doing it. I didn't need the Wild Bunch out there getting paid overtime on Lee's nickel. That was one favor too far.

The bartender deposited our beers on the bar and Mace slipped him a bill, then he ignored the drink, and I did too.

"If this is dangerous, we'll leave," I told him.

He shook his head.

"Finish what you start," he said. "We have it covered."

"You have *what* covered?"

"Don't know. When we do, it'll be covered."

Eek.

"What's going on?" I asked.

"You're here to talk to your Dad. Lee's out there, somewhere, and so are Vance and Matt. I'm assigned to you. Something happens, I grab you and we go to the safe point."

Safe point?

Safe point?

This did not sound good.

In fact, it sounded really not good.

I opened my mouth to speak but he wasn't finished.

"Something happens and I have to grab you, you come with me. No argument, no struggle, no worrying about your friends or I'll neutralize you, no hesitation. Got me?"

Oh... dear... Lord.

I was pretty certain I didn't want Mace to neutralize me. I didn't know how he'd do that and I didn't want to learn.

I decided to pull out the attitude. "I'm calling it off. No neutralizing, no worrying about my friends and no owing Lee the overtime he's paying you," I declared.

He watched me for a beat and something happened to his expression. His face became hard, but the look in his green eyes went soft. I watched, fascinated, and I felt the change throughout my entire system.

"Get that out of your head and focus. This is voluntary overtime. For all of us."

I stared, trying to process his words, but he didn't give me a chance.

He got closer and his voice dropped to a whisper.

"Babe, watching you these past months has been like watching a flower bloom. Don't disappoint us."

Then he was gone.

I stood and stared in the space he'd been occupying.

"Um... *hello?*" Tod called to me, drawing out the "hello".

I snapped to and stared at them all. They were all looking at me.

"Mace was just here," I said.

"He was?" Indy asked looking around.

I couldn't believe they hadn't seen him, but I ignored that as there were slightly more pressing things at hand.

I told them all what he said.

They all continued to stare at me.

"We gotta go," I decided.

They looked at each other.

"We ain't gonna go, Sugar. He's right, finish what you start," Daisy said.

Lottie was watching me, then a slow smile spread on her face. "I couldn't put my finger on it, but it's true. You *are* a flower. I thought it was the hair, but it isn't the hair, it's *you*."

My sister.

"Pu-lease," I muttered and rolled my eyes.

She just nodded, looking all happy in the face of certain danger.

My eyes moved to Indy. "What the hell did he mean, watching me these past months has been like watching a flower bloom? Who talks like that? And, anyway, he barely comes into Fortnum's."

"Um, I kinda forgot to tell you." Indy was shifting uncomfortably and it worried me.

"What?" I prompted.

"Lee has surveillance on Fortnum's," she began. "Cameras and bugs, twenty-four, seven. He put it in when I was going through my drama and never took it out. The boys at the office watch for security purposes and, um… for kicks."

I stared at her.

"You're joking," I breathed, at the same time silently asking God to make Indy tell me she was joking.

She shook her head.

I knew it was selfish, but I really wished God would pay more attention to me.

I was processing this, thinking about all that went down at Fortnum's; Eddie Torture, me running and hiding from Eddie, Dad's serenade, Lottie and me wrestling.

"Holy crap," I breathed.

Indy bit her lip.

Daisy tensed.

"We got the high sign," Daisy whispered.

I didn't have time to worry about being on show nearly every day for the Wild Bunch.

It was confrontation time.

We all shuffled around mentally preparing.

"Everybody got their stun guns?" Tod asked.

"I can't wait to get my hands on Dad," Lottie announced.

"Let's rock," Indy said.

Dear Lord.

⋈

We walked down the back hall and Shirleen was standing in it.

"They're on a bathroom break. Ray's at the table. Get in there," she said.

Daisy nodded and everyone stepped aside to let me go first.

I looked at Shirleen.

"Thank you," I told her, and there was a lot of feeling in it.

She turned her eyes to me and her face was gentle. "Child, you got nothin' to thank me for. You get a chance to do a good deed, you do it. That way, when you need a good deed done, it'll come back to you. Karma."

I wasn't certain I wanted to have a discussion about karma at that particular moment, and luckily Shirleen didn't wait for my comment. She stepped aside.

I walked into another dark, smoky, sweat-smelly room.

Dad was alone, sitting at the table, looking dirtier and far more worn down than he had a week ago.

"Dad," I called.

He looked up, his eyes grew bright and my heart clutched.

Then he caught sight of my carefully closed face, the brightness died and he stood up.

"Princess Jet," he said, then his gaze went beyond me and his eyes grew bright again, "Lottie!"

He looked like he was going to go for her, but her body language didn't invite approach.

I spoke. "You gotta get out of town, Dad. This has got to stop. Mom's in a safe house and I'm staying with Eddie because it's too dangerous to be at home. Eddie's sorting things out, but the more trouble you cause, the harder that's going to be for him. You have to go."

I sounded calm, cool and collected.

Inside, I was anything but. I wanted to start bawling. I wanted to stuff him in a car and go on the run with him. I wanted to get him to a Gambler's

Anonymous meeting. I wanted to put my arms around him and have him dance me around, singing Paul McCartney songs. I wanted to ask him why he left Mom, Lottie and me. I wanted to know why he was a bum.

Instead, I stood and stared at him.

"I'm gonna sort it out, Princess Jet. I'm workin' on it," he told me.

"You aren't going to sort it out gambling and stealing," I returned. "Someone shot at me and someone else wants to rape me."

His lips pressed together then he stated, "That's not gonna happen, Jet. I've got my eye out for Fratelli."

"Yeah, right," Lottie mumbled.

I looked over my shoulder at her. She was standing one foot out, arms crossed on her chest, face angry. The rest of the posse stood behind Lottie, their eyes not on Dad, but on me. Tod gave me an encouraging smile and winked.

I looked back to Dad and saw him try his smooth-it-over smile. "You girls gotta give me some time. I'll hit it big and I'll take you to the French Riviera."

Without hesitation, Lottie reminded him, "We've heard that before."

She was right, we had. We'd heard it a lot. I'd just never known what he thought he was going to hit big.

Dad's face got tight and he threw Lottie an angry look.

"Dad… " I started.

"Give me time!" he yelled and both of us jumped.

Dad was a good ole boy. He didn't yell. Ever.

"I'll sort it out," he went on, his face getting red. "You don't know. You don't fuckin' get it. I'm gonna come back, but only when I hit it big. Only when you girls and Nancy can be proud of me, when we can live large, like you deserve."

His words hit me like he was pelting me with rocks.

I mean, really, was he crazy? What kind of fucking nonsense was he going on about?

I put both hands on my hips and leaned forward.

"It's too late! The time to do that was fourteen years ago. You've been gone half my life!" I shouted, "We've moved on. It's over! You've got to get out of town, Dad, and stay gone. For your own good, but especially for ours."

He flinched like I'd hit him. "You don't mean that Princess Jet."

I didn't mean it. I didn't mean a word of it. I wanted him to come back. I wanted to live large with Mom and Lottie and Dad all together again.

But that was a dream and I knew dreams didn't come true.

Dad taught me that.

I didn't get time to go back on what I said, soften the blow or finish my point.

It was at that moment I found out what war felt like.

⟝⫤⟞

Looking back, it was surprisingly clear, every bit of it.

You would think that in the middle of bedlam you would lose track, but I remembered every moment in a way I knew I'd never forget.

There was the time when it was just me, Dad, Lottie and the gang standing in the smoky room. Shirleen had closed the door on us.

Then the door was opened and Slick was there, Slick and his friends. Slick had apparently gone to ground and gathered reinforcements. Too many, too much for all of us.

He'd also decided that tactically a knife was not the chosen weapon. He went with guns.

Unfortunately, somewhere along the line, Dad had decided to arm himself as well.

Eddie was right. The stun gun in my purse wasn't shit when bullets started flying. It wasn't like the movies. There were no clever comments to give you the chance to prepare. Slick was done fucking around and that was that.

They fired upon entry and Dad yanked his gun out of his waistband and randomly returned fire shouting, "Girls, get down!"

I threw myself at Lottie and we both went down. I rolled away from the legs charging in the door, taking her with me. We ended facedown and started to crawl, low on our bellies, Lottie moving underneath me. I held most of my body over her.

There was more gunfire, a lot of it, too much. It was so loud it rang in my ears and I could smell the gun powder in my nose.

Then I heard shouts, screams, running footsteps, thuds of flesh against flesh. I saw Lee, running low, snatching up Indy on the go as if she weighed no more than a feather. He turned and they vanished.

I saw Matt, crouched low with Daisy in a fireman's hold over his shoulder. Then, quick as a flash, they disappeared around the corner of the door.

Then a hand wrapped around my ankle and I was pulled back. My arms let go of Lottie and I rolled, thinking Mace had got to me, but it wasn't Mace. It was Vince.

Just my *fucking* luck.

He pulled me to my feet, an arm around my waist, and started running, me tucked under his arm. I noticed he jumped over a prone Shirleen, lying on her side in the hall.

Fuck!

I didn't let the surprise at seeing him get to me and I didn't let my worry for Shirleen break my focus.

This was about life, death and rape. I wanted no part of the second two and the first one was just getting interesting and I wasn't about to let it go.

I twisted, struggled and screamed at the top of my lungs.

That was when Mace arrived.

I saw him, Vince saw him and Vince stopped. He jerked me upright and pulled me back against his body, an arm around my ribcage.

"Not another step," Vince warned, and I felt the cold against my temple.

Mace froze.

Mace was carrying a gun, held up and pointed at us, left hand to his right wrist, head cocked to the sight of the gun but his eyes shifted to my temple.

My eyes slid there too.

I could see Vince's gun held to my head.

Wonderful.

Now, at this juncture I had two choices. I could get dragged out of there and hope someone found me and took care of Vince before I got raped, and possibly killed. Or I could fight, maybe get killed, but at least I wouldn't spend the last hours of my life being scared out of my mind and violated.

No choice, really.

I brought my head forward then back with a vicious snap. I cracked my skull against Vince's chin and for some reason, it didn't hurt.

The gun fired and I felt the burning pain at my temple.

Now *that* hurt.

I thought surely I was dead, but my limbs were still taking orders from a brain that was still working and positioned in my skull and I noticed Mace move, fast as lightning.

Vince's arm around me went slack when he went into defense mode, forgetting me when faced with an aggressor who one second was five feet away, the next second, on top of us.

Mace grabbed me and threw me free, and since apparently I could run, I did.

I heard a struggle, a grunt of pain, but I kept going and didn't look back.

I went down running, doing a sliding skid on my knees, stopping next to Shirleen. I had time to get my hands on her and noticed she was breathing when a strong arm came around my waist. I was pulled to my feet and redirected.

It was Mace. He was running, half dragging me along with him. I remembered his orders and didn't try to go back even though I really, *really* wanted to.

We cleared the bar, running flat out, Mace's hand in mine, to an SUV. The locks and lights were bleeping as we ran toward it (I found, in a desperate situation I *could* run in stiletto heels).

He directed me straight to the driver's side. He picked me up and shoved me through to the passenger side, got in, started the truck and took off without either of us wearing seatbelts.

He drove down Colfax then swung into an empty parking lot and round the back of some building. He braked, killed the lights and turned to me.

Before I knew what he was doing, his fingers closed on my chin and he gently pulled my face around. It was the dead of night and there were no lights where we were. There was no way he could see but I could tell he was looking.

"Graze," he said, though I didn't know how he could determine that in the dark. Then he muttered, "Fuck."

He let me go, looked forward, and I got the weird feeling he slipped somewhere else for a moment.

Then he shouted, "*Fuck!*" And that one word was like a controlled, muted, explosion that I was surprised didn't shake the windows.

I put my hand to my head, tentatively exploring the wetness there but I could feel it wasn't that bad. I'd skinned my knees worse.

"I've skinned my knees worse," I told him.

At my words, he turned. His arm went around my waist, he yanked me across the seat and then he kissed me.

Eek!

It was a full-on kiss, tongues and everything. I shouldn't have responded but I did. Maybe it was the life or death situation, the thrill of being alive, desperate gratitude. Or maybe it was because it was a great kiss. It was likely all of that and more. I wasn't going to analyze it. I was going to go with it then bury it. Deep.

His head came up, but he didn't let me go and stayed firmly in my space.

For my part, I had both hands curled on his neck, just below his ears, and I found I *couldn't* let go.

We both sat there, silent, staring at each other in the dark and breathing heavy.

There was something important about that moment for Mace. I felt it. I didn't entirely get it but I was honored by it.

The only thing I knew was that, for me, it was about him saving my life and me being alive.

Then Mace broke the moment.

"You tell Chavez I kissed you, we're disappearin' in Mexico where no one can find us."

Sweet Jesus.

He said "us".

I couldn't blame *that* on the Smithie's uniform.

"What was that about?" I whispered.

He was quiet for a beat.

"I'm just glad you got a face left to kiss."

Hmm.

Guess, for Mace, it was the thrill of me being alive.

Yeesh, men were so weird.

He let me go and I dropped my hands. He yanked his t-shirt out of his jeans, pulled a penknife out of his pocket, cut away the hem and pressed it against my temple. This must have meant he didn't have tissues in the glove compartment.

I took over with the pressing. He turned away and buckled up.

I put on my seatbelt too and off we went.

He drove to the parking lot at the Kmart strip mall off Alameda and Broadway by Indy's house. There was a clutch of vehicles parked haphazardly, close to the entrance off Alameda, all SUVs except for the red Dodge Ram.

I scanned the huddle of people, counting. Lottie was there, her arms wrapped around her middle, standing next to Vance. Indy was being held by Lee. Tod had hold of Daisy. Matt was leaning against one of the SUVs.

No Dad.

Everyone was alive and breathing and I appeared to be the only member of the walking wounded.

Eddie was close to Indy and Lee, pulling a hand through his hair, but when our lights flashed into the lot, his head jerked around. He started walking toward us before Mace had a chance to get close.

Mace swung the truck around, positioning my door close to Eddie and stopped. I didn't even get a chance to put a hand out when the door swung open, the interior lights went on and Eddie saw me.

"*Dios mio*," he said, soft and quiet.

"It's nothing, just a—"

He didn't let me finish. He reached around, released the belt, pulled me out of the cab and into his arms which went around me so tight, I could barely breathe.

"Graze," I finished on a poof of expelled breath.

He leaned back, took my hand away from my temple and looked at my wound.

"We're going to the hospital," he said.

"Eddie, it's nothing. I just need to clean it and…"

His eyes cut to mine and I quit talking.

"We're going to the fucking hospital," he repeated in a voice you just did not argue with, even me, and I seemed to be able to argue with Eddie all the time.

"Okay," I replied.

He moved away, his arm around me and everyone crowded in.

Tears started falling from Lottie's eyes. Indy's face went so pale, it shone in the dark and Tod cursed.

Daisy snapped, "That just cuts it. I'm done fuckin' around with this business. Sugar, you had it your way now I'm callin' Marcus. This means *war*."

Eddie didn't break stride, even with the threat of Marcus entering the mix. He ignored her comment and kept on going, straight toward the truck. He bleeped the locks, opened my door and helped me in. Before he closed it, Lee was there.

Eddie looked at him.

"I'll wanna know how you let this get out of hand," Eddie said to him, and I could tell he was angry and placing blame square on Lee's shoulders.

A muscle jumped in Lee's cheek, he gave one nod, accepting blame.

"No," I said.

Eddie started to close the door but I put my foot out to stop it.

"No," I said again.

"Move your leg, *chiquita*." There was no anger when he addressed me. He was back to using his soft voice.

"You aren't blaming Lee and you aren't blaming Mace. You aren't blaming anyone. Mace told me shit would go down, I told everyone else and we decided to stay. It's my shit that brought everyone out in the first place. If there's anyone to blame, it's me."

Eddie wasn't listening to me. Eddie was focused.

"Move your leg," he repeated.

Then I thought about what I said.

"Actually, if there's anyone to blame, it's my Dad," I amended.

Eddie's eyes cut to me. "*Mi amor*, I'm askin' you, move your leg."

I scanned the crowd and saw Lottie was standing behind Lee, next to Indy.

"Our Dad is a fucking shithead," I told her.

Seriously, if there was an f-word moment in my life, this was it.

"Jet, let Eddie take you to the hospital," Lottie urged.

It was all hitting me, delayed reaction.

"He thought he could gamble himself into the big time and we'd all 'live large'. What kind of stupid, fucking moron is he?" I asked her.

"Jet, get to the hospital," Lottie repeated.

"I've been working since I was fourteen fucking years old and he gambled away every fucking dollar I gave him. What a fucking *dick!*" I shouted.

To punctuate my point, I brought my hand down on the window ledge and then cried, "Ow!" mainly because it hurt.

I looked at Eddie. "I hurt my hand," I informed him unnecessarily.

His dimple appeared first then his lips formed a grin. "Maybe we'll get the doctors to look at it after they check the bullet wound to your head."

I blinked at him then nodded, "That's a good idea."

"You gonna move your leg now?" he asked.

"Sure," I answered, the soul of amenity, and then I moved my leg.

He slammed the door and walked around the front of the truck.

Everyone was gathered at the side. Mostly they looked shell-shocked. Except Daisy, she looked pissed right the hell off. And not Lee and his boys. I noticed they were all trying to hide grins.

Eddie got in and started the truck.

To let them know everything was all right, I flashed a smile and gave a jaunty wave as Eddie pulled away.

⋙⋘

It wasn't until a lot later that I saw (regardless of the fact that it *was* just a graze) the amount of blood that had leaked down my face. I was sitting on the end of a bed in the emergency room at Denver Health and the nurse was cleaning me up.

"That's a lot of blood," I remarked, staring clinically at the towel she was using as if it was someone else's blood.

"Head wounds bleed," she replied in battle weary tones, the voice of experience.

That was all I heard, because it was then that I fainted.

Eddie was sitting by the bed when I woke up.

"Hey there, *cariño*," he whispered.

"Don't tell anyone I fainted," I whispered back.

His eyes smiled even though his lips didn't.

"They must have thought I was a lunatic, ranting about Dad with blood running down my face," I noted.

"I don't expect they thought much of anything except bein' glad you were alive to rant."

I figured he was right.

He helped me sit up and then took off to go to the waiting room to tell everyone I was okay while I filled out forms. I was praying, since I was on an unplanned, unscheduled vacation, that Smithie still had me insured.

Told you he took care of his girls; probably no other strip joint had good insurance.

Then Eddie came back. "You should know, someone told Duke and Tex and they were both out there. Your Mom too. I told 'em you were fine, I'd take care of you and sent them home. You can talk to them tomorrow."

I pushed back the alarm of Mom knowing I'd been grazed by a bullet and focused on feeling grateful. Grateful I had friends who would sit around in the waiting room of a hospital to hear news of a graze and grateful that Eddie took care of them so I didn't have to. Because I was grateful, I found his hand and I gave it a squeeze. He one-upped my squeeze by bringing my fingers up and brushing his lips against my knuckles.

The gesture was so intimate, my belly curled and the oxygen burned in my lungs.

It was then, Detective Marker arrived.

Eddie stood with me while Detective Marker talked to me, *again*.

The only good news Jimmy Marker gave me was that Shirleen was okay. She sustained a blow to the head. She was taken to Presbyterian/St. Luke's Hospital and admitted for observation only, a minor concussion.

"Do you know where Dad is?" I asked Detective Marker.

He looked at me.

"Usually that's my line," he returned, trying to joke.

I stared at him.

He sighed, looked at Eddie, then back at me.

"We got witnesses who say he was taken by Slick. He was alive, but looked injured. No word, no sign. We're lookin' and we'll keep lookin'," he promised me.

I felt his words slice through me like a knife.

Eddie's hand went into my hair and, very gently, he pressed the uninjured side of my head against him.

"I'm okay," I lied, looking up at him.

He looked down. "You're so full of shit."

That got him a grin.

He took me to his place, helped me undress and stepped into the shower with me. He turned me away from the spray and used the showerhead on me, and, careful to avoid the dressing at my temple, he shampooed the blood out of my hair. We patted ourselves dry, I combed out my hair and Eddie put me to bed naked and held me tight.

After a while, his warmth seeped into me and I started to feel safe again.

"I'm worried about Dad," I whispered as if I was admitting to a grave sin. "I know I shouldn't be, but I am."

"You wouldn't be you if you didn't," he replied, his voice gentle and, I swear, maybe even a little bit affectionate (or maybe even a lot).

I lay there awhile, suddenly feeling even warmer.

"Eddie?"

"*Sí, mi amor?*"

"I've got to tell you something and you have to promise me you won't get mad."

He was silent.

"Promise?" I pushed.

He sighed. "You're killin' me," he muttered.

I pressed into him. "You have to promise."

"I promise."

He may have promised but he clearly wasn't happy about it.

I told him what happened, in detail, with Vince and Mace. He listened without making a single noise but his body got more and more tense.

Then I told him about the kiss and he went totally still.

"It was just... not what you think... it was... I don't even know what it was. Mace told me not to say anything but—"

Eddie interrupted me, "Mace's sister was murdered while Mace was forced to watch. Got her head blown off. Shot to the temple."

It was my turn to go totally still while I felt my blood run cold.

Eddie went on, "Probably not fun to relive and probably worth a kiss from you when the ending was different."

I couldn't help it. It was the flashbacks that kept entering my head. It was the ugly knowledge of why Mace was pissed off all the time. I burst into tears.

Eddie stroked my back and spoke softly to me in Spanish until, finally, I stopped crying and the adrenalin subsided. I started to get drowsy and snuggled deeper into him.

Right before I fell asleep, he said quietly, "Tomorrow, we need to have a chat."

"I thought we were chatting," I mumbled, half asleep.

"This isn't a lyin'-in-bed-naked-after-getting-a-gunshot-wound-to-the-head kind of chat. This is a wide-awake-and-listen-to-Eddie kind of chat."

Dear Lord.

Not another one of those.

I suppose if I could survive being held at gunpoint, I could survive a listen-to-Eddie chat.

On that thought, I fell asleep.

Chapter 21

The G-word Turns into the W-word (Um … Eek!)

The alarm went off. Eddie touched a button and rolled into me.

I tensed, waiting for him to throw back the covers and drag me out of bed.

Instead he pulled my back to his front and asked softly, "How's your head?"

I did a full body scan. My knees hurt, my head hurt and my entire body felt stiff. On the other hand, I was breathing and not locked in a scary, sideways refrigerator at the morgue so I figured I was feeling pretty good.

In answer I said, "I cannot *believe* I have to get shot for you to hit the snooze button."

His body went still.

"Can we make a deal?" he asked, his voice still quiet.

I wasn't awake enough to make a deal with Eddie, but was also not feeling like arguing.

"Maybe," I hedged, thinking that was a good compromise.

"The deal is that was the last joke we'll make about you gettin' shot."

My breath caught and I held it.

His lips came to my neck.

"Deal?" he asked.

"Okay," I agreed on a big exhale.

I had to admit, his words and the meaning behind them shook me straight to my soul. I didn't have time to focus on my shaken soul, Eddie's lips started roaming, gliding up my shoulder.

"Are we going to take a shower?" I asked.

He carefully turned me around so we were face-to-face and his hands slid down my back to my bottom. I tilted my head up to look at him and his eyes were on my temple.

"I figure it's best we do this lyin' down."

I nodded, because he was probably right. I'd survived a shooting. I didn't need to die a tragic death while being given an orgasm in the shower.

Then he kissed me and I wasn't thinking about tragic *anything*.

Then he made love to me.

It wasn't hot, fast or rough like it seemed both Eddie and I liked it.

It was about a slow burn. It was gentle. And it was sweet. It was so slow, gentle and sweet that, in the end, it garnered an "ohmigod, ohmigod" neck arching orgasm, which was good since, after, my body didn't feel stiff anymore.

<hr />

"We're going to be late for work," I said to Eddie's throat when we were done and I was lying in his arms. His arms got tighter, indicating we weren't going anywhere.

"Indy doesn't care when you show up, and everyone knows my girlfriend got shot last night. I don't think they'll be expecting us first thing."

There it was again, the g-word.

"Everyone knows?" What I meant was... everyone knew I was his... g-word.

"Cops talk. You've been the main topic of conversation since I got pulled in after the bachelor party brawl."

Oh... dear... Lord.

I went up on my elbow. Eddie rolled to his back and I looked down on him.

"What do you mean, pulled in after the bachelor party brawl?" I asked.

He was wearing his satisfied look and my belly curled. He tucked my hair behind my ear and then cupped my jaw, running his thumb across my bottom lip.

My belly curl turned into a twist.

"They're not exactly gonna give me a commendation for starting a fight and breakin' some guy's nose a few days before his wedding."

I blinked then I stared. "You got in trouble?"

"Relax *chiquita*." He grinned and pulled me down to him. "Nothing came of it. The groom wasn't fired up to tell his bride he'd got his nose broke because he put his hand down the shirt of a cocktail waitress at a strip joint. And Smithie didn't push it, likely because of you."

I thought about Bachelor Number One, or *The* Bachelor, getting married with a big old swollen nose. That would be a serious bummer for the wedding photos.

But I had to admit, I liked the thought. Mainly because he was a jerk, even if I felt sorry for his bride for a variety of reasons.

I couldn't help it, a wedding photo appeared in my head and it made me smile. As my face was against Eddie's chest, he felt it and kissed the top of my head.

Then I lost my smile as my thoughts drifted.

Eddie got into trouble at work for me. Eddie also paid for my car, which had to cost at least a thousand bucks, not to mention the coffeemaker. Eddie was a cop. I figured cops probably did all right money-wise, say, in comparison to bums like my Dad. They weren't known to be bazillionaires. And last night, Eddie was supposed to be somewhere where something was "going down", but instead he was at the hospital with me.

Seriously, this could not go on.

I figured it was time to have a Jet Chat.

"Eddie?" I started.

"Shit, I thought I had your 'Eddies' down but that sounds like a new one," he teased.

I ignored him. "I thought you had something going on last night."

"I did."

"Did it 'go down'?" I asked.

His hand slid up my back and started to play with my hair. "Heard the call go over the radio. Indy's got her own code, which shouldn't surprise you. I knew you were with her so I blew out."

I closed my eyes.

"I *am* a pain in the ass," I whispered.

He pulled gently on my hair and I looked up at him. He had his chin dipped, looking down at me. His face was mellow yet serious. It was a new look, and, just like any of his looks, I liked it.

"I was on a stakeout, nothin' was happening, it was becoming clear nothin' was gonna happen and it was boring as hell. Although I would rather have come home to you jazzed like you were the other night, you didn't interrupt anything."

Well, that was a relief.

I decided to hit on topic number two. I didn't know how to broach it so I decided just to be direct. "You have to quit spending money on me."

He rolled me over to my back, his body mostly on me. "*Chiquita*—"

"No, really. I know you want me indebted to you, but it's getting ridiculous. The car was too much. The coffeemaker..."

He started laughing. Not out and out but his body was moving with it.

I wasn't sure what was so damn hilarious. According to Daisy, coffeemakers were pretty serious and Daisy knew just about everything.

"What's funny?" I asked. "No, wait. I'll tell you what's *not* funny and this is not funny. I'm being serious."

"You really have a problem with that coffeemaker, don't you?" Eddie asked back.

"Eddie—"

"*Cállate, mi amor.*" he said and there it was again. I could hear affection in his voice. I wasn't ready for amused affection, not when we were discussing something as important as coffeemakers.

"Don't tell me to shut up," I said to him.

He ran his knuckles down my jaw and looked into my eyes. His were still full of laughter. "I know you work hard for your money. But you should know that it means more to you than it probably means to me."

"Money means a lot to everyone and I know you aren't rolling in it, so you have to stop blowing it on me."

The laughter died out of his eyes.

I had, of course, in the throes of performing my Jet Chat, forgotten that Eddie was a Mexican-American man and they tended to be both proud and macho, and I'd just stepped all over both of those.

Still, I didn't care. This was going a lot further and a lot faster than made me comfortable. In fact, this happening *at all* made me uncomfortable. I had to set the brakes, pronto.

"We're not talking about this, *chiquita*," he said to me.

"Yes we are," I shot back.

His eyes started to get a little glittery.

"Okay then, we are," he said.

Uh-oh.

I didn't think I had control of the Jet Chat anymore.

"Time for our chat," he announced.

I was right. I didn't have control of the Jet Chat anymore. The Jet Chat had just taken a scary turn down the road leading straight to the Eddie Chat.

Damn.

"I think I need coffee before our chat," I said hoping to buy time.

"After. We're gonna get a few things straight, you and me."

Damn, shit, fuck *and* hell.

I wasn't doing very well with things crooked between Eddie and me. I really didn't want things straight. I didn't know for certain how I wanted things. What I did know was how I didn't want them and that was Relationship Overdrive while the rest of my life was chaos.

"Eddie—"

"I know the meaning of *that* 'Eddie'," he started, "and you can save it. You're not getting out of this."

Exactly *how* did he have me *so* figured out?

I gave up and glared at him.

He ignored The Glare.

"See, even with bullets flyin', I've had the chance to get to know you. Call me crazy but I'd like to do it better."

My glare deepened.

He continued to ignore it.

"That said, bullets *are* flyin'. One nearly blew your pretty face off last night, so, I gotta tell you, I'd like it a fuck of a lot more if you saw your next birthday. The way I see it, that gives you two choices. First choice, you cool it with this 'get control of my life' business and let me keep you safe, which means you do what I say and you don't go out on the town with your gang in high heels. Second choice, you go your own way. You do that, I have Lee pick you up and put you in his safe room until I sort this shit out. If that means we're over, I'm willin' to take that chance, knowin' after it's done you'll be somewhere alive and breathing even if you're doin' it in someone else's bed."

I gasped through The Glare and said, "Eddie—"

"No 'Eddie'. You choose, right now, door number one or door number two, no discussion."

Really.

I did *not* think so. He was *not* going to lie there and give me an ultimatum.

I pushed him off, sat up, taking the sheet with me, and turned to him but he sat up too so I lost my leverage.

So be it, I was used to no leverage.

"There's always room for discussion," I told him.

"Not this time," he returned.

I narrowed my eyes at him and then said something immensely stupid. Do *not* ask me why, I just did. Maybe it was my newfound attitude. I didn't have it under control just yet. It leaked out willy-nilly at *the* worst possible times.

In my defense, Eddie *was* being kind of bossy.

"Door number three is I do what I want and get Daisy to help me avoid you while I'm doing it. And door number four is turn tail and run, escaping it all by talking Mace into helping me and Mom disappear in Mexico like he said last night."

Eddie's eyes were no longer a little glittery. They were full-on glittery.

"I'm sorry?"

Um… maybe it was time to put away the attitude and keep my mouth shut.

"I'd like to hear that part again about Mace helping you disappear," Eddie told me.

I didn't actually think he'd like to hear it again so I decided not to say it again.

"Tell me about Mace," he persisted.

"No," I said.

"I think I missed something, maybe we should go back over that kiss you shared," he suggested and I could feel the negative vibes rolling off him in waves, pounding against me.

"Eddie."

"*For fuck's sake, Jet!*" he exploded and I'd never heard him talk so loudly. I mean, I'd heard him yell but this was a *roar*. "You were *shot* last night!"

"Believe me, I know!" I yelled back but mine wasn't as good.

"You are not puttin' yourself out there and you are not goin' anywhere near Mace again," he shouted.

"You can't tell me what to do!"

His eyes narrowed. "You better fucking believe I can."

I felt my temple throb and I chose to drop back to the pillows instead of having another staring contest. I never won those anyway.

I closed my eyes and put my hand to my head.

He was right, of course, and that totally pissed me off. I had no business putting myself out there. I didn't know what I was doing. He tried to tell me with the pepper spray incident, but did I listen? *No.* So I ended up on the floor of a dirty, smoky room, shielding my sister from bullets, my friends in the line of fire; Shirleen, who I barely even knew, lying unconscious out in the hall and finally with a gun to my head. A gun that went off in front of Mace, making him relive a nightmare.

Damn, shit, fuck, hell and back again.

"All right," I snapped, opening my eyes. "I'll be cool but you have to promise me you won't tell Mace I told you all this."

He dropped to his side and rolled over me, pinning me to the bed.

"No fuckin' way, Mace and I are gonna have a talk."

"No! You have to promise."

"You just chose door number one, which means you chose me, which means you stayin' in my life and my bed. I know you aren't gonna like it, *chiquita*, because you look like you're preparin' to bolt any time anything looks or sounds serious about us, but that also means you are now officially my woman and as such, Mace and I are gonna have words."

I didn't have time to freak out about being Eddie's woman. That was worse than his girlfriend. Far worse. A thousand times worse. The w-word was to the g-word what the f-word was to the c-word. I couldn't even say the c-word in my head!

I had to let the w-word go and tackle one thing at a time.

"He said if I told you, we were going to disappear in Mexico! You can't tell him. It'll break it, whatever it was for him. He wasn't there. He'd slid into another moment. I saw it, I felt it. It just happened that I was there when he did, it could have been anyone. But it was me and that connects us, but not in a bad way. You can't understand it, you weren't there. But I told you what happened. I didn't lie and I didn't hide. Don't make me sorry I didn't."

He did a jaw clench and stared at me.

"Eddie, promise me," I pushed.

"Jet, you aren't just anyone to those boys. Lee's got cameras and bugs in Fortnum's. They've been watchin' you for months and likin' what they see. I know, I heard 'em say it. When Lee told me he'd got word that Slick was on the move and he was asking for volunteers to run protection for your crew, every fuckin' guy on his payroll volunteered. He got to hand pick a team of his best men, all of 'em puttin' themselves on the line for you for free."

Sweet Jesus.

He had to be joking.

"You're joking," I whispered.

He shook his head.

I found I was having trouble breathing. I would never process this. This was beyond processing.

"Why?" I asked.

"I'm thinkin' it's because they'd like to be where I am right now. Lucky for me, I got there first and made it clear I was interested. That is, I made it clear to everyone but you." He stopped and watched me closely. "Jesus, Jet, you don't have a clue, do you?"

I found I didn't want to chat anymore. I was done chatting.

I needed to get up. I had to get to work, go check on Shirleen, make sure my Mom and Lottie were okay and process the fact that I was now "officially" Eddie's w-word. I did not want to be having this discussion.

To communicate all of this to Eddie, I said, "I need coffee."

He kept looking at me for a while then something changed in his eyes. The glitter went out and the warmth went back in, warmth *and* tenderness. I was beginning to miss the terror of having a gun held to my head.

"*Chiquita,* women spend a lot of time sittin' around bitchin' that there are no good men out there. I hate to tell you this, but there aren't a lot of good women either. The difference is when a man sees one, he knows it. Then he goes after her and wears her down until she's his. Then, if he's any man at all, he won't let her go."

Eek!

This just got worse and worse.

"I really need coffee," I said.

His eyelids lowered a bit and the dimple came out, but his lips didn't form a smile.

"I see you're in ready-to-bolt mode so I'll let you off the hook. Just to finish this, I hope you can understand now why I'm gonna get things straight with Mace."

I sighed, knowing that this was another argument I wasn't going to win, and deciding to save my energy for one I could win.

Whenever that would be. Likely when I was ninety-eight and wearing black flats.

Then I said, "If he grabs me and we disappear in Mexico, you'll only have yourself to blame."

The smile came out. "I'll take that chance."

I used the best word a woman had in her argument arsenal, undoubtedly its own special kind of f-word for men.

"Fine," I clipped, meaning anything but. "Can I have coffee now?"

Somehow, it seemed Eddie found my "fine" amusing. I could tell by the warmth and tenderness being joined by an affectionate gleam in his eye.

Wonderful.

So much for me putting on the brakes. It seemed instead I somehow shifted us up from relationship overdrive straight to relationship hyperdrive.

His lips touched mine then he said, "Yeah, you can have coffee."

Chapter 22

One of My Girls

Late morning, Eddie and I walked into Fortnum's; my arm was around Eddie's waist, my other hand on his abs. Eddie's arm was curled around my neck, his hand hanging loose in front of me, which meant I was tucked super close to his side.

I'd decided to call this the Eddie's Woman Hold, and even though the w-word was seriously flipping me out, I had to admit, The Hold wasn't so bad.

The minute we entered, my musings on The Hold ceased and I wanted to turn around and run.

I wasn't a big fan of being the center of attention. I much preferred to fly below radar. That, obviously, was not going to happen the morning after I'd been grazed by a bullet.

I'd looked in the mirror that morning and I thought I looked like I normally looked. I just had a white dressing taped to my temple. It wasn't *that* bad, certainly not as bad as the looks on everyone's faces made it out to be.

Duke and Tex were behind the espresso counter. Jane and Ally behind the book counter. Mom, Trixie, Ada, Blanca and Lottie formed one huddle in the seating area, Eddie's sister Gloria, Tod, Stevie and Indy in another, and the Wild Bunch, plus Hank, in the last.

When we walked in, everyone stared at us.

Eddie and I stopped.

I did a store sweep.

Then I did a vague hand wave.

Then I called, "Hey."

No one moved.

I sighed. "I'm perfectly fine," I told them.

This prompted action, but only from Duke.

He walked from behind the espresso counter, grabbed a broom that was against the wall and stormed outside. He swung the broom like it was a baseball bat against a telephone pole. He did this with such force it split in half, the broom portion flying out into Broadway, where luckily the cars were stopped across the intersection at a light. Then he did an under arm toss, throwing the remaining portion into the street and stormed back in.

Everyone watched this. Therefore, everyone was watching Duke when he came back. He pointed to me, brows drawn under the trademark rolled, red bandana that was tied around his forehead.

"You're done," he declared, his gravelly voice low and barely controlled.

I nodded. I was too scared to do anything else.

Then he pointed to Eddie. "You got two days to sort this shit out. You don't, Jet and her Mom are disappearing. Got boys everywhere who owe me favors. She stays in this kind of danger, I'm putting her on the back of a hog and she's gone. Got me?"

This outburst took me by surprise.

First, I didn't know Duke liked me so much. Duke was kind of surly, so I figured mostly he put up with me, not that he liked me. Not enough to break a broom and definitely not enough to go head-to-head with Eddie. Second, I was flipping out because Duke was going head-to-head with Eddie. I didn't think Eddie would like that.

"Calm down, *hombre*," Eddie said in a warning tone.

I was right, Eddie didn't like that.

"I'll calm down when I don't hafta jump on my bike in the middle of the night to make sure one of my girls didn't get her head blown off," Duke shot back.

"Duke, it's just a graze," I put in, feeling the words "one of my girls" slide through me like silk.

His eyes cut to me. "I don't fuckin' give a shit. Do you *see* where it is? An inch and half your head would have been gone. *Jesus fucking Christ!*" he exploded.

I had no chance to defuse the situation I felt hands on me then. I was shifted outside of Eddie's arm and then engulfed in a hug. I felt Tex's flannel shirt against my cheek and then I felt his beard press against my forehead.

"Fuckin' A, Loopy Loo," he said, absolutely no boom to his voice.

I couldn't withstand it. Tex *always* had a boom to his voice. Tears hit my eyes and I couldn't control them.

"I'm okay," I whispered.

"World would be a poorer place without you in it," he whispered back, actually *whispered*.

"I'm okay," I repeated, putting my arms around his waist, or trying to. He was a big guy they didn't fit all the way around.

If you told me two weeks ago I'd be hugging Tex, I would have laughed in your face. But there you go.

His arms loosened and he turned me towards Mom who was standing there. She pulled me to her, one-armed, and this started the rounds of hugs, cheek kisses (except for Blanca, who laid one right on my lips) and a lot of me saying, "I'm okay."

I had to admit, this brought it all home to me. You get caught up in your chaos, you don't realize just how much you're dragging everyone along with you.

In the end, I was slouched, exhausted, on a couch between Mom and Trixie, my head on Mom's shoulder, her head resting against mine. Ada's handkerchief with most of my mascara on it was clutched in my hand.

"I'm sorry," I told Mom. "I just wanted to fix things."

Her head came up and she looked down at me.

"Can you do me a favor, dollface?" she asked.

I nodded.

"This time, can you let someone else fix things?"

I looked to Eddie, who was the someone else who was going to fix things. He was talking low-voiced to Mace. They broke off and stepped outside.

Damn.

I sighed.

As Eddie would say, one thing at a time.

"Sure," I said to Mom.

Mom relaxed into me. "That makes me feel a whole lot better."

Blanca, sitting across from us, said something in Spanish. I looked at her.

"Pardon?" I asked.

She shook her head but Gloria answered, "She said you were worth the wait."

I clutched the handkerchief tighter.

Yeesh.

Was I in trouble or what?

"Thank you," was all I could think to say.

It was then Ada shuffled up, her eyes gleaming and she pointed to Vance.

"That boy over there is a *bounty hunter* and he's got a *motorcycle* and he said he'd take me for *a ride*."

Dear Lord.

I visualized Ada on the back of Vance's Harley and I couldn't help it, I burst out laughing.

Mace disappeared, but Eddie came back and I wasn't certain I could read his face, except for the fact that whatever he was thinking was not good.

I got up and went to him. The minute I came within reach, he grabbed my hand and pulled me closer, sliding an arm low around my waist. He drew me into his body and touched his lips to mine.

"Gotta get to work," he said when he was done.

Hmm. He was trying an avoidance tactic.

"How'd it go with Mace?" I asked, not letting him get away with it.

His eyes flickered, not a good sign.

"He's clear where I stand."

This wasn't a lot of information.

"Eddie..."

The hand not around my waist went to my neck and his eyes locked on mine.

"Stay away from Mace," he ordered.

Uh-oh.

"What's that mean?" I asked.

"It means stay away from Mace," he said.

"Eddie."

He pulled me deeper. "Mace knows where I stand. I know where Mace stands. Now that I know, I'm asking you, stay away from Mace."

My eyes bugged out.

What did *that* mean?

No, I didn't want to know.

I tried for assurance. "I never see Mace, he's a nighttime person."

"Good." He did another lip touch, so I guess he was assured, then he said, "I talked to Lee. You got protection anytime you aren't with me. First up is Matt."

No.

No, no, no.

"Eddie! I can't—"

"I'm not arguing about this *chiquita*. I've been a party to scenes like we just had when we walked in here, but I've always been the man removed. Don't like bein' part of the scene or people I respect breaking brooms and gettin' in my face. You're not with me, you got a bodyguard. End of discussion."

I pulled out The Glare, it was really just for show and Eddie knew it, which had to be why he smiled.

"You're adorable," he said.

"Am not," I returned.

He did another lip touch. This one was a new one. It lasted longer and included a tongue touch.

It was *yum*.

I hit a full-on Eddie Daze. He tucked my hair behind my ear then he was gone.

⋈

Ten minutes after Eddie left, Daisy strolled in.

It was bad timing. Things were beginning to calm down.

Trixie went back to her salon and Gloria took Blanca home. Ada was spending the day at the coffee house with Mom while Tex and I worked. Lottie and Indy had gone down the street to Walgreen's to get a newspaper so Lottie could look for apartments. Tod and Stevie both had flights so they went home. The Wild Bunch and Hank dispersed, leaving Matt behind.

Daisy took one look at me and skidded to a halt on her platform, denim-covered boot that had shiny rivets and rhinestones up the sides.

"Well, ain't that just peachy!" she snapped in a tone that said she felt it was anything but peachy. "You get a scar, Sugar, I'm rippin' Vince Fratelli's face off with my goddamned fingernails!"

Um... eek!

"Daisy, I'm okay," I said for the millionth time that day.

She put up The Hand.

"This is all Marcus's fault. I gave him what for last night and don't think I didn't. He's promised to fix it. He don't, I'm cuttin' off his water, you know what I'm sayin'?"

Actually, I didn't, but she was on a roll so I didn't have to wait for an explanation.

"He don't get a piece of me until I make sure no more pieces of *you* come flying off. Comprende? You and me just got to set a meeting between Marcus and Eddie and we'll get this shit *sorted*."

This was not good. I didn't think Eddie was going to be jumping for joy at the idea of a sit down with Marcus.

Of course, Daisy, who knew everything, already had it figured out.

"Don't you worry 'bout a thing, darlin'. I know our boys aren't the best of friends. We just need to get them both seconds. Keep the peace. Marcus has picked Smithie. I figure Lee'll sit in for Eddie."

"Daisy—"

Up came The Hand again.

"Too late, Marcus has already got the ball rollin'. He likes his water, he ain't messin' around. I figure Eddie should be gettin' a call just about now. You just got to talk him into it."

Wonderful.

I had no more chance to argue, Daisy was finished and glancing around. Her eyes locked on Mom. "Is this your Mama?" she squealed, in an abrupt change of mood and marched over to Mom, leaned over and gave her a big hug. "Oowee, been lookin' forward to meeting you."

Ada was staring at Daisy with huge eyes. Mom looked dumbstruck or perhaps her face had been frozen in place after coming into contact with Daisy's super-hold hairspray.

"I like your boots," Ada said.

Daisy turned blue eyes to Ada. "Well, ain't you sweet? I'm Daisy."

I left them to introductions and retreated to the espresso counter.

"I feel like I'm standing on quicksand," I told Duke, Tex and Jane.

"That's 'cause you are," Duke shot back, scowling at Daisy. He stomped into the bookshelves and disappeared.

Shit and damn.

My cell was in my back pocket and I heard it ring. I pulled it out and the display said, "Eddie calling".

I sighed then I flipped it open and said, "It wasn't my idea. I didn't have anything to do with it, I swear."

"*Chiquita*—" Eddie started.

"You don't have to do it," I whispered so Daisy wouldn't hear me. "I'll think of something. I'll get you out of it."

"I already took the meet."

I was silent.

Then I said, "Eddie."

"Remember what I said about wantin' you to see your next birthday?"

The quicksand slurped up my shoes and headed for my knees.

"Eddie—"

"Stay close to Matt. Don't worry, *chiquita*, it's gonna be fine. I'll call you later."

Then there was a disconnect.

I flipped my phone shut and looked at Tex. He was watching me.

"Eddie just took a meeting with his mortal enemy for me. Daisy cut off Marcus's water. Duke broke a broom. Lee's hemorrhaging money to keep me in bodyguards. It goes on and on and on. How is this happening? Why is it happening?" I asked, and I really wanted to know.

Tex laid a big, beefy hand gently on the top of my head. "What goes around comes around, Loopy Loo." Then his hand went away and he boomed across the store, "Yo, Daisy. What'll it be?"

I stood behind the espresso counter, letting my second, far briefer lecture about karma wash over me.

Well, then, fuck it. If everyone was so intent on being nice to me, let them. I'd deal with the consequences later. I mentally pulled myself out of the quicksand while Daisy walked up to the espresso counter and ordered a mocha, double chocolate, skimmed milk.

I stared at her.

"Chocolate's good for you, milk's not. I don't care what those stupid celebrity mustache ads say," Daisy told me.

Whatever.

"Do you know where Shirleen lives?" I asked her.

"No, but I can find out," she said. "We gonna pay a visit?"

I hadn't expected it to be a "we' situation but then again, with Daisy in the mix, it was never anything but.

I turned to Tex. "Put it in a to go cup."

I turned to Daisy. "Make the call."

I turned to Matt. "Fire up the SUV, we're rollin' out."

Daisy was watching me.

"Shit, Sugar, did Vince blow some bossy into you, or what?" Daisy asked.

Tex chuckled low.

"I'm not allowed to joke about the shooting," I told her as Tex handed her the cup.

"Says who?" Daisy asked.

"Says Eddie," I answered.

She cocked her head a bit and nodded. "What'd I say about the coffee-maker?"

Wonderful.

⋈

Shirleen lived in a gated community; new, big, fancy homes built so close to each other you could pass the gravy through the window to the neighbors next door. Still, they were better than anything I'd ever lived in so I suspected running a bar with a poker table in the back paid well.

Daisy, Matt and I marched up to the house.

Well, Matt didn't march. After listening the whole way to Daisy talk a mile a minute, bouncing around subjects ranging the scope of revenge threats to skincare tips, he followed us looking like he'd much rather be anywhere else; in the middle of another shootout, having his nails yanked out by the roots, anywhere.

Daisy rapped on the door and within seconds, it opened.

Darius stood there.

What in *the hell?*

"What are you doing here?" I asked, too shocked at his presence to be polite.

"Shirleen's family," he answered, obviously not surprised at my surprise.

Wonderful.

Only I'd get a scary drug dealer's family member conked unconscious while my shit went down.

My *fucking* luck.

I couldn't dwell, I just had to go with it.

"Can we talk to her?" I asked.

He stepped wide and we marched through.

Half a dozen people were hanging around in the living room/kitchen open plan area that had high, cathedral ceilings. They all watched as we strolled in.

Shirleen was lying on a big, poofy couch decorated in bold black swirls against a white background. It made me dizzy just looking at it.

She looked fine, but how would I know? I was no nurse.

"Hey Shirleen," Daisy called.

"Hey Daisy-girl," Shirleen replied, a big smile on her face then her eyes slid to me and the smile died.

I didn't take that as a good sign.

I didn't know what to say, so I said, "Hey Shirleen."

"What happened to your head?" she asked.

I looked to Daisy then back to Shirleen. "Fratelli held me at gunpoint. I got grazed trying to get away."

Her eyes grew wide then her lips went thin.

"You okay?" she asked.

I nodded.

"Are you okay?" I asked.

"Head hurts and I'm pissed off, other than that, fine."

"I'm sorry," I said.

"What you sorry for?"

If she didn't know, I wasn't certain I wanted to enlighten her.

Oh well, in for a penny, in for a pound.

"It's my fault you were hurt."

At that, she burst out laughing.

"Girl, you got a screw loose. You hit me on the head?"

"No," I said.

"Don't you worry about Shirleen. Shirleen can take care of herself. If she can't, she'll find someone who can."

That's when Shirleen looked to Darius.

"You know 'bout Jet gettin' shot?" she asked.

He nodded.

"That's it, son, you hear what I'm sayin' to you?" she went on.

He nodded again. This time his lips were turned up a little at the ends.

Something scary was going on and I knew it was the truth when Matt tensed and Daisy's wide eyes swung to me.

"Shirleen," Daisy started, turning back to her, "I got Marcus on the case."

"Well, then, I got Darius on the case. This is good. This means them stupid-ass motherfuckers won't get away, will they? Think they can fuck around at Shirleen's table, shoot my friends. I don't *think* so."

No.

No, no, no.

I mean, okay, I liked it that Shirleen wasn't mad at me and thought of me as a friend, but I figured we were talking about someone getting whacked. Although I wanted my problems to go away, and I wanted the fix to be permanent, I wasn't ready for that.

"What are we talking about here?" I asked.

Shirleen opened her mouth to speak but Daisy cut in, "Her man is Eddie Chavez."

Shirleen's mouth snapped shut and her eyes grew wide.

Wonderful. Now, Eddie was "my man".

I took in a deep breath.

Whatever.

"Really, I can't——" I started to say.

"Shut your mouth, get yourself an iced tea and sit your ass down. We're gonna watch *Days of Our Lives*."

Without further ado, she flipped on the TV and someone handed me an iced tea. I was a little too scared of Shirleen to disobey her order to watch *Days of Our Lives*, even though I had other things to do; *a lot* of other things, like tell Eddie that I was pretty certain I just saw Shirleen give the order for Vince Fratelli to be whacked. Instead, I walked forward and sat down in a chair that was upholstered in Barney the Dinosaur purple.

Shirleen's eyes watched Matt and Darius move toward the door.

"She's got Nightingale's protection," Daisy said, settling in on the migraine couch at Shirleen's feet with her own iced tea.

"Figured that after I heard his army swept through last night. That boy rocketed straight from wild child to badass motherfucker, now he scares the shit out me." I was a little surprised to hear Lee could scare the shit out of Shirleen. Shirleen didn't seem to be scared of anything. Though I knew where she was coming from and I nodded to her in agreement. She caught my nod and looked at me. "What's the story with you and Eddie?"

Before I could answer, Daisy got there.

"They bought a coffeemaker together the other day."

Shirleen's eyes nearly popped out of her head and then she roared with laughter.

"Eddie Chavez and a coffeemaker! Holy fuck! Darius, you hear that?" she called.

Darius was standing at the door with Matt. He looked down the hall, not pleased at being interrupted.

"I heard it," he replied.

"Jet, girl, you're workin' on becomin' a legend. Kneein' Fratelli in the balls, traipsin' around with Nightingale protection and buyin' kitchen appliances with fuckin' Eddie Chavez. Shee-it. Darius!" Shirleen yelled, displaying no sign of concussion or that she had a care in the world that Scary Darius didn't want to be interrupted. I decided to focus on that semi-positive fact rather than the new frightening turn in the conversation. "How many girls wished they'd bought a coffeemaker with Eddie? What, a hundred?"

I sent word to the Good Lord that I really, *really* needed deliverance.

Darius didn't answer.

At least that was something.

Then Shirleen leaned into me and I realized I should have been more specific about my heavenly request.

"Darius is my nephew. I know Eddie from way back. That boy nailed every piece o' booty that moved. Made Lee Nightingale look like a choirboy. Eddie sent his mother into despair. Think they wrote to the Pope claimin' it was a miracle when he became a cop. Still, even after he got the badge, he fucked everything that breathed, no coffeemakers in *sight*. Jet, girl, you are the shit!"

Daisy leaned back and tucked her denim, platform boots under her skinny ass, preparing to stay awhile. I realized immediately I should have come alone but I was thankful I hadn't shared about the toaster.

"She thinks she's boring and out of his league," Daisy threw in.

I shot her a killing look.

She let out a tinkly-bell laugh.

Shirleen matched it with another burst of hilarity.

I sat back, put my iced tea on a coaster, crossed my arms and legs, one foot bouncing with angry impatience and pulled out The Glare.

"I don't know what's so fucking funny," I said to them, and maybe it wasn't worth the f-word and maybe I shouldn't have confronted the likes of Daisy and

Shirleen with the f-word, but I was feeling a bit ticked off. "You'll see. When this is all over, he'll be gone like a shot."

They took no notice of the f-word or my attitude. They burst into gales of laughter and if they'd started rolling around the floor giggling, I wouldn't have been surprised.

When they got control of themselves, Shirleen held out her hand to one of the hangers-on and snapped her fingers. "Get me the phone, Wanda. I gotta call Dorothea. This shit's too good not to share."

Wonderful.

"Dorothea?" Daisy asked, carefully wiping away a tear of humor, so as not to smudge her mascara.

Wanda handed Shirleen the phone.

"Darius's mother. She's gonna *love* this." Shirleen's eyes came to me while she punched buttons with her thumb. "What brand of coffeemaker was it, girl?"

I looked at the TV set.

"KitchenAid," I muttered.

"Oowee! No silly-ass Mr. Coffee for Eddie Chavez. When that boy does somethin' he goes whole hog," Shirleen hooted, putting the phone to her ear. "Dorothea? You are *not* gonna believe this!"

Daisy giggled and I clenched my teeth.

My life sucked.

Chapter 23

Gray

I listened to Shirleen tell Darius's mother about the coffeemaker, clearly both of them appreciating the story a lot more than I ever would.

Then we watched *Days of Our Lives.*

Then Dorothea came over.

She was pretty; soft-spoken, with eyes that went bright when she met me then settled into what I suspected was a permanent sadness that she tried to hide, but it didn't work too well.

She wasn't what I would expect a drug dealer's mother would look like. She looked normal and kind, a lot like Darius looked when he wasn't being scary.

We left, with Dorothea making me promise to tell everyone she said hello and Shirleen making me promise to come back and watch *Days of Our Lives* with her and to keep her informed of any new kitchen appliances Eddie and I bought together.

Darius was long gone.

Matt was looking like he was going to ask for a raise.

Daisy took off the minute we got to Fortnum's and I found out from Indy that Mom, Tex and Lottie were at our place for Mom's PT, then they were going to hit the El Camino to cruise neighborhoods looking at apartments.

Jane and Duke went home and I called Eddie.

No answer.

I left a message. "Call me."

When I flipped my phone shut, I worried that I should have said good-bye or offered something witty and amusing. Then I spent a while trying to think of witty and amusing things to say next time I had to leave a message for Eddie. Then I gave up because I wasn't witty or amusing.

Indy and I closed the store and we were standing outside, locking the doors when something down the sidewalk caught Matt's attention and he did the chin lift.

"Later," he said and that might have been the first thing he said all day. Then he took off.

"Lee's boys aren't fond of bodyguard duty. They're action men," Indy explained.

I nodded and saw Hank walk up to us.

Hank was the same height as Eddie, maybe taller by an inch. He had an athlete's body, lean and muscled. He also had thick, dark brown hair and whisky-colored eyes. Hank wasn't a badass, bad boy. Hank was the to-die-for boy-next-door. Hank was every mother's dream and every girl's wet dream. And, I had the sneaking suspicion, Hank was my next bodyguard.

Indy greeted him and I stared at him.

"You got Jet Duty?" Indy asked.

Hank cut his eyes to me. "Yeah."

He didn't sound happy about it.

Indy laughed and looked at me. "Don't take it personally. Last time Hank played bodyguard, I led him to a pot farm and it was on all three networks. Don't ask, I'll tell you later." She gave me a hug and took off.

I stood there and looked up at him, feeling uncomfortable.

"What now?" I asked.

"Dinner," he answered, took my arm and guided me down the sidewalk to a black Toyota 4Runner that was parked on the street. His head was up, his eyes alert.

"Um... where's Eddie? I called him—"

"Eddie's busy," Hank replied, bleeping open the doors and walking into the street to escort me to the passenger side.

"Busy with what? The meeting with Marcus?"

He looked at me. "That's later."

"How much later?"

"A lot later," he said.

He opened the door for me.

Guess that was all I was going to learn about Eddie's plans for the evening.

I got in, he did too. He pulled out and started driving.

"I'm sorry you have to do this," I told the windscreen, feeling weird. I'd been around Hank, a lot, but never alone. And anyway, Ally said he thought I was hot. What did I do with that?

"Everyone's gotta eat dinner. Might as well do it with a pretty girl even if she is a friend's woman."

Yeesh. The w-word.

He took me to Bonnie Brae Tavern, a no-nonsense family business on University Boulevard that hadn't changed in seventy years. It specialized in piz-za that some would come to blows about if you told them it wasn't the best in Denver.

I preferred Famous.

I wasn't going to tell Hank that.

Luckily, they had a greasy spoon menu that hadn't changed in seventy years either. There was a lot of choice and most of it was damn good.

We settled in a green booth, the plethora of neon beer and Colorado sports team signs providing Denver atmosphere. I ordered a Reuben. Hank or-dered a cheeseburger. Then I checked my phone.

"Expecting a call?" Hank asked, sitting back, arm stretched out along his side of the booth, watching me.

"I left a message for Eddie," I said.

"May be a while before he gets back to you."

I nodded.

Hmm.

Dilemma.

See, first, I didn't have a lot of experience conversing with hot guys. Well, I guess I was amassing experience lately, but mostly arguing with Eddie when we weren't having sex, or when I was in the middle of a life and death situa-tion. *Not* hanging out at a pizza joint. Second, I was pretty certain that a crime was going to be committed, partially because of me, and Hank was a cop. I was thinking I should report it, though I liked Shirleen and didn't want to be a snitch.

Still.

I looked anywhere but him, trying to think of what to say. When I ran out of places to look, I caught him grinning at me.

"What?" I asked.

"It's cute," he answered.

"What?" I asked again.

"You bein' shy. I like it. It's better than the attitude, though that works too."

My mouth dropped open.

I snapped it shut and focused on a Coors beer sign with the intent of memorizing it.

He leaned forward and I looked at him. "Relax, Jet, I'm not gonna bite you."

Eek.

The dinner was hard enough. I didn't need visions of Hank biting me in my head.

"I have a problem," I blurted out, deciding to be a snitch rather than spending any more time thinking of Hank's straight, white teeth sinking into my flesh.

"You got a lot of problems," he told me.

I gave him a glare. I wasn't fully committed to it because I didn't know him very well but it was a glare all the same.

"Yeah," he muttered, his eyes going a funny kind of flirty-lazy while he looked at me. "That works too."

Sweet Jesus.

I focused on my goal. "I need to talk about my problem."

He sat back again. "Fire away."

"You're a cop," I told him.

His lips twitched and he nodded.

I kept going. "Well, say someone, I'm not saying who, but *someone* kinda knows something bad is going to happen. Something really bad. Then, say that bad thing happens. Will that someone be in trouble if she... or he... didn't report it to the cops, like, right away?"

His eyes changed again. He wasn't playing at flirting anymore. He was watching me closely.

"How bad is this something?"

"Bad," I said.

"Steal a candy bar bad or worse?"

"Worse, a lot worse." Then I leaned across the table and motioned to him to do the same. He did and when he was a couple inches away I whispered, "Murder."

Then I sat back.

There, I did it.

Whew. That was a load off my mind.

Hank stayed where he was, stony-faced and serious and he crooked a finger at me.

Uh-oh.

The load settled right back on my mind.

I didn't want to, but I leaned forward again.

"Talk to me," he demanded.

I sighed.

Then I told him about Darius and Shirleen, keeping names out of it, but it wouldn't take a genius to figure it out.

When I was done, he sat back and his arm went along the seat again. He looked away and muttered, "Fucking hell."

The waitress served our food, snatched up our drinks and shot off to get us refills even though we'd both only taken a few sips. I understood her. I knew from experience what it could do to your tips if you weren't super careful with refills.

"That why you want to talk to Eddie?" Hank asked.

I nodded.

"Lee know about this?" he went on.

"Matt was there," I shared.

"Lee knows about it," he said to himself. He dug into his jeans and pulled out his phone. He was ignoring his food and so was I, even though I'd missed lunch due to iced tea and *Days of Our Lives,* so I was really hungry.

He hit a button and put the cell to his ear, his eyes flashed on me and he said, "Eat. I have a few calls to make."

I ate.

The waitress brought back our drinks.

Hank made a few calls.

Then he ate.

"I don't want them to be mad at me," I said after we finished.

"Who?" he asked.

"The people who... well, I think they're kinda my friends and in a way doing this for me. I think they're good people doing bad things."

Kristen Ashley

"It's simple. A bad thing is a bad thing, no matter who does it or why. And homicide is the worst thing there is."

He was right. Though I figured forcing a girl to live in fear of being raped was pretty high up there.

"Jet," Hank called and I looked at him. "Fratelli has one true friend right now and that's you. Marcus isn't happy because not only is Daisy pissed at him, Vince is making him look bad. Eddie and Lee are gonna spend the meeting trying to talk Marcus out of giving the same order you heard today. Marcus is gonna pretend to play the game, because if he doesn't, Eddie'll be all over him. He's just looking for an excuse. But Marcus is gonna make the order anyway. It's the only way to send the message. Vince is in a load of hurt, with both Darius and Marcus ordering the kill. You keep Eddie, or me, informed of this shit when you hear it, maybe we can stop it before it happens."

I nodded.

He watched me.

"You don't look happy," he noted.

"I think I betrayed a friend," I whispered.

Hank caught my hand on the table and tugged at it. I came forward and so did he, but he didn't let go of my hand.

"Eddie tell you about Darius?" he asked.

I nodded.

Hank continued, "I've known both Darius and Shirleen what seems my whole life. Darius came from a good family, but Shirleen married badly. Her husband, Leon, was a sonovabitch. Mean as hell and dirty as they come. He's the one that turned Darius. Shirleen was a different Shirleen back then, beaten down and powerless. She couldn't control what happened to Darius, and Leon had long since tied her up in that shit as well. Leon was whacked two years ago and Shirleen and Darius assumed their positions when the king was dead. They did it because it's all they know and the only place they feel safe. They got a different set of rules, but it's the wrong set."

I swallowed and his hand squeezed mine.

"Jet, it's the wrong set," Hank reiterated. "You did the right thing. I like both of them and I'd hate to see either of them go down, but if they did, they'd deserve it."

I moved forward a bit more and asked, "How do you live this life all the time? They're your friends. How do you do it? I couldn't stand it."

His eyes changed and his hand tightened even more on mine. "I can do it because their shit doesn't stay in their circle. It filters down to kids in schools, and old people wanting quiet lives forced to live next to crack houses, and pretty girls who work in bookstores who have shitheel fathers. Someone has to protect those people."

"That's you," I said.

"That's me and that's Eddie," he replied.

"You don't see gray," I told him.

His hand let go of mine. "Sorry?"

"You see black and white, you don't see gray," I said.

"No. I don't see gray. It's not my job. It's the judge's job to see gray," he said it and he meant it. I could tell because his face went hard and kinda scary.

I stared at him. He was the boy-next-door. The boy-next-door with an edge.

"You're scary too," I told him.

He grinned, taking us out of the moment. "I'm the good guy."

"You're the scary good guy," I amended.

He motioned to the waitress. Our conversation was over.

"Let's get you home."

⌫⌦

By "home" Hank meant Eddie's. He parked on the street. I let us in using my key for the first time.

He sat down and immediately found a ballgame on TV and I thought, why was there always a ballgame on TV? Didn't these sports people take a night off?

I got Hank and myself a beer and called Mom and Lottie. They were playing Trivial Pursuit with Tex. I called Daisy. She was waiting in the Denver Castle for Marcus to get home and giving herself a do-it-yourself facial. I called Ally. She was shouting to me over the crowd at Brother's. I called Indy. She was watching Chowleena while Tod and Stevie were flying off to God-knew-where (Indy's words) and making cookies to bring into Fortnum's the next day.

I ran out of people to call so I took off my shoes, put my feet up on the table, sat back on the couch and took a pull on my beer.

I watched the game for about five seconds.

It was boring.

"I'm bored," I told Hank.

Hank's eyes slid to me, then back to the game.

"Not sure I can pull off your brand of excitement," he said.

"What brand is that?"

"Stun-gunning, running for your life, bar brawls. We could go out and try to rustle something up but I think Eddie'd frown on that."

"You got any perps to stake out?" I asked hopefully, sounding depressingly like Ada. It wouldn't be a great deal of fun, but it'd be something. "I'll make a thermos of coffee," I offered.

His lips turned up. "I'm off-duty tonight."

Hmm.

"You know how to play poker?" I tried.

His eyes slid to me again. "You play poker?" he asked.

"No, I thought you could teach me."

His eyes went that lazy-flirty again. I immediately thought it was a bad idea, but it was too late. He clicked off the TV, got up, grabbed my hand and pulled me up.

"Let's see if Eddie's got some cards."

⇥⇤

"Shit, Hank. Seriously?"

I was dreaming, Eddie was speaking and Eddie sounded kind of pissed off.

"She fell asleep. I didn't want to wake her."

That was confusing, now Hank was speaking and he sounded kind of amused.

I was used to dreaming of Eddie. I hadn't dreamt of Hank yet. Dreaming of Hank *and* Eddie was probably not a good thing.

I tried opening my eyes.

They opened all right and I could see down a long leg, at the end of which was a foot wearing a brown boot that was sitting on a coffee table. Beyond the coffee table was another pair of legs in faded jeans. I looked up the jeans to see Eddie's belt, then Eddie's abs, then Eddie's chest, then Eddie.

"Hey," I said to Eddie, still half asleep.

He was staring down at me and I was right, he was kind of pissed off.

I blinked.

"What?" I asked.

"You wanna get your head out of Hank's lap?"

I shot up and twisted around, and I did it so fast I became dizzy and had to throw my hand out to steady myself. It landed on Hank's thigh. I pulled it away like it burned and stared at Hank.

He was grinning at me.

My fucking luck.

Definitely the boy-next-door with an edge.

His hand came out and he wrapped it around my head. Then he leaned forward, kissed my forehead, pulled back and looked in my eyes.

"Fun night, Jet," he muttered. Then he got up and grinned at Eddie too and said, "We had dinner. We played poker. We didn't get shot at and she fell asleep watching a movie. You should be thanking me."

Eddie just stared at him, obviously not feeling thankful. This made Hank's grin turn into a full-on smile.

"I'll let myself out," Hank offered, the smile firmly in place. He thought this was hilarious.

I stood up and looked from Eddie to Hank. Eddie was also not feeling in the mood to be polite, so I followed Hank to the door.

"Thanks Hank," I said, when he'd cleared the door.

He turned, winked and he was gone.

I locked up behind him, started to turn back into the room and my shoulder bumped into Eddie.

I looked up at him.

Uh-oh.

"Have fun?" he asked.

Actually, I did. Hank beat the shit out of me hand after hand in poker, but since we were playing for pretzel sticks, I didn't mind too much. He also flirted with me outrageously, which, at first, freaked me right the hell out. Then I realized he was just playing with me and I found that kind of fun too.

I didn't tell Eddie any of that.

I was reading loud and clear that Eddie wouldn't have thought any of that was fun.

"Eddie—"

He didn't let me finish, his hands came to my waist and he pulled me to him, and then they came up and with them came my t-shirt. Then it was gone.

Kristen Ashley

"Eddie—"

"Sat down with Marcus tonight," Eddie said, walking backwards and taking me with him. "Marcus who runs guns, drugs and whores. Dabbles in drugs, mainly focuses on flesh and selling shit that tears through it."

Eek!

We cleared the coffee table and couch and I thought we were heading to the bedroom but I was wrong. Instead, he turned, my back came up against the wall and Eddie pressed into me.

"Made a deal with him. He finds Vince, Slick or your Dad, he hands them over to me. Since he's lookin' for all of them, mostly for Daisy, this wouldn't be so bad, 'cept he has to hand them over to me."

His hands were at my jeans, he undid my belt and then my jeans while he was talking. When he stopped, he bent low to pull them down, snagging my underwear with them and keeping me against the wall with his other hand at my belly.

Dear Lord.

"Eddie—" I tried again.

He came up and both of his hands went to my bottom and he yanked me up. I threw my arms and legs around him to hold on and he pressed me tight against the wall. My stomach pitched in a not altogether unpleasant way (in fact, it was altogether pleasant).

His mouth went to my neck and he kept talking.

"Problem is, Marcus doesn't do somethin' for nothin'."

His teeth gently nipped my earlobe and I shivered.

He went on whispering in my ear, "So, in order for him to give me these guys, and there's a good chance he'll find 'em before I do, I gotta do something for him in return."

He paused to run his tongue down my jaw and, I couldn't help it, I wanted to be angry or outraged, but I was turned on. I didn't know what that said about me, but I didn't care.

His lips went from my jaw to my cheek and then he said against my mouth, "I don't like owing Marcus."

I held my breath, opened my eyes and looked into his.

They were glittery *and* liquid. Another new look.

"I'm sorry," I whispered.

He let go of my bottom, but I held on tight.

His hand went between us and worked at his jeans.

"Sorry about me owin' Marcus or comin' home to you with your head in Hank's lap?" he asked.

I should have said, "Both."

Instead, I said, "Marcus. I didn't start out in Hank's lap. It just happened."

His fingers went from his jeans to me and, without warning, one slid inside.

"Ohmigod," I whispered. I couldn't help it. It felt so good it deserved an "ohmigod".

"A lot of shit just happens when you're with other guys," Eddie said low, his mouth still against mine, then his fingers moved. His thumb got involved and my bones dissolved. I closed my eyes and pressed my hips against him.

"It's nothing," I breathed.

"Jet, open your fuckin' eyes and look at me."

I did.

His eyes were burning into me. I realized in the middle of a turned on daze that something was happening, and it had a lot to do with Eddie being hot-blooded, me being his w-word and Eddie not liking coming home after a shitty task he did for me to find me with my head in some other man's lap.

I couldn't say I blamed him.

His fingers kept up their torture as he spoke.

"You're gonna have to wake up to the shit happenin' around you. You think Hank doesn't want this..." His finger went out and then back in, and I was pretty sure it was joined with another one. "You're wrong."

I was finding it difficult to keep my concentration on our conversation but felt it was important I do so.

I tried to explain.

"Hank's your friend. He sees in black and white. He plays by the good guy's rules. He told me so. He wouldn't try anything with me."

Eddie wasn't convinced.

"I think I've been pretty fuckin' tolerant of your shit until now, but I'm warnin' you, tonight it ends. Do you understand?"

I nodded, though I didn't really understand. I was beginning to.

His fingers went away but then *he* filled me and immediately started moving.

"You don't understand. You don't have a fuckin' clue," he said against my neck.

I'd never had sex against a wall, or anywhere other than a bed. Except, of course, the stuff Eddie and I did in the shower. The shower stuff wasn't sex as such, as it didn't involve penetration and acrobatics, just fingers, mouths and eventual orgasms. Mostly, *my* orgasms.

Okay, *all* my orgasms.

This was all new to me.

New and *yum.*

I chanced moving my arm from hanging on for dear life around his shoulders and slid my fingers into his hair.

"Eddie," I whispered.

His head came up. "What?" he asked, still moving.

"Are you done talking?"

He ground his hips into me and I bit my lip.

"Yeah," he said.

"Then, would you please kiss me?"

The glitter went out of his eyes, leaving only the liquid. I felt a deep relief in my belly, then a deep thrust somewhere else and then he obliged.

Chapter 24

Bloody T-shirts and Biohazard Bags

The alarm went off. Eddie touched a button and rolled out of bed.

I tensed, waiting for him to yank me out with him, but he didn't.

I heard him moving around the room and I opened my eyes, noticing it was dark, way early and I sincerely hoped he was only getting up either to use the bathroom or program the coffeemaker for later.

I fell back to sleep.

Then I heard beeping buttons like someone pressing them and I opened my eyes.

I was on Eddie's side of the bed, hugging Eddie's pillow and smelling Eddie, probably both on his pillow and on him. He was crouched by the bed, fully clothed and fiddling with the alarm.

"Eddie?" I murmured.

His head turned toward me. "Shh, *cariño*, go back to sleep."

I noticed the clock. It was still way early.

I got up on my elbow.

"Whas goin' on?" I mumbled. It was so early I couldn't fully form words.

He came out of the crouch but sat on the side of the bed.

"I'm goin' to work," he said.

I blinked, coming quickly awake. "What about our shower?"

"Maybe we'll shower later."

Something was wrong. Eddie liked our showers, a lot (or, as far as I could tell he did).

I sat up feeling strange and, maybe, a little scared. "Are you mad at me?" I whispered.

His hand came out and tucked hair behind my ear. "Why would you think that?"

I felt something lodge in my throat.

I knew what it was.

It was fear.

Okay, so maybe I was a lot scared.

"Last night… Hank," I answered.

For a second he didn't move then he put his hands at my waist and pulled me around so I was sitting on his lap.

His lips touched my neck and he said, "I wasn't mad at you last night."

"You sure seemed mad."

"That wasn't mad, that was frustrated."

Dear Lord, if that wasn't mad, I wasn't sure I wanted to see mad.

His head came up and he looked at me in the dark.

"I don't like Marcus," he shared.

"I think I got that."

I could swear, even in the dark, I could see him smile. "I also don't like seein' you with other guys."

"I haven't been with other guys."

"Vance?"

Hmm.

"Mace?"

Well, what could I say? That was a life or death situation.

"Hank?"

I didn't really have an excuse for that one.

"I'll try to do better," I promised.

"Try real hard."

Eek.

Time for a new subject.

"Eddie?"

"Yeah?"

His arms tightened and I came closer. I slid my hands around his middle and put my head on his shoulder.

"Yesterday, nothing happened. No one shot at me and I didn't wrestle with anyone and my stun gun stayed in my purse the whole day. Except for seeing Shirleen tell Darius to whack Vince, yesterday was a good day."

Eddie's body grew still when I talked about Shirleen and Darius.

"Don't worry, I told Hank about it. He made some calls," I assured him.

"Lee told me last night. That why you left me a message?"

I nodded against his shoulder.

His body relaxed.

"I think we should celebrate," I decided, lifting my head to look at him. "Not about Darius whacking Vince, but for a day with no hair-raising experiences. I'll make you dinner tonight."

He ran a hand through the side of my hair and then rested it against my neck.

"Dinner would be good," he said in a soft voice.

My belly did a curl.

"Maybe Mom and Lottie will come over. And Tex."

"I thought your sister was moving to Denver?" he asked.

"She is."

"They can come over another night."

My belly curl graduated to a doo-da spasm.

"Okay," I agreed.

He touched his lips to mine.

"Why are you leaving so early?" I asked when he was done.

"Got shit to do."

"My shit?"

"Your shit."

Wonderful.

I really *was* a pain in the ass.

I tucked my face in his throat.

"I'm sorry," I said against his skin. "I hate this."

"*Mi amor*, it'll be over soon."

"I hope so. Who would have thought it, but I want my boring, old, normal life back."

His body shook with soft laughter. "*Chiquita*, I'm not sure you're capable of boring and normal."

I wished he was right.

"Just you wait," I mumbled.

He didn't say anything, but I could tell, even in his silence, he didn't believe me.

"I've set the alarm so you can get up later. Bobby'll be here at seven thirty to take you to Fortnum's."

Bobby was another of Lee's men and I was guessing Bobby pulled Jet Duty that morning.

I sighed. "All right."

He kissed me, the touch-on-the-lips, touch-the-tips-of-the-tongue kiss. It was one of my favorites.

Who was I kidding? They were all my favorites.

"Be good," he said against my mouth.

I sighed again. "I'll try."

He was laughing when he put me back into bed.

It was only when he was gone that I realized I still had fear lodged in my throat. It wasn't fear of men with guns and knives and rape on their mind.

It was a whole other kind of fear that, call me crazy, was far worse.

⊱⊰

The alarm went off and I hit the snooze, thanking God for one small favor, that the snooze button was always the biggest one.

The alarm went off again, and again I hit the snooze.

This happened two more times.

At seven fifteen, I stared bleary-eyed at the clock, let out a little scream and jumped from the bed.

I was in my underwear and one of Eddie's flannel shirts, hair wet from a fast shower and in a complete tizzy, when there came a pounding at the door.

It was Bobby.

Bobby was built like a tree and he looked like a member of the Tex Family, except younger and before the crazy kicked in. *Just* before.

He did a body scan and his eyebrows went up.

"I'm running late, can you wait?" I asked.

He shrugged, sat down on the couch, grabbed a remote and found a ballgame.

"How can there be a ballgame on at seven thirty?" I enquired, exasperated, staring at the screen.

"English football, it's later there. Man U vs. Arsenal, a friendly."

It was like he was speaking in code but I wasn't really listening. I was staring at the screen.

These guys didn't wear pads and helmets that hid their faces. These guys didn't wear silly pants with gathers at the ankles.

These guys wore shorts and shirts, no hats or helmets and you could see, straight out, they were hot.

I sat down on the arm of the couch and watched.

Some official looking guy threw a yellow flag.

"What's that mean?" I asked.

Bobby explained someone did something bad but I wasn't listening. All the players were pissed off and getting in each other's faces.

I pushed Bobby over and sat down fully on the couch.

Twenty minutes later, Bobby looked at me. "Don't you need to get to work?" he asked.

"Shit!" I cried, jumped up and ran to the coffeepot. I made Bobby a coffee, made one for me and did the getting ready business.

It was nippy and not the normal, bright, sunshiny Colorado day. I put on a fitted heathered gray t-shirt, a wool, aubergine, ribbon cardigan, jeans and my high-heeled black boots. Hair back in a ponytail, minimum makeup, spritz of fancy perfume and ready to roll.

We swung into Fortnum's way late.

No one noticed.

Mom was on the couch, Lottie next to her and I gave them both a kiss and went behind the espresso counter to help Duke and Tex with the line of customers.

"I see you're still alive," Duke remarked, obviously still feeling crotchety about my recent troubles and deciding to blame it on me.

I felt the best course of action was not to answer.

It proved not to be the best course of action.

Duke stared at me a beat then turned to the CD player, yanked out Tex's Steppenwolf and put in Charlie Daniels.

Normally, this was indication of a throw down. Once a CD was on, it was *on* and the only reason you were allowed to turn it off was if it wasn't some of Duke's country or some of Ally, Indy and Tex's rock 'n' roll.

I held my breath waiting for Tex to react.

Tex wasn't biting.

This was weird. Tex *always* bit.

Both Duke and I stared at him.

"Are you okay?" I asked Tex.

He turned to me. "Gonna ask your mother to dinner and I want your blessing."

My mouth dropped open.

Duke made a sound like someone punched him in the gut.

"Well?" Tex prompted me.

I struggled to find my voice. "Um… you two are consenting adults. You don't need my blessing."

"Don't want you and your sister playin' snotty tricks on me like those brats on TV," Tex replied.

I blinked. "The brats on TV are usually kids, not adults approaching thirty like Lottie and me."

His bushy eyebrows hit his hairline. "Wasn't very adult, pullin' each other's hair and having a fuckin' catfight on the floor, Loopy Loo."

He had a point.

"You have my blessing," I told him.

Then I smiled liking the idea of Tex dating my Mom.

He scowled.

"What? I said you have my blessing," I reminded him.

"Now I gotta ask her."

I looked at Mom. She was watching us. Or more likely, watching Tex. She looked away the minute she saw me looking at her.

I looked back at Tex. "I think she'll say yes."

"Yeah?" he looked uncertain.

I did my best not to laugh.

It didn't work.

"Shee-it," Tex said, turning away from me.

The door opened and Daisy strolled in, her hair barely tamed by two pigtails sticking out the sides of her neck. I left Tex to his worried thoughts and Duke to his pissed off state of mind and walked out from behind the counter.

Daisy waved to me and then looked to Lottie.

"You ready, Sugar?" she said to Lottie.

"What's happening?" I asked.

"Daisy's going to take me to Smithie's, show me some moves, make sure I get my Porsche," Lottie explained. "Mom's gonna come with us."

I thought about Mom hanging out at Smithie's watching her daughter practice strip routines.

My family.

Then I turned to Daisy. "Would you mind swinging by our apartment building? Ada might want to come. With Mom out of the house, she doesn't have much company and she might be bored. She'd probably like to see your moves."

This was weird, but this was true.

"No problem, darlin'," Daisy replied then looked to Tex and called, "Tex, you playin' bodyguard?"

"Fuck yeah," Tex boomed.

"Let's go," Daisy ordered and off they trotted.

Jane came in ten minutes later, Ally ten minutes after that.

Ten minutes after that, my cell rang and I flipped it open because it said, "Eddie calling."

"Hey," I greeted.

"You okay?" he asked.

Uh-oh.

"Should I not be?"

"With you, *chiquita*, it's a crapshoot."

Wonderful.

I strolled from behind the counter, letting Ally deal with the customer there so I could deal with Eddie. He took my full attention at the best of times.

I stood at the window, looking out.

"How's your day?" Eddie asked.

"I hit the snooze button, like, ten times. Then Bobby introduced me to soccer and I got to work way late. Now, I'm at Fortnum's. Tex asked for my blessing to date Mom and then Daisy came in and gathered up Mom, Lottie and Tex to go to Smithie's so she could teach Lottie how to strip. They're swinging by to pick up Ada, just in case she wants to go."

Silence.

"Smithie says Lottie'll be driving a Porsche in a week," I told him.

More silence.

I kept going. It was like I couldn't stop, even if I tried.

"Smithie says if I make it a sister act, he'll put me in his will."

Now, there was Spanish.

This made me smile.

"What's happening with you?" I asked, starting to feel funny and the smile died away.

This was a strange conversation because it was a normal conversation. This was the kind of conversation normal, average, everyday g-words had with their b-words, or worse, w-words had with their m-words.

He answered, but I didn't hear him. I noticed a car braking funny in the middle of Broadway, directly across from where I was standing. The car didn't come to a complete stop, but the backdoor opened and a body was flung out.

A body that looked like my Dad's body.

"Dad," I whispered into the phone and watched as Dad tumbled, limbs jiggling uselessly, not trying to break or control his roll.

"*Dad!*" I shouted as I watched him roll.

The door to the car closed and the car sped away.

I had the cell away from my face. I flipped it shut and shoved it into my jeans, running outside.

"Get her!" Duke yelled, but I was gone, out the door, running into traffic, straight to my Dad's prone body.

Cars swerved and honked and I went down on my knees in the middle of the left lane, next to Dad's body.

He was on his side and there was blood *everywhere*. On his clothes, in his hair, the blood was wet and dry, new and old.

I gently rolled him over and what I saw caused a wave of nausea to roll up my throat. Frantically, I swallowed it down. His face was beaten to a bloody pulp. He was barely recognizable. Eyes swollen shut. Lips cracked and ripped. Nose smushed flat. The flesh of his cheeks cut and mangled. Most of his clothes were ripped and cut and blood was flowing freely from the holes.

I bent low, putting my cheek to his and listened for his breathing while my hand went to feel for his pulse.

I heard Bobby issuing orders, "Call 911," and, "Control traffic."

I felt Dad's pulse. I didn't know anything about pulses, but I figured him having one at all meant God had finally come through in a clinch.

I sat up, pulled off my cardigan and bunched it under his head.

"Jet," Bobby said, hand on my shoulder.

I pulled my shoulder from his hand and carefully ripped Dad's shirt down his chest, seeing what looked like knife wounds and bullet wounds, old and new, all over; blood seeping from them, some maroon, some red, too much of it. No one could lose that much blood and survive.

"Jet," Bobby said again, crouching down beside me.

I heard sirens and sat down, pulling Dad's dead weight up to a sitting position using all my strength, pressing his torso to me, wrapping my arms tight around him and putting my mouth to his ear.

Not knowing what else to do, I started to sing softly Paul McCartney's "Jet".

"Get her outta there," Duke growled from somewhere close.

I skipped a bit of the song and went to the good part about wanting Jet to always love him.

It was then Dad was gently pulled away from my arms by a uniformed officer and I was helped to my feet by another. I was turned and Duke's arms were there, going round me tight.

We watched as the police worked, then the ambulance was there. Duke helped me into Bobby's SUV and Bobby took off behind the ambulance, following close.

He was on his cell, listening to someone then he murmured, "It's bad."

Yes, he was right. It was bad. It was very, very, *very* bad.

Bobby angled into an illegal spot outside Denver Health, but I was out of the truck before he came to a full stop. He caught up to me and we entered the emergency room together.

The receptionist stared at me, her eyes rounding with horror and she began to stand.

"She's unhurt. It's someone else's blood," Bobby took over, talking to reception.

I pulled my cell out of my back pocket and scrolled down to Daisy and hit the button.

Daisy answered on the second ring. "Hey, Sugar. We just picked up Ada and we're headin'—"

I interrupted her, "Fifteen minutes ago, Dad was flung out of a moving car on Broadway. He's been beaten, stabbed and shot. I'm at Denver Health. Can you find a good way to break it to Mom and Lottie and get over here?"

Silence for a beat, then, quietly, "You betcha, darlin'."

I flipped the phone shut and saw Bobby take a piece of fabric from the receptionist. He grabbed my arm and pulled me in the direction where she was pointing. We went into the emergency ward. He opened a door and we went into an empty room with an exam table, a bunch of medical stuff and a sink. He took me to the sink.

"Shirt off," he ordered.

"What?"

His hands went to my t-shirt at my hips and he whipped it over my head. I stood frozen and stared at the t-shirt in his hand. It was covered in blood.

"You don't want your mother seeing you in that shirt. Let's get you cleaned up."

He handed me the fabric. It was a green scrubs top. I put it on while he walked to a biohazard bag, opened the top and shoved my shirt in. He grabbed some gauze on the way back, shoved it under the tap, wet the gauze and turned back to me.

"You're fuckin' covered," he muttered, wiping at my neck, eyes on his task, face set like it was carved from stone.

I looked down. He was right. The shirt was gone but there was blood all over my arms, neck and jeans.

"Bobby…" I said and my voice broke on his name.

His eyes came to me.

"Don't. Don't do it, Jet. You're hangin' in there. Don't break now."

I nodded and swallowed.

Bobby's eyes dropped to my neck and he started wiping, the door opened and Eddie was there.

I looked at him. Bobby looked at him. Eddie looked at us.

"Jesus fucking Christ," Eddie whispered but I could hear it from across the room.

"It's not my blood," I told him.

He came forward. Bobby gave him the gauze and vanished.

Eddie didn't hesitate and he didn't look at me, he just started wiping.

Then he tossed the bloody gauze in the sink and went to get more.

When he'd wiped off all the blood, I said, "There was a lot of blood."

His eyes came to mine. "I could see."

"No, I mean, on Dad."

His hand came to my jaw. "I know what you mean."

I stared at him. "I want to cry."

His eyes went from carefully blank to warm. "Have at it, *chiquita*."

"Bobby told me not to break."

"Bobby's a macho idiot."

His hand moved from my jaw, slid into my hair and he pulled my head to his chest. I wrapped my arms around his middle and he moved his arm around my waist. The other hand stayed in my hair.

I took a deep breath. It broke in the middle a couple of times, but I didn't cry.

We stood there, holding onto each other for a good long while.

Then I realized something. Something tremendously good and something frighteningly bad.

Eddie was my anchor. I was a boat, tossed on the seas in an ugly storm that wanted to engulf me, and Eddie was keeping me tethered and safe.

How did *that* happen?

I'd been tossing on the seas for twenty-eight years. I was used to flipping around on the waves by myself, bailing out the water like a mad fool.

How did I get used to an anchor?

What if that anchor broke off?

Shit and damn.

Bobby was right, I couldn't break.

I had to keep bailing, I couldn't get used to an anchor.

"Mom and Lottie might be here," I mumbled to Eddie's chest.

"*Cariño...*"

I lifted my head, put my hands to his waist, pushed away a bit and looked at him.

"I have to go out there and talk to them. See if the doctors have anything to say yet."

He stared at me a beat and then, finally, he said, "You aren't in this alone."

I tried to pull away, but he brought me back with his arms tightening.

"Jet, you aren't alone."

I nodded and tried to smile.

It didn't work.

His hands came to my face, holding me by the jaw and he did a lip touch.

"I'm fine," I whispered.

His lips twitched but it wasn't exactly amused and it wasn't exactly unamused.

Then he whispered back, "You're so full of shit."

Chapter 25
Chili

By the time we got to the waiting room, Mom, Daisy, Tex, Ada and Lottie were there. They'd been told Dad was in surgery. That was it, nothing else. It was now a waiting game.

Eddie took his badge out of his back pocket, hooked it onto his belt and walked to reception to see if he could get more answers.

I caught the gang staring at the blood on my jeans then Mom moved forward and pulled me into a one-armed hug, Lottie joined us and we became the McAlister huddle.

Tex engulfed us with his wide arm span and Daisy burrowed in, bringing Ada with her.

Tex, Daisy and Ada gave the only thing they had to give, seeing as they weren't surgeons, nurses or miracle workers. They gave comfort and we took it.

Eddie walked up to us. Tex noticed and we disengaged. Eddie put me into the Eddie's Woman Hold and said, straight out, "Gunshot wounds were from the other night and shoulda been treated, stab wounds more recent. He lost a lot of blood and Slick did a lot of damage. It doesn't look good."

I was glad he said it straight out. I wanted to know and it said a lot that he trusted me enough to say it, though tears started rolling from Lottie's eyes.

Indy came in a few minutes later with the cookies she'd made the night before. Ally followed her with a cardboard tray filled with lattes that Jane had made.

It was the beginning of the parade.

Mom made some calls, and Trixie, Lavonne and Bear showed up. Lavonne and Trixie stationed themselves like sentries next to Mom, and Bear sat alone with his head in his hands, probably thinking twice about his career choice as a bum.

Vance and Matt did fly-bys, doing chin-lifts to me and talking to Bobby and Eddie, then they peeled off and disappeared.

After a while, Daisy took off with Ada and Trixie in tow and came back with bags filled with burgers and fries and more cardboard trays of drinks.

Daisy handed me a burger saying, "Nothing says 'hospital waiting room' like greasy fries and a burger with cheese."

I doubted the burger joint was going to use that in their next advertising campaign.

Lee showed up and Indy immediately walked over to him. Eddie was standing next to me. He grabbed my hand and walked me over.

"Hey," Lee said softly, then, I kid you not, he slid an arm around my waist and kissed my temple, right above the bandage that was still there.

"Hey," I replied when he let me go. His eyes were warm and concerned and I thought maybe he wasn't so scary.

He looked to Eddie and the warmth and concern melted out of his eyes and I thought maybe I was wrong.

"We got Slick."

Both Eddie and I tensed.

"You bringin' him in?" Eddie asked.

Lee shook his head once.

"He's in the holding room. We have a few more questions to ask and then we'll take him to the station."

I didn't know what the holding room was but it didn't sound like a good place to be. I didn't feel too sorry for Slick. It might make me a bad person, but I didn't feel sorry at all.

Eddie didn't seem overwhelmed with happiness about this statement. He seemed resigned to it, like it wasn't the first time it happened.

Lee's eyes turned to me. "He's done with your Dad and there'll be no further involvement with your family."

I didn't know if Slick was done with Dad because he beat the shit out of him and carved him up or because Lee made it so. I didn't ask either, mainly because the expression on Lee's face wasn't inviting my participation in the discussion.

"He formed an alliance with Vince," Lee continued. "Vince convinced him they had the same goal and Slick was looking for reinforcements, so he didn't need a lot of convincing. That's why Vince was there the other night." He paused. "We haven't found Vince."

This was not good news.

Lee looked back to Eddie. "Mace is taking vacation days. He's after Vince. He's on a fuckin' mission. I'm two men down with Mace gone and providing protection for Jet. I have to pull Bobby. Mace had an assignment and Bobby needs to cover. Ike'll be available when you need him."

Eddie wasn't happy about this news either.

"What's on Mace's mind?" Eddie asked.

"Mace is working through some issues," Lee told him.

This *really* made Eddie unhappy, I could tell by the way his jaw clenched.

"Vince is fucked unless I find him," Eddie said.

"Vince is fucked unless you find him," Lee agreed.

Eddie said a few bad words in two languages then he said, "I cannot believe I have to protect that fuckin' asshole."

I couldn't believe it either.

"I gotta get on the street," Eddie finished, his arm coming around me.

Both of mine went around him as well and I looked up at him.

"Go. I'll be okay." Then I turned to Lee and said, "You don't have to send more bodyguards, I have Tex and—"

Lee interrupted me, "Primary objective for Nightingale Investigations right now is your protection. You're okay in this waiting room but once you leave it, you have cover."

"But "

He turned to Indy. "She doesn't leave unless she has cover."

Indy nodded.

"I can't ask you to—"

He interrupted me again, "You didn't ask."

"Lee…" I tried.

His eyes cut to me and I shut up.

Yep, I was wrong about Lee not being scary.

Indy obviously didn't think he was scary. Indy was grinning.

〜✴〜

Eddie, Lee and Bobby left and we settled in for the long haul.

Lavonne went outside every twenty minutes to have a cigarette.

I considered joining her. Even though I'd never smoked the situation seemed to warrant it. Though I pictured the Nightingale Investigation Team swooping down on me in black SWAT clothes, rappelling off the side of the hospital, shackling me and taking me to the safe room if I even stepped foot out of the waiting room. I decided to start smoking the next time someone I loved was flung out of a moving vehicle.

Eddie obviously made a couple calls himself and Blanca and Elena showed up and took turns with Indy, Ally, Daisy and Ada getting us coffees and making certain no one was alone with their thoughts for too long.

I spent most of my time sitting with Lottie and holding her hand.

"I wasn't very nice to him the last time I talked to him," she said to me.

I squeezed her hand. "Stop it. There's no use to it so stop."

She squeezed my hand back.

"Love you, Jet," she whispered, looking at the wall.

I swallowed my tears. Again.

"Love you too."

A couple of hours later, the doctors came out. They told us a bunch of stuff about Dad's injuries and what they did to him, but all I heard was that he was alive.

He was in ICU, in critical condition. We were allowed to go in, one by one. First Lottie (because she had things to say), then Mom (because I suspected she had things to say) and then me.

I didn't say anything. I just held his hand for a while. He was asleep but he looked better. Mainly because there wasn't blood all over him anymore.

I walked out of ICU, away from everyone and down a hall.

I called Eddie.

"Yeah?"

"Alive, critical, ICU." I didn't have it in me to use fancy language, like verbs.

He was quiet a beat then he asked, "You stayin'?"

I thought about it.

"I think I need to make chili," I replied. "Do you mind if I use your kitchen?"

"No."

"Do you mind if I invite everyone over?"

"No."

"If you don't get home in time, I'll save you some."

"Your chili as good as your chicken fried steak?" he asked.

What could I say? Even I really liked my chili.

"It's okay," I lied.

"You are so full of shit."

⊰⊱

Ike showed up and everyone broke off to perform the tasks I assigned. A contingent to my apartment to pick up my huge, heavy-bottomed pot that I made chili in and other kitchen utensils that would be needed (because Lord knew, Eddie didn't have what I'd need). A contingent to the liquor store (because Lord knew, we'd need booze). And I took Lottie and Ike to King Soopers and whisked them through in my normal mad dash.

Ike was another of Lee's boys that I didn't know too well. I didn't tag Ike as being the kind of guy who drank coffee. More like raw eggs, and we didn't serve those at Fortnum's.

He was a light-skinned black man, a few inches taller than me; wiry, bald and he had one of those tattoos that originated somewhere else, but you could see where it slithered partially up his neck and down his arm.

We descended on Eddie's and everyone went in. Mom and Trixie immediately started looking around with expressions that could only be described as awe, as if we'd entered the Taj Mahal.

"Eddie own this place?" Trixie asked, or more like *breathed*.

Wonderful.

"Yeah," I answered, lugging groceries into the kitchen.

Daisy was already there.

"Is that the coffeemaker?" She was pointing to the KitchenAid.

I knew it was pushing it, considering God let my Dad live that day, but I still sent word.

"What about the coffeemaker?" Mom asked.

"Eddie and Jet bought that together," Daisy answered.

God's answer was that he didn't feel like working overtime.

Mom and Trixie stared at me.

I couldn't do it. They had hope glittering in their eyes and we needed hope that day, so I nodded and let the coffeemaker work its magic.

I made vast amounts of chili.

Usually, chili was easy to make.

It was harder when Blanca was hovering around me.

"You need more cayenne," she told me, after taking a spoonful of the simmering stew.

"Okay." I didn't argue. I dumped more in and stirred.

She took another spoonful. "More cumin."

I did a mental sigh and dumped more in.

She took another spoonful. "Needs jalapeños. I'll go to the store."

Then she nabbed Elena and they were off.

They came back with seven bags of groceries. Some for the party, most for Eddie and me so we could shack up and have uninterrupted sex for the next month, the better to give Blanca grandbabies.

We ate. We drank. Vance popped by and had a bowl of chili and decided to stay. He must have called Matt and Bobby because they came by, too. The beer was running out so Lottie took off to get more and to replenish the quickly dwindling Frito supply.

Duke and Dolores showed up and I ran to the kitchen and spooned out a mass of chili into a Tupperware to put in the fridge so Eddie could have some when he got home.

That was when my cell phone rang.

⇥⇤

I knew it wasn't smart.

Ike, Vance, Bobby and Matt were all in the other room, not to mention Tex and Duke. I had so much protection; it was an army of protection. I could have walked in there. I could have asked. I could have taken the risk.

But I didn't. The risk was too great.

The risk was Lottie.

See, my phone said, "Lottie calling".

I flipped it open and the minute I put it to my ear, Vince said, "Got your sister. You don't want what's supposed to happen to you to happen to her, you meet me in the parking lot of the 7-Eleven on Louisiana and Pearl. No tail, no protection, right now. Got me?"

Disconnect.

Fuck.

Fuck, fuck, fuck.

At that point in my life, I was beyond worrying about the f-word.

I stood in the kitchen and wasted two seconds deciding. Then I grabbed Blanca's keys that were on the countertop and hightailed it out the backdoor.

Blanca parked in the back drive, next to the garage. I saw her do it when she came back with the groceries. She drove a silver Honda Accord. It was new-ish and it was nice and I really hoped she didn't mind me stealing it. I hoped more that I'd be alive to find out.

The 7-Eleven on Louisiana and Pearl was less than a five minute drive away but I still made it in record time.

I pulled in. There were a bunch of cars in the parking lot and I saw one at the end with people sitting in it, Lottie's blonde hair visible.

I got out, pocketed the keys and walked to it.

Vince got out too, dragging Lottie across the driver's seat with him. She was pale and trembling visibly, eyes wide, hands obviously cuffed or tied behind her back.

"Jet, you shouldn't—" she started.

I was within reaching distance. Lottie was shoved forward before she could finish. My arm was grabbed and I was pushed into the car through the driver's side. This all happened in seconds. I didn't even make a noise.

I could see Lottie was on her knees and struggling to get up without the use of her arms. Vince had the car idling, and we rocketed out of the 7-Eleven parking lot so fast he narrowly missed her.

He drove like a crazy man and I held on for dear life, but still had my head together enough to check and see if I could open the door and throw myself out of the car. I didn't figure it would kill me. It would hurt, but would leave less mental scars than what Vince had planned.

There was no handle and no lock.

Wonderful.

I could throw myself at him, force an accident, but I wasn't buckled in and an accident, at the speed he was driving, might kill me, so that idea was out the window.

I decided to try to talk my way out of it.

"Vince…"

That's all I got out. He whacked me with the back of his hand against my mouth and I immediately tasted blood.

Guess talking was out too.

Kristen Ashley

I decided to wait for my opportunity. There had to be one, there just had to.

I hung onto that thought as he drove.

⚑

He took me somewhere I'd never been; no reason to be there and I hoped I'd never have the choice of whether or not to go back (I'd pick *not*).

We went underneath the mousetrap interchanges. A mass of highway above us, nothing around us but hardscrabble cement and litter, likely left by homeless people and drug addicts, none of whom were in attendance for the evening's festivities.

Vince stopped. He pulled me out of the car through the driver's side and before I could struggle or break away, he yanked a gun out of the waistband of his pants.

Then he put it to my head.

"Been lookin' forward to this for a long time," he said as he walked me forward. "Undo your jeans."

I was getting a little fidgety.

My opportunity wasn't arising and I was beginning to get scared.

Therefore, I hesitated.

He took the gun away from my head and squeezed off a round.

I jumped, thinking he'd shot me, but realized he'd fired away from me.

He put the gun back to my head.

"Undo your fuckin' jeans."

I did what I was told. Maybe death before defilement was the way to go, but I couldn't think at that moment.

The minute I unbuckled my belt and slid the zip down my jeans, he whipped me around and forced my torso to the hood of the car. He pressed his crotch into my behind, the rest of his body against my back and the gun against my temple.

"Gonna fuck you against the car, *then* I'll do you doggie style," he said into my ear.

My heart was racing, my breath coming in jerks and my mind was absolutely blank.

He wasn't done.

354

"Then, got me a bottle and I'm gonna fuck you with that, too, break it and fuck you with it. Hard. Tear you apart. The next time your wetback boyfriend puts his dick in you, you'll fuckin' scream."

It was then I decided death before defilement was the way to go.

"First, you gotta beg," he said.

He tried to pull down my jeans. Problem was, it wasn't easy with one hand pointing a gun to my head and my body bent at the hips.

"Beg, bitch!" he demanded.

Really.

Enough was enough.

"Fuck you!" I shouted and then did a backwards head butt, catching him somewhere pointy, and I hoped it hurt because for me it hurt like hell.

I lifted up, taking him with me.

He tried to force me back and I started to go with him, but I got turned a bit and was wedged sideways against him and the car.

I struggled, managed to slide around front-to-front and got my hand on the gun.

Both our hands scrabbling for control of the gun, I put my ass on the car, forced my knees up, put my feet to his belly and pushed.

He went flying. I came off the car and jumped on top of him before he could recover.

Maybe I should have run, but I didn't. I was *way* too pissed off to run. He'd made my life a living hell and that's all that was in my head. It was probably stupid but I didn't really care. I straddled him, reared back a fist and slammed it into his face.

"Fucking bitch!" he snarled and brought up the gun, trying to point it at me.

I saw it, did a sideswipe, hit his forearm and the gun went flying.

"*Motherfucker!*" I shouted, my hands going to either side of his head. I lifted it up and cracked it against the cement.

I'd never cracked anyone's head against cement and it caused a weird sensation that could only be described as a repulsive, but kickass rush.

I didn't have to ask myself if I was a bad person. At that moment I just was.

My arm went back, cocked at the elbow to hit him in the face again, but he grabbed my wrist, bucked and rolled me over onto my back, him on top.

Hmm.

This was probably *not* an advantageous position.

I had little time to muse on it because one second he was there, the next second he was flying through the air.

I blinked and looked up.

Mace was standing over me, looking down, face rock-hard. He must have ascertained I was okay because he moved around my body and advanced on Vince.

I laid there a beat, breathing hard and feeling weird as the sudden relief that I wasn't alone tore through my body.

Okay, so I learned my lesson.

God didn't deal with the piddly-ass stuff. God kicked in when shit was important.

Good to know.

I got up shaky and realized that not only were we not alone; we were *really* not alone.

People where forming from shadows. Darius came forward, and so did Lee. Hank came from behind me. Willie Moses, the police officer that came to Eddie's house what seemed ages ago, also materialized, this time, in plain-clothes.

Eddie was also there. By the time I'd scanned the scene, he already had Vince cuffed and pressed against the hood of the car exactly as Vince had pressed me (except for obvious differences).

A squad car, driven by Willie's partner Brian, swung in next to Vince's car.

"Holy crap," I whispered.

It was like the Justice League of Super Heroes, but instead it was the Justice League of Hot Guys.

My heart was still racing and I was still panting and I felt strangely super cold.

I stood there staring at them all, stunned immobile, except for the trembling.

Eddie looked at me, yanked Vince from the car and shoved him toward Willie, turning away from him and not looking back.

Then he came to me.

He got close, blocking everyone from view and his hands went to my jeans. I didn't move, maybe didn't even breathe as he buttoned then zipped them up and did the buckle, his eyes looking into mine the whole time.

"You okay?" he asked when he was done.

I nodded.

It was a lie. I was seriously full of shit. I wasn't okay. I was terrified.

"I'd be more assured if you'd breathe," Eddie said.

I let out of a gush of air.

He closed his eyes, put his forehead to mine, then opened them.

"Better," he murmured.

"Takin' him to the station," Willie called.

Eddie turned and nodded. Willie walked away talking to Vince, and Brian had the backdoor of the squad car open.

It was over.

Dear Lord, it was finally over.

I didn't know what to do, laugh out loud or burst out crying.

I didn't have a chance to decide.

Lee got close.

Eddie turned to Lee, his face changing, registering anger, as in, *a lot* of anger.

Okay, maybe it wasn't over.

"You and me got to have words," Eddie declared.

Uh-oh. Words with Eddie.

Eek!

"It was under control," Lee returned.

I looked from one to the other in confusion. Confusion was good. I was embracing confusion. It made the super cold and trembling go away.

Darius, Hank and Mace also got close, but I think they got close in case Lee and Eddie came to blows.

"*Hombre*, he shouldn't've got his hands on her and he *definitely* shouldn't've got her pants unzipped," Eddie said in Scary Eddie voice.

Maybe Eddie wasn't feeling anger. Maybe it was something else a few notches above anger.

"He went from two counts of kidnapping to two counts of kidnapping and attempted rape with her pants unzipped," Lee answered, calm as you please.

I blinked.

357

Um… pardon me?

"Pardon?" I whispered.

Eddie moved about an inch, but it was a frightening inch. He ignored me, and his body and face now registered out-and-out hostility, but his voice was still quiet.

"Yeah? That okay with you? You all right with that?"

"Darius was here the whole time," Lee said.

"Fuck, Lee! You used my woman as bait!" Eddie shouted.

Eek!

The w-word with an even more scary b-word.

"What are you talking about?" I asked.

Lee turned to me and Eddie pulled a hand through his hair. "I slipped a tracking device in your jeans today at the hospital and Vance told Lottie the plan at Eddie's place. Mace had found Vince and we knew he was watching you. Lottie went out unprotected with her own device. Vince took the bait. Now, it's done."

At his words, a red film covered my eyes.

Scary or not, Lee was going to get a dose of Jet's Newfound Attitude.

"You used my sister as bait?" I shouted, took my life in my hands for the second time that night and shoved his shoulder.

Eddie grabbed my wrist and pulled my back to his chest, wrapping my arm around my waist at the front.

"I had her tracked, Lee. She was covered. Willie had her," Eddie ignored me and (selfishly, if you asked me) kept on his own subject.

"Willie was five minutes late," Lee replied.

I struggled against Eddie's hold.

"You used my sister as bait?" I shouted again, feeling, for the first time in my life, that attention should be centered on me.

Lee's eyes turned to me. "I was covering your sister."

Oh.

Well then.

That was something.

I stopped struggling.

"It's over," Darius finally spoke. "What's it matter how it's done? Everyone's breathin'. Quit fuckin' fightin'," he said this as if he'd had a lot of practice stopping Eddie and Lee from fighting.

Eddie and Lee stared at each other.

I waited, tense.

Hmm.

They didn't look like they were ready to stop fighting.

Yeesh. Men.

"I made chili," I blurted out.

Everyone looked at me, and, after a second, Eddie's arm around me relaxed.

"If everyone at Eddie's hasn't hoovered through it, there should be some left," I carried on.

I was trying to defuse the situation.

It wasn't working.

"Gotta go," Darius muttered, looking ready to fade back in the shadows.

I turned to him. "There's plenty."

I saw a white flash of teeth then he was gone.

See, I was right. Darius was a good guy.

I gave Hank a look, communicating without words that life definitely held shades of gray.

Hank just winked at me.

Whatever.

I turned and Eddie's arm stayed around me, but slid around my back.

I looked up at him. "Eddie, stop fighting with Lee. Let's go to the hospital and check on Dad and then let's go home."

I tried to use a sweet, coaxing voice, but Eddie didn't feel in the mood to be sweet-talked and coaxed.

"You wouldn't have allowed Indy to be put in that position," Eddie said to Lee, pushing the point.

"You're right. I wouldn't," Lee replied. "Indy would have put herself in it. And two days ago, when we knew Vince had aligned himself with Slick and we wanted to offer this choice to Jet, you wouldn't allow it, but I'm guessin' she would've taken it."

I twisted around to look at Lee, my eyes nearly popping out of my head.

What he said surprised me. What surprised me more was that he was right, I would have taken it.

"I would have preferred you to know," Lee told me.

Wow. That was huge. It was even kind of earth-shattering, not only that I would have taken it, but that he thought I would.

"Thank you," I said and meant it.

At that, Eddie was done. He moved, grabbing my hand and taking me with him.

Guess I was done too.

"Don't forget the chili!" I called back to Lee, Hank and Mace.

They'd formed a huddle and turned their heads to look at me. All of them gave me the chin lift and grinned.

Eddie walked me away, far away, to where he'd parked the truck. He helped me in the passenger side and then he got in the driver's side.

He turned to me before he started the truck. "You sure you're okay?"

I nodded and smiled.

"It's over," I told him, feeling almost giddy and thinking now was the appropriate time to either burst into laughter or tears, or both.

Wrong again.

All of a sudden, he yanked me across the seat, twisting me and pulling me into his lap. His arms went around me tight and his face went to my neck.

"Fucking hell," he muttered.

He was right. It was the F-word Moment to end all F-word Moments.

"You can say that again," I said to him.

His head came up and his hand went through my hair, his fingers curled around the back of my head and he kissed me. It wasn't deep, passionate, full-on tongue. It was sweet and soft and really nice.

"I would have taken Lee up on the offer," I told him after he lifted his head.

"I know. That's why I didn't let him give it to you."

Wow, that was kind of earth-shattering too.

Regardless, I pulled out the glare.

He shook his head, completely unaffected by the glare.

I didn't push it. Now wasn't the time to argue, especially with an outstanding issue at hand.

I put my hands to his shoulders, the fingers of one fiddling with the neckline of his t-shirt.

"Um… there's a slight problem," I shared.

Eddie stilled. "You *are* joking, right?"

Hmm.

Oh well, nothing for it…

"I kinda stole your Mom's car," I admitted.

His hand at my hair slid down my back and he pulled me deep into him.

"I think she'll forgive you," he told me.

That was a relief.

Chapter 26

The Empty Space Where My Bag Used to Be

The alarm went off, Eddie touched a button and rolled out of bed.

I snuggled into the pillow, figuring Eddie would give me a reprieve. I mean, I did just survive the most traumatic two weeks of my life, culminating in being kidnapped and nearly raped.

Eddie's hand wrapped around my wrist and he pulled me out of bed.

"Eddie!" I cried while being dragged across the room. "I deserve at least one snooze button hit. I was kidnapped and nearly raped last night."

He stopped. I bumped into him and looked up.

Um… eek!

"We don't joke about that either," he said.

"I wasn't joking," I told him.

His hands went to the t-shirt I was wearing, then up, and then it was gone.

"You'll feel better after the shower."

He wasn't wrong.

⚜

I went back to bed after the shower and Eddie went to work.

When I finally woke up and stumbled into the bathroom, I realized after I looked into the mirror that Trixie's new hairdo did have a weakness. You didn't sleep on it after it got wet.

One word: scary.

I pulled the bandage off my temple to see the graze had scabbed over. I wet my hair, picked up the discarded t-shirt on the way back to the bedroom, put it on and stared at my bag on the floor. Somewhere along the line, it had exploded. There hadn't been a whole lot of time to keep things tidy.

Kristen Ashley

Therefore, I tidied.

First, I called Fortnum's and told them I'd be in late, or maybe not at all.

Then, I stripped the bed, found the stairs off the kitchen that led to the basement and stuffed the sheets in the laundry. I found some more sheets and made the bed, then I cleaned the house.

The whole time I was thinking.

The night before, Eddie took me to the station to talk to Detective Marker and make my statement so they could press charges. Then he took me for a quick visit to Dad who was still asleep and his condition was unchanged. After, we went to Eddie's, and Eddie had chili while everyone put me under the microscope.

Once they'd ascertained that I was okay and not under imminent threat of suffering nervous collapse, they all went home. Eddie gave me a t-shirt and we went to bed.

Now, it was over and I was safe. Slick and Vince were locked up and Dad was hanging in there.

Over.

Safe.

Back to Just Jet.

It actually didn't take a lot of thought to make my decision. It was easy.

I got dressed, put on some makeup and pulled my hair in a ponytail. I called Lottie to pick me up, packed my bag and all my junk from the kitchen and cleaned out the coffeemaker.

Lottie showed up in her rental and took me back to my apartment.

"You okay?" she asked on the way home, sliding her eyes to me.

"I'd be more okay if everyone would quit asking me if I was okay," I told her.

"We care," she sounded kind of pissy.

I sighed. "I'm okay."

"What's with all the stuff? You moving back home?"

"Yeah," I said.

"Why?"

"It's over."

"What's over?" she asked.

I looked out the side window. "All of it."

"Jet—"

364

"I don't want to talk about it."

"Jet—"

I turned to her. "I said, I don't want to talk about it."

She gave me a glare. "You're a pain in the ass, you now that?"

"Yeah," I said, my heart breaking, "I know."

⌖

We lugged my stuff up the stairs.

I avoided a Mom Talk (even though I could tell she really wanted one) by putting in a load of laundry and hightailing it back out.

I got in my car for the first time in two weeks and started it. It purred like a kitten.

Wonderful. Who would have ever thought I'd want my car to be cantankerous?

I went to the Credit Union and waved to Jody and Amy and knocked on Nicki, the Manager's, door.

"Hey Jet!" she exclaimed when she saw me then her eyes got big, "Holy cow! What happened to your head?"

"Gunshot wound," I replied as if I suffered one every day, and her big eyes nearly popped out of her head.

I ignored it.

"Can I talk to you?" I asked.

We talked. I asked for my job back. She said they didn't have any positions open. Then she told me she'd give me a call when they did.

I talked with Jody and Amy for a while, keeping the subject off my recent travails and my gunshot wound even though both their eyes kept straying to it.

Then I went to Smithie's. Smithie was open all day, but his day crew was second string. It wasn't a nice thing to say, but it was an honest thing to say.

I swung in.

"Well look who's here. I hear you got your shit sorted last night," Smithie remarked when I walked in.

I was learning quickly that Darius had a big mouth.

I nodded to him.

LaTeesha, one of Smithie's women, was standing in front of him at the bar. Smithie had clothes in the closets of four different women and they didn't seem to mind sharing. This could be because a little of Smithie went a long way. It also could be that Smithie had a big enough heart to keep them all happy. It could be a bit of both.

"Hey girlfriend, how's it goin'?" LaTeesha asked, pulling me into a hug.

"Much better now, thanks," I told her and hugged her back.

When she let go, I turned to Smithie.

"Can I have my job back?" I asked.

His eyebrows shot up. "Thought your sister was gonna help out."

"I'm sure she is."

"Then why do you need two jobs?"

"I'm quitting Fortnum's, this pays better."

Smithie stared at me, then he looked at LaTeesha, then back at me. "What does your cop boyfriend think of that?"

"We're breaking up," I told him.

Smithie looked back at LaTeesha. She was biting her lip and looking at me.

"Come a-fuckin'-gain?" Smithie asked, his eyes back to me.

"We're breaking up," I repeated.

"Breaking, not broken?" Smithie queried.

"I haven't told him yet," I shared.

More looks between Smithie and LaTeesha.

"You wanna tell LaTeesha about it?" she asked.

I shook my head, but smiled. "I just want to know if I can come back to work here."

Smithie sighed. "Once a Smithie's girl, always a Smithie's girl. You want to come back you start Monday night. You don't want to come back, I don't fuckin' care. You'll always be welcome here, wearin' an apron or havin' a drink. Though, I think you should let your sister work for a while and just have the drink, but what do I fuckin' know? I also don't think you should be breakin' up with a boyfriend who'd put his ass on the line for you."

"Smithie," LaTeesha said softly.

I ignored him.

Well, I didn't really ignore him because I felt his words in my gut, but I didn't let him know that.

I nodded and said, "I'll be here at seven on Monday."

"Or not, your call," Smithie returned before he looked away.

LaTeesha squeezed my arm.

I left.

⋈

I went to King Soopers and bought a whole load of stuff. I dragged it back up to the apartment and went straight into the kitchen, calling a hello to Mom, Lottie and Ada who were all sitting in the living room.

I pulled the stuff out of the bags and started preparing to bake like a baking fool.

Mom, Lottie and Ada came into the kitchen.

"What are you doing?" Mom asked.

"Baking," I answered, opening up the flour with a little more force than it needed so it gave a dusty, white "poof".

"Baking?" Mom repeated in a question.

"I can't afford to buy nice things to say thank you to everyone, so I'm gonna make stuff for them," I explained.

"That's nice," Ada said.

Lottie leaned a hip against the counter. "Mom and I've been talking."

Wonderful. Mom and Lottie talking. This spelled Disaster for me with a capital "D".

"About what?" I asked, though I didn't want to know.

"Well," Lottie started. "Mom called the landlord to this place and gave up the lease. He's got a waiting list and wants to jack up the rent, so he's pleased as punch."

I turned and stared. "What?"

"I'm moving in with Trixie," Mom informed me.

"You can't move in with Trixie!" I kind of yelled.

"Why not?" Mom asked.

I didn't have an answer to that. She was getting around better all the time. Eddie was right. She didn't need me as much as I thought she did.

I knew I couldn't fight it and didn't have the energy anyway.

I turned back to baking.

"Where am I going to live?" I asked.

"We found you a sweet one bedroom, in a big old Victorian house close to Eddie," Lottie told me.

I closed my eyes.

I opened them.

"Where are you going to live?" I asked Lottie.

"I got some money stashed. I'm going to buy a place. I'm also going to pay for Mom's OT, PT and medical stuff and give Trixie a little bit extra until Mom gets fully back on her feet. I'll stay with them until I get my place. You're off the hook."

I turned to them.

"Who said I want to be off the hook?" I enquired.

"No one, we're just letting you off the hook," Lottie replied.

I stared at them then turned back to baking.

"Whatever," I mumbled.

"Listen, Missy…" Uh-oh, Mom used the m-word. "You're all-fired determined not to live your own life, so we're making you and you don't have anything to say about it. Got me?"

I nodded. I knew better than to argue during a Missy Moment.

"Henrietta Louise…" Mom knew I wasn't fully committed to the nod.

Dear Lord.

I turned and looked at Mom and asked, definitely snippy, "What?"

"Don't 'what' me," Mom returned. "I don't know what's going on with you and that bag of yours being back in the house, but I'm going to tell you now, you're all kinds of fool if you don't hold on to Eddie Chavez and hold on tight."

"Mom—"

She gave me The Hand.

"You let go of Oscar for no good reason." Mom informed me.

"He was possessive," I explained.

"So what?" Mom shot back. "Good trait in a man if you ask me. Anyway, he *adored* you. Still does if you want the God's honest truth."

Yeesh.

I went back to measuring, Mom went back to lecturing.

"You let go of Luis after he asked to marry you."

"He lived with his mother," I reminded her.

"So? He would have moved out for you," Mom retorted.

"Do we have to go through this?" I asked.

Mom started talking to the ceiling. "I don't even know what was wrong with Alex, he was a nice boy."

Guess we had to go through it.

It was then Ada came forward and wrapped her hand around my wrist. I stopped measuring and looked at her.

She stared into my eyes, smiled a small, kind of sad, smile, let go of my wrist and turned. "There's a *World's Most Unbelievable Police Chases Caught on Video* starting about now. Let's watch it at my place." she said to Mom and Lottie.

Both my mother and sister opened their mouths to argue but Ada must have given them a look. I didn't know Ada was capable of giving a look, but whatever she did, it worked.

They left.

I watched the space they were in for a long time forcing, with a superhuman effort, my mind to go blank.

Then I baked.

⇥⇤

I swung by the hospital to visit Dad.

They said it was good he made it through the night. They took him off the critical list and would move him out of ICU if things kept on as they were.

They told me he'd been awake for a while but he was asleep when I went in to see him.

I sat, holding his hand and telling him about my day.

Then I told him about my decision.

He didn't respond. He didn't give me any judgments, attitude or advice and certainly not The Hand.

This, I thought was good, even though I'd rather he didn't do it because he didn't have any judgments, attitude or advice, not because he was a couple of brain pathways shutting down away from a coma.

Then, I left.

I walked into Fortnum's about half an hour before closing, carrying bags filled with tins and boxes that were stuffed full with cookies, cakes and pies.

Everyone was there. Lee, Indy, Ally, Tex, Duke, Jane and Hank.

"Jet!" Indy yelled when she saw me and ran up to me, giving me a big hug.

I was about to tell her I was okay, but she pulled away and shoved her hand in my face.

There was huge rock on her ring finger.

"Ohmigod!" I yelled, dumped the bags and hugged her, shaking her body from side to side and laughing. "You're getting married!" I cried when I pulled back a bit.

She nodded. "Lee asked me over a champagne breakfast." Then she leaned in. "We just got out of bed, like, an hour ago," she whispered.

She leaned back, eyes bright and happy, and I nodded the knowing girl-friend's nod.

"Nice," I drawled.

"You better believe it," she replied.

Everyone was in celebration mode and it was far, far better than despera-tion mode, so I went with it. I'd tell Indy I was quitting later.

I handed out cookies, cakes and pies, giving Lee a big bag all to himself to take to the office. At first, I was glad I had Indy and Lee's news to take attention off the gifts. It didn't really work, considering the looks and hugs I got, but they knew me enough by now not to make a big deal of it.

We were locking up and going to Indy and Lee's for a celebration drink when Daisy came storming up, carrying what looked like twenty magazines.

"Ally texted me. I got *Bride*, *Modern Bride*, *Contemporary Bride*, *Today's Bride*, *Denver Bride*, *Wedding*, *Martha Stewart Wedding* and *Vogue*, really just for the pic-tures 'cause who dresses like that? And *People* 'cause some fancy-ass celebrity is probably gettin' hitched and we can steal ideas," she announced.

Ally smiled. "Righteous."

"I think that covers it," Indy said.

"Fucking hell," Hank muttered, sounding horrified.

I shot him a grin.

He caught it, threw his arm around my neck and gave me a sideways hug, keeping me held against him in a modified, friendly Eddie's Woman Hold.

My grin turned false and I ignored the painful crunch in my belly.

I was going to miss these guys.

Tod and Stevie showed up, Chowleena in tow, a half an hour after we all got to Indy and Lee's. They were carrying, between them, what looked like a dozen bottles of chilled sparkling wine and a Yahtzee game.

"Since Lee moved in, we've been preparing. Now, we'll have room in our fridge," Stevie said.

He and Tod took in the female huddle sitting in Indy's living room, pouring over wedding magazines.

The men, (Lee and Hank had been joined by Vance, Matt and Bobby), were upstairs watching a ballgame and drinking beer. Duke had gone home to Dolores. Tex had gone home to the cats. And Jane just went home (she didn't do crowds).

"Aiyeee!" Tod screamed. "Is that *Modern Bride?* I *love Modern Bride.* Move over," he ordered, not exactly moving me over, but shoving me off an armchair so I landed on my ass on the floor and he confiscated the magazine I was flipping through by ripping it out of my hands.

"I'm thinking wedding colors green and yellow," Tod decided. "No, no, pale blush and burgundy," he changed his mind. "No, sapphire and ice," he changed his mind again.

I didn't know "ice' was a color.

Indy started giggling.

Stevie popped open a bottle of sparkling wine.

"Get the glasses!" he shouted then looked around. "What the hell, we're celebrating and we have enough so that everyone can have their own."

Then he took a swig straight out of the bottle.

⚑

We were all playing Yahtzee.

I was well into my personal bottle of wine, wedged between Hank and Vance at Indy's dining room table. She'd opened it up so that it was huge, but still it was a crush with eleven people sitting around it. It was my turn in a few goes when the phone in my back pocket rang.

I pulled it out and saw the display said, "Eddie calling".

"Damn," I whispered.

Then I took a hearty tug on my bottle with both Hank and Vance watching. I was pretty sure they'd seen the display on my phone, which meant I couldn't ignore it like I wanted to.

I flipped it open.

"Hey," I said.

"Where are you?" Eddie asked.

I looked at the table. Everyone had their eyes on me.

Wonderful.

I *hated* that.

"I'm at Indy and Lee's, drinking sparkling wine and playing Yahtzee. Indy and Lee got engaged today and we're celebrating," I answered.

Silence.

"Eddie? Did you hear me? Indy and Lee got engaged."

More silence.

Hmm.

"Where are you?" I asked.

"I'm standin' in my bedroom lookin' at the empty space where your bag used to be."

Eek!

I gave a weak smile to the table, got up and started towards the kitchen.

"I meant to tell you," I said as I was walking.

"When?" Eddie asked.

I hadn't actually meant to tell him. I had meant to avoid him until I had a chance to figure out what I meant to tell him. Which meant figure out my life, sort out Fortnum's and Smithie's and then say good-bye. I got sidetracked by the informal engagement party, the sparkling wine and Yahtzee.

I cursed wedding magazines, champagne and dice games and hit the kitchen.

"Maybe we can talk about this later," I suggested.

"When?"

I figured Eddie was pretty good in an interrogation room.

"Eddie—"

"I'll be there in ten."

No.

No, no, no.

"I'm leaving in a few minutes," I lied. I didn't intend to leave. I had the bonus points all tied up in that game and I was cruising to a win (or, at least, one of the top three). I only had a full house and a chance left, and Tod said full houses were easy to get.

"You're not there when I get there, I'll find you and it won't be good when I do," he warned.

Dear Lord.

"Eddie—" I tried again but he'd disconnected.

Eddie showed up, and, luckily, he was forced into the celebration by the very fact that it was a celebration. He gave Indy a hug and Lee a man-hug (one-armed, hearty slap on the back that would probably leave a bruise, all the while shaking hands).

Then his eyes locked on me.

They were glittery.

Not good.

I was back to being wedged between Vance and Hank. Hank slid his seat away from me, Lee found a chair and Eddie flipped it into a super-wedge in the space Hank left. He sat beside me, *close* beside me. His hand curled around my neck and he pulled me to him. His lips hit my cheek and moved to my ear.

"Don't even think about it," he stated.

My stomach clutched and I was pretty sure I was having heart palpitations.

"Yahtzee!" Stevie shouted and I jumped.

Eddie let me go and sat in the next game, drinking from my bottle of wine.

I kind of wanted to ask for another one. I was thinking drunk was definitely the way to go.

Once the game was over, Daisy got up and declared, "Marcus'll be wonderin' where I am."

She said her good-byes with hugs and air kisses and left.

Tod and Stevie followed her and Bobby and Matt went home to their girlfriends (this was a surprise; I didn't know they had girlfriends).

Vance took a call that changed the expression on his face. He sent a meaningful glance to Lee and left.

"Let's play strip poker," Ally suggested when the door closed behind Vance.

"That'd be a good idea. Jet's a shit poker player," Hank replied.

Dear Lord, save me.

"But I'm not playin' strip poker with my sister," Hank finished.

Thank you God for one small favor.

"Time to go home," Eddie announced, pushing his chair back to get up.

I looked at him. He may have been playing at being in the celebratory mood, but one look at him told me he simply was *not*.

I looked at the table.

"Maybe we could play just poker, poker," I tried.

His hand grabbed mine and he pulled me up.

"Indy and Lee probably want to be alone," Eddie said.

He was probably right. One look at Lee's face said he was definitely right.

Everyone dispersed, more hugs and kisses, and Eddie and I went out the front.

"My car is at Fortnum's," I told him.

"I'll take you to get it tomorrow morning," Eddie replied, walking me to the truck. He bleeped its locks and I pulled hard on my hand in his. It didn't work.

He stopped at the passenger side door.

"I'm going home," I told him.

"Already told you, I prefer my bed," he returned.

"Okay, you sleep in your bed and I'll sleep in my bed."

Wrong answer.

He pushed me against the truck with a hand at my belly. "You want to have this talk out here in the street, or do you want to do it at my place?"

I didn't want to have the talk at all. But I was willing to have the talk in a delayed-type fashion.

I went for it. "I was thinking maybe tomorrow."

"You were thinkin' wrong."

Sweet Jesus.

"Eddie."

He opened the truck door. "Get in the truck, Jet."

I pulled out the attitude. Certainly, the scaredy-cat gambit wasn't getting me anywhere.

I gave him a glare. "You're incredibly pushy!" I snapped.

"Get in the truck," he repeated.

I turned to walk away.

"I'm going to my car," I announced.

I was pulled back at the middle, his finger snagging the belt loop of my jeans.

He pushed me back against the side of the truck and got close.

"Remember what I said about no longer bein' tolerant of your shit?"

He sounded pretty angry, so angry that words escaped me, so I nodded.

"I meant this shit, too, now get in the truck."

"I really don't like you," I told him, still trying to go with the attitude.

Again, it was the wrong choice.

His body got still for a beat and then he got even closer.

"Now," he said quietly, "you just threw down. So, I'm gonna have to prove you wrong. After I do that, we're gonna talk."

Eek!

What could I say?

I'd walked right into that one.

Still, I gave him a glare before I got in the truck.

Just because.

Chapter 27

The Talk

I came up with a strategy on the silent ride to Eddie's.

He parked in the garage and we went into the kitchen. I put my purse down on the counter and he walked into the living room. I took a deep breath and followed him.

He turned to me, planted his hands on his hips and stared at me.

"You wanna explain why I came home to find you'd moved out?" he asked.

The good news was he'd given up on the idea of proving me wrong about not liking him.

The bad news was we weren't going to sit down and relax in front of a ballgame before our talk.

Oh well, it was now or never.

I walked up to him and slid my arms around his middle. I pressed my body to his. I tucked my face into his neck and, with my lips pressed against the side of his throat I replied, "Not really."

"*Chiquita...*"

I went up on tiptoe, my lips moved and I kissed him behind his ear.

I'd never had to seduce Eddie. Eddie was kind of a take-charge type of guy when it came to sex (well really, Eddie was kind of a take-charge type of guy all the time), as in, he wanted it, he took it.

I'd never actually had to seduce anyone and I didn't exactly know what to do. I was hoping just to get the ball rolling and then Eddie could take over.

"Jet, I asked you a question," he prompted.

My hands moved up his back. He had a nice back and I could feel the definition of the muscle under my fingers. I could also smell him, and the combination of the two was pretty heady stuff.

"I heard you," I said against his skin and then moved my mouth around the front and kissed his throat in the dent where it met his neck.

"You gonna answer me?" he asked and I got the feeling he wasn't going to fall in line with my plan. The reason I thought this was because he still had his hands planted on my hips.

That was a bummer considering I was liking my plan more and more as the seconds ticked by.

I pulled my arms from his back and put them around his neck. My fingers went in his hair and I tilted my head back as I pressed his down.

"I'll answer... later."

Then I kissed him.

I should have tried that first.

In the beginning, he didn't respond, but then I got going and touched the tip of my tongue to his closed lips. The second I did that, his arms went around me and he kissed me back. Then he took over the kiss, his mouth opening over mine, his tongue sliding inside.

My body melted and my stomach curled.

He lifted his head and I whispered, "Yum."

I didn't really mean to, it just came out.

I opened my eyes and his were liquid.

Then he started walking us toward the bedroom, arms still around me. I was moving back, he was moving forward, his hands were active and he kissed me again.

This was more like it.

It was a while later (a *long* while), after he'd let me take over again (for a *little* while), then he took over (for a *longer* while), when he flipped me on my back, spread my legs and finally, slowly, slid inside me.

"*Chiquita.*"

I opened my eyes at his call as he pressed deep.

"Yeah?" I whispered, wrapping my calves around his thighs.

"I like where you were goin' with this but you're still gonna talk," he told me.

Eddie had me *so* figured out.

⚜

After, I was pressed up against his side, Eddie was on his back. He had his hand low on my hip and his fingers were moving absently.

My plan was to distract him from the talk, at least until the morning. In the bright light of day, I could figure out how to say what I wanted to say.

There were also other, better, more important parts to my plan.

It would give me one last time to be with Eddie. I needed it. I deserved it. To make love and sleep next to him, smell him in my nostrils and feel him against my skin. To make one last memory so I could keep it with me for a long, long time.

And we'd made a really good memory. I wrapped my arm around him and snuggled into his side.

His fingers curled on my hip.

"You think you got away with it," he muttered and I could tell he found this amusing.

"No," I said honestly. "But I'm hoping you're feeling mellow enough to wait until the morning."

"Jet..."

I pulled up and looked down on him.

"Eddie, please. Can I have this one night where we don't argue? Please?"

He looked at me a beat then his hand came up and slid in my hair and pulled my face down for a lip touch.

"One night," he said against my mouth.

I smiled at him.

His hand moved to my jaw and his thumb traced my smile while his eyes watched.

"I'm hopin', with your shit finished, I'll see more of that smile."

I dropped down and snuggled into him.

He wouldn't be seeing any of my smile, but where I'd be (that was, away from him and all his friends), I probably wouldn't be smiling much anyway.

I could hear the ring tone from his phone. He dislodged me, leaned down, grabbed his jeans and pulled the cell out of the back pocket. He came back, brought me to him again and flipped the phone open one-handed.

"Yeah?"

He listened for a bit then I felt his body tense.

I came up on my elbow to look at him and his gaze locked on mine.

"You're shittin' me," he said into the phone.

He listened more and then he took his arm from around me and wiped his eyes.

"Right. Yeah. Later." Then he flipped the phone shut and threw it on the nightstand.

"What?" I asked.

He looked at me. "They found Fratelli dead in his cell. Someone broke his neck."

I sucked in breath.

"Dear Lord," I said on an exhale.

His arms came around me and he rolled into me so we were both on our sides, front-to-front. "You okay?" he asked.

"How did that happen?"

"They don't know. They're investigating. He wasn't in lock up. He was in a private cell. I made arrangements. I figured Marcus would renege on the deal."

"Do you think he did?"

Eddie gave a single shoulder shrug.

"I don't believe it," I said, and I didn't. I didn't want Vince dead. Maybe, if I was honest with myself, roughed up a bit, but not dead.

"Are *you* okay?" I asked.

"It doesn't matter to me. It's just one more piece of shit washed away."

But Eddie was one of the good guys.

I stared.

Then I told him, "Homicide is a bad thing."

He rolled me to my back, coming over me, his body mostly pressed against mine.

"Yeah," he agreed.

"The worst thing," I went on.

His hands slid into the hair on either side of my head. "You aren't okay," he noted.

"I don't care about Vince. He told me he was going to rape me with a broken bottle."

Eddie's eyes changed, instead of partially wary and partially resigned, they became active, as in, *scary* active.

"He said that?"

I nodded.

"Then I really don't give a shit that he's dead."

"But you're a cop!" I cried.

"So?"

"Hank says you guys are the good guys. You play by the right set of rules and homicide is wrong, no matter who does it or why."

He did a lip touch and then rolled again, taking me with him so that I was on top.

"Hank's a different kind of cop than me," Eddie shared. "Some dickhead makes my woman's life a living hell and threatens to rape her with a broken bottle, I'm not fuckin' losin' sleep over the fact he isn't breathin' anymore."

"So, Hank plays by the rules and you see shades of gray," I summed up.

His body moved with laughter.

"Hank plays by the rules," he repeated this like it was funny.

"He doesn't?" I asked.

"*Chiquita*, Hank's got a rule book, and I bet he studies it, but he's also got a lot of shit scratched out and a fuck of a lot of notes in the margin."

Hmm.

"Oh," I mumbled.

See, I was right. Hank was a scary good guy.

"Let's talk about what Vince said to you," Eddie suggested.

I sighed and pressed my face in his neck and shoved my arms around him. "Let's not."

"You got to talk about it."

"Why? It's over. You deal. You move on. I'm fine. Everyone I love is fine. Except Dad, and there's hope he'll be fine too. Vince was a jerk. Now he's dead. The end."

Eddie's arms tightened around me and he said some stuff softly in Spanish.

My head came back up. "What? I didn't catch any of that."

He did another roll, him getting on top again.

Then, he said, "You don't wanna talk? We won't talk."

Then he kissed me.

Then, for the next hour, there were some words muttered, but you couldn't really call them talking.

⌖

The alarm went off, Eddie touched a button and rolled into me, wrapping his arms around me and pulling my back to his front.

It was Saturday. Saturday meant there wasn't even the need for the snooze button.

I nestled my bottom into his groin and started to drift back to sleep.

Then I heard Eddie say, "Wake up, *cariño*, time for our talk."

Shit, hell and damn.

"I want to sleep more," I mumbled.

"After our talk and after I make love to you, then you can sleep. First, the talk."

My belly did a curl.

I ignored it.

"But I want to sleep more *now*."

I was partly trying to avoid the talk, partly trying not to think of Eddie making love to me and partly, I really did want more sleep.

He moved away and rolled me onto my back. He was up on his elbow and looking down on me. "Later," he declared.

I threw an arm over my eyes. "I need coffee."

"Later."

I wasn't going to get out of it, I wasn't going to delay it and I wasn't going to get more sleep.

I took the arm away and looked at him.

It was a serious look, no attitude, no bullshit.

"I need coffee before we talk."

He looked at me, registered the seriousness, then rolled out of bed and pulled me with him.

I put on one of Eddie's flannel shirts (thinking I'd steal that too if I could get away with it) and a pair of panties and Eddie tugged on a pair of jeans.

We made coffee.

We used the delicious in-store bakery bread Blanca bought and made toast, breaking the seal on Eddie's new toaster. We smeared it with real butter (that Blanca also bought) and grape jelly (again, that Blanca bought).

We sat at the dining room table with our coffee and toast. Eddie sat back, his legs out in front of him and his feet crossed at the ankles. It wasn't a good position because it *was* a good position and it was a new position.

I hadn't had the opportunity to be around an Eddie who was relaxed, sitting back at his dining room table, wearing nothing but jeans. All I knew was Eddie at Fortnum's, Eddie Action Man or at most, Eddie lounging on the couch holding me while watching a ballgame. Still, even lounging on the couch, there was something active about him, alert, aware, focused, whatever.

He was focused now, but we'd had a lot of sex last night and I'd agreed to talk. Not to mention I was sitting at his dining room table eating toast and wearing his shirt.

He was focused but laidback. He looked really handsome and both were going to make things a lot harder for me.

He took a bite of toast and watched me.

"You're gettin' that about-ready-to-bolt look again," he remarked when he swallowed and then he took a sip of coffee, all the while, his eyes on me.

"I didn't really think you'd be mad that I moved out. I wasn't really moved *in*. I was just staying here—" I started but he interrupted.

"You weren't moved in. We're not ready for moved in. Still, you could have told me and you could have stayed a while. At least until your sister found a place to stay."

"Mom gave up the apartment. She and Lottie are moving in with Trixie."

His eyes didn't leave me but they became active. "That was fast. Where are you gonna live?"

"They found me an apartment. I'm quitting Fortnum's and working at Smithie's until the Credit Union has an opening. Then, I'm going back there."

He still watched me. "Prefer it to the other way around, you stay at Fortnum's and quit Smithie's."

"Smithie's is more money."

"Then you *are* moving in until you can afford your own place."

I shook my head.

"It wasn't an offer, *chiquita*. I don't want you workin' at Smithie's."

"Eddie," I began, putting down my toast, "You don't have much to say about it."

His eyes started changing.

Uh-oh.

I leaned back, took a huge breath and then said it, straight out, "I'm breaking up with you."

His eyes finished changing, quick as a flash.

"I'm sorry?" he asked quietly.

"I'm breaking up with you," I repeated.

Not only had his eyes changed, but his body wasn't laidback anymore. He was still in the same position, but he was back to alert and aware. *Very* alert and aware.

"I..." I started, swallowed then started again, "I want to thank you for all you've done for me. I have cookies in my car—"

"I don't want your fuckin' cookies."

Hmm.

Not good.

Eddie liked my cookies. I made the peanut butter and Hershey's square ones for him especially.

"Eddie—"

"What the fuck are you afraid of?" he asked.

I blinked. "Pardon?"

He stared at me a beat then said, "You're fuckin' unbelievably clueless."

I straightened in my chair. "That's not nice."

"This is good," he declared.

"What's good?"

"Us."

I did a head jerk.

He was right. It was good. That was the point.

I stood up. "I think I should go."

I started to walk to the bedroom, rethinking stealing his shirt. He was a little harder to break up with than Oscar, *or* Luis, and Luis had asked me to marry him. At that juncture, I didn't think Eddie would appreciate me stealing his clothes.

I got about three steps before my arm was grabbed and Eddie swung me around.

I didn't want to hear what he had to say, so I started talking immediately, "I'm going to go. I'll call Lottie. She can pick me up."

"You're not goin' anywhere, we're gonna talk this shit out."

"There's nothing to talk about."

"You fuckin' better believe there is."

"Eddie, please. Don't."

"*Chiquita*, you're a pain in the ass, but you aren't boring, you aren't normal and you aren't average. That's the point. It would be cute that you don't realize how fuckin' pretty you are, except you get yourself kissed and end up with your head in other guy's laps. You bein' shy is sweet, but the attitude is better."

"The attitude was all about Slick and Vince and now that they're gone—"

"The attitude was latent. Slick and Vince, and likely Indy and Ally, brought it out."

"Really, I don't think—"

His arms came around me and he pulled me, hard, up against his body and his head tilted down to mine as I looked up.

"Eddie."

"You aren't breakin' up with me and you aren't leavin'. We're gonna finish our toast and coffee and then I'm takin' you into the bedroom and fuckin' you so hard that idiot brain of yours won't think of anything but me movin' inside you. Then after that, we're gonna have a normal, average day doing some normal, average shit before some other crisis blows us back into pandemonium."

"There won't be another crisis," I said.

"There's always another crisis."

"Eddie, let me go."

"That's not gonna happen."

I started panicking. It was a delayed reaction panic, but I'd finally realized that this was not going well.

At all.

"Eddie, *let me go!*" I kind of shouted.

His arms tightened and he shook me a bit. "It's not gonna happen!" he shouted back.

Okay, I was full-on panic at that point.

"You have to let me go!"

Definitely a shout.

"Why?" he asked.

"You just have to."

Another shake. "Why?"

I felt tears burn in my throat.

No, this was *seriously* not going well.

"Jet, talk to me," he demanded.

I shook my head and tried to pull away.

He brought me even closer.

"Eddie, let me go!"

"You like me. You don't want to, but you do and this is total bullshit."

"I don't like you!" I yelled.

"You fucking well do!" he yelled back.

385

Kristen Ashley

I gave a vicious yank and the tears burning my throat started to burn my eyes. I couldn't swallow them down and they started flowing.

He caught me again and brought me back.

"Do I have to prove it to you?" His voice was back to quiet and it was far more scary than him shouting.

"I don't like you."

Another shake.

I pulled away again, but stood in front of him and shouted, "I don't like you! I love you! I've loved you since the minute I saw you. God!" I looked to the ceiling and swiped a hand across my face to wipe away the tears. "You're a good guy, I could tell right off. You're nice to your friends and they love you. You're handsome and you stepped up for me, going all out to keep me safe and... and..." I faltered and then rallied, "You have a fancy truck!"

For a second he looked shocked then the warmth came into his eyes and he reached out to me.

I whirled; totally panicked, beyond freaked out, straight to temporary insanity.

What was I thinking, blurting out that I loved him?

Totally temporary insanity.

I started to run but he caught me, swung me around again and walked me back until I was pressed against the wall, his body against mine.

"*No!*" I screamed. "We can't have sex against the wall again. I have to go."

"We're not havin' sex against the wall."

I looked at him and shouldn't have. The warmth was there, but he was also amused, he thought this was funny.

This was anything but funny.

"I have to go."

"You aren't goin' anywhere."

"Eddie—"

"*Chiquita*, calm down."

I shook my head. Calm was not an option. My heart was beating so hard I thought I could hear it, even though I couldn't hear anything but the blood rushing to my ears.

"Why are you scared?" he asked.

I shook my head.

"Why do you want to break up with me?"

I shook my head again but answered.

And I answered honestly.

"It isn't going to work. I know it. I'd rather have it end now when it'll hurt, but I don't want it to end later when it'll tear me apart."

I was struggling against him to get away but he pressed deeper. I could smell him and I stopped. I had to hold on to my reserves. I couldn't burn out too fast. I had to keep enough energy to find a way to walk out of there.

"Why isn't it going to work?" he asked.

"It never works."

"Why?"

"I don't know. It just doesn't. You can love someone a lot and treat them nice and do everything for them and then they just go. It happens. I saw it happen to my Mom and I don't want it to happen to me. She came undone. It was like watching her unravel. And she was strong, *is* strong, and it destroyed her."

I was talking to his throat. It was the only way to get it out. His body still pressed against mine, his hands came to my face and tilted it up, forcing me to look at him.

"Jet, I don't know what's gonna happen and I can't promise anything, but I do know I don't want this to end. What we have is good, it's so fuckin' good, it's great."

"Eddie—"

"No 'Eddie', listen to me. You go, I follow and bring you back. You leave, I'll do it again. You want to quit workin' at Fortnum's, do it. But I'll be at Smithie's every night to pick you up. I told you I'd wear you down and I thought I was gettin' somewhere but it seems I got work to do."

"Don't," I whispered.

"I know you love him, but your Dad's an asshole."

I shook my head, but I was beginning to feel it, coming up, willy-nilly and uncontrollable.

The attitude.

No one called my Dad an asshole.

Okay, well, maybe Eddie could get away with it, but not without a little 'tude thrown at him.

"And your Mom has shit taste in men," he went on.

I stopped shaking my head and stared at him.

He did a lip touch and my body froze.

"But you don't," he whispered.

He pulled me away from the wall and in his arms.

Then, he grinned. "You have fuckin' great taste in men," he finished.

That brought me out of my freeze and I glared at him. "This isn't funny," I snapped.

"You're wrong. This is hilarious. You love me and you're tryin' to break up with me."

I put my hands on my hips in a Double Diva Threat.

"I'm not trying. I *am* breaking up with you."

The grin broke out into a smile, white teeth, dimple and all. "You are so full of shit."

Really.

Was he serious?

"Eddie—"

"*Cállate, mi amor.* We're done talkin' now. I'm takin' you to the bedroom."

I planted my feet. "We are *not* done talking!"

He pressed me back.

"You wanna do it against the wall again?" he asked softly then his lips went to my neck.

"Don't ignore me while I'm trying to break up with you," I snapped at him.

His hands went under the shirt. "I'm not ignoring you. I'm just not listenin' to your shit."

"Eddie."

He kissed me.

It was a good kiss.

No, it was a great kiss.

My fingers curled into the waistband of his jeans.

"I really don't like you," I whispered against his mouth as his hand cupped my breast.

"I know. You love me."

I tried to give attitude, I even tried to hold on to the panic, but it was just melting away.

And then it was gone.

Just like that.

"I'm never going to hear the end of that, am I?" I asked.

His thumb did a nipple swipe.
I did a gasp.
"Probably not," he said.
Oh well.
Whatever.

The Rock Chick ride continues
with **Rock Chick Redemption**
the story of Hank and Roxie

22979394R00243

Made in the USA
San Bernardino, CA
29 July 2015